Richard Bradley

The Country Housewife and Lady's Director in the Management of a House, and the Delights and Profits of a Farm

Richard Bradley

The Country Housewife and Lady's Director in the Management of a House, and the Delights and Profits of a Farm

1st Edition | ISBN: 978-3-73409-007-3

Place of Publication: Frankfurt am Main, Germany

Year of Publication: 2019

Outlook Verlag GmbH, Germany.

Reproduction of the original.

Management of a House, and the
Delights and Profits of a Farm.

CONTAINING

Instructions for managing the Brew-House, and Malt-Liquors in the Cellar; the making of Wines of all sorts

Directions for the Dairy, in the Improvement of Butter and Cheese upon the worst of Soils; the feeding and making of Brawn; the ordering of Fish, Fowl, Herbs, Roots, and all other useful Branches belonging to a Country Seat, in the most elegant manner for the Table.

Practical Observations concerning Distilling; with the best Method of making Ketchup, and many other curious and durable Sauces.

The whole distributed in their proper Months, from the Beginning to the End of the Year.

With particular Remarks relating to the Drying or Kilning of Saffron.

By R. BRADLEY,

Professor of Botany in the University of *Cambridge;* and F.R.S.

The Sixth Edition With Additions.

* * * *

* To

The
LADY *WAGER*,
Consort to the Right Honourable
Sir *CHARLES WAGER*,
One of the Lords Commissioners
of the Admiralty,
AND
One of His Majesty's Most Honourable
PRIVY-COUNCIL;

This Book is most humbly Dedicated, by Her Ladyship's most Obedient, and most Humble Servant,

R. BRADLEY.

* * * * *

AN INDEX TO THE FIRST PART.

A.

Asparagus, preserv'd.

Ditto Drest the *Dutch* way.

Ditto with Cream.
Artichoakes, to dry.
Ditto preserv'd.
　Ditto pickled.
　Ditto fryed.
　Ditto in Suckers, to eat raw.
Apricot Wine.
Alamode Beef.

B.

Brandy, Laurel.
Birch-Wine.
Brewing.
Beef Cake-Soup.
　Ditto to Pot like Venison.
Beef, to Collar.
Brocoli, to boil.
Butter, good in *Suffolk*.
Buckingham-Cheese, to make.
Butter, why good or bad.
　Ditto in general.
Butter, what Milk is good.
　Ditto made over the Fire.
　Ditto wash'd.
　Ditto churn'd in Summer.
Ditto churn'd in Winter.
Beans, preserv'd, the Winter.
Berberries, to pickle.
Beet-Roots, red, to pickle.
　Ditto fryed.
Boar's-Head imitated.
Brawn, to Collar.
Boar, when to be put up for Brawn.

C.

Capon, to dress.
Carps, to stew.
Cellars, which are best.

Cowslip-Wine.
Cheese, spoiled.
  Ditto what concerns its Goodness.
  Ditto why bad in *Suffolk*.
  Ditto Good from one sort of Cattle.
  Ditto preserv'd in Oil.
  Ditto Marygold.
  Ditto Sage.
  Ditto Sage in figures.
  Ditto *Cheshire*.
  Ditto *Cheshire* with Sack.
  Ditto *Gloucestershire*.
Cheese, Cream.
  Ditto Why the Aversion to it.
Churns, the Sorts.
Clove-Gilly-Flower Syrup.
Cucumbers, to pickle.
Codlings, to pickle, green.
  Ditto to pickle Mango.
Cherry-Brandy.
Cherry-Beer.
Cherry-Cordial.
Cherries distill'd.
Cherry, Cornelian, in Brandy.
Calf's Feet Jelly.
Cockles, pickled.
Capons, to set upon Eggs.

D.

Dairy, how to build.
Different Sorts of Goosberries.
Different Sorts of Currans.
Ducks, wild, to roast.
Ducks, wild, hash'd.

E.

Eels, their time of Breeding.
  Ditto in plenty.

Eggs, to prepare six ways.
Eels, to clear from Mud.
  Ditto to roast.
  Ditto to Pitchcot.
  Ditto to Collar.
Elder-Flowers, to dry.
Elder Vinegar.
Elder-Wine, red.
  Ditto white.
English-Wine.

F.

Fowls and Birds, the Difference.
Fowl, to dress.
  Ditto to farce.
Fricassee of Chickens, brown.
  Ditto white.
Fish Gravey for Soups.
Flounders, pickled.
Frontiniac-Wine imitated.
Fruits preserv'd for Tarts.
Florence-Wine imitated.
Frontiniac-Wine to make.
Fowls, the Sorts.
Fish, to boil firm.
Fish boiled, the Sauce.

G.

Geese, when to buy.
  Ditto to fat.
  Ditto to roast.
Ditto how to kill.
Grapes, ripe early.
Grape-Wine.

H.

Herb-Soup, the Foundation.
Hops.
Hare, to pot.
Herbs, to dry.
Hare coursed, how to keep.
  Ditto hunted, to dress.
  Ditto the Pudding for it.
  Ditto to roast.
Hare, to stew.
Hung-Beef.
Herbs infused in Spirits.

L.

Larks, to dress.

M.

Malt, which is good.
  Ditto Liquor, to bottle.
Mountain-Wine, to imitate.
Milk, to be examin'd.
Mace in Rennet.
Mead, small, to make.
Metheglin or strong Mead.
Mushrooms.
Mushroom-Gravey.
  Ditto Ketchup.
Mushrooms, stew'd.
  Ditto broiled.
  Ditto fry'd.
Mushrooms, a Foundation for Sauce.
Mushrooms, to powder.
  Ditto to pickle.
Melons, green, to pickle, like Mango.
Mussels, scallop'd.
  Ditto fryed.
Ditto pickled.
Morillas, to dress.
Morillas, to dry.

Ditto in Ragoust.
Ditto to fry.

O.

Orange-Flower Cordial.
Onions, pickled.
Oysters, from *Colchester.*
Oysters, to stew.
Orange-Wine.
Oysters, in Scallop Shells.
Oysters, roasted.
Oysters, pickled.
Onion-Soup.

P.

Pidgeon, wild.
  Ditto tame, the Sorts.
  Ditto Carrier, its use.
  Ditto broiled.
  Ditto in Paste or Dumplings.
  Ditto stew'd.
Portmanteau Pottage.
Pike, to roast.
  Ditto to bake.
Pease, preserved all the Year.
Pickled Walnuts.
  Ditto Cucumbers.
  Ditto for Mangoes.
  Ditto Kidney-Beans.
  Ditto *Nasturtium*-Seeds.
Partridges stew'd with Sallery.
Ditto roasted.
Pheasants, their Sauces.
  Ditto to dress.
Potatoes.
Perch, with Mushrooms.

Q.

Quince-Wine.

R.

Rennet, how made in *Essex.*
  Ditto another way.
Rennet-Bags, which are good.
Rennet-Bags, how to make them good.
Rennet with Spice.
Red Surfeit-Water.
Rosa Solis, to distil.
Raspberry-Wine.
Red Goosberry-Wine.
Rabbit, roasted with a Pudding.

S.

Sausages of Fish.
Sausages, of Pork.
Soup of Herbs.
Shrub, to make.
Sauce Royal, or Travelling-Sauce.
Spinach, stew'd.
Sallads, to dress.
Sage-Wine.
Skerrets, to dress.
Salsify, to dress.
Scorzonera, to dress.
Saffron, to cure.
Snipes, to roast.
Soup, *a L'Hyvrogne.*

T.

Tokay-Wine, to imitate.
Travelling-Sauce.
Tench, which is best.

Trout in Season.
Trouts, to pot.
Tragopogon, to dress.
Truffles, to broil.
Truffles, to stew.
Truffles, ragou'd.
Turkey, to dress.

U.

Veal-Glue.
Visney.
Venison, and its Sauces.

W.

Water-Soochy.
Wines, boiled.
Wines, fermented.
Wines, to help, by Sugar.
Wines, of *St. Helena,* reform'd.
Woodcocks, to roast.

* * * * *

TO THE
LADIES
OF
GREAT BRITAIN, &c.

The Reason which induces me to address the following Piece to the Fair Sex, is, because the principal Matters contained in it are within the Liberty of their Province. The Art of Oeconomy is divided, as Xenophon tells us, between the Men and the Women; the Men have the most dangerous and laborious Share of it in the Fields, and without doors, and the Women have the Care and Management of every Business within doors, and to see after the good ordering of whatever is belonging to the House. And this, I conceive, is no less the Practice of these Days, than it was in the time of that great Philosopher; therefore it may seem necessary that I make some Apology for the Work I now publish, which, for the most part, falls within the Ladies Jurisdiction: but I hope I am the more excusable, as my Design is rather to assist, than to direct. I may call myself rather their Amanuensis, than their

Instructor; for the Receipts which I imagine will give the greatest Lustre or Ornament to the following Treatise, are such as are practised by some of the most ingenious Ladies, who had Good-nature enough to admit of a Transcription of them for publick Benefit; and to do them justice, I must acknowledge that every one who has try'd them, allow them to excel in their way. The other Receipts are such as I have collected in my Travels, as well through England, *as in foreign Countries, and are such as I was prompted to enter into my List, as well for their Curiosity as for their extraordinary Goodness.*

I could have launched much further in this Attempt, but that I confined myself to publish only such as were necessary for the Use of a Farm; or, in other terms, for the good ordering of every thing which is the Produce of a Farm and Garden: And especially I am Induced to publish a Tract of this nature for two Reasons, which I think carry some sway with them.

The first is, that I find many useful things about Farms, and in Gardens, whose Goodness is so little known, or understood, that they are seldom reckon'd of any account, and in most places are looked upon as Incumbrances; such as Mushrooms, Lupines, Brocoly, Morilles, Truffles Skirrets, Scorzonera, Salsifie, Colerape, Charddones, Boorencole, and many other such like things, which are excellent in their kind, when they are well dress'd, and admired by the greatest Epicures.

The other Reason which has induced me to publish this Piece, is, the Difficulties I have undergone in my Travels, when I have met with good Provisions, in many Places in England, which have been murder'd in the dressing.

I could mention many Instances as bad as the common Story of Bacon and Eggs strewed with brown Sugar: But as this was done through Ignorance, as the Story relates, I hope I need make no further Apology, or have occasion to give any other Reason for making this Treatise publick, but that it may improve the Ignorant, and remind the Learned how and when to make the best of every thing: which may be a means of providing every one with a tolerable Entertainment founded upon Practice and Fashion; which can never fail of Followers, and of making us fare much better upon the Roads in the Country than we were used to do.

* * * *

* THE
Country Lady's
DIRECTOR

* * * * *

JANUARY

I Shall in this Month take particular notice of the Pigeon, whose Characteristicks are chiefly to have short Legs, and their Feet of a reddish Colour, to have long Wings, and to be quick of Flight; in which the spreading of their Tail-Feathers greatly contribute, as well as to guide them in the Air. They by for the most part two Eggs for one sitting, and so more; but breed often in the Year. When Pigeons are once paired, it is observed they are very constant to one another, and assist each other in the Incubation or Sitting on the Eggs, as well as in bringing up and feeding the young ones; and moreover it is remarkable, that a Pigeon has no Gall-Bladder.

The sorts are, first, the blue wild Pigeon, which is the most frequent in Dove-Cotes, but is not very large, nor disposed to breed so early in the Spring as some others: they are, however, a hardy kind, and will thrive any where, if there is plenty of Water; for tho' they are not of a watery Race, yet it is observable, that they covet to be where it is, and that they feed frequently upon the Banks of Rivers and Ponds. I have known that where there were two Dove-Cotes, that stood within a Mile of one another, and one of them was near a River, and the other remote from it, the Pigeons of the House distant from the Water, left their Habitation to reside in that next the River, even tho' they had an Allowance of good Feed at home.

Among the tame Pigeons, those which the *Italians* call'd *Tronfo*, and we Runts, are the largest; but these may be again distinguish'd under the Characters of greater and smaller: those which are commonly call'd the *Spanish* Runts, are very much esteem'd, being the largest sort of Pigeon, and are sluggish, and more slow of flight, than the smaller sort of Runts; but the smaller Runts are better Breeders, and quick of flight, which is to be esteem'd; because if they were to seek their Food far, they can range much more Ground, or return home much quicker on occasion of stormy or wet Weather. As for the Colours of their Feathers, they are uncertain, so that one cannot judge of the sort by them.

The next, which makes the largest Figure, but is not in reality the largest Bird, is the Cropper; it is so named, because they usually do, by attracting the Air, blow up their Crops to an extraordinary bigness, even so sometimes as to be as large as their Bodies. This sort is esteemed the better, as it can swell its Crop to the largest Size. The Bodies of this sort are about the bigness of the smaller Runt, but somewhat more slender. This sort, like the former, is of various Colours in the Feathers.

The next are those Pigeons call'd Shakers, and are said to be of two sorts, *viz.* the broad-tail'd Shaker, and the narrow-tail'd Shaker: The reason which is assign'd for calling them Shakers, is, because they are almost constant in wagging their Heads and Necks up and down; and the Distinction made between the broad and narrow-tail'd Shaker, is, because the broad tail'd sort abounds with Tail-Feathers, about twenty-six in number, as Mr. *Ray* observes, and the narrow-tail'd Shakers have fewer in number. These, when they walk, carry their Tail-Feathers erect, and spread abroad like a Turkey-Cock. They likewise have diversity of Feathers.

The next I shall take notice of, are the Jacobines, or Cappers: These are called Cappers from certain Feathers which turn up about the back part of the Head. There are of these that are rough-footed: these are short-bill'd, the Iris of their Eye of a Pearl Colour, and the Head is commonly white.

The next is the *Turbit*, commonly so call'd, but what is the occasion of the Name, is not known, unless *Turbit*, or *Turbeck*, is a Corruption of the Word *Cortbeck*, or *Cortbeke*, which is the Name the *Hollanders* give them, and seems to be derived from the *French*, where *Court-bec* would signify a short Bill, which this Pigeon is remarkable for; the Head is flat, and the Feathers on the Breast spread both ways. These are about the bigness of the Jacobines.

The Carrier Pigeon is the next I shall take notice of; it is so call'd from the Use which is sometimes made of them in carrying of Letters to and fro: It is very sure that they are nimble Messengers, for by experience it is found, that one of these Pigeons will fly three Miles in a Minute, or from *St. Albans* to *London* in seven Minutes, which has been try'd; and I am inform'd, that they have been sent of a much longer Message: however, they might certainly be made very useful in Dispatches, which required speed, if we were to train them regularly between one House and another. We have an account of them passing and repassing with Advices between *Hirtius* and *Brutus*, at the Siege of *Modena*, who had, by laying Meat for them in some high Places, instructed their Pigeons to fly from place to place for their Meat, having before kept them hungry, and shut up in a dark Place. These are about the size of common Pigeons, and of a dark blue or blackish Colour, which is one way of distinguishing them from other sorts: they are also remarkable for having their Eyes compass'd about with a broad Circle of naked spungy Skin, and for having the upper Chap of their Beak cover'd more than half from the Head with a double Crust of the like naked fungous Body. The Bill, or Beak, is moderately long, and black. These Birds are of that Nature, that tho' they are carried many Miles from the place where they were bred, or brought up, or have themselves hatch'd, or bred up any young ones, they will immediately return home as soon as we let them fly. Perhaps this may, in some measure, depend upon the Affection the Male or Female bear to one another. When they are to be used as Carriers, two Friends must agree to keep them, one in

London, and the other at *Guilford*, or elsewhere; the Person that lives at *Guilford* must take two or three Cocks or Hens that were bred at his Friend's at *London*, and the other two or three that were bred at *Guilford*; when the Person at *London* has occasion to send an Express, he must roll up a little piece of Paper, and tie it gently with a small String pass'd thro'it about the Pigeon's Neck. But it must be observ'd before, that the Pigeons you design to send with a Message, be kept pretty much in the dark, and without Meat, for eight or ten Hours before you turn them out, and they will then rise and turn round till they have found their way, and continue their Flight till they have got home. With two or three of these Pigeon's on each side, a Correspondence might be carried on in a very expeditious manner, especially in Matters of Curiosity, or those things which tend to publick Good. I know a Gentleman that has set out on a Journey early in the Morning, where it was judged to be dangerous travelling, that has taken one of this sort of Pigeons in his Pocket, and at his Journey's End, which he tells me was near thirty Miles distant from his House, has turn'd off the Pigeon, and it has been at its feeding Place in nine or ten Minutes, with an Account of his safety. In *Turkey* it is very customary for these Pigeons to be taken on board a Ship that sails, by the Captain, and if any thing extraordinary happens within the distance of six or eight Leagues, the Pigeon is sent back with Advice, which sometimes may be a means of saving a Ship from being taken by the Pyrates, or other Enemies, and expedite Trade.

The *Barbary* Pigeon, or *Barb*, is another sort, whose Bill is like that of the *Turbit*, i.e. short and thick, and a broad and naked Circle of a spungy white Substance round about the Eye, like that in the Carrier Pigeon. The Iris of the Eye is white, if the Feathers of the Pigeon are inclining to a darkish Colour; but is red, if the Feathers are white, as we find in other white Birds.

Smiters are another sort of Pigeon, suppos'd to be the same that the *Hollanders* call *Draijers*. This sort shake their Wings as they fly, and rise commonly in a circular manner in their flight; the Males for the most part rising higher than the Females, and frequently falling and flapping them with their Wings, which produces a noise that one may hear a great way; from whence it happens that their Quill-Feathers are commonly broken or shatter'd. These are almost like the Pigeon call'd the Tumbler; the difference chiefly is, that the Tumbler is something smaller, and in its flight will turn itself backward over its Head. The diversity of colours in the Feathers makes no difference.

The Helmet is another kind of Pigeon distinguish'd from the others, because it has the Head, the Quill-Feathers, and the Tail-Feathers always of one colour: Sometimes black, sometimes white, or red, or blue, or yellow; but the other

Feathers of the Body are of a different colour.

The next Pigeon I shall take notice of, is that which is call'd the light Horseman; this is supposed to be a cross strain between a Cock Cropper and a Hen of the Carrier Breed, because they seem to partake of both, as appears from the exerescent Flesh on their Bills, and the swelling of their Crops; but I am not determin'd concerning that point, nor can give any good Judgment about it, till I have seen whether the Cropper be the Male or Female, upon which depends a Debate in Natural Philosophy, which has not been yet decided; this sort however is reckon'd the best Breeder, and are not inclin'd to leave the place of their Birth, or the House where they have been accustom'd.

The *Dastard bill Pigeon* is another sort, which is somewhat bigger than the *Barbary* Pigeon; they have short Bills, and are generally said to have red Eyes, but I suppose those colour'd Eyes are belonging only to those which have white Feathers.

There is also a Pigeon call'd the *Turner*, which is said to have a Tuft of Feathers hanging backward on the Head, which parts, as Mr. *Ray* says, like a Horse's Main.

There is a smaller sort than the former call'd the *Finikin*, but in other respects like the former. There is a sort of Pigeon call'd the *Spot*, suppos'd, and with good Judgment, to take its Name from the Spot on its Forehead just above its Bill, and the Feathers of its Tail always of the same colour with the Spots, and all the other Feathers are white.

Lastly, I shall take notice of the Pigeon call'd the *Mawmet*, or *Mahomet*, supposed to be brought from *Turkey*; however, it is singular for its large black Eyes; the other parts are like those of the *Barbary* Pigeon.

These are the sorts of Pigeons generally known, for the large *Italian* Pigeons are only the larger Runts; and I am of opinion, that the diversity of colours in Pigeons only proceeds from the diversity of kinds of Pigeons, that couple with one another; for I have known Swine that have been whole-footed, that have coupled with those that were clovenfooted, and the Pigs that were produced, were partaking of whole and cloven Hoofs, some one, some two cloven Hoofs, and the rest whole Hoofs.

Concerning the Life of a Pigeon, *Aristotle* says, that a Pigeon will live forty Years, but *Albertus* finishes the Life of a Pigeon at twenty Years; however, *Aldrovandus* tells us of a Pigeon, which continued alive two and twenty Years, and bred all that time except the last six Months, during which space it had lost its Mate, and lived in Widowhood. There is a remarkable Particular mention'd by *Aldrovandus* relating to the Pigeon, which is, that the young Pigeons always bill the Hens as often as they tread them, but the elder

Pigeons only bill the Hens the first time before coupling. *Pliny* and *Athenaeus*, from *Aristotle*, tell us, that it is peculiar to Pigeons not to hold up their Heads when they drink as other Birds and Fowls do, but to drink like Cattle by sucking without intermission; it is easily observed, and worth Observation.

To distinguish which are the Males and Females among Pigeons, it is chiefly known by the Voice and Cooing; the Female has a small weak Voice, and the Male a loud and deep Voice.

The Flesh of Pigeons is hard of Digestion, and therefore is not judged a proper Supper-meat; it is said to yield a melancholy Juice, but if boil'd are very tender, or roasted while they are called Squabs, *viz.* Pigeons about four days old, they are much better for the stomach, and then commonly yield, among the Curious in eating, about eighteen Pence, or two Shillings a piece. The Food which is generally given to Pigeons is Tares; but if we were to mix Spurry-Seeds with it, or Buckwheat, those Grains would forward their breeding, as has been try'd: however, if Pigeons are fed only with Tares, and are of a good kind, we may expect them to breed nine or ten times in a Year; but sometimes, perhaps, not hatch above one at a time, tho' if they were in full Vigour, they would breed up a Pair at one sitting.

In the feeding of Pigeons, it is adviseable not to let them have more Meat at one time than they can eat, for they are apt to toss it about, and lose a great deal of it; so that the contrivance of filling a stone Bottle with their Meat, and putting the Mouth downwards, so that it may come within an Inch of a Plain or Table, and will give a supply as they feed, is much the best way. And their drinking-water should be dispensed to them in the same way out of a Bottle revers'd with the Mouth into a narrow shallow Cistern; but at the same time they should not want the conveniency of a Pan of Water, if there can be no better had, to wash themselves in, for they are of themselves a Bird subject to contract Dirt and Fleas. This is what I shall say of the breeding of tame Pigeons at present.

As to the preparing of Pigeons for the Table, they are commonly either roasted, boiled, baked, or broiled; these are so generally understood, that I need not mention them, nor that Parsley is almost become necessary with them either to be roasted or boiled in the Body of the Pigeon, or put in the Sauces for them: this every one knows, but that the Liver of the Pigeon should be always left in the Body of it, is not known every where, otherwise it would not be so generally taken out and lost, as it is in many places remote from *London*; but this may be, perhaps, because every one does not know that a Pigeon has no Gall. As to particular ways of Dressing of Pigeons, there are two or three which I think are excellent. The first I had from a Lady in *Essex*, whom I have had occasion to mention in this and other Works, and that is in respect to broiling of Pigeons whole. When the Pigeon is prepared for the Kitchen, tye the Skin of the Neck very tight with Packthread, and put into the Body a little Pepper, Salt, Butter, and a little Water at the Vent, and tie it up close at the Neck, broil this upon a gentle Fire, flowring it very well, and basting it with Butter. When this is brought to Table, it brings its Sauce in itself. To those who are not lovers of Spice or Salt, the Butter and Water will be sufficient to draw the Gravy in the Pigeon: but a Pigeon that is split and broiled is of a very different Taste from this, and not worthy, in my opinion, to be reckon'd with it.

Another way of ordering Pigeons, which I met with by accident, and pleased me as well as several Gentlemen in my Company, was the boiling of Pigeons in Paste: The Receipt the People gave me for it, was, to fill the Belly of the Pigeon with Butter, a little Water, some Pepper and Salt, and cover it with a thin light Paste, and then to put it in a fine Linen Cloth, and boil it for a time in proportion to its bigness, and serve it up. When this is cut open, it will yield Sauce enough of a very agreeable Relish.

Stewing of Pigeons, from Mons. *La Fountaine,* an excellent Cook in *Paris.*

Pick and wash half a dozen Pigeons, and lay them into a Stew-Pan, with a Pint or more of good Gravy, an Onion cut small, or three or four large Shalots, a little Bunch of sweet Herbs, some Pepper and Salt, a Pint of Mushrooms that have been well clean'd, and cut into small Pieces, and a little Mace; let these stew gently till they are tender, and add to them about half a Pint of White-Wine just before you take them off the Fire; then lay your Pigeons in your Dish, and brown your Sauce after 'tis discharged of the Bunch of sweet Herbs and the Spice, which should be tied in a little Linen Cloth; pour then your Sauce with the Mushrooms over the Pigeons, and strew the whole over with grated Bread, giving it a browning with a red-hot Iron; or the grated Bread may be omitted.

Another Way of dressing Pigeons, from the same.

Take young Pigeons and par-boil them, then chop some raw Bacon very small, with a little Parsley, a little sweet Marjoram, or sweet Basil, and a small Onion; season this with Salt, and Pepper, and fill the Bodys of the Pigeons with it. When this is done, stew the Pigeons in Gravy, or strong Broth, with an Onion stuck with Cloves, a little Verjuice and Salt; when they are enough, take them out of the Liquor, and dip them in Eggs that have been well beaten, and after that roll them in grated Bread, that they may be cover'd with it. Then make some Lard very hot, and fry them in it till they are brown, and serve them up with some of the Liquor they were stew'd in, and fry'd Parsley.

In the beginning of this Month, as well as in *December*, the Eel is commonly laid up in the Mud, and we find them there in Clusters folded one over another, which I suppose is the manner of coupling; for in the beginning of *March*, or end of *February*, we see young ones as small as Threads on the edges of the Waters. I think it is no longer to be doubted, but that the Eel is viviparous; that is, it brings its young ones perfectly framed, and does not lay Spawn like other Fish: and the Resemblance the Eel bears to that Fish, which is call'd by the Fishermen the Coney-Fish, and is found at this time about the *Buoy in the Nore* full of young ones, makes me the rather conclude the Eel brings forth its Young perfectly form'd. This Fish is not accounted wholesome at this time of the Year, nor fit for eating till they begin to run in *March*, therefore what I have to say relating to preparing Eels for the Table, will be set down in the Month of *March*.

* * * * *

FEBRUARY.

As our Poultry will begin to lay plentifully in this Month, it may not be improper to say something of them before we proceed to give the Receipts for dressing and preparing their Eggs for the Table. It is necessary to be known first, the Difference between Fowls and Birds; a Fowl always leads its young Ones to the Meat, and a Bird carries the Meat to the Young: for this reason, we find that Fowls always make their Nests upon the Ground, while Birds, for the most part, build their Nests aloft; so then our common Poultry are Fowls, the Pheasant, Partridge, Peacock, Turkey, Bustard, Quail, Lapwing, Duck, and such like are all Fowls: But a Pigeon is a Bird, and a Stork, or Crane, and a Heron, are Birds, they build their Nests aloft, and carry Meat to their young Ones.

The Characteristick Marks of the Poultry Kind are, besides what I have said above, to have short, strong, and somewhat crooked Bills, which are best adapted to pick up Grains of Corn, Pulse, and other Seeds, which is chiefly what these Fowls feed upon; and we may observe, that as neither Birds nor Fowls have Teeth to macerate their Food with, so Nature has provided them not only with a Crop to soften their Meat, but a Stomach furnish'd with thick strong Mucles, whose use is to grind the Grains of Corn, or any hard Meat swallow'd whole, which they perform by the help of little Stones, which Birds and Fowls swallow now and then, and which supply the defect of Teeth. It is observable, that Fowls, for the most part, lay a greater number of Eggs than Birds, even many more than they can sit upon at one time. I have known about thirty Eggs lay'd by one common Poultry-Hen, but it is seldom that any Bird lays more than five or six, except the Wren, and the Tom-tit, andthe

Pigeon not more than two. Again, the Poultry, contrary to others of the winged Race, are armed with Spurs; and it is observable, that the Cocks of the common Poultry distinguish themselves from diurnal Fowls, by crowing or singing in the Night, as the Nightingale distinguishes itself from the rest of the Bird-kind. As for the length of Life in common Poultry, *Aldrovandus* makes it to be about ten Years, but that the Cock becomes unfit for the Hens when he is four Years old; and we find by experience the same, as well as that a Cock should not have more than six or seven Hens, if we expect healthful and strong Broods of Chickens. About the Laying-time of these Fowls, Spurry-Seed and Buckwheat is an excellent strengthening Food for them.

There is another thing relating to Fowls of this kind well worthy observation; and that is, of Capons being made to bring up a Brood of Chickens like a Hen, clucking of 'em, brooding them, and leading them to their Meat, with as much Care and Tenderness as their Dams would do. To bring this about, *Jo. Baptista Porta*, in *lib. 4. Mag. Nat.* prescribes to make a Capon very tame and familiar, so as to take Meat out of one's Hand; then about Evening-time pluck the Feathers off his Breast, and rub the bare Skin with Nettles, and then put the Chickens to him, which will presently run under his Breast and Belly; the Chickens then rubbing his Breast gently with their Heads, perhaps allay the stinging and itching occasioned by the Nettles, or perhaps they may contribute to warm that part where the Feathers are away; however, the bare part must be rubb'd with Nettles three or four Nights successively, till he begins to love and delight in the Chickens.

When a Capon is once accustomed to this Service, he will not casuly leave it off; but as soon as he has brought up one Brood of Chickens, we may put another to him, and when they are fit to shift for themselves, we may give him the Care of a third.

The sorts of the House Pullen, or common Poultry, are many; but as the use of them for the Table is the same, I shall only take notice of such as are of the large Dunghill kind, or of the *Hamburgh* sort, of the Game kind, and of the small *Dutch* kind; which last is admired by some for the fineness of their Flesh, and for being great Layers, especially in the Winter: But it is certain that the larger sort sell the best at Market, and lay the largest Eggs, and therefore should be the most cultivated about a Farm. As for the Game Breed, some fancy that their Flesh is more white and tender than the other sorts; but they are always quarrelling, which contributes to make themselves and their Brood weak.

Where we propose to raise a large Stock of Poultry, we should be careful to secure our Hen-House from Vermin of all sorts, and keep it dry and clean, allowing also as much Air as possible; for if it is not often clean'd, the scent of the Dung will give your Fowls the Roop: So likewise there must be easy Convenience for perching of the Fowls, disposed in such a manner, that the Perches be not placed over any of the Hen's Nests, which must always lie dry and clean, bedded with Straw, for Hay is apt to make the sitting Hens faint and weak. When we design to set a Hen, we should save her Eggs in dry Bran, and when she clucks, put no more in her Nest than she can well cover; for as to certain numbers to be more lucky in hatching, there is nothing in that: And if we fat Fowls, then use the Method prescribed in my *Country Gentleman and Farmer's Monthly Director*, in the Month of *January*, which is much the best way of any that has yet been discovered. In the choice of Fowls for eating, those which are white feather'd and white legg'd, are much tenderer and finer in their Flesh than those of other Colours, and are much weaker; for which reason, those who understand Cocking, do not approve of such as happen to be white feather'd: and those which are black feather'd, are accounted the hottest and most fiery, and their Flesh is coarser than in other Fowls. But let us now come to the use of the Flesh of these Fowls, which is either eaten roasted, boiled, fricasseed, baked, or broiled either slit or whole. It is to be noted, that the Flesh of these Fowls or Chickens boiled is more easily digested than the Flesh of those that are roasted, and the Flesh of the Legs is more easy of Digestion than that of the Breast. Mr. *Ray* takes notice, that those parts of Fowls, which are continually in Action, are esteem'd the best, for which reason he prefers the Legs of tame Fowls, and what we call the Wings in wild Fowl, that is, the fleshy part on the Breast. *Gefner* and *Aldrovandus* have both largely treated of the use of the Flesh and Eggs of these Fowls, but I believe some of the following Receipts for dressing them, will not be unacceptable, they being more adapted to the Taste of our Times.

I shall begin with some curious ways of dressing of Eggs, which I had from a Gentleman of *Brussels*, who had collected them from most parts of *Europe*.

First Way of dressing of Eggs.

Boil your Eggs till they are hard, and cut the Whites only into Rings or large pieces; then cut some Parsley and Onions small, and stew them with a little Salt, Pepper, and Nutmeg in half a Pint of Water, till the Onion and Parsley is tender; when this is done, put in your Eggs well flower'd, and as soon as they are hot, put half a Pint of Cream to them, and thicken them for serving at the Table. The Yolks may be fry'd to garnish the Dish.

Second Way of preparing of Eggs.

Boil your Eggs hard as before, and cut the Whites likewise as directed in the above Receipt, and then prepare some Gravy, a bunch of sweet Herbs, a little Salt, some Lemon Peel, some *Jamaica* Pepper beaten small, an Onion shred small, and let these stew together till it is sufficiently season'd; after which, strain it off, and put in the Eggs to heat them thoroughly, and then thicken the whole with burnt Butter.

Third Way of preparing of Eggs.

Break some Eggs, beat them well, and season them with Salt and some *Jamaica* Pepper finely powder'd, then make some Butter very hot in a Pan, and pour in the Mixture to fry, till it is hard enough to hold together; then it must be taken out, and cut into several Pieces, and served with the same Sauce directed in the foregoing Receipt.

Fourth Way of dressing of Eggs.

Take the Hearts of two or three Cabbage-Lettuces, a little Sorrel, Parsley, Cherville, and a large Mushroom, put them in Water over the Fire till they are tender, then chop them together very small with some Yolks of hard Eggs, and season the whole with Salt, Pepper, or Nutmeg; and when the Mass is well mixt together, put them in paste, making them into small flat Puffs, and fry them. This may be diversify'd, by adding some sweet Herbs chop'd small to the Mixture, before it is put into Paste.

Fifth Way of dressing of Eggs.

Beat as many Eggs as you think convenient, and at the same time squeeze the Juice of an Orange among them; being well beaten, season them with a little Salt, then take a Stew-Pan, and if it is a Fast-day, put some Butter into it and pour in your Eggs, keeping them stirring continually over the Fire till they are enough, then pour them into a Plate upon Sippets. But on Flesh-days, instead of Butter use strong Gravy, or on Fish-days some Mushroom-Gravy may be used instead of Butter, or with it.

Sixth Way of ordering of Eggs.

Boil Eggs till they are hard, peel them, and cut them lengthways, then quarter each half, and dip the several quarters in Batter, made of Flower, Eggs and Milk; fry them then in Butter very hot, over a quick Fire, and lay them a while before the Fire to drain. In the mean while prepare for them the following Sauce of burnt or brown Butter, seasoned with Sweet-herbs, Salt, Pepper, Nutmeg, and a little Elder-Vinegar, with some Mushrooms stew'd and hash'd; and garnish your Dish, or Plate, with fry'd Bread, Parsley, and fry'd Mushrooms.

These are a few out of many Receipts, which the above Gentleman gave me, and may serve as Directions for many others; for by what I can find, all the others depend upon the same Principles. The variation of these depends upon the variety of Tastes: Some like Amletts, or Frazes of Eggs, with Bacon, or with Clary, or other high-tasted Herbs, which every good Housewife knows how to direct. The same Gentleman observes, that Amletts with boiled Artichoke Bottoms sliced, Amletts with the Tops of boil'd Asparagus, green Pease boiled, Mushrooms stew'd and sliced, or Truffles, these he tells me are extraordinary.

As to the particulars relating to the dressing of farced Fowls, the methods which most agree with my Palate, and have been admired by the best Judges of my Acquaintance, are the following, which I had from *France*.

To dress a Capon, or other Fowl.

When your Fowl is truss'd for Roasting, cover the Breast with a thin slice of fat Bacon, and put an Onion stuck with Cloves into the Belly, with some Salt and Pepper; when it is roasted enough, take off the Bacon, and strew it with grated Bread, till it is brown. This is eaten, either with Orange-Juice and Salt, or if Oysters are at hand, as they are about many Farms in *England*, they may be stew'd gently with a little White Wine, Spice, and a little Butter, which will make an agreeable Sauce for it. Or else it may be eaten with a very good Sauce, which I have often met with, and have lik'd as well; which is made with small Beer and Water, equal quantities, an Onion slic'd, some Pepper and Salt, and about an Ounce of Flesh, either of Mutton or Beef, to boil till it comes to about half, supposing at first 'tis not above half a Pint; and at some places, instead of Mutton, &c. this Sauce has been only made of the Neck of a Fowl. This Sauce, in my Opinion, has a very rich Taste, and has been well approv'd of by some curious Travellers: Where we could have this, we rather chose it than Wine-Sauce. Capons, Pullets, or others of this sort of Fowl, may be also larded with Bacon, if they are roasted; but the Gentleman aforesaid, who gave me this Receipt, told me that no Water-Fowl must be larded with Bacon.

To farce or stuff a Fowl. From Mr. *Agneau.*

When your Fowl is made ready for Roasting, take the Liver boil'd, a Shallot, a little Fat of Bacon, some grated Bread, the Bottom of a boil'd Artichoke, and some Mushrooms, chop these very small, and make a forc'd Meat of them, season'd with Salt and Spices at pleasure; fill the Belly of the Fowl with this, and then truss it, covering the Breast with a thin slice of fat Bacon, and over that put a piece of writing Paper. Roast this, and serve it up with the following Sauce: Make a hash of Mushrooms, an Anchovy, a few Capers and some Gravy, boiled together with such Seasoning as you approve; the Sauce should be thicken'd or brown'd, and it is fit for the Table.

To farce Fowls another way. From the same.

Take Pullets and roast them, then take the Flesh of the Breast, and mince it small, with some Fat of Bacon boil'd, a few Mushrooms, a little Onion and

Parsley, and some Crumb of Bread soak'd in Cream over a gentle Fire; when all these are well minc'd, add the Yolks of two or three Eggs, and mix all together; then with this forced Meat fill the Breast of the Fowls in their proper shape, and beat some Whites of Eggs to go over them, and then cover them thick with Crumbs of Bread, having first laid your Fowls commodiously in a Dish, and then put them in the Oven till they have taken a fine brown Colour. If you have more of this farced Meat than you use in making good the Fowls, either make it into Balls and fry them, or else make a Batter of Eggs, Milk, and Wheat-Flower, and dip small parcels of the Farce into it to fry for garnishing. You may make a Sauce to these farced Fowls with stew'd Mushrooms toss'd up with Cream; the same may be done with Turkeys, Pheasants, &c.

To make a brown or white Fricassee of Chickens. From the same.

Strip the Chickens of their Skins as soon as they are kill'd, and when they are drawn, cut their Wings, Legs, and most fleshy parts in Pieces, then fry them a little in Hog's-Lard; after which, put them to stew with a little Butter and Gravy, for a brown Fricassee, or Butter and Water for a white Fricassee; to either of these add a Glass of White Wine, with a Seasoning of Salt, Pepper, Nutmeg, Cherville cut small, and three or four young Onions whole, that they may be withdrawn when the Fricassee is enough: Then brown the Sauce with some of the same Lard the Chickens were fry'd in, and thicken it with burnt Flower; to this you may add fry'd or stew'd Mushrooms. But for a white Fricassee, instead of the browning with the Lard and burnt Flower, thicken the Sauces with three or four Yolks of Eggs, and a little Verjuice; or else when the Fricassee is stew'd enough, take off the Fat as much as possible, and toss it up with Cream; this will serve to fricassee Rabbits.

In Lent, and on Fast-days, I have eaten very good Soups abroad, that were made without any Flesh. And as that is not very common in *England*, I thought it convenient to bring over the Receipts with me, that we may know how to make the best of every thing about a Farm.

To make Fish-Gravy for Soups.

To make this Fish-Gravy, which may serve for a Foundation of all Fish Soups, take Tench or Eels, or both, well scour'd from Mud, and their Outsides scour'd well with Salt; then pull out their Gills, and put them in a Kettle with Water, Salt, a bunch of sweet Herbs, and an Onion stuck with Cloves; boil these an hour and a half, and then strain off the Liquor thro' a Cloth: add to this the Peelings of Mushrooms well wash'd, or Mushrooms themselves cut small; boil these together, and strain the Liquor thro' a Sieve into a Stew-Pan, upon some burnt or fry'd Flower, and a little Lemon, which will soon render it of a good Colour, and delicate Flavour, fit for Soups, which may be varied according to the Palate, by putting in Pot-Herbs and Spices to every one's liking; this will keep good some time. When you make any of this into Soup, remember to put a Glass of white Wine into your Soup a little before you serve it.

A Foundation for Herb Soups.

Take a quantity of good Herbs, such as Cherville, Spinage, Sallery, Leeks, Beet-Cards, and such like, with two or three large Crusts of Bread, some Butter, a bunch of sweet Herbs, and a little Salt; put these, with a moderate quantity of Water, into a Kettle, and boil them an hour and half, and strain off the Liquor thro' a Sieve, and it will be a good Foundation for Soups, either of Asparagus Buds, Lettuce, or any other kind, fit for Lent or Fast-days. These Herb Soups are sometimes strengthened with two or three Yolks of Eggs, a little before they are serv'd to the Table.

As in this Month there is plenty of Oranges, so it is a proper Season to make Orange-Wine, which is a most pleasant and refreshing Liquor in the Summer Season. The following Receipt is an approved one for it.

To make Orange Wine. From Mrs. *E. B.*

Take twenty Gallons of Water, and forty Pounds of fine Sugar, mix these together, boil and clarify it with the Whites of Eggs: against this is done, have two hundred middling Oranges, pared so thin that no White appear upon the Rinds; and as soon as the Syrup is taken off the Fire, put the Peels of five and twenty Oranges into it; and when the Liquor is quite cold, put in the Juice of the Oranges, with some fresh Ale-Yeast spread upon a warm Toast of white Bread; let this work two days, and then put it into the Vessel or Cask, adding at the same time, two Gallons of white *Port* Wine; and then to every Gallon of Liquor, add an Ounce of Syrup of Citron, or Syrup of Lemon, and in two Months time it be fit to bottle.

In this Month it may not be unneccasary to observe that Oranges are declining, and waste apaces; but they are commonly very cheap, and therefore such as have a great Call for Orange-peel, as Confectioners, &c. now buy them in quantities; but a little Carriage by Land will contribute to their quicker decay. The Orange, tho' it is not found in every Garden, yet I esteem it as a necessary Fruit in many Cases, and what a Family can hardly be without; and truly considering how good Oranges we might have in our Gardens, and how easily they may be cultivated against Garden-walls, I much wonder that they are not more generally planted with us. There is a very good Instance of their prospering well against a Wall, and thriving in the natural Ground, at Mr. *Heather*'s, a curious Gentleman at *Tiwittenham*, which Trees bear very well, and bring very large Fruit.

But as I have observ'd above, that this is the Season when foreign Oranges are generally in the greatest plenty about *London*, it is a good time to preserve their Juice; especially it may prove useful to such as have opportunities of vending *Punch* in large Quantitles, or for such who find that Liquor agreeable to them: For tho' I have known several who have express'd the Juice of Oranges and Lemons, and bottled it up against a dear Time, yet such Juice has turn'd to be of a very disageeable Sourness in a short season. The Method which I have taken to preserve this Juice to be used in Punch, was to express the Juice, and pass it thro' a Jelly-bag, with about two Ounces of double-refined Loaf-Sugar to each Pint of Juice, and a Pint of Brandy, or Arrack; bottle this up, and cork it well with sound Corks, and you may keep it a Year. Before you pass this Liquor thro' the Bag, you may put about the Rind of two Oranges to steep for two Hours, into each Quart of Liquor, which will give it a rich Flavour. When you have occasion to use it for Punch, it is at the discretion of the Maker to add what quantity of Brandy, or Arrack, he thinks proper, only remembring that there is already a Pint in each Bottle. This may be of good advantage to Inn-keepers, &c. who live remote from *London*; and by this way they need not run the hazard of losing this sort of Fruit, by bruising or rotting, which they will be subject to, if they are not well pack'd, and have bad Roads. And besides, considering the vast difference that there is in the Price of Oranges, so much, that at some Seasons you must pay as much for one, as will at another time purchase near a Dozen, it is the best to consider of this when they are at the cheapest Price. We may likewise use the same Method with Lemons; but it is not convenient to steep any of the Peels in the Liquor, for they will give it a disagreeable Flavour. But it is to be understood also, that Lemons are to be met with in perfection all the Year; only this Season they are at the cheapest Price. The Peel of an Orange or two may be put to each Quart of Juice, to steep as above directed, bruising every piece of Peel as you put it into the Juice. Note, that the Lemon and Orange Juice must not be mix'd together in the same Bottles.

* * * * *

MARCH.

This Month all sorts of Pond-fish are in Season; *viz.* the Jack, the Carp, the Tench, the Perch, and the Eel; but it must be noted, that both the Males and Females of every kind of Fish are in their greatest Perfection before the Spawning-time, and they are sick and unwholesome for three Weeks after Spawning. The Eel, indeed, has not yet been known to lay any Spawn, but is likely to be Viviparous, as I have mention'd in the Month of *January*. The Jack, or Pike, this Month runs, as the Sportsmen call it; that is, they retire into the Ditches, if there are any in their way, and feed upon Frogs; or else, in warm Days, lie upon the top of the Waters, and are easily taken by Snares: However, they are this Month full row'd, and are then in their greatest Strength, and in the best condition for the Table. We judge those are the best which are broad-back'd, and deep Fish; for those that are long and slender, have not their Flesh firm, which is reckon'd the Perfection of a Fish. The way of preparing this Fish in the best manner, in my Opinion, if it is large, is to roast it according to the following Receipt, which I had from Mr. *John Hughs*, an excellent Cook in *London*.

When a Jack or Pike is discharged of its Scales and Entrails, and well clean'd, prepare a Mixture in the following Manner, to be sew'd up in the Belly of the Fish: Take of grated Bread about one third part, the Rivet, or Liver of the Fish cut small, with Oysters chopped, or the Flesh of Eels cut small; mix these with three or four Eggs butter'd in a Sauce-pan, to which add Pepper and Salt with some dry'd Sweet Marjoram well pouder'd, or such other Sweet-herbs as are most grateful to the Palate, an Anchovy shred small, and fill the Belly of the Fish with the Preparation, and sew it up. When this is done, cut two small Laths of Willow, or any other Wood, except Deal, or such as has a Turpentine Juice in it, of the length of the Fish, and lay the Fish upon the Spit, with the two Laths upon the Fish, and bind them together with a Fillet of Linnen, about an Inch wide, which must be wrapp'd round them in a Screw-like manner, and then laid down to the Fire, and basted very well with Butter, and drudged with Crumbs of Bread, and the same sort of Sweet-herbs that were used in the Mixture abovemention'd. Where you have not the conveniency of Oysters, or Eels, to compose the aforemention'd Mixture, you may add a larger quantity of butter'd Eggs. Where there is the conveniency of an Oven, we may bake such a Fish with less trouble than roasting it; and in that case rub the outside with the Yolk of an Egg, and roll it in some of the Mixture abovemention'd, the Anchovy and butter'd Eggs excepted, putting some Vinegar and Butter in the Pan. The Sauce to this Fish is Butter melted, a little White-wine, and mix'd with a third part of season'd Beef Gravy, with a Spoonful or two of Mushroom Ketchup, and an Anchovy or two dissolved.

The smaller Sort of these Fish, *i.e.* such as are about a Foot long, are most commonly boiled, but they will do well baked, as above directed. The same Sauce may be used with the boil'd Fish; or instead of Beef Gravy, may be used the Mushroom Gravy, as directed in this Work, which will have a much finer Relish than the Beef Gravy.

In this Month likewise, the Carp is fit for the Table, and is commonly much admir'd, if it be well stew'd; otherwise I think it makes but an indifferent Dish, being a Fish full of Cross-bones. The Head is accounted much the best part of the Fish, and is therefore presented as a Compliment to the greatest Stranger at the Table. The Carp, as it is a Fish which thrives best in black, deep, standing Waters, is therefore commonly given to taste of the Mud; but to cure this, those Carps you intend for the Table should be put into a clear Water for a Week before you use them, that they may purge themselves. You may keep two Brace of large Carps well enough in a two-dozen Hamper, plung'd into any part of a River where there is a clear Stream, or Trench that is fed by a Spring, and they will become of an extraordinary sweet Taste. And so we may do with Tench and Eels, when we catch them in foul feeding Waters. When your Fish are thus purify'd, dress your Carps after the following manner:

To Stew Carps or Tench.

Take a Brace of live Carp, scale them, gut and wash them, and bleed them in the Tails, so that the Blood be not lost; for according to all the Receipts for stewing this kind of Fish, the Blood, however small the Quantity is of it, must make part of the Sauce: Lay these in a Stew-Pan with the Blood, a Pint of Beef-Gravy, a Pint of Claret, a large Onion stuck with Cloves, three large Anchovies, a Stick of Horse-radish sliced, the Peel of half a large Lemon, Pepper and Salt at pleasure, a Bunch of Sweet-herbs, two or three Spoonfuls of Vinegar. This Liquor should nearly cover the Carps; so that if the Gravy and Claret, mention'd above, be not sufficient, add equal quantities of each till you have enough; cover this close, and set the Stew-pan over a gentle Fire, till the lower-side of the Fish are stew'd enough; then turn them, and keep them stewing as before, close cover'd, till they are enough; after which, lay them in a Dish upon Sippets of fry'd Bread, and strain off the Sauce to be thicken'd and brown'd with burnt Butter. This must be poured over the Fish, and the Dish garnish'd with the Row or Milt, Barberries, and Lemons sliced.

The same Method is also used for stewing of large Roach, Dace, and Chubb; but a Tench stew'd this way, is much better than a Carp, The Back of this Fish, and the Head, are the Pieces which are most in esteem.

It is worth our remark, that when we find our Tench cover'd with black Scales, they Will always taste muddy, which is the fault of the River-Tench about *Cambridge*; but where we find Tench of a golden Colour, we are sure of good Fish, that will eat sweet without the trouble of putting 'em into clear Water to purify.

As there is some trouble in the dressing of this Fish, they may be stew'd the Night before they are to be eaten, and will keep very well; and half an hour before they are to be serv'd up, set them over the Fire to be thoroughly hot, and then brown their Sauce as before directed.

It is to be observ'd, that to bake these Fish with the above Ingredients is as good a Way as the stewing them. It is likewise necessary to observe, that all Fish which will keep a long time alive out of Water, will sicken, and their Flesh become unfirm by lying in the Air; therefore, if Fish are to be sent a Day's Journey, or kept a Day before they are used, kill them as soon as they are taken out of the Water, and the Flesh will be firm.

I shall add one thing more concerning the boiling of Fish, which was communicated to me by a very ingenious Gentleman, who has made Fishing his Study for many Years: He says, that the Goodness of boil'd Fish consists chiefly in the Firmness of the Flesh; and in the next place, that the Flesh parts easily from the Bone; to do which, he directs to kill the Fish immediately after they are taken out of the Water; and when you design to boil 'em, put a large handful of Salt into about two or three quarts of Water, and so in proportion: Put in the Fish while the Water is cold; then set them over the Fire, and make them boil as quick as possible, without any Cover over the Pan. This is approved to do very well. This Receipt is particularly good for boiling of Flounders. His Receipt for Sauce for boil'd Fish, is the following.

Sauce for boil'd Fish.

Take Beef-Gravy, an Onion, a little White-wine, some Horse-radish sliced, Lemon-peel, an Anchovy, a Bunch of Sweet-herbs, boil them well together, and strain off the Liquor, then put a Spoonful of Mushroom Ketchup to it, and thicken it with Butter mix'd with Flower: or for Fast-days the Gravy may be omitted, and in the place of it put Mushroom-Gravy, or a larger quantity of Mushroom-Ketchup, or some of the Fish-Gravy mention'd in *February*, which is good to put in Sauce for any sort of Fish.

As this is the Month when Eels begin to be good, I shall give two or three Receipts for the Dressing of them in the best manner: The first for Roasting of Eels, or Pitchcotting them, I had from the Crown at *Basingstoke* some Years ago; and that for Collaring of Eels, from Mr. *John Hughs*, a celebrated Cook in *London*. But I shall first observe, that the Silver Eel is counted the best; and that all such as lie and feed in clear Streams, may be used without purging them, as I have directed above; but all Pond Eels must be put into clear Waters for a Week, at least, before they are used, if you would have them in perfection. And now to the Receipts.

To Roast or Broil an Eel, from the *Crown* at *Basingstoke, An. 1718.*

Take a large Eel, rub the Skin well with Salt, then gut it and wash it well; cut off the Head and skin it, laying by the Skin in Water and Salt; then lay your Eel in a clean Dish, and pour out about a Pint of Vinegar upon it, letting it remain in the Vinegar near an hour; then withdraw your Eel from the Vinegar, and make several Incisions at proper distances in the Flesh of the Back and Sides, which Spaces must be fill'd with the following Mixture:

Take grated Bread, the Yolks of two or three hard Eggs, one Anchovy minced small, some Sweet-Marjoram dry'd and pouder'd; or for want of that, some Green Marjoram shred small: to this add Pepper, Salt, a little Pouder of Cloves, or *Jamaica* Pepper, and a little fresh Butter, to be beat all together in a Stone Mortar, till it becomes like a Paste; with which Mixture fill all the Incisions that you cut in the Eel, and draw the Skin over it: then tie the end of the Skin next the Head, and prick it with a Fork in several Places; then tie it to a Spit to roast, or lay it upon a Grid-iron to broil, without basting. The Sauce for this is Butter, Anchovy, a little Pepper, and Lemon-juice.

To Pitchcot Eels.

Take a large Eel, clean well with Salt and Water both the Skin and the Inside, then pull off the Skin, and prepare the following Mixture of Bread grated, Sweet-herbs pouder'd, or minced small, such as Sweet-marjoram, Sage, and some Pepper and Salt; then rub your Eel with Yolks of Eggs, and after that, roll it in the Mixture, then draw the Skin over it, and cut your Eel in several pieces about three Inches in length, dipping them again in Yolks of Eggs, and after that, in the above Mixture: then lay them on the Gridiron, and when they are enough, serve them to the Table, with the Sauce prescribed for the roasted Eels, abovemention'd.

To Collar Eels, from Mr. *John Hughs,* a famous Cook in *London.*

Take a large Eel, and scour the Skin and the Inside very well with Salt, cut off the Head, and split it down the Back, then lay it abroad upon your Dresser, and season it well with Spice, Salt, and a good quantity of Red Sage minced small: mix these well, and sprinkle the Mixture thick upon your Eel, then roll it up, and tye it close in a thin Cloth at each end, and in the middle; boil it then in a strong Pickle of Vinegar, Water, Salt, some Spice, and a Bay-leaf or two; and when it is boiled enough, take out the Eel, and let it stand till it is quite cold, and when the Pickle is cold likewise, pour the Pickle into a glazed Earthen-Pan, and put your Eel into it to keep for Use; this will remain good several Weeks, if it is kept close cover'd. When the Eel is quite cold, take off the Cloth.

The Eel is also good in Pyes, fry'd and boil'd, which every one knows how to prepare.

About the end of this Month, the Trout begins to come in Season; for before this time, its Body is cover'd with little Insects, which is a Demonstration of its being sick and unwholesome. The best way of eating this Fish is to boil it, and serve it with Butter and an Anchovy for Sauce; as is commonly practis'd about *Hungerford, Spenham-Land*, and other noted Places for Trout.

If the Season is now mild, about the end of the Month the Sap in the Birch-Tree will begin to be very fluent. And so in the Choice of Fish to be seasonable, we must have regard to the Temper of the Air; for if the Air be mild and gentle, sooner or later all parts of the Creation are govern'd by it: but when I direct for this Month or another any thing to be done, I suppose the Temper of the Air to be what it is for the generality; but the Birch-Tree Sap we will suppose begins now to flow, and then we are to take the opportunity of making Wine of it. The best Receipt I have met with for making this Wine, is the following.

To make Birch-Wine. From Lady *W*.

When the Sap of the Birch-Tree will run, cut a large Notch in the Bark of the Trunk of the Tree, in such a place as one may conveniently place a Vessel to receive the Sap; which Will flow at the Incision very plentifully, without doing any harm to the Tree. If the Trees are pretty large, you may expect about a Gallon of Liquor from each of them, which must be order'd in the following manner. Take five Gallons of the Liquor, to which put five Pounds of Powder-Sugar, and two Pounds of Raisins of the Sun stoned; to this, put the Peel of one large Lemon, and about forty large fresh Cloves: boil all these together, taking off the Scum carefully as it rises; then pour it off into some Vessel to cool, and as soon as it is cool enough to put Yeast to it, work it as you would do Ale for two days, and then tunn it, taking care not to stop the Vessel till it has done Working, and in a Month's time it will be ready to bottle. This is not only a very Pleasant, but a very Wholesome Wine.

This Month is esteemed one of the principal Seasons for brewing of Malt Liquors for long keeping; the Reason is, because the Air at this time of the Year is temperate, and contributes to the good Working or Fermenting the Drink, which chiefly promotes its Preservation and good Keeping: for very cold Weather prevents the free Fermentation or Working of Liquors, as well as very hot Weather; so that if we brew in very cold Weather, unless we use some Means to warm the Cellar while new Drink is Working, it will never clear itself as it ought to do; and the same Misfortune will it lie under, if in very hot Weather the Cellar is not put in a temperate state, the Consequence of which will be, that such Drink will be Muddy and Sour, and, perhaps, never recover; or if it does, perhaps not under two or three Years. Again, such Misfortunes are often owing to the badness of the Cellars; for where they are dug in springy Ground, or are subject to Wet in the Winter, then the Drink will chill, and grow flat and dead. But where Cellars are of this sort, it is adviseable to make your great Brewings in this Month rather than in *October*; for you may keep such Cellars temperate in Summer, but cannot warm them in Winter, and so your Drink brew'd in *March* will have due time to settle and adjust itself before the Cold can do it any great harm. It is adviseable likewise to build your Cellars for keeping of Drink, after such a manner, that none of the external Air may come into them; for the variation of the Air abroad, was there free admission of it into the Cellars, would cause as many Alterations in the Liquors, and so would keep them perpetually disturb'd and unfit for drinking. I know some curious Gentlemen in these things, that keep double Doors to their Cellars, on purpose that none of the outward Air may get into them, and they have good reason to boast of their Malt-Liquors. The meaning of the double Doors, is to keep one shut while the other is open, that the outward Air may be excluded; such Cellars, if they lie dry, as they ought to do, are said to be cool in Summer, and warm in Winter, tho' in reality, they are constantly the same in point of Temper: they seem indeed cool in hot Weather, but that is because we come into them from an hotter abroad; and so they seem to us warm in Winter, because we come out of a colder Air to them; so that they are only cold or warm comparatively, as the Air we come out of is hotter or colder. This is the Case, and a Cellar should be thus dispos'd if we expect to have good Drink. As for the Brewing Part itself, I shall leave that to the Brewers in the several Counties in *England*, who have most of them different Manners even of Brewing honestly. What I shall chiefly touch upon, besides what I shall speak of Cellaring, will relate to Water, Malt, Hops, and the keeping Liquors.

The best Water, to speak in general, is River Water, such as is soft, and has partook of the Air and Sun; for this easily insinuates itself into the Malt, and extracts its Virtue; whereas the hard Waters astringe and bind the Parts of the Malt, so that its Virtue is not freely communicated to the Liquor. It is a Rule with a Friend of mine, that all Water which will mix with Soap is fit for Brewing, and he will by no means allow of any other; and I have more than once experienc'd, that where the same Quantity of Malt has been used to a Barrel of River Water, and the same to a Barrel of Spring Water, the River Water Brewing has excell'd the other in Strength above five degrees in twelve Months, as I prov'd by a small Glass-Tube with a Seal, and was much preferable to the Taste, I must observe too, that the Malt was not only in Quantity the same for one Barrel as for another, but was the same in Quality, having been all measur'd from the same Heap; so also the Hops were the same both in Quality and Quantity, and the Time of boiling, and both work'd in the same manner, and tunn'd and kept in the same Cellar. Here it was plain that there was no difference but the Water, and yet one Barrel was worth two of the other.

There is one thing which has long puzzled the best Brewers, which I shall here endeavour to explain; and that is, where several Gentlemen in the same

Town have employ'd the same Brewer, have had the same Malt, the same Hops, and the same Water too, and brew'd all in the same Month, and broach'd their Drink at the same time; and yet one has had Beer which has been extremely fine, strong, and well tasted, while the others have hardly had any worth drinking. I conjecture there may be three Reasons for this difference: One may be the different Weather which might happen at the different Brewings in this Month, which might make an Alteration in the Working of the Liquors: Or, secondly, that the Yeast or Barm might be of different sorts, or in different states, wherewith these Liquors were Work'd: And, thirdly, that the Cellars were not equally good: for I am very sensible, the goodness of such Drink, as is brew'd for keeping, depends upon the goodness of the Cellars where it is kept; for at a Gentleman's of my Acquaintance, who for many Years has used the same Brewer, and the same Method, his Beer is always of the same Taste, his Cellars, or Vaults, are very dry, and have two or three Doors to them.

The *Dorchester* Beer, which is esteem'd preferable to most of the Malt-Liquor in *England,* is for the most part brew'd of chalky Water, which is almost every where in that County; and as the Soil is generally Chalk there, I am of opinion, that the Cellars being dug in that dry Soil contributes to the good keeping of their Drink, it being of a close texture, and of a drying quality, so as to dissipate Damps; for damp Cellars, we find by experience, are injurious to keeping Liquors, as well as destructive to the Casks. The Malt of this Country is of a pale Colour; and the best Drink of this County that I have met with to be sold, is at a small House against the Church at *Blackwater,* four Miles beyond *Dorchester,* in the Road to *Bridport,* in *Dorsetshire*; they broach no Beer till it is a Year old, and has had time to mellow. But there must be such Cellars as I speak of, which inclose a temperate Air, to ripen Drink in; the constant temperate Air digests and softens these Malt Liquors, so that they drink smooth as Oil; but in the Cellars which are unequal, by letting in Heats and Colds, the Drink is subject to grow stale and sharp: For this reason it is, that Drink, which is brew'd for a long Voyage at Sea, should be perfectly ripe and fine before it is exported, for when it has had sufficient time to digest in the Cask, and is rack'd from the Bottom or Lee, it will bear carriage without injury. It is farther to be noted, that in proportion to the quantity of Liquor, which is enclosed in one Cask, so will it be a longer or a shorter time in ripening. A Vessel which will contain two Hogsheads of Beer, will require twice as much time to perfect itself as one of a Hogshead; and from my experience I find there should be no Vessel used for strong Beer, which we design to keep, less than a Hogshead: for one of that quantity, if it be fit to draw in a Year, has Body enough to support it two, or three, or four Years, if it has strength of Malt and Hops in it, as the *Dorseshire* Beer has; and this will bear the Sea very well, as we find every day.

There is one thing more to be consider'd in the preservation of Beer; and that is, when once the Vessel is broach'd, we ought to have regard to the time in which it will be expended: for if there happens to be a quick Draught for it, then it will last good to the very bottom; but if there is likely to be a slow draught, then do not draw off quite half, before you bottle it, or else your Beer will grow flat, dead, or sour. This is observed very much among the Curious.

One great piece of Oeconomy is the good management of Small Beer; for if that is not good, the Drinkers of it will be feeble in Summer-time, and incapable of strong Work, and will be very subject to Distempers; and besides, when Drink is not good, a great deal will be thrown away. The use of Drink, as well as Meat, is to nourish the Body; and the more Labour there is upon any one, the more substantial should be the Dyet. In the time of Harvest I have often seen the bad Effects of bad Small Beer among the Workmen; and in great Families, where that Article has not been taken care of, the

Apothecaries Bills have amounted to twice as much more as the Malt would have come to, that would have kept the Servants in strength and good health; besides one thing more, which I observed above, good wholesome Drink is seldom flung away by Servants, so that the sparing of a little Malt ends in loss to the Master. Where there is good Cellaring, therefore, it is adviseable to brew a flock of Small Beer, either in this Month or *October*, or in both Months, and to be kept in Hogsheads, if possible: The Beer brew'd in *March* to begin drawing in *October*, and that brew'd in *October* to begin in *March*, for Summer drinking; having this regard to the quantity, that a Family of the same number of working Persons, will drink a third more in Summer than in Winter,

If Water happens to be of a hard nature, it may be softened by setting it exposed to the Air and Sun, and putting into it some Pieces of soft Chalk to infuse; or else when the Water is set on to boil, for pouring upon the Malt, put into it a quantity of Bran, which will help a little to soften it.

I shall now mention two or three Particulars relating to Malt, which may help those who are unacquainted with brewing: In the first place, the general Distinctions, between one Malt and another, is only that one is high dried, the other low dried; that which we call high dried, will, by brewing, produce a Liquor of a brown, deep Colour; and the other, which is the low dried, will give us a Liquor of a pale Colour. The first is dried in such a manner, as may be said rather to be scorch'd than dried, and will promote the Gravel and Stone, and is much less nourishing than the low dried, or pale Malt, as they call it; for all Corn in the most simple way is the most feeding to the Body. I have experienc'd too, that the brown Malt, even tho' it be well brewed, will sooner turn sharp than the pale Malt, if that be fairly brewed. I am told, that a Gentleman in *Northamptonshire* has dried Malt upon the Leads of a House, and has made very good Drink of it: And the Method of drying Malt by hot Air, which was once proposed to the Publick, will do very well for a small quantity, but 'tis much too tedious to be ever rendered profitable; however, any means that can be used to dry Malt without parching of it, will certainly contribute to the goodness of the Malt. At the *Greyhound* at *Marlborough* I have drank of the palest-colour'd Ale I ever saw, and the best tasted, and the strongest that I have met with. In that place they dry their Malt very tenderly, and brew with chalky Water, and their Cellars are dug in Chalk: So at the *Crown* at *Hockrell* near *Bishop-Starford* in *Hertfordshire*, is excellent Beer of a pale Colour, strong, and well tasted; there the Malt is tenderly dried and the Soil chalky: likewise at *Nottingham* and *Derby* they brew with pale Malt, chalky Water, and their Cellars are dug in Chalk.

These Places are noted for the Goodness of their Ale all over *England*, insomuch that it has been computed, that there has been above two Hundred Thousand Pounds worth of Ale sold in and about *London,* under the Denomination of *Nottingham, Derby, Dorchester, &c.* in one Year's time: but it is not in *London* that we must expect to taste these Liquors in perfection; for it is rare to find any of them there without being adulterated, or else such Liquors are sold for them as are unskilful Imitations of them; and I may add, are unwholesome into the bargain. While I am writing this, a Gentleman of good Judgment in this Affair informs me, that the Brown Malt he finds makes the best Drink, when it is brew'd with a coarse River Water, such as that of the River *Thames* about *London*; and that likewise being brew'd with such Water, it makes very good Ale: but that it will not keep above six Months, without turning stale, and a little sharp, even tho' he allows fourteen Bushels to the Hogshead. He adds, that he has try'd the high-dry'd Malt to brew Beer with for keeping, and hopp'd it accordingly; and yet he could never brew it so as to drink soft and mellow, like that brew'd with Pale Malt. There is an acid Quality in the high-dry'd Malt, which occasions that Distemper commonly called the Heart-burn, in those that drink of the Ale or Beer made of it. When I mention Malt, in what I have already said above, I mean only Malt made of Barley; for Wheat-malt, Pea-malt, or these mix'd with Barley-malt, tho' they produce a high-colour'd Liquor, will keep many Years, and drink soft and smooth; but then they have the Mum-Flavour. I have known some People, who used brewing with high dry'd Barley-malt, to put a Bag, containing about three Pints of Wheat, into every Hogshead of Drink, and that has fined it, and made it to drink mellow: others I have seen put about three Pints of Wheat-malt into a Hogshead, which has produced the same Effect. But all Malt-Liquors, however they may be well-brew'd, may be spoiled by bad Cellaring, and be now and then subject to ferment in the Cask, and consequently turn thick and sour. The best way to help this, and bring the Drink to it self is to open the Bung of the Cask for two or three Days, and if that does not stop the Fermentation, then put about two or three Pounds of Oyster-shells wash'd and dry'd well in an Oven, and then beaten to fine Pouder, and stirring it a little, it will presently settle the Drink, make it fine, and take off the sharp Taste of it; and as soon as that is done, draw it off into another Vessel, and put a small Bag of Wheat or Wheat-malt into it, as above directed, or in proportion, as the Vessel is larger or smaller.

Sometimes such Fermentations will happen in Drink, by change of Weather, if it is in a bad Cellar, and it will in a few Months fall fine of it self, and grow mellow.

It is remarkable, that high-dry'd Malt should not be used in Brewing till it has been ground ten Days, or a Fortnight, it yields much stronger Drink than the same quantity of Malt fresh ground; but if you design to keep Malt some time ground before you use it, you must take care to keep it very dry, and the Air at that time should likewise be dry. And as for Pale Malt, which has not partaken so much of the Fire, it must not remain ground above a Week before you use it.

As for Hops, the newest are much the best, tho' they will remain very good two Years; but after that, they begin to decay, and lose their good Flavour unless great Quantities have been kept together; for in that case they Will keep much longer good than in small Quantities. These, for their better preservation, should be kept in a very dry Place, tho' the Dealers in them rather chuse such Places as are moderately between moist and dry, that they may not lose of their Weight. I cannot help taking notice here of a Method which was used to some stale and decay'd Hops the last Year 1725, to make them recover their Bitterness; which was to unbag them, and sprinkle them with Aloes and Water, which, together with the badness of the Malt of the same Year's growth, spoil'd great quantities of Drink about *London*; for even where the Water, the Malt, and the Brewer, and Cellars are good, a bad Hop will spoil all: So that every one of these Particulars should be well-chosen before the Brewing is set about, or else we must expect but a bad Account of our Labour. And so likewise the Yeast or Barm that you work your Drink with, must be well consider'd, or a good Brewing may be spoil'd by that alone; and be sure that be always provided before you begin Brewing, for your Wort will not stay for it.

In some remote Places from Towns it is practised to dip Whisks into Yeast, and beat it well, and so hang up the Whisks with the Yeast in them to dry; and if there is no Brewing till two Months afterwards, the beating and stirring one of these Whisks in New Wort, will raise a Working or Fermentation in it. It is a Rule that all Drink should be work'd well in the Tun, or Keel, before it be put in the Vessel, for else it will not easily grow fine. Some follow the Rule of beating down the Yeast pretty often while it is in the Tun, and keep it there working for two or three Days, observing to put it in the Vessel just when the Yeast begins to fall. This Drink is commonly very fine; whereas that, which is put into the Vessel quickly after 'tis brew'd, will not be fine in many Months.

We may yet observe, that with relation to the Season for brewing of Drink for keeping, if the Cellars are subject to the Heat of the Sun, or warm Summer Air, it is best to brew in *October*, that the Drink may have time to digest before the warm Season comes on: And if Cellars are inclinable to Damps, and to receive Water, the best time is to brew in *March*, and I know some experienced Brewers, who always chuse the brewing of Pale Malt in *March*, and the Brown in *October*; for they guess that the Pale Malt, being made with a lesser degree of Fire than the other, wants the Summer Season to ripen in;

and so on the contrary, the Brown having had a larger share of the Fire to dry it, is more capable of defending itself against the Cold of the Winter-Season. But how far these Reasons may be just, I shall not pretend to determine; but in such a Work as this, nothing should be omitted that may contribute to give the least Hint towards meliorating so valuable a Manufacture; the Artists in the Brewing Way are at liberty to judge as they please.

But when we have been careful in all the above Particulars, if the Casks are not in good order, still the Brewing may be spoil'd. New Casks are apt to give Drink an ill Taste, if they are not well scalded and season'd several days successively, before they are put in use; and for old Casks, if they stand any time out of use, they are apt to grow musty: unslack'd Lime, about a Gallon to a Hogshead, with about six Gallons of Water put in with it, and the Hogshead presently stopp'd up, will clear it of its Taint, if the same be repeated four or five times; or burning of Linnen dipp'd in Brimstone, to be close stopped in a Cask, three or four times repeated, will do the same: or else put Water in your Vessels, and throw in some burning Coals, and stop them close, will do the like, if it be often repeated.

I have now but little more to say about the Management of Drink, and that is concerning the Bottling of it. The Bottles first must be well clean'd and dry'd; for wet Bottles will make the Drink turn mouldy, or motherry, as they call it; and by wet Bottles, many Vessels of good Drink are spoiled: but if the Bottles are clean and dry, yet if the Corks are not new and found, the Drink is still liable to be damaged; for if the Air can get into the Bottles, the Drink will grow flat, and will never rise. I have known many who have flatter'd themselves that they knew how to be saving, and have used old Corks on this occasion, that have spoiled as much Liquor as has stood them in four or five Pounds, only for want of laying out three or four Shillings. If Bottles are cork'd as they should be, it is hard to pull out the Corks without a Screw, and to be sure to draw the Cork without breaking, the Screw ought to go through the Cork, and then the Air must necessarily find a Passage where the Screw has pass'd, and therefore the Cork is good for nothing; or if a Cork has once been in a Bottle, and has been drawn without a Screw, yet that Cork will turn musty as soon as it is exposed to the Air, and will communicate its ill Flavour to the Bottle where it is next put, and spoil the Drink that way.

In the choice of Corks, chuse those that are soft, and clear from Specks, and lay them in Water a day or two before you use them; but let them dry again before you put them in the Bottles, lest they should happen to turn mouldy: with this care you may make good Drink, and preserve it to answer your expectation.

In the bottling of Drink, you may also observe, that the top and middle of the

Hogshead is the strongest, and will sooner rise in the Bottles than the bottom: And when once you begin to bottle a Vessel of any Liquor, be sure not to leave it till all is complcated, for else you will have some of one Taste, and some of another.

If you find that a Vessel of Drink begins to grow flat, whilst it is in common draught, bottle it, and into every Bottle put a piece of Loaf-Sugar, about the quantity of a Walnut, which will make the Drink rise and come to itself: and to forward its ripening, you may set some Bottles in Hay in a warm Place; but Straw will not assist its ripening.

Where there are not good Cellars, I have known Holes sunk in the Ground, and large Oil Jars put into them, and the Earth filled close about the sides: One of these Jars may hold about a dozen quart Bottles, and will keep the Drink very well; but the tops of the Jars must be kept close cover'd up. And in Winter time, when the Weather is frosty, shut up all the Lights or Windows into such Cellars, and cover them close with fresh Horse-Dung, or Horse-Litter; but 'tis much better to have no Lights or Windows at all to any Cellar, for the reasons I have given above.

If there has been opportunity of brewing a good stock of Small Beer in *March* and *October*, some of it may be bottled at six Months end, putting into every Bottle a lump of Loaf-Sugar as big as a Walnut; this especially will be very refreshing Drink in the Summer: Or if you happen to brew in Summer, and are desirous of brisk Small Beer, bottle it, as above, as soon as it has done working.

* * * * *

APRIL.

From the beginning of this Month the Perch is in great Perfection, and holds good till Winter. One of the ways of dressing this Fish, according to the *Hollanders*, and which is much admired by Travellers, is after the following manner, and is called *Water-Soochy*.

To make a Water-Soochy.

Take Perch about five Inches long, scale and clean them well; then lay them in a Dish, and pour Vinegar upon them, and let them lie an Hour in it; after which put them into a Skillet with Water and Salt, some Parsley Leaves and Parsley-Roots well wash'd and scraped: let these boil over a quick Fire till they are enough, and then pour the Fish, Roots, and Water into a Soop-Dish, and serve them up hot with a Garnish about the Dish of Lemon, sliced. These Fish and Roots are commonly eaten with Bread and Butter in *Holland*, or there may be melted Butter in a little Bason for those who chuse it. It is to be noted, that the Parsley-Roots must be taken before they run to Seed; and if they happen to be very large, they should be boiled by themselves, for they will require more boiling than the Fish, This I had from Mr. *Rozelli* at the *Hague*.

The following Receipt for dressing of Perch, I had likewise from the same Person, and is an excellent Dish.

To prepare Perch with Mushrooms.

Pick, and clean, and cut your Mushrooms into small pieces, and put them in a Saucepan to stew tender without any Liquor, but what will come from them; then pour off their Liquor, and put a little Cream to them; having ready at the same time a Brace of large Perch well scaled, wash'd, and cut in Fillets or thick Slices, and parboil'd: Put your Perch thus prepared to your Mushrooms, and with them the Yolks of three Eggs beaten, some Parsley boil'd and cut small, some Nutmeg grated, a little Salt, and a little Lemon-Juice: keep all these stirring gently over a slow Fire, taking care not to break your Fish; and when they are enough, garnish them with Slices of Lemon and pickled Barberries.

The following general Sauce I had from the same Person; it is always ready to be used with every kind of Flesh, Fowl, or Fish that require rich Sauces, and will keep good twelve Months.

A Travelling Sauce.

Take two Quarts of Claret, a quarter of a Pint of Vinegar, and as much Verjuice; put these together in a new Stone-Jar that will admit of being stopp'd close: Put to this a quarter of a Pound of Salt that has been well dry'd over the Fire, an Ounce of Black-Pepper, a Drachm of Nutmeg beaten fine, and as much Cloves, a Scruple of Ginger, two or three little Bits of dry'd Orange-Peel, half an Ounce of Mustard-Seed bruised, half a dozen Shallots bruised a little, five or six Bay-Leaves, a little Sprig of Sweet Basil, or Sweet Marjoram, a Sprig of Thyme, and a little Cinnamon; then stop your Jar close, and let the Mixture infuse for twenty-four Hours upon hot Embers: when this is done, strain your Composition through a Linnen Cloth, till you have express'd as much Liquor as possible, and put it in a dry Stone Bottle or Jar, and stop it close as soon as 'tis cold. You must keep this in a dry Place, and it will remain good twelve Months. This is a good Companion for Travellers, who more frequently find good Meat than good Cooks. My Author adds, that those who are Admirers of the Taste of Garlick, may add it to this Sauce, or diminish, or leave out any particular Ingredient that they do not approve of. It may also be made of Water only, or of Verjuice, or of Wine, or of Orange or

Lemon-Juice; but if it is made of Water, it will keep but a Month good: if it be made of Verjuice, it will last good three Months; if we make it of Vinegar, it will last a Year; or of Wine, it will last as long. Use a little of this at a time, stirring it well when you use it.

In this Month I likewise judge it will be a good Season to make the following curious Preparation for the use of Gentlemen that travel; the use of which I esteem to be of extraordinary Service to such as travel in wild and open Countries, where few or no Provisions are to be met with; and it will be of no less Benefit to such Families as have not immediate Recourse to Markets, for the Readiness of it for making of Soups, or its Use where Gravey is required: and particularly to those that travel, the lightness of its Carriage, the small room it takes up, and the easy way of putting it in use, renders it extremely serviceable. This is what one may call Veal-Glue.

To make Veal-Glue, or Cake-Soup, to be carried in the Pocket.

Take a Leg of Veal, strip it of the Skin and the Fat, then take all the Muscular or Fleshy Parts from the Bones; boil this Flesh gently in such a quantity of Water, and so long a time, till the Liquor will make a strong Jelly when 'tis cold: this you may try by taking out a small Spoonful now and then, and letting it cool. Here it is to be supposed, that tho' it will jelly presently in small quantities, yet all the juice of the Meat may not be extracted, however, when you find it very strong, strain the Liquor thro' a Sieve, and let it settle; then provide a large Stew-pan with Water, and some China-Cups, or glazed Earthen-Ware; fill these Cups with the Jelly taken clear from the Settling, and set them in the Stew-pan of Water, and let the Water boil gently till the Jelly becomes thick as Glue: after which, let them stand to cool, and then turn out the Glue upon a piece of new Flannel, which will draw out the Moisture; turn them in six or eight Hours, and put them upon a fresh Flannel, and so continue to do till they are quite dry, and keep it in a dry warm Place: this will harden so much, that it will be stiff and hard as Glue in a little time, and may be carry'd in the Pocket without Inconvenience. We are to use this by boiling about a Pint of Water, and pouring it upon a piece of the Glue or Cake, of the bigness of a small Walnut, and stirring it with a Spoon till the Cake dissolves, which will make very strong good Broth. As for the Seasoning Part, every one may add Pepper and Salt as they please, for there must be nothing of that kind put among the Veal when we make the Glue, for any thing of that sort would make it mouldy. Some of this sort of Cake-Gravey has lately been sold, as I am inform'd, at some of the Taverns near *Temple-Bar*, where, I suppose, it may now be had. As I have observ'd above, that there is nothing of Seasoning in this Soup, so there may be always added what we desire, either of Spices or Herbs, to make it savoury to the Palate; but it must be noted, that all the Herbs that are used on this occasion, must be boiled tender in plain Water, and that Water must be used to pour upon the Cake Gravey instead of simple Water: so may a Dish of good Soup be made without trouble, only allowing the Proportion of Cake-Gravey answering to the abovesaid Direction. Or if Gravey be wanted for Sauce, double the Quantity may be used that is prescribed for Broth or Soup. I am inform'd by a Person of Honour, that upon this Foundation, there has been made a Cake-Gravey of Beef, which for high Sauces and strong Stomachs, is still of good use; and therefore I shall here give the Method of it.

To make Cake-Soup of Beef, &c.

Take a Leg, or what they call in some Places a Shin of Beef, prepare it as prescribed above for the Leg of Veal, and use the muscular Parts only, as directed in the foregoing Receipt; do every thing as abovemention'd, and you will have a Beef-Glue, which, for Sauces, may be more desirable in a Country-House, as Beef is of the strongest nature of any Flesh. Some prescribe to add to the Flesh of the Leg of Beef, the Flesh of two old Hares, and of old Cocks to strengthen it the more; this may be done at pleasure, but the Foundation of all these Cake Graveys or Glues is the first. These indeed are good for Soups and Sauces, and may be enrich'd by Cellary, Cherville, beat Chards, Leeks, or other Soup-Herbs. A little of this is also good to put into Sauces, either of Flesh, Fish, or Fowl, and will make a fine mixture with the Travelling Sauce. So that whenever there is mentioned the Use of Gravey in any of the Receipts contained in this Treatise, this may be used on Feast-days, and the Mushroom Gravey, or Travelling Sauce on Fast-days.

This is also a time of the Year when potted Meats begin to come in fashion; to do which, the following Receipt may be an Example.

To pot a Leg of Beef to imitate potted Venison, from Col. *Bradbury* of *Wicken Hall*.

Provide a Leg of Beef, and take off the Skin as whole as you can, then cut off all the Flesh, and season it with Pepper, Salt, and Allspice; then break the Bones and take out what Marrow you can to mix among your slices of Beef, which must be put in a deep Earthen Pot; cover then the whole with the Skin, and lay the Bones over that, covering all with Paper, and tying it down close; after which, bake it with great Bread, and let it stand in the Oven all Night. When this is done, take off the Bones and the Skin, and clear it from the Liquor as well as you can, then put the Meat into a Wooden Bowl, and beat it as small as possible with a Wooden Pestle, often putting in some Butter, and some of the Fat of the Marrow, which will swim upon the Gravey, but suffer none of the Gravey to go in with it: when this is beat enough, while it is warm, butter the Bottom and Sides of the Pan which you design to keep it in, and press down your Meat in it as hard as possible; when that is done, cover it with melted Butter. If you would have your Meat look red, rub it with a little Salt-peter before you season it. By the same Method you may pot Venison, Mutton, or what Flesh else you please, observing that 'tis only the fleshy or muscular Parts that are used in that way; and that they must be season'd and baked till they are tender, and then beat into a sort of Paste, with a little Butter added now and then while the Meat is beating. Keep these Meats in a cool dry Place, and you may preserve them good several Weeks. If you desire to pot a Hare, take the following Receipt.

To Pot a Hare, from the same.

Take a Hare and bone it, then mince the Flesh very small, with a Pound of the Fat of Bacon; after which, beat these in a Mortar, and then season your Meat with Pepper, Salt, Cloves and Mace, adding to it an Ounce of Salt peter: mix all these well, and let the Meat lie twenty-four Hours, then put it in an earthen glazed Pot, and bake it three Hours; after which, take it out, and dry it from the Gravey, then return it to the Pot again, and then cover it with clarified Butter. This Receipt might have been put in some of the former Months, as the Hare is then in season; but as it depends upon the foregoing Receipt, I thought convenient to insert it in this Place: however, a Jack-Hare may now be dress'd in this fashion, but the Doe-Hares are now either with Young or have Young ones, so that they are out of Season. These Potted Meats are useful in Housekeeping, being always ready for the Table: So likewise the following Receipt for Collar'd Beef is of the same service.

To Collar Beef.

Get the Rand or Flank of Beef cut about a foot in length; bone it, and then mix two Ounces of Salt peter, with a good handful of common Salt: after which, carbonade the outward Skin of the Beef, and rub the whole well with the Salts, letting it lie for twenty-four hours in Salt before you collar it; but observing to turn it twice a day, at least, whilst it is in Salt. When it has lain thus to season, get some Sweet-Marjoram, a little Winter-Savoury, some Red Sage-leaves, and a little Thyme, and shred them small; among which put an Ounce of Pepper ground small, half an Ounce of Cloves and Mace beat, and a Handful of Salt; mix these together, and stew the mixture thick over the inside of your Meat, that when it is roll'd up, it may be equally bound in with the Turnings of the Beef: then provide some thin Slices of the same Beef to lay before the first Turn, that the Collar may not be hollow in the middle. This must be roll'd as hard as possible, so that every Part is equally press'd to each other; then get some Tape about an Inch wide, and bind it hard about your Collar of Beef, in a Screw-like manner, till you have closed your Collar from top to bottom as tight as can be; observing to bind the top and bottom in an extraordinary manner with strong Packthread. Put this in a glazed earthen Pan, with as much Claret as will cover it, putting over the whole some coarse Paste, and send it to the Oven to stand five or six Hours. When it is baked enough, take out your Collar, and set it upright till it be cold, and then take off the Fillets, or the Tape that braced it together, and keep it for use. This is cut in thin Slices, and eaten with Vinegar, as are most of the Collar'd meats and Potted meats. This Example is enough for any one either to Collar other Meats by, only observing that such Flesh as is tender, as Pig and a Breast of Veal, must not be salted before they are collar'd, and the Spice or Herbs to be roll'd up with them, may be at discretion; but for the boiling or baking, the Time must be in proportion to their Size, or natural Tenderness. It must nevertheless be observed, that they must be baked or boiled till all the Gravey is out of them; for the Gravey being in them, will contribute to their spoiling by growing musty, or otherways foetid.

We have now Flounders in good Perfection, and besides the common Way of Dressing them, either by boiling them, as mention'd in the former Months, they are also sometimes fried, and sometimes broil'd; but the following is after such a manner, as is extremely agreeable, and will preserve them good a long time. These, or other Fish fry'd, are kept after the same manner: the Receipt I had from a worthy Gentleman, where I eat some in great Perfection.

Pickled Fish. From *Aaron Harrington,* Esq.

Let the Fish be fry'd after the common manner, and when they are cold lay them in a Dish, and pour on the following Pickle: Water and Vinegar equal quantities, *Jamaica* Pepper, Pepper and Salt, a little Mace, a few Bay-leaves, and some White-wine: when these have boiled together, pour the Pickle on the Fish while it is not too hot; these eat extremely well.

Trouts are now in good perfection in the South parts of our Country; that is, where the Weather has been favourable in the former Month; and then besides the common way of boiling them we may have them potted, which will make them as valuable as potted Charrs, which are a sort of Trout.

To pott Trouts. From Mrs. *R. S.* of *Preston* in *Lancashire.*

Scale and clean your Trouts very well, wash them in Vinegar, and slit them down the Back, after which put Pepper and Salt into the Incision, and on their Outsides, and let them lie upon a Dish three Hours; then lay them in an earthen glaz'd Pan, with pieces of Butter upon them, and put them in an Oven two Hours, if they are Trouts fourteen Inches long, or less in proportion, taking care to tie some Paper close over the Pan. When this is done, take away from them all the Liquor, and put them in a Pot, and as soon as they are quite cold, pour some clarified Butter upon them to cover them: These will eat as well as potted Charrs. Some will take out the Bone upon slitting the Back, and these have been often taken for Charrs; tho' I don't know above two Places where the Charrs are, one is a Pool where a River or Brook runs thro' in *Lancashire,* and the other is in a Pool at *Naant,* within four Miles of *Caernarvon.* But the Charr is of the Trout kind, and it must be a good judge in Fish to distinguish one from another; however, there is some small difference, which the Criticks in fishing take notice of.

Fish may also be kept in Pickle several Weeks, as the Jack and Trout especially are agreeable Varieties.

This time is a proper Season for making a pleasant and strong Wine of *Malaga* Raisins, which will keep good many Years, and among the best Judges of Wine is much admired; it is not unlike a strong Mountain Wine: at this time also the Raisins are very cheap.

To make Raisin Wine.

Take half a hundred weight of *Malaga* Raisins, pick them clean from the Stalks, and chop the Raisins small, then put them into a large Tub, and boil ten Gallons of River Water, or such Water as is soft, and pour it hot upon them; let this be stirr'd twice or thrice every Day for twelve Days successively, and then pour the Liquor into a Cask and make a Toast of Bread, and while it is hot, spread it on both sides with Yeast or Barm, and put it into the Vessel to the Wine, and it will make it ferment gently, which you may know by its making a hissing Noise; during the time of working, the Bung of the Vessel must be left open, and as soon as that is over, stop it up close. This will be fine and fit for Drinking in about four Months time; but if you make twice the quantity, it should stand five or six Months before you broach it: Observe that you set it in a good Cellar, such as I have mentioned in the Month of *March*, under the Article of Brewing.

To make Fronteniac Wine.

The foregoing Receipt must be followed in every particular, only when you put it into the Vessel, add to it some of the Syrup of the white Fronteniac Grape, which we may make in *England*, tho' the Season is not favourable enough to ripen that sort of Grape; for in a bad Year, when the white Fronteniac, or the Muscadella Grapes are hard and unripe, and without Flavour, yet if you bake them they will take the rich Flavour, which a good share of Sun would have given them. You may either bake the Fronteniac Grapes with Sugar, or boil them to make a Syrup of their Juice, about a Quart of which Syrup will be enough to put to five Quarts of the Raisin Wine. When these have work'd together, and stood a time, as directed in the foregoing Receipt, you will have a Fronteniac Wine of as rich a Flavour as the *French* sort, besides the Pleasure of knowing that all the Ingredients are wholesome.

This Month is the principal time for Asparagus, which every one knows how to prepare in the common way; but there are some particulars relating to the fitting them for the Table, which I had from a curious Gentleman at *Antwerp,* which I shall here set down.

To preserve Asparagus.

Cut away all the hard part of your Asparagus, and just boil them up with Butter and Salt, then fling them into cold Water, and presently take them out again and let them drain; when they are cold, put them in a Gallipot, large enough for them to lie without bending, putting to them some whole Cloves; some Salt, and as much Vinegar and Water, in equal quantities, as will cover them half an Inch; then take a single Linnen Cloth, and let it into the Pot upon the Water, and pour melted Butter over it, and keep them in a temperate Place: When you use them, lay them to steep in warm Water, and dress them as you would do fresh Asparagus. It is to be noted, that in *Holland,* and most places abroad, the Asparagus is always white, which is done according to a method that I have inserted in my other Works; the method of bringing them to Table the foreign way, is to serve them with melted Butter, Salt, Vinegar, and Nutmeg grated.

The Tops or Heads of Asparagus being broken in small pieces and boil'd, are used in Soups like green Pease.

Asparagus in Cream. From the same.

Break the Tops of your Asparagus in small Pieces, then blanch them a little in boiling Water, or parboil them, after which put them in a Stew-Pan or Frying-Pan with Butter or Hog's-Lard, and let them remain a little while over a brisk Fire, taking care that they are not too greasy, but well drain'd; then put them in a clean Stew-Pan with some Milk and Cream, a gentle Seasoning of Salt and Spice, with a small Bunch of sweet Herbs; and just when they are enough, add to them the Yolks of two or three Eggs beaten, with a little Cream to bind your Sauce.

The Greens, which are now fit for boiling, are Sprouts of Cabbages, and young Cabbage-Plants, which every one knows how to prepare. There is also Spinage, which is best stew'd without any Water, its own Juice being sufficient; and we have still plenty of Lupines, that is, the flowring Stalks of Turnips, which eat very agreeably; they should be gather'd about the length of Asparagus, when the Tops are knotted for flowering, and the strings in the outside of the Stalks stripp'd from them; then tie them in Bunches, as you do Asparagus, and put them in boiling Water with some Salt, and let them boil three or four Minutes, then lay them to drain, without pressing, and serve them to Table as you would do Asparagus. The same way is used in the management of Brocoli.

The middle of this Month the Cowslip is in Flower, or as some call it the Peigle; and now is the Season to make a most pleasant Wine of the Flowers. This Receipt is the best I have met with.

To make Peigle, or Cowslip Wine, From Mrs. *E. B.*

To three Gallons of Wine, put six Pounds of fine Sugar, boil these together half an hour, and as the Scum rises, take it off; then set the Liquor to cool, and when it is quite cold, take a Spoonful of the best Ale-Yeast, and beat it well with three Ounces of Syrup of Citron, or Syrup of Lemon; mix these very well together with the Liquor; and then put into it a Pound and three quarters of the yellow part of the Cowflip, or Peigle Flowers, which must be cut from the Stalks a little beforehand, but no other part must be used: let these infuse and work three days in an Earthen Vessel, cover'd with a Cloth; then strain them, and put your Liquor into a clean dry Cask, and let it stand to settle three Weeks or a Month before you bottle it.

* * * * *

MAY.

As this is the busy Month in the Dairy, I shall here insert the Remarks I have by me concerning the making of Cheeses; and in this Work it is first necessary to know how to manage the Rennet. The Rennet is made of the Calves Bag, which is taken as soon as the Calf is kill'd, and scour'd inside and outside with Salt, after having first discharg'd it of the Curd, which is always found in it; this Curd must likewise be well wash'd in a Cullender with Water, and the Hairs pick'd out of it till it becomes very white, then return the Curd again into the Bag, and add to it two good Handfuls of Salt, and shut the Mouth of the Bag close with a Skewer, then lay the Bag in an Earthen-Pan, and cover it close, and keep it in a dry place; this will remain fit for use twelve Months. When you would use it, boil a Quart of Water, after you have salted it, so as to bear an Egg, and letting it stand to be quite cold, pour it into the Bag, and prick the Bag full of very small Holes, and lay it in a clean Pan for use. While this Rennet is fresh, a Spoonful of the Liquor will turn or set about sixteen or twenty Gallons of Milk; but as it is longer kept, it grows weaker, and must be used in greater quantity: this Rennet will last good about a Month. This is the *Essex* and *Hertfordshire* way.

Another way of preparing of Rennet Bags, is to take the Calves Bag, and wash and scour it with Salt, and the Curd likewise, as directed above; and then salting it very well, hang it up in the Corner of a Kitchen Chimney, and dry it; and as soon as you want to use it, boil Water and Salt, as before, and fill the Bag with it, making small Holes in the Bag, as before directed, and keeping it in a clean Pan.

It is to be noted, that the Bag of the Calf, which is the part that receives the Milk, is so disposed, as to change the Milk into Curd, as soon as it is received into it; and the Curd, which is found in it, partaking of that quality of the Bag, which disposes it to harden the Milk; these are therefore to be preserv'd for the same use, when we employ common Milk to be made into Curd: but as the Calves Bag is warm, when it naturally receives the Milk from the Cow, and it then curdles in it; so, when we want to set or turn Milk, for Cheese or other use, we must have the Milk warm as one may guess the Body of the Calf was, and the Milk was likewise, when the Calf receiv'd it from the Cow. There is great danger if the Milk be too hot when the Rennet is put to it, for then it sets or turns to Curd very quick, and the Cheese will be hard; but it is good to let the Milk be of such a warmth as not to come too soon, as it is called in the Dairies, but to have it of such a warmth, as to let the Curd set easily, and come moderately, for the quicker the Curd comes, the harder it is, and the harder the Curd is, the harder is the Cheese. Again, we must have some regard to the Pasture where our Cows feed; those that feed in rank Grass have more watery parts in their Milk than those Cows which feed on short Grass; and sometimes, as I have observed before, in my other Works, the Cows feed upon Crow Garlick, or the Alliaria, or Sauce alone, or Jack in the Hedge, or Goose-grass, or Clivers, or Rennet Wort, and their Milk will either be ill tasted, or else turn or curd of itself, altho' the Cow has had a due time after Calving; and if the Goose-grass or Clivers happen to be the occasion of the turning of the Milk, then a less quantity of Rennet should be used: for the only use of Rennet is to fix the Milk, and turn it to Curd, and if already there is near an equivalent for Rennet in the Milk, by the Cow's eating such Herbs, then a little of it will do. But as I have observ'd above, where Cattle feed upon long rank Grass, the Milk is watery, and does not contain two thirds of the Cream, or Richness that there is in the same quantity of Milk from Cows fed upon short fine Grass: So that if one was to make Cheese, one would chuse the Milk of Cows that fed upon the purest fine Grass. Here the Milk would be rich, and if the Rennet is good and well proportion'd, the Cheese will be so too. It is to be observ'd likewise, that when Cows feed upon such Weeds as I have mention'd, I mean the Clivers, which turn their Milk, the Curd is always hard and scatter'd, and never comes into a Body, as the pure Milk will do that is set with Rennet, and consequently the Cheese will be hard. There is one thing likewise to be taken notice of, with regard to the Rennet, that as the Bag, of which it is made, happens to be good, so is the Rennet good in proportion. I mean the Bag is good when the Milk of the Cow, that suckled the Calf, is good; for the goodness of the Feed of the Cow does not only dispose the Body of the Calf to produce a gentleness or softness in the Acid, which promotes the curdling of the Milk, when it is received into the Body of the Calf, but makes the Rennet more tender to the setting of the Cheese-Curd, and so the Cheese will consequently be the better for it: And I judge that one reason why the *Suffolk* Cheese is so much noted for its hardness, is on account of the badness of the Rennet, tho' it is certain, that the worst Cheeses of that Country are made of Skim-Milk; however, the nature of the Milk is such, according to my Observation, that it makes very rich Butter, but the Cream rises on it so quickly, and so substantially, that it leaves no fatness or richness in the other part, which we call the Skim-Milk, but that remains little better than Water: so that 'tis no wonder in this case, and thro' the rank Feed of the Cows, that the Cheeses of those parts are not good. I think however the Cheese of *Suffolk* might be help'd in a good measure, if the Farmers there were to have their Rennet Bags from places where the Grass was short and fine; for I guess then, from the above reasoning, that the Curd would be of a more tender nature, or not of so binding a quality as it now is, and the Cheese consequently would be the better. But besides the goodness of the Milk and the Rennet, if a Cheese is over press'd, it will be hard and unpleasant; but it is to be remark'd, that all Cheeses that are hard press'd will keep longer than those that are gently press'd, and bear transporting thro' the hottest Climates, which the more tender-made Cheeses will not without corrupting, unless they are put into Oil. There is one thing which I may observe particularly, relating to the Rennet Bag; which is, that the Calf should suck it full about an hour before it is kill'd, that there may be more and fresher Curd in it; tho' in the killing of Calves it is a Rule to let the Calf fast some time before killing, which we are told contributes to the Whiteness of the Flesh. Again, it would be an advantage in the making of Cheese to have your Cattle all of one sort, and to feed all upon the same sort of Pasture; for when it happens to be otherwise, the Cheeses are apt to decay, from the different Tempers of the Milk; but let our Milk be what it will, be careful of the former Method prescribed, *i.e.* to break the Curd by gentle degrees, and as equally as possible every where: the little pains extraordinary will be paid in the goodness of the Cheese, for then it will not be full of Eyes or Hollows, and will sell the better.

But besides the way of preparing the Rennet, as I have here set down, it is practised to make an artificial Rennet, which will do very well for making of Cheese; and that is, to boil the Cliver, or as some call it Goose-grass, or others Rennet-Wort, in Water, and you may add some Tops of Sweet Bryar; about a Spoonful of which Decoction, or boiled Liquor, will turn a Pail-full of Milk, of about five Gallons, without any other help; but in the Preparation of this, as well as the other, for the Improvement of the Cheeses, in giving them rich Flavours, it is adviseable to insert, while we are boiling the Waters for them, either some of such Sweet Herbs as we like, or such Spices as we most covet the taste of. As for the famous *Stilton* Cheese, which I have already published the Receipt of, we are to make the Rennet strong of Mace, by boiling the Mace in the Salt and Water, for without that is done, the Cheese will not have the true Relish that the first famous *Stilton* Cheeses had; and without the People of *Stilton* keep up the antient way of making it, agreeable to the old Receipt, they must of necessity lose the Reputation they have gain'd by their Cheeses. I shall not pretend to affirm why the Cheeses now in that Town are not generally so good as they were formerly; but perhaps it is because some of the Cheese-Sellers there depend upon the reputation of the first Cheeses, and now buy Cheeses from other parts, where nothing of the true Receipt is known but the Figure. However, it would be injustice in me if I did not take notice, that the Master of the *Blue-Bell Inn* in *Stilton* provided me with one that was excellent in its way, and yearly furnishes as many Customers with them as give him timely Notice: But as these Cheeses require time in the Dairy, before they are fit for eating, and the Season of making them is in the Bloom of the Year, so it is necessary to speak for them betimes, to have them to one's mind. I shall not give the Receipt of it at this time, as it has already fallen into a good number of hands with my former Pieces, and has been thought good enough to have been copied from me, with many other Articles, and published by Mr. *Lawrence*. I shall proceed therefore to give the Receipts for making of some other kinds of Cheeses, which yet have not appear'd in the World, which I have collected from some of the best Dairies in *England*. The following is the famous *Buckingham* Cheese, which I had from Mr. *Foord,* a very curious Gentleman of that place.

To make *Buckingham* Cheese. From Mr. *Foord* of that Place.

Prepare a Cheese Vat or Cheese Mote of a square Figure, six Inches over, and nine Inches deep, full of small Holes for the convenience of letting out the Whey when the Curd is put into it: Then take the Night's Cream, and mix it with the Morning's Milk, and put the Rennet to it to cool. When the Curd is come, take it gently from the Whey, and fill the Cheese Vat with it, and lay a Board up on the Curd, and as that sinks, fill up the Cheese Vat with fresh Curds; this should be done once every Hour till Night. The next Day turn your Cheese upside down, and continue turning it every Night and Morning till it shrinks from the Vat or Cheese Mote, and is stiff enough to take out without breaking, and then lay it upon the Shelf to be turn'd, and shift it Night and Morning till 'tis dry for use. This Mr. *Foord* tells me is the best sort of Cheese he has met with in *England*.

The following I have experienced to be an extraordinary Cheese; in some places 'tis call'd the Golden Cheese, and in others the Marygold Cheese, which it is properly. The Juice of the Marygolds adds a very great richness to the Milk, and contributes almost as much to it as Cream would do. The following is the Receipt to make it.

To make Marygold Cheese.

Gather your Marygold Flowers in a dry Day, and pick the golden-colour'd Leaves from them, (these we call the Petals of the Flowers:) As soon as you have pick'd a sufficient quantity of these Leaves for your use, bruise them in a Mortar, or grind them, if you have Conveniency, and strain out the Juice; this Juice, when you put the Rennet to the Milk, must be put into the Milk, and stirr'd into it. The Milk must then be set, and as soon as the Curd is come, break it gently, and as equally as possible, and put it into the Cheese Vat, and press it with a gentle Weight, letting the bottom part of the Vat have such a number of Holes in it, as will let out the Whey easily, or else a Spout to carry off the Whey; but the Holes are much better than the Spout. This Cheese, which is made in a Cloth, must be used like other Cheeses made after that manner.

As for the making of Sage-Cheese, the following is the best way that I have met with, and therefore I think the Receipt may be useful to the Publick.

To make a plain Sage-Cheese.

Gather the young Tops of red Sage, and bruise them in a Mortar till you can press the Juice from them; then take Leaves of Spinach or Spinage, and bruise them likewise, and press out the Juice to mix with the Sage Juice; for the Sage Juice of it self is not of a pleasant green Colour, and the Spinach Juice is added to it to render it more bright to the Sight; it also serves to take off the bitterness of the Sage. When this Juice is prepared, put your Rennet to the Milk, and, at the same time, mix as much of your Sage and Spinach Juice with it, as will give the Milk the green Colour you desire. If you would have it strong of the Sage, you must have the greater share of Sage Juice; or weaker of the Sage, the greater share of Spinach Juice. When the Curd is come, break the Curd gently, and when it is all equally broken, put it into the Vat or Cheese Mote, and press it gently: remember that the equal and due breaking of the Curd will keep your Cheese from having Hollows or Eyes in it, and the gentle pressing of Cheese will make it eat tender and mellow. This, as well as the Marygold Cheese, must be salted, when it has been press'd about eight Hours.

To make Sage-Cheese in Figures.

Those that are willing to have figur'd Cheeses, such Cheeses as are partly green and partly otherwise, must take the following method. Provide two Cheese Vats of the same bigness, and set your Milk in two different Vessels; one part with plain Rennet only, and the other with Rennet and Sage Juice, as directed in the above Receipt; make these as you would do two distinct Cheeses, and put them into the Presses at the same time. When each of these Cheeses has been prest half an hour, take them out and cut some square Pieces, or long Slips, quite out of the plain Cheese, and lay them by upon a Plate; then cut as many Pieces out of the Sage Cheese, of the same Size and Figure of those that were cut out of the plain Cheese, and presently put the pieces of the Sage Cheese into the holes that were cut in the plain Cheese, and the pieces cutout of the plain Cheese into the holes of the Sage Cheese, contriving to make them fit exactly: for this use some have Tin Plate, made Into Figures of several Shapes, with which they cut out the pieces of their Cheeses so exactly, that they fit without trouble. When this is done, return them to the Presses, and treat them like common Cheeses, so will you have one Cheese Sage, with white or plain Figures in it, and the other a white Cheese, with green Figures in it. In the making of these Cheeses you must particularly observe to break your Curd very equally, and press both your Cheeses as equally as possible before you cut out the Figures; for else when they come to be press'd for the last time, your Figures will press unequally and lose their Shapes. When these Cheeses are made, they must be frequently turn'd and shifted on the Shelf, and often rubb'd with a coarse Cloath. These Cheeses may be made about two Inches thick, for if they are thicker, it will be more difficult to make the Figures regular; these will be fit to eat in about eight Months.

To make Cheese in imitation of *Cheshire* Cheese.

When your Milk is set, and the Curd is come, it must not be broken with a Dish, as is usual in the making of other Cheeses, but drawn together by the Hands to one side of the Vessel, gently and regularly broken; for if it is roughly press'd, a great deal of the richness of the Milk will go into the Whey. As you thus gather your Curd, put it into the Vat or Cheese Mote till it is full, then press it and turn it often, salting it at several times. It is to be noted, that the Cheeses should be six or eight Inches thick, and will be fit to eat in a Year; they must be frequently turn'd and shifted upon the Shelf, and rubb'd often with a dry coarse Cloath, and at the Year's end may have a hole bored in the middle, so as to contain a quarter Pint of Sack, which must be pour'd into it, and then the hole stopp'd close with some of the same Cheese, and the Cheese set in a Wine Cellar for six Months to mellow; at the end of which time, the Sack will be all lost, and the hole will be in a manner clos'd up.

To make Cheese in imitation of those made in *Gloucestershire*.

These Cheeses are to be about two Inches thick, and the Vats or Cheese Motes must be provided accordingly; set your Milk as directed in the former Receipts, and breaking it as equally and tenderly as possible, put it in a Cloth into the Vat, and set it in the press for an Hour; then take it out of the Press, and cut it in small Pieces, as big as Nutmegs, into a Pan of scalding Water, taking them again soon out of the Water, and sprinkle them with Salt at your pleasure, and return them again to the Vat or Cheese Mote, and keep them in the Press till the next Morning, and after that turn them and wipe them often, till they come to be very dry; or else when you have let one of these Cheeses press about two Hours, salt it on the upper side, and turn it at Night, and salt the side that lies uppermost, to lie in the Press till Morning; but the first way of cutting and salting it is much the best. These Cheeses will be fit to cut when they have been made eight Months; it is to be observ'd, that if we salt them in the manner first mention'd, that is, by cutting the Cheese, such Cheeses will be smooth-coated.

To make Slip-Coat Cheese, which is the thin Summer Cheese, call'd in *London* Cream Cheese. From the Farm call'd the *Vaises* in *Essex*.

Take six Quarts of new Milk, and a Pint of Cream, put it together with a Spoonful of Rennet just warm, and let it stand till the Curd is come; then lay a Cloath in your Cheese Vat, and with a Skimming-Dish cut out the Curd, and lay it in the Vat till it is full, turning your Cheese-Cloath over it; and as the Curd settles, lay more on, till you have laid on all. When the Whey is drain'd out, turn the Cheese into a dry Cloath, and then lay a weight of a Pound upon it; at Night turn it into another dry Cloath, and the next Morning salt it a little, then make a Bed of Nettles or Ash-Leaves to lay it on, and cover it with the same, shifting them twice a day, till the Cheese is fit to eat, which will be in about ten days. This Cheese is approved to be the best of the kind in the whole Country, and may be made all the Summer.

It is to be observ'd, that if in any sort of Cheese, which is here mentioned, there is not a strength or briskness of taste agreeable to every Palate, it may be strengthned, by putting either Spice into the Rennet Bag, as Pepper, or Mace, or Cloves, which will make the Rennet very strong, and the Cheese of consequence more sharp to the Palate; or else add the Juices of strong sweet Herbs to the Milk, when the Rennet is put in: the Juice of Marygolds especially helps the richness of the Milk, or Cheese. The Mace in good quantity put into the Rennet will give the Cheese a most agreeable warmth.

As for the Antipathy which some People bear to Cheese, I judge that it must proceed from the first impression made from the Nurse that suckles Children, or from the first Cow's Milk that is given them: for as the Stomach is the first part which the Nourishment is received into; so, as that Nourishment is at first favourably receiv'd into the Stomach, so the Tone of the Stomach will ever remain afterwards, unless it could be so clear'd from the first impression by such a Tryal as Human Nature can hardly bear. I guess too, that from this Prejudice in the Stomach proceeds the Aversion which some People have to the Smell of Cheese; and if I may go a little farther this way, I suppose that the Dislike to Cats, and the Antipathy some People bear to them, is from Frights which the Mothers have receiv'd from them during their Pregnancy: concerning which last Particular, I have offer'd my Sentiments in the Article of the Longing of Women, in my *Philosophical Account of the Works of Nature*. But as for the other things, which some People bear an Aversion to, as the Mutton of black Sheep, or a Breast of Mutton, &c. they depend upon the loathing of the Stomach, from the first Impression. What I have remark'd here, concerning the preparing and softning of the quality of the Rennet Bag, is in part a reason for the first good or bad Impression that may be made upon Mankind with regard to Cheese; and I think the following relation, which I had from a noble Peer, from whom I have learnt many curious and useful things, tending to the good of my Country, will be acceptable to the World.

Some Gentlemen that had been hunting, and were led by their Sport to a retir'd part of the Country, where they found only a Cottage to refresh themselves in, were forc'd to take up with Bread and Cheese; there was nothing else to be had, and they had craving Stomachs; but one of the Company was so unfortunate as to have an aversion to Cheese, and could never bear either the taste or smell of it; however, at this time feeing how heartily it was eaten by his Companions, and being very hungry, he resolved to venture upon it, and eat heartily of it; but about an hour after was taken so very ill with Purging and Vomiting, that in a short time his Life was despair'd of. He had the Advice of the best Physicians, but no Medicine took place, and he was given over, after he had lain in that condition a Week; however, at length the Distemper went off, and by degrees he get strength enough to go homeward, and in his way happening to stop at an Inn, where there stood a Waggon Load of *Cheshire* Cheeses, he found that he had a strong Appetite to eat some of that sort, and had one cut on purpose, and eat heartily of it, without suffering the least inconvenience, and has ever since been a great lover of Cheese. So that there is an Example of getting over this Aversion; but considering the difficulty he went thro', it shews the danger of such an Attempt: Nothing less than the violent Scouring he underwent could have chang'd the first Impression made in his Stomach. But thus far of Cheese.

It is necessary, in the next place, to say something of Butter, and how far that may be mended in many parts of *England*, as well for private as for more general use.

In the first place it is to be remark'd, that some Grounds will never produce good Butter, and others will not produce good Cheese, tho' there is the best management in the Dairy. Again, there is one sort of Cattle, which tho' we feed them in the finest Grass, and best Pasture, will never yield a rich Milk; while on the other hand, there are some sorts of Cattle which will yield a rich Milk for Butter in any Pasture: tho', as I have observ'd before, the Milk and Butter will be ill tasted if the Cows fed upon Crow-Garlick, Alliaria, or Saxifrage. What I have said of this, with regard to the making of Cheese, must here be consider'd; that is, if the Cows feed upon short fine Grass, there will be more Cream in the Milk than if they feed upon long rank Grass. Indeed the long rank Grass will give more Milk than the short, but less Butter, and worse into the bargain. Again, the Milk of one Cow shall give richer and better Butter than the Milk of others, tho' they all feed on the same Pasture, even so that the Milk of one Cow will cover or enrich the Butter made from nine or ten other Cows; her Milk will make Butter of a rich yellow Colour, full of Fatness, and the others will only produce a pale, lean Butter, but all together will be good: I know several Instances of this, and every one who is skilful in a Dairy may observe it. I have already treated largely concerning this Particular, in my Works of Husbandry, and I shall therefore proceed to speak of the Management of Milk in the Dairy for making Butter; for I am very sensible, that many Farmers might have twice the Benefit from their Dairies, if the Articles of Butter and Cheese were consider'd in a rational way, and the old Custom could be broke through; and moreover, if the best Rules for managing of the Dairy were known, and put in practice, the whole Country would be the better for it, every one might enjoy the benefit of good things: whereas for want of knowledge among some Farmers, their Goods are of small value, and the People are also disatisfied.

In many parts of *England*, it is common to set Milk in Brass Pans, and that gives an ill Taste to the Milk; and again, there is a custom of setting the Cream in Brass-Kettles over the Fire, and as it warms to stroak the Butter as it rises to the edge of the Kettle: this way is very bad for Butter, for the warm Brass assuredly will spoil the Taste of the Cream, and it is often smoak'd. The surest way is to set the Milk in glaz'd Earthen Pans or in Leaden Pans, but the Earthen Pans are preferable. It should be particularly observ'd, that the Dairy be kept cool, for that in hot Weather contributes greatly to the Advantage of the Butter: I have known some that have had Streams of Water running thro' them, and at the same Places, instead of Glass Windows, there have been no Lights at all to them but thro' Wyer, and Shutters to them, to open or close as the Sun chang'd its Course. The thatching of the Dairy is much cooler also than Tyling; and whatever will contribute to keep off the Sun, should be practis'd. There are yet in some Places in *England* some Farmers that do not know the use of the Churn; however, it is certain, that there is no better way of making Butter than by that means, or something equivalent to it; that is, by beating the Cream, so that the Oily, or Fat Parts separate from the Watery Parts, in the most constant and gentle way that is possible, for to use this beating of the Cream too violently, will make the Butter like Grease; whereas a gentle beating of the Cream will render it more firm or stiff: and besides, when the Cream is beat with too much hurry, the Butter will ferment, and presently change to be of a bad Taste; but if it be gently beat or churn'd, it will be firm, and will be fit for keeping. Again, it must be observ'd, that as the beating or churning of Cream, to bring it to Butter, is only to separate the oily from the watery Parts of the Cream, so when once you begin to churn, or beat the Cream, you must continue to churn or beat it in the most constant manner you can, till the Butter is made: for if you had perhaps beat the Cream within three or four Minutes of its becoming Butter, if you leave off the Work but a Minute, the oily and watery Parts will return to one another, and will require as much Labour as before to separate them: it is like Oil and Vinegar that have been mix'd by Labour, and then let alone for a Minute or two, they will divide and separate from one another, as much as if they had never been mix'd; but the beating of it too violently, will make the Butter oily, as observ'd before. As for the Figure of our common Churn, I shall not give a draught of it, because such as are unacquainted with it may understand it much better by seeing a Model of it, which may be had at any Toy-Shop in *London*; nay, the very beating of Cream with a Spoon, in a small Bowl, will bring it to Butter; but it must be beat regularly.

In the great Dairies in *Holland*, where one Farmer keeps four or five hundred Cows, the Cream is put into a large Well, lined with Lead, and a large Beam set with cross Bars is turn'd in the Cream by a Horse; but the violence of the Motion makes the Butter rather like Oil than Butter; and the consequence is, that it will not keep long, and as I have heard say, will not melt well, like the Butter that is made by more gentle means. Where a gentle way is used in making Butter, it will cut like Wax, and it should especially be well wrought with the Hands, when it is fresh, taken from the Churn and salted for common use; for if the Milk be not well work'd out of it, the Butter will not keep. However, if Butter begins to decay in goodness, or change to an ill Taste, let it be work'd well, and wash'd with Water, and it will come to itself, and will bear salting and potting as well as fresh Butter; but always observe not to put up Butters of several sorts into the same Pot or Vessel, but chuse that of the same Dairy, and of the same making, if possible. One of the most curious Women I have met with in this way, is Mrs. *Cowen,* a Shopkeeper at *Newport Pond* in *Essex,* who pots great quantities every Year; there are undoubtedly many others who are very good in this way, but as I do not know them, therefore I may be excus'd if I mention her in particular.

Again, Butter that was good originally, and well potted, may be wash'd and beaten in the Winter, so as to be made more sweet and palatable than fresh Butter, made in many Places, at that time of the Year; and this is frequently practiced about *London,* where the workers of it get more than twice the first Price of the Butter, by their Care and Labour.

Before I conclude this Article, it may be necessary to observe, that the best managers of the Dairy frequently fill up their Churns with cold Water, before they put in the Cream to churn, in the heat of the Summer, for fear of over-heating the Butter in the making, and in the Winter heat their Churns with warm Water before they use them, but the over-heating of the Churns spoils the Butter; she best way is to set the bottom of the Churn in warm Water, when you churn in cold Weather, to save Trouble.

I shall now proceed to say something of preparing Cordial Waters; for this Month gives us a vast variety of Herbs in full perfection, and in the most proper condition for the use of the Shops, whether for drying, infusing, distilling, &c.

In the first place, all Herbs design'd to be dried, must be gather'd in dry Weather, and laid in some Room, or cover'd Place, to dry in the Shade, to be afterwards used for infusion or distillation, for which Business the dried Herbs are as useful as the green Herbs, if they be such as are Aromatick, *viz.* Thyme, Sweet Marjoram, Savory, Hysop, Sage, Mint, Rosemary, the Leaves of the Bay-Tree, the Tops of Juniper, Gill, or Ground Ivy, and such like: The Infusions, or Spirits, drawn from dried Herbs are more free from the Earthy and Watery Parts, than the Infusions, or Spirits drawn from green Herbs. I observe, that in making such Infusions as Teas of dried Herbs, the best way is to pour boiling Water upon them, and in half a Minute, at most, pour out the Water again from the Herbs, if we have them in small quantities, as we do Sage Tea, or other Tea; such Tea will then be of a fine green Colour, and full of Spirit: but if the Herbs stand longer with Water upon them, the Water will change of a brownish Colour, will lose the fine Flavour of the Herb, and become ill-tasted; so that in the making of Sage Tea, for example, pour on your boiling Water, and when it has been half a Minute upon the Sage-Leaves, pour it off and fling away the Leaves; for if you pour more Water upon them, you must expect your Tea of a dark Colour and ill tasted: therefore have fresh Sage to every fresh quantity of Water. And the same method should be used in the making of all kinds of Teas, to make them palatable and more wholesome. But when I speak of Teas having good qualities in them, I must not be understood to mean any of the Foreign Teas, such as Green, and Bohea Teas, &c. for I have had experience enough in them to know that they are injurious to the Body, of which I shall say more in a Treatise by it self. What I mention here, is only with regard to the infusing of Herbs in the Tea manner; but there are Infusions of Herbs in Spirits: here the Spirit that the Herbs are put into, must be cold, or used without any Fire at all, and the Herbs in this case may be used either green or dry; here they may stand several days before the Spirit that they are infus'd in be drawn off, as the following Cordial, call'd Surfeit Water, may serve to instance.

To make red Surfeit-Water. From Mrs. *B*.

To three Gallons of Brandy, put the Flower Leaves of a Bushel of red Poppies, one Pound of Raisins of the Sun stoned, a large Stick of Liquorice sliced, a quarter Pound of Caraway-Seeds bruised, a large Handful of Angelica, Sweet Marjoram, red Sage, Dragon's Mint, and Baulm, of each a handful; let all these be cover'd close in a Glass, or glaz'd Earthen Vessel, and stand to infuse or steep in the Brandy for nine Days, keeping it, during that time, in a Cellar; then strain it off upon a Pound and half of Loaf-Sugar, and put it into Bottles. This is a good Cordial, if used only when occasion requires.

In this Month, Orange-Flowers are in the greatest plenty; about half a Pound of them put into a Gallon of Brandy, with a quarter Pound of Orange-Peel, and half a Pound of double refin'd Loaf-Sugar, makes a very agreeable Cordial: We may let these Ingredients infuse in the Brandy nine or ten days before we pour the Brandy from them. Some chuse rather to put the Sugar to the Brandy after it is pour'd from the Orange-Flowers.

As for the distilling part, we have already several Books which treat largely of that Business, both with respect to the management of what is call'd the cold Still, and the Alembick, to which I shall refer: but in this place I shall only take notice, that whereas several kinds of distill'd Waters are drawn from many Herbs, which do not appear all the Year about; so if one has not an opportunity of collecting all our Herbs together, just when we want them, we may yet distil those we can get at one time, and make another Distillation of those we collect at another time, and so mix both Spirits or Waters together: For Example, in those Cordial Waters where the Ros Solis, or Rosa Solis is used, which is an Herb not always to be found, and will not keep above a day or two after 'tis gather'd, this I say may be distill'd by itself, and kept to use with other Waters at pleasure; putting of this such a proportion as would have been produced from the quantity directed, of the Plant, in the Receipt, if it had been distill'd with the other Herbs: and so of any other Herb that is hard to come by.

This Herb, however, I may inform my Reader, grows in Bogs, and when we find it we may preserve it artificially, by either planting it immediately in other boggy places, or else in artificial Bogs, made of Earth and Water in

Tubs, or Earthen Pots, made without holes at the bottom.

This Season affords us great variety of Necessaries for Food, in the Farm and Garden; the Pond Fish, as Pike or Jack, Carp, Tench, and Perch, as well as Eels are in Season, and may be prepared for the Table, as directed in *March;* there are likewise green Geese, young Ducks, Chickens, Pigeons, and Rabbits in the artificial Warren; and in the Garden, Spinage and Cabbage-Lettuce to boil, some forward Pease and Beans, Asparagus, Artichokes, the first Cabbages, and Caulyflowers, Cucumbers for stewing and in raw Sallads: however, in this Season all raw Sallads should yet partake of some warm Herbs, as I have directed in my *New Improvement of Planting and Gardening.* The Method which I most approve of for dressing a Sallad, is, after we have duly proportion'd the Herbs, to take two thirds Oil Olive, one third true Vinegar, some hard Eggs cut small, both the Whites and Yolks, a little Salt and some Mustard, all which must be well mix'd and pour'd over the Sallad, having first cut the large Herbs, such as Sallery, Endive, or Cabbage-Lettuce, but none of the small ones: then mix all these well together, that it may be ready just when you want to use it, for the Oil will make it presently soften, and lose its briskness. Onions should always be kept in reserve, because it is not every one that like their relish, nor is Oil agreeable to every one; but where Oil is not liked, the Yolks of hard Eggs, bruis'd and mix'd with the Vinegar, may be used as above. The difficulty of getting good Oil in *England,* is, I suppose, the reason why every one does not admire it; for I was once of opinion I could never like it: but when I was once persuaded to taste such as was of the best sort, I could never after like a Sallad without it. The best Oil that I have met with in *England,* is at *Mr. Crosse's,* a *Genouese* Merchant, at the *Genouese Arms* in *Katherine-Street,* in the *Strand, London.*

As for the ordering of the above Animals and Vegetables for the Table, we may find Directions in this Work.

In this Month gather Elder-Flowers when they are dry, and pick them from the Stalks; let them dry in the Shade, and then put an Ounce to each Quart of White-Wine Vinegar, to stand in the Vinegar for two Months, then pour the Vinegar from them for use.

About the end of this Month is a proper time to make Sage-Wine, which is a very pleasant one, and I think worthy a place among the best Receipts.

To make Sage-Wine. From Mrs. *E. B.*

To three Gallons of Water put six Pounds of Sugar, boil these together, and as the Scum rises take it off, and when it is well boiled put it in a Tub boiling hot, in which there is already a Gallon of red Sage Leaves clean pick'd and wash'd; when the Liquor is near cold, put in the Juice of four large Lemons, beaten well with a little Ale Yeast, mix these all well together, and cover it very close from the Air, and let it stand forty eight Hours; then strain all thro' a fine Hair-Sieve, and put it into a Vessel that will but just hold it, and when it has done working, slop it down close, and let it stand three Weeks or a Month before you bottle it, putting a Lump of Loaf-Sugar into every Bottle. This Wine is best when it is three Months old. After this manner you may make Wine of any other Herb or Flower.

* * * * *

JUNE.

This Month is a proper Season for making several sorts of Wine, whether it be that of Goosberries, Currants, Cherries, Apricots, or Rasberries, all which are very agreeable and worth the trouble; the Expence, where these Fruits are growing, being very inconsiderable. The following Receipts are approved to be very excellent.

Preliminaries to the making of Goosberry-Wine.

Goosberry-Wine is one of the richest and strongest Wines made in *England*, it will keep many Years, and improve by keeping, if it be well made; and is not, in my opinion, inferior to Mountain *Malaga*.

To make this Wine, we must have regard to the sort of Goosberry we design to use, for there is a great deal of difference in the time of one sort's ripening and another: the earliest ripe are the Champaign, the Green, the Black, and Red hairy Goosberries, every one of which has a Flavour distinct from the other sorts, and so will yield each of them a Wine of as different a relish from the rest, as one may expect to find among the several Varieties of the *French* growth. The most forward of these kinds about *London* ripen early in this Month, if the Season be good; but the later forts are not generally ripe till the end of the Month, or in *July.* The later sorts are commonly the white Dutch, the Amber, and the Walnut-Goosberries, each of which has likewise a different fort of taste: of the Amber especially I have known an excellent Wine to be made. Again, we must consider, that as to the time of their ripening, the diversity of Situations will forward or retard them a Fortnight or three Weeks; and beside, as we have observed above, every Season is not alike, and we must have regard also to the difference of Climate, one part of *Britain* is three Weeks sooner or later than another: and when I say in any one of my Kalendars, or Monthly Directories, that any particular Fruit is ripe, or any particular thing is to be done in such a Month, it must be understood that it is generally so, but will vary now and then, as the Season is more or less forward. There is likewise another thing to be consder'd relating to the ripeness of Fruits, and that is, the different Opinions or Tastes of Mankind; some call them ripe when they just begin to turn: but what I mean by ripeness, is, when a Fruit is as tender as it can be, and possessing its highest Flavour: And by those Fruits which I call half ripe, I mean such as have their inward Juices sweet, and their outward Parts a little hard and sour. In this state should the Goosberry be gather'd for making of Wine, See the following Receipt.

To make Goosberry-Wine.

Gather your Goosberries in dry Weather, when they are half ripe, as I have explained in the above Preliminaries, pick them and bruise them in a Tub, with a wooden Mallet, or other such like Instrument, for no Metal is proper; then take about the quantity of a Peck of the bruised Goosberries, put them into a Bag made of Horse-Hair, and press them as much as possible, without breaking the Kernels: repeat this Work till all your Goosberries are press'd, and adding to this press'd Juice, the other which you will find in the Tub, add to every Gallon three Pounds of powder Sugar, for *Lisbon* Sugar will give the Wine a taste which may be disagreeable to some People, and besides it will sweeten much more than the dry powder Sugar; stir this together till the Sugar is dissolved, and then put it in a Vessel or Cask, which must be quite fill'd with it. If the Vessel holds about ten or twelve Gallons, it must stand a Fortnight or three Weeks; or if about twenty Gallons, then about four or five Weeks, to settle, in a cool Place: then draw off the Wine from the Lee, and after you have discharg'd the Vessel from the Lees, return the clear Liquor again into the Vessel, and let it stand three Months, if the Cask is about ten Gallons; or between four and five Months, if it be twenty Gallons, and then bottle it off. We must note, that a small Cask of any Liquor is always sooner ripe and fit for drinking than the Liquor of a larger Cask will be; but a small

Body of Liquor will sooner change sour, than that which is in a larger Cask. The Wine, if it is truly prepared, according to the above Directions, will improve every Year, and last several Years.

Preliminaries to the making of Currant Wine.

It is to be noted, that tho' there are two sorts of Currants, which may be used for making of Wine, that is, the Red and the White; yet the Taste and Goodness will be the same, whether 'tis made of the White or the Red, for they have both the same Qualities, except in the Colour. Observe also, that the Fruit be gather'd in a dry time, and that if you make a large Quantity, it must stand longer in the Vessel, before bottling, than a small Quantity.

To make Currant Wine

When your Currants are full ripe, gather them, and pick them from the Stalks and weigh them, in order to proportion your Water and Sugar to them. When this is done, bruise them to pieces with your Hands, and add to every three Pounds of Currants a Quart of Water, stirring all together, and letting it stand three Hours, at the end of which time, strain it off gently thro' a Sieve, and put your Sugar into your Liquor, after the rate of a Pound to every three Pounds of Currants. This Sugar should be powder Sugar, for *Lisbon* Sugar would give the Wine an ill Taste. Stir this well together, and boil it till you have taken off all the Scum, which will rise plentifully; set it then to cool, at least sixteen Hours, before you put it into the Vessel. If you make the Quantity of twenty Gallons, it may stand in the Vessel three Weeks before it will be fit for bottling; and if you make thirty Gallons, then it must stand a Month before it be bottled off, observing then to put a small Lump of Sugar into every Bottle; it must be kept in a cool place, to prevent its Fretting. By this Method it will keep good many Years, and be a very strong and pleasant Wine, at a very cheap rate.

It is necessary to observe, that the same sort of Currant is not always of the same Sweetness when it is ripe, those growing in the Shade will be less sweet than those that are more exposed to the Sun. And when the Summer happens to be wet and cold, they will not be so sweet as in a dry warm Season; therefore tho' the Standard of the above Receipt be one Pound of Sugar to three Pounds of pick'd Currants, yet the Palate of the Person who makes the Wine should be the Regulator, when the Sugar is put to the Juice, considering at the same time, that it is a Wine they are making, and not a Syrup. The Sugar is only put to soften and preserve the Juice, and too much will make the Wine ropey.

This Season is proper for making Cherry Wine, the *Kentish* and *Flemish* Cherries being now full ripe, which are much the best for this purposes:

This is a very pleasant strong Wine.

To make Cherry Wine.

Gather your Cherries in dry Weather, when they are full ripe, pick them from the Stalks, and bruise them well with your Hands till they are all broken; then put them into a Hair Bag, and press them till you have as much Liquor from them as will run without breaking the Stones. To every Gallon of this Juice, put one Pound of powder Sugar, and having stirr'd it well together, boil it and scum it as long as any Scum will rise; then set it in a cool Place till it is quite cold, and put it into your Vessel, when it will presently begin to work. When the Working is over, slop the Vessel close, and let it stand four Months; if it holds the Quantity of twenty Gallons, or more or less, as the Quantity happens to be, then bottle it off, putting a Lump of Loaf-Sugar into each Bottle. It will keep two or three Years, if it be set in a cool Place.

I have now done with the Wines that are to be made in this Month: I shall in the next place set down the Method of keeping or preserving Fruits for Tarts all the Year about, as I had it from a very curious Person, in whose House I have seen it practised with extraordinary Success. The Fruits which are chiefly to be put up this Month, are Goosberries, Currants and Cherries.

To preserve Fruits for Tarts all the Year.

The Goosberries must be full grown, but not ripe, they must be gather'd in dry Weather, and pick'd clean of their Stalks and Tops; then put them into Quart Bottles, that are made on purpose, with large wide Necks, and cork them gently with new sound Corks, and put them into an Oven after the Bread is drawn, letting them stand there till they have shrunk about a fourth part; observing to change them now and then, because those which you set at the further part of the Oven, will be soonest done. When you find them enough, according to the above Direction, take them out, and immediately beat the Corks in as tight as you can, and cut the Tops off even with the Bottles, and pitch them over; you must then set your Bottles by, in a dry Place. I have tasted of Fruits done this way, that have made as good Tarts at the Year's end, as those that were fresh gather'd: The only difference between the preserving Goosberries and Currants, is, that the Currants must be full ripe when we put them into the Bottles, and so likewise the Cherries.

There is another way of putting up Fruits for this use, which is, by half preserving them with Sugar, *i.e.* half a Pound of Sugar to every Pound of Fruit. Apricots especially, when they are near ripe, make excellent Tarts; being split and pared from the Skin, and boiled in a Syrup, they will keep the Year round, as an ingenious Lady has told me. It is also to be remark'd, that ripe Goosberries make very fine Tarts.

The beginning of this Month, when the Goosberries are full grown, but not ripe, is the right Season for preserving of them in sweet-meat: The white *Dutch* Goosberry is the best for this use.

So likewise if you have plenty of *Kentish* Cherries, pick some of them from the Stalks, and lay the Cherries upon a fine Wire Sieve, and dry them in an Oven; when they are dried enough, and quite cold, put them in an Earthen glazed Jar, and stop them up close: These must be kept in a dry place.

Upon the foot of the above Receipt, for preserving of Fruits, I have a Notion that we may preserve green Pease, after the same manner, in Bottles, that I have mention'd for the preserving of Goosberries, Currants, &c. So that they will eat tender and well tasted at *Christmas:* it is well worth the tryal, seeing that a Bottle or two cannot be any great Expence, and that Pease are acceptable almost to every one. This I have persuaded some of my Acquaintance to try, but particularly a very curious Person in such matters, who tells me, that provided this method answers what we aim at, he supposes they will be the most agreeable, either to be boiled with Cream, or stew'd in Gravey, after the *French* manner, for it is a dispute with him, whether they will hold their green Colour; but, as I observ'd before, it may be try'd at an easy Expence.

The beginning of this Month is the time to pickle Walnuts, for then the Walnuts have not began to shell, and moreover are not so bitter nor hollow as they will be afterwards; they will now be full flesh'd, and you will have no Loss. The following Method I learnt from Mr. *Foord,* a curious Gentleman of *Buckingham,* and has been experienced to be the best way. There is one thing indeed which must be regarded in this Pickle, which is, that every one does not love the Taste of Onion or Garlick; but that may be omitted as we please, only supplying the place with Ginger.

To pickle Walnuts.

The Walnuts being fit for pickling, wash them, and put them into a Kettle to scald; then with a piece of Flannel rub off the outer Skin, and let them lie till they are quite cold, after which put them into a Vessel of Salt and Water, and let them stand 24 Hours; then take them out, and put them again into fresh Salt and Water for 24 Hours more; then shift them as before, and continue this Practice for fourteen Days, at the end of which time wipe them dry, and lay them in a glazed earthen Pot, *Stratum super Stratum,* with Spice, whole Mustard-Seed, Horse-Radish slic'd, and Garlick, or Eschalots: that is to say, make a Layer of Walnuts, and strew over it whole Pepper, Ginger slic'd, Horse-Radish slic'd, some whole Mustard-Seed, and three or four Cloves of Garlick; or if Garlick be too strong, as many Cloves of Shalots. Then lay upon these another Layer of Walnuts, and upon them the Roots and Spices as before, and so continue till your Pot is full; then pour over the whole, as much boiling Vinegar as will cover them, and immediately cover the Pot close, and let it stand till the next Day, when we may again pour off the Vinegar from them, without disturbing them; and making it again boiling hot, pour it upon them, and stop them close, as before, to be set by for use. But these will not be fit for eating under three Weeks or a Month, and will be much better by keeping a few Months.

This Month is a proper time to make Syrup of Clove-Julyflowers, and likewise to make Julyflower Wine, which is a very rich Liquor, and may be made in the best manner, by the following Receipt from Mrs. B. B.

To make Julyflower Wine.

Take nine Gallons of Water, and twenty four Pounds of Sugar, boil these on a gentle Fire till one Gallon is lost, or evaporated, taking off the Scum as it rises. Then having prepared a Bushel of Clove Julyflowers, the red Flower Leaves only, pour the Liquor scalding hot upon them, and cover them close till the next Day, then pressing them with a Screw-press. When this is done, bake a piece of Bread hard, without scorching, before the Fire, and while it is warm, spread some Ale-Yeast upon it, and put it into the Liquor, in an open Tub, till it begins to worker ferment; the next Day after which, add two quarts of Sack, and one of *Rhenish* Wine, and barrel it for three Weeks or a Month; let it then be bottled, and kept in a cool Place.

In this Month such Carp and Tench are good as have not lately spawn'd; the dressing of them, and of Pikes, or Jacks, see in *March*. Perch are now very good, the large ones for stewing, as recommended for Carp, or boiled or fry'd, or else in the *Dutch* manner, call'd Water Soochy; which is to boil the Perches with Salt in the Water, and Parsley-Roots and Parsley Leaves, to be brought to Table in the Water they are boiled in, and eaten with Bread and Butter. 'Tis an odd way to the *English*, but is much admir'd by many Genlemen who have travell'd.

The Garden is now very rich in Eatables, as may be seen in my *Gardener's Kalendar*, printed for Mr. *Mears*.

The Trasopogon, or Goatsbeard, is now, as well as in the former Month, fit for boiling; it is in much request in some of the Western parts of *England*, especially about *Bristol*, as I am inform'd, where the Country People call it Trangompoop, or Crangompoop, a corruption, as I suppose, from the true Name above written: This is eaten like Asparagus, and dress'd the same way, the part which is eaten is the blossomy Bud a little before it would flower, with about six Inches of the Stalk to it.

There are now Chickens, Pigeons, Ducks, and some young wild Ducks, and

Rabbets, which may not only make great Variety at a Table, to be drest after the common plain way, but may also be made into elgant Dishes, after the several manners mention'd in this Work, if there is an occasion to entertain particular People of fine Taste.

The Ronceval and Mooretto Pease, and *Windsor* Beans, are also good helps to a Table: I need say nothing of their dressing; but that I am of opinion, that the *Windsor* Beans, when they are blanch'd, that is, boiled long enough till we can take off their Skins, and then put into large-neck'd Bottles, and order'd as I have prescrib'd for the preserving of Pease; by this means I suppose they may be preserv'd many Months: but we may defer this Experiment till the end of *September*, to be try'd upon the latter Crops.

Near the Sea we have Mackrel in the height of perfection, and Mullet, Turbut, Herrings, Scate, and Soles, as also Lobsters and Crabs; and in the Rivers, Salmon and Trout are still good, and some Cray-Fish.

'Tis now a proper Season to put up Rasp-berries, either in Sweetmeat, or to infuse in Brandy; but they must be gather'd dry. There are certain People who know how to mix these with *Port* Wine, and imitate the richest *Florence* Wine.

About *Midsummer* is a proper time to put up a Boar for Brawn against *Christmas*, or against the beginning of *December*, for then is the Season it sells best, and is chiefly in request, selling at that time for twelve Pence *per* Pound.

For this end we should chuse an old Boar, for the older he is, the more horny will the Brawn be: We must provide for this use a Frank, as the Farmers call it, which must be built very strong to keep the Boar in. The figure of the Frank should be somewhat like a Dog-Kennel, a little longer than the Boar, which we put up so close on the Sides that the Boar cannot turn about in it; the Back of this Frank must have a sliding Board, to open and shut at pleasure, for the conveniency of taking away the Dung, which should be done every Day. When all this is very secure, and made as directed, put up your Boar, and take care that he is so placed, as never to see or even hear any Hogs; for if he does, he will pine away, and lose more good Flesh in one Day than he gets in a Fortnight: He must then be fed with as many Pease as he will eat, and as much skim'd Milk, or flet Milk, as is necessary for him. This method must be used with him till he declines his Meat, or will eat very little of it, and then the Pease must be left off, and he must be fed with Paste made of Barley Meal, made into Balls as big as large Hen-Eggs, and still the Skim-Milk continued, till you find him decline that likewise, at which time he will be fit to kill for Brawn; the Directions for making of which, with the Pickle for it, see in the Month of *December*. During the time he is thus feeding, great care must be taken that he has always Meat before him, for neglect in this will spoil the whole Design.

This is the way of feeding a Boar for Brawn, but I cannot help thinking 'tis a little barbarous, and especially as the Creature is by some People put in so close a Pen, that as I hear, it cannot lie down all the while 'tis feeding; and at last, considering the expence of Food, Brawn is but an insipid kind of Meat: however, as some are lovers of it, it is necessary to prescribe the method which should be used in the preparing it.

In this Month we have plenty of Artichokes and it is a good Season to put them up for Winter use, to be used simply, or to be put in Sauces, or in compound Dishes; they are easily dried or pickled, to be kept, and if they are not gather'd as soon as they are in their perfection, they will lose the goodness of their Hearts, or the Bottoms, as some call them. In a plentiful Year of them I have had a great number dried for Winter use, in the following manner.

Concerning the gathering, and ordering Artichokes for drying.

In the gathering of Artichokes, observe, that the Leaves of what is call'd the Artichoke be pointing inwards, and lie close at the Top, for then the Bottom will be large and full; but if you find many of the Leaves of the Artichoke spread from the Top, then the Choke, or bristly part is shot so much, that it has drawn out much of the Heart of the Artichoke; and as the Flower comes forward, the more that grows, the thinner will be the Bottom, which is the best part of it.

When you cut the Artichoke, cut it with a long Stalk, that when you use it you may clear it well of its Strings, which will else spoil the goodness of the Bottom, wherein the Strings will remain; to do this, lay the Artichoke upon a Table, and hold it down hard with one Hand, while with the other Hand you pull the Stalk hard up and down, till it quits the Artichoke, and will then pull away the Strings along with it; this being done, lay the Artichokes in Water for an Hour, and then put them into a Kettle of cold Water to boil, till they are tender enough to separate the Leaves and the Chokes from them. When this is done, lay the Hearts, or Bottoms upon a Cullender, or some other thing, to drain conveniently; then dry them upon a Wire Sieve, or Gridiron, in a gentle Oven, by degrees, till they are as hard as Wood. These will keep good twelve Months if they are laid by in a dry Place.

When we want to use these for boiling, frying, or to accompany other Meats, we must put them into warm Water, often repeating it to them for eight and forty Hours, by which means they will come to themselves, and be as good when they come to be scalded as if they were fresh gather'd. But they may also be preserv'd after the following manner.

Second Way to preserve Artichokes.

Having chosen your Artichokes according to the above Directions, cut the Bottoms, with a sharp Knife, clear of their Leaves and their Chokes, flinging them immediately into cold Water, to prevent their turning black. When they have lain in the Water for seven or eight Minutes, wash them and drain them a little, and then fling them into Wheat or Barley Flower, so that they be all over cover'd with it; after which, lay them upon Wire Sieves, or Pieces of Wicker-work to dry in an Oven gently, till they are quite dry and hard: these must be kept in a dry Place, and when they are to be used, steep them in Water four and twenty Hours, and boil them till they are tender, they will eat as well as if they were fresh cut.

The Artichoke may likewise be pickled in the following manner.

To preserve Artichokes by Pickling.

Gather and prepare your Artichokes as before, and put them into cold Water to boil, with a moderate quantity of Salt; then take them off the Fire, and let the Water stand in the Kettle for a quarter of an hour, till the Salt is settled to the bottom; then pour off your Water clear into an Earthen glazed Vesel where you design to put your Artichokes, and clearing them from the Leaves and Choaks, wash them well in two or three Waters, and put them in the Brine or Pickle they were boiled in, when both are quite cold; upon which pour as much Oil as will cover it half an Inch thick, or where Oil is wanting, melted Butter will serve: be sure you put so much as will keep the Air from the Artichokes. Some will add some Vinegar to the Water, but that is at pleasure; when this is done, cover the top of the Earthen Pot close with Paper, and lay a Board over it to keep it from any Air, or else cover the Pot with a wet Bladder, and tie it down close. They will keep good a Year, and when we want to use them, lay them to steep in cold Water to take out the Salt; you may shift the Water three or four times, they will be the better for it, and then use them in Pyes, or other compound Dishes.

In *Holland* I have often eaten the small Suckers of Artichokes fry'd, which have made an agreeable Dish. The Receipt for preparing them is the following.

To fry small Suckers of Artichokes, or small Artichokes.

Gather the young Heads of Artichokes, and boil them with Salt and Water till they are tender; these Artichokes should be no bigger than middling Apples; split these in four or six Parts each, flower them well, and fry them crisp in Hogs-lard, and eat them with Butter, Pepper, and a little Verjuice or Orange-

Juice.

It is a common practice in *France* to eat the small Heads of Artichokes raw, with Vinegar, Pepper, and Salt; the Method is to pull off the single Leaves, and dip the fleshy part of the Leaves into it and eat that. They are agreeably bitter, and create an Appetite.

This Month Rasberries are ripe; and as they make a most pleasant Wine, I shall here give the Receipt for making it.

To make Rasberry Wine.

To every Quart of the Juice of Rasberries, put a Pint of Water, and to every Quart of Liquor a Pound of fine Sugar; then set it on the Fire to boil half an hour, taking off the Scum as it rises: then set it to cool, and when it is quite cold, put it in a Vessel and let it stand ten Weeks or something more if the Weather prove cold; when it is settled, bottle it, and it will keep two Years. Altho' I have set down in this Month a good experienced way of making Goosberry Wine, which will keep twenty Years, and grow better by Age; yet I cannot pass by a Receipt which is highly commended for making Wine of Red Goosberries, which I had from an Acquaintance who frequently makes it.

To make Red Goosberry Wine.

When the Red Goosberries are well colour'd and not over-ripe, but grateful to the Taste, gather them in a dry Day; take a Peck of these, and slit them a little more than half thro' the middle, putting them into a large glazed Earthen Pan, with eight Pounds of fine powder'd Sugar strew'd over them; then boil four Gallons of Cyder, and pour it boiling hot upon the Sugar and Goosberries: this must stand eight or ten Days, stirring it once each Day, and at length strain it thro' a Flannel in a Press, and put the Liquor into the Vessel with a warm Toast of Wheat-bread, spread on both sides with Ale-Yeast; this must stand two or three Months till it is fine, and then bottle it. This is a very strong Wine, and of a bright red Colour.

* * * * *

JULY.

This Month is the principal Season for pickling of Cucumbers, for that Fruit is now in the greatest Perfection, as well for pickling them in imitation of Mango's, or as Girkins. They are now to be had in great plenty, and are free from Spots.

The following is an extraordinary Receipt for pickling of Cucumbers to imitate Mango's.

Gather large Cucumbers of as green a Colour as may be, wash them well in common Water, and then either cut off their Tops, and scoop out all the seedy part, or else cut a Slice out of the Side of each of them, and scrape out the seedy part with a small Spoon, taking care not to mismatch the Slices or Tops of the Cucumbers, that they may tie up the better when we come to fill them with Spices, &c. When we have thus prepared enough to fill the Jar or Earthen Vessel which we design for them, peel some Garlick or Shalots, which you like best, and put either two Cloves of Shalot into each Cucumber, or one middling Clove of Garlick; and also into every one put a thin slice or two of Horse-radish, a slice of Ginger, and, according to custom, a Tea Spoonful of whole Mustard-seed; but, in my opinion, that may be left out. Then putting on the tops of the Cucumbers, or the Slices that were cut out of them, tie them close with strong Thread, and place them in your Jar. Then prepare your Pickle of Vinegar, which we suppose to be about five Quarts to two dozen of large Cucumbers, to which put about a Pound of Bay-Salt, half an Ounce of whole Pepper, about an Ounce of Ginger sliced, and a large Root of Horse-radish sliced; boil these in a brass Sauce-pan for about fifteen Minutes, taking off the Scum as it rises, and then pour it upon your Cucumbers, and cover the top of the Vessel with a coarse Linnen Cloth four or five times double, and set the Vessel near the Fire to keep warm; the day following you will find them changed to a yellow Colour, but that will alter in a day or two to be much greener than they were at first, If you use the following Method: Pour all your Pickle into a brass Skellet, and add to it a piece of Allum as big as a Walnut, and set it over the Fire till it boils, then pour it on your Cucumbers as before, and repeat the same every day till the Cucumbers are of the Greenness you desire. When you have pour'd on your Pickle for the last time, the Jar must be cover'd as before, but remain without Corking till it is quite cold, then stop it close and set it by, in a dry place. The Corks for the stopping of these Jars should be cover'd with soft glove-leather, for the naked Corks will make the Pickles musty. See the Mango's made of green Melons in the Month of *September*.

To preserve Green Cucumbers for slicing in the Winter, by Mr. *Foord* of *Buckingham*.

Gather Cucumbers half grown, that is, before they incline to be seedy, put them in Salt and Water for five or six days, shifting it every day; then wipe them dry, and put them in Vinegar with a little Allum to green over the fire; then take out the Cucumbers, and boil the pickle to pour hot upon them, covering the Mouth of the Jar with a coarse Cloath four or five times doubled, and let the Jar stand near the fire. When this Pickle is quite cold, stop the Jar close with a leather'd Cork, as mention'd in the foregoing Receipt for Mango Cucumbers. These Cucumbers may be used in the Winter to be pared and sliced like those gather'd fresh from the Garden; you may cut an Onion with them, and eat them with Pepper, Vinegar and Oil.

To Pickle Cucumbers, from Mr. *Foord* of *Buckingham.*

Gather the smallest Cucumbers you can find, for it is the smallest Size, which is most commonly brought to table among People of the first Rank; tho' a Cucumber of two Inches long will do very well, or even one of three Inches. These must be put in Salt and Water, to be shifted every day till they change to a yellow colour: wipe them dry, and prepare Pickle of Vinegar, a piece of Allum as big as a Wallnut to a gallon, or in proportion, Ginger diced, Mace, whole Pepper, a few Bay-leaves, and some Dill-Seed, which will do better than the Herb it self. Tye the Seeds in a piece of Muslin, that when the Pickle by boiling is strong enough of the Dill, you may take it out. This Pickle, when it is of a right flavour, must be pour'd boiling hot upon the Cucumbers, which must be laid in a Stone Jar or Gallypot proper for them, and then cover'd with a coarse Linnen Cloth folded in several Doubles, and let them stand near the fire: Repeat the boiling of the Pickle every day, pouring it hot upon the Cucumbers, and covering them as before, till they become of the green colour you desire. When they are quite cold, stop them up close with a leather'd Cork, as directed in the former Receipt, if you use a Jar, or else if you make use of a Gallypot, tye them down with Leather or a wet Bladder. It is to be understood, that Allum and boiling Vinegar will strike a green colour to any unripe Fruit; but care must be taken that too much Allum be not used, left the stomach be offended by it. It is a custom in some places to pickle the green Pods of *Capsicum Indicum* with their Cucumbers, which will contribute to make them much hotter or warmer to the Stomach, and promote Digestion in cold Constitutions. But the *Capsicums* should be boiled in Water gently, and wiped dry, before you put them among the Cucumbers, where they must be placed before the Pickle is poured upon them.

Kidney-Beans are pickled the same way as the Cucumbers, only leaving out the Dill; and the Dill also may be left out of the Cucumber-Pickle, if it is not agreeable to the Palate; and so likewise in other Pickles, Garlick or Onions, or any particular Spice may be left out which is disagreeable, for it is not the business here to pin down the Palate of any one to a certain Relish that I may like my self, but to put it in the power of every one to preserve or order such things as a Farm or Garden affords, so that they may be pleased with them. The Receipts which I have here given, are what I have generally found to be the most approved. We have some who pickle the green Fruit of the Passion-Tree, the Berougella, and Fig: but for my part I can find nothing to recommend them, but the relish of the Pickle, neither are they by any means wholesome.

The Flowers of the *Nasturtium Indicum* make an excellent Sallad in this Month, and the Seeds of the Plant, while they are green, may be pickled to our satisfaction: the Receipt for pickling them is as follows.

To pickle Nasturtium Seeds.

Gather the Seeds when they are full grown and green, in a dry day, and lay them in Salt and Water for two or three days; then boil Vinegar, with some Mace, Ginger sliced, and a few Bay-Leaves, for fifteen Minutes, and pour it boiling hot upon them, covering them with a Cloth, as prescribed in this Month for the other Pickles, and repeat the boiling of the Pickle, and scalding them with it for three days successively; and when the last is poured on, let it be cold before you cork it up. The folded Cloth which should be put over the Mouth of the Jar, will suffer some of the Steam of the Pickle to pass thro' it, and by that means the Pickles will not turn mouldy, so soon as they might otherwise do, and besides will be much greener than if they were to be close stopped. All these Pickles should be kept in a dry Place, and look'd into every Month, lest by chance they turn mouldy; which if you find they incline to, boil the Pickle afresh, and pour it on them as before.

There is now the Skerret fit to be eaten; it is a very nourishing and pleasant Root, and is prepared in the following manner for the Table: the Culture of it is set forth at large in my new *Improvements of Planting and Gardening*, printed for Mr. *Mears*, near *Temple-Bar*,

The Skerret, tho' it is none of the largest Roots, yet is certainly one of the best Products of the Garden, if it be rightly dress'd; the way of doing which, is to wash the Roots very well, and boil them till they are tender, which need not be very long. Then the Skin of the Roots must be taken off, and a Sauce of melted Butter and Sack pour'd over them. In this manner are they serv'd at the Table, and eaten with the Juice of Orange, and some likewise use Sugar with them, but the Root is very sweet of itself.

Some, after the Root is boil'd, and the Skin is taken off, fry them, and use the Sauce as above: So likewise the Roots of Salsify and Scorzonera are to be prepared for the Table.

The Apple call'd the Codlin is in good perfection for scalding, the manner of doing which, that they may be brought to Table, of a fine green Colour, is as follows.

Gather your Codlins half grown, and without Spots, for if they are spotted, they are commonly Worm-eaten; scald them in Water till the Skin will come off easily, then put them again into cold Water, and a small piece of Allum to green in a Brass Pan over the Fire; which they will soon do if they are kept close cover'd.

The following Receipt is sent me by a curious Person for pickling of Codlins, in imitation of Mango.

Gather Codlins green and near full grown, blanch them, that is, scald them in soft Water till the Skin will peel off, then prepare your Pickle of Vinegar and Bay Salt, about a large Spoonful of Salt to a Quart of Vinegar, three or four Cloves of Garlick, a quarter of an Ounce of Ginger sliced, and as much whole Pepper; boil this in a Brass Pan, with a piece of Allum as big as a Horse-Bean, for half a quarter of an hour, and pour it hot upon your Codlins, covering the Mouth of the Jar with a Cloth, and let it stand by the Fire-side; boil the Pickle again the day following, and apply it as before, and repeat the same till your Codlins are as green as you desire, and when they are quite cold, cork them close, and set them by in a dry place. There is one thing must however be observed in all these Picklings, which is, that if the Pickles do not come to their fine green Colour presently, by boiling often of the Pickle at first, yet by standing three or four Weeks, and then boiling the Pickle afresh, they will come to a good Colour; and then your Pickles will eat the firmer and keep the longer, when they are not too soon brought to Colour.

In this Month we have the Morello and Black Cherry ripe, which both are pleasant in Brandy; to those who would have Drams by them, the way of making Black-Cherry Brandy, is only to pick the Cherries from the Stalks, and put them whole into the Brandy, about a Pound of Cherries to a Quart; this may remain for about a Month before it is fit to drink, and then the Brandy may be pour'd from the Cherries, and the Cherries put then into a Vessel of Ale will make it extremely strong, only about the proportion of a Pound of Cherries to a Gallon of Ale; but some will put fresh Brandy to them, and the Cherries will turn the Brandy of a deep Colour, and give it a strong taste of Ratafia; others will distill these Cherries in a cold Still, with as much Water as will cover them, and draw a fine Cordial from them.

To make Visney.

This Visney is made of pure Brandy, and as many Morello Cherries as will fill the Bottles or Casks, with one Ounce of Loaf-Sugar to each full Quart; these Vessels or Bottles must be gently stopp'd, when the Cherries are put in, and stand in a cool Cellar for two Months before the Liquor is poured from them, and then the Liquor may be put in small Bottles for use: It is not very strong, but very pleasant. The Cherries, when they are taken out, may be distill'd, and will yield a fine Spirit.

In some places, where there are Laurels grow wild, without Cutting or pruning, I mean, the *Lauro-Cerasus*, as we find in many old Gardens, that Plant is apt to bear Berries, which in reality are Cherries, from whence it has its Name; these Berries, or Cherries, are ripe about this time, and make a fine

Cordial, if we infuse them in Brandy for two or three Months with a little Sugar; this will have a Flavour of Abricot Kernels, and be of a rich red Colour. While I am speaking of this, I cannot help taking notice of a particular Dram which I tasted at a curious Gentleman's House at *Putney* in *Surrey*, _W. Curtis _Esq; which he made by infusing of the Cornelian Cherry in Brandy; that Gentleman is the only one who I think has yet tried it, and to my Palate it seems to be so like *Tockay* Wine, that it must be a very good judge who can discover the difference. I have drank that Wine in perfection, and this preparation has both the Colour, Taste, and Proportion of strength equal to it; for the great strength of the Brandy is lost in the Cornelian Cherry, and tho' the Cornelian Cherry is of a bright red Colour, yet this Liquor is of the Colour of *Tockay* Wine.

Those who live near *London*, may, about this Season, buy Geese out of the Flocks, which are now drove up to that City, at about five and twenty, or thirty Shillings a score; and till the Season we are to turn them into the Stubble, we may feed them chiefly with the Offals of the Garden, Lettuce especially, which will fatten them, if you have enough: but as for their particular Feed for fatting, I shall speak of that in another place.

About this Season Abricots are ripe, and where there are plenty of them, we may make a pleasant Wine with them. The following Receipt is a very good one.

To make Apricot Wine. From Mrs. *J. L.*

To every Quart of Water put a Pound and half of Apricots, that are not over-ripe, let them be wiped clean, and cut in pieces; boil these till the Liquor is strong of the Apricot Flavour; then strain the Liquor thro' a Sieve, and put to every Quart four or five Ounces of white Sugar, boil it again, and scum it as it rises, and when the Scum rises no more, pour it into an Earthen Pot; the Day following bottle it, putting into every Bottle a lump of Loaf-Sugar, as big as a Nutmeg. This will presently be fit for drinking, is a very pleasant Liquor; but will not keep long.

* * * * *

AUGUST.

In this Month there are many Delicacies about a Country Seat; all kinds of Pond-Fish are good, there is plenty of Poultry of all kinds, wild and tame, except the Water-Fowl, which should yet remain untouch'd. Turkey Poults, Pheasant Poults, Partridges, and some sort of Pigeons, are good; but for the most part the Dove-cote Pigeons are distemper'd, and are now full of Knots in their Skins, and unwholesome. The Eggs of Fowls likewise at this Season, as well as in the former Month, are unhealthful. Towards the end, Pork comes again in Season, and young Pigs also are pretty plentiful; 'tis a good time likewise to save young Pigs to grow up for now you may turn them with their Dams into the Stubbles, and soon after into the Woods. About the end of this Month, you have Rabbets full grown in common Warrens, and young wild Ducks; and those who live near the Sea, have plenty of Oysters, and in great perfection, much better, in my opinion, than in the Winter. Hares are also now good, and Buck Venison is still good. Turnips, Carrots, Cabbages, Caulyflowers, Artichokes, Melons, Cucumbers, and such like, are in prime; Sallary and Endive, *Nasturtium Indicum* Flowers, Cabbage Lettice, and blanch'd sweet Fennel is now good for Sallads. Peas and Beans, and Kidney-beans, are likewise to be met with, so that a Country Gentleman and Farmer may have every thing at home, and let out a Table fit for a Prince, without being beholden to the Markets; and the great variety of Fruits which this Season produces, renders it still more delightful and profitable.

Now Elder-berries are ripe and fit for making of Wine, as well the white as the red sort: these are both very good, if they are rightly managed. The following drinks very much like the *French* Wine call'd *Hermitage*, and is full as strong.

To make red Elder Wine.

Take twenty Pounds of *Malaga* Raisins pick'd and rubb'd clean, but not wash'd; shred them small, and steep them in five Gallons of Spring Water, putting the Water cold to them, and stirring them every day; then pass the Liquor thro' a Hair Sieve, pressing the Raisins with your Hands, and have in readiness six Pints of the Juice of Elder-Berries that have been first pick'd from the Stalks, and then drawn by boiling the Berries in a glaz'd Earthen Pot, set in a Pan of Water over the Fire. Put this Juice cold into the Liquor, stirring it well together, and then tunning it in a Vessel that will just hold it, and let it stand six Weeks or two Months in a warm place; then bottle it, and it will keep a Year if the Bottles are well stopp'd. Note, that the Elder-Berries must be full ripe, and gather'd in a dry day; and when you have tunn'd your Wine, let the place where you set it be warm and dry, where no external Air is admitted, that it may ferment or work duly, for that is a material point. If it be otherwise disposed, so that it stands in a place which is subject to Heats and Cold, the Ferment will stop upon Cold, or be too violent upon Heats; but in cold Weather put some Straw about it. See more of the working of Liquors in *March*, in the Article of Brewing, and likewise take care that your Bottles are dry when you bottle your Wine, and that you have good Corks; take care likewise that your Wine be clear before you bottle it, or it will be good for nothing. If this Wine be rightly managed according to the above Directions, it will be fit for drinking after it has been bottled a Month.

In the making of white Elder-Wine, there is no difference if you make it with Raisins; but it is much the best, in my Opinion, if you make it with Sugar after the following manner: only it is to be consider'd, that white Elder-Berries are yet very scarce, and there must be more of them used in the Sugar Wine than in the Raisin Wine.

To make white Elder-Wine, or red Elder-Wine, with Sugar.

Gather the Elder-Berries ripe and dry, pick them, bruise them with your Hands, and strain them; then set the Liquor by in glaz'd earthen Vessels for twelve hours to settle, then put to every pint of Juice a pint and half of Water, and to every Gallon of this Liquor put three Pounds of *Lisbon* Sugar: set this in a Kettle over the Fire, and when it is ready to boil, clarify it with the Whites of four or five Eggs; let it boil an hour, and when it is almost cold, work it with some strong Ale-Yeast, and then tun it, filling up the Vessel from time to time with the same Liquor saved on purpose, as it sinks by working. In a Month's time, if the Vessel holds about eight Gallons, it will be fine and fit to bottle, and after bottling, will be fit to drink in two Months: but remember, that all Liquors must be fine before they are bottled, or else they will grow sharp and ferment in the Bottles, and never be good for any thing.

N.B. Add to every Gallon of this Liquor a Pint of strong Mountain Wine, but not such as has the Borachio or Hogskin flavour. This Wine will be very strong and pleasant, and will keep several Years.

We must prepare our Red Elder-Wine in the same manner that we make with Sugar, and if our Vessel hold about eight or ten Gallons, it will be fit for Bottling in about a Month; but if the Vessel be larger, it must stand longer in proportion, three or four Months at least for a Hogshead.

This Month Barberries are ripe and fit for pickling; they make a pretty Garnish, and are prepared as follows.

To pickle Barberries, or Pipperages, as call'd in some places.

Gather your Barberries in dry Weather, and lay them in their Bunches into an earthen glazed Pot, then boil a quantity of Water made strong with Salt, scumming it as it rises, and let it stand to be quite cold; then pour it upon the Barberries, so as to cover them an Inch, and cover it close. Some use half Vinegar and half Water for this Pickle, but it is at every one's pleasure, I think one is as good as the other.

Partridges are now in Season, and are prepared after several manners; some of the principal are the following.

Boil'd Partridges with stew'd Sallary, from Lady W———.

The Partridges being clean'd and trussed, boil them tender, and make the following Sauce for them. Take half a score large Sallary Plants that are well whiten'd or blanched, boil them first in Water and Salt, and then stew them tender with Gravey, Salt, some Pepper, and a Spoonful or two of White wine; and when they are enough, thicken and brown the Sauce they are stew'd in with burnt Butter, lay your Sallary at the bottom of the Dish, and your Partridges upon that, then pour your Sauce over all, and garnish with Lemmon or Orange slic'd. This is the method of stewing Sallary, which is an agreeable Plate of itself.

From the same Lady I had the following Directions for roasted Partridges: Partridges which are designed for roasting may be larded with fine Bacon Fat on the Breast, or roasted without larding; but in a Dish of these Fowls, there should be some of one and some of the other. The Sauce for them should be of two sorts, one of Gravey in the Dish with them, and the other of Bread in Saucers on the sides of the Dish. The Gravey is made of Beef, an Onion, a Bunch of sweet Herbs, some Salt and Pepper, stew'd half an hour together, in a little more Water than will cover them, then strain off the Liquor into the Dish.

The Pap-Sauce, or Bread-Sauce, is made of grated Crumb of Bread, boiled with as much Water as will cover it, a little Butter, an Onion, and some whole Pepper; this must be kept stirring often, and when it is very thick, withdraw the Onion, and serve it in a Saucer with your Partridges. These Sauces may likewise be served with Pheasants, or Quails. These may also be stew'd, farced, baked, or put in Soups, or used in Fricassees. Thus far the Lady.

Hares begin now to be in Season, and are well dress'd by the following Receipt, which I purchased a few Years ago, at a noted Tavern in *London*.

A Hare and its Sauces.

If you kill a Hare by Coursing, you may keep it if the Weather be cool three days before you roast it; or if it has been run hard by the Hounds, then it will not keep so long. When the Skin is taken off, it is the fashion to leave the Ears on, but that is at pleasure; then truss it for Roasting, and take the Liver and boil it, and mince it very small; add to this grated Bread, a little All-Spice, but fine, some butter'd Eggs, a little dry'd sweet Marjoram, with a Seasoning of Pepper and Salt at discretion, and some Parsley shred small: Mix this well together, and add the Yolk of an Egg to it to bind it; then fill the Body of the Hare moderately with this Farce, and sew up the Belly. When the Hare is first laid down to the fire, put about three pints of Water with an Onion, some Salt and whole Pepper, in the Dripping-pan, and baste the Hare with this till it is near roasted enough, and baste it with a piece of fat burning Bacon, or in the place of that, common Butter; but the Bacon is best, if the Person knows how to use it. When it is enough, pour the following Sauce into the Dish with it: Take the Liquor, with the Onion and Pepper in the Dripping-pan, out before you baste the Hare with Butter or Bacon, and boil it with a glass of Claret; it will be very rich when it comes to be mixt with the Farce out of the Belly of the Hare, and is little trouble. You may thicken this with a little Butter and Flower, if you please.

The following is also a very good one: Take a pound of lean Beef, boil it in about three pints of Water with an Onion, a Bunch of sweet Herbs, some Allspice, Pepper and Salt, till the Beef is boil'd half enough; then cut the Beef in several places to let out the Gravey, and continue to boil all those till the Liquor has lost a third part; then add a little Claret to it, and strain the Liquor through a Sieve, pouring the Gravey hot into the Dish before you put the Hare in it; and when you lay in the Hare, cut away the part that was sew'd up, or take away the thread that sew'd it. Some chuse to skewer up the Belly of the Hare, rather than sew it. You may serve this with Lemmon sliced, and in a plate by it have the following Sauce.

Sweet Venison Sauce.

Take half a pint of Claret, a little Stick of Cinnamon, and boil them together till the Flavour of the Cinnamon is in the Claret; then sweeten it to your mind with double-refined Loaf-sugar. Or else,

Grate some Crumb of Bread, and put to it as much Claret as will make it like thin Pap; add to this a small piece of Cinnamon, and boil it well, then sweeten it with double-refined Loaf-sugar grated small. These are the sweet Sauces used for Hare, and all other Venison.

To dress a Hare with White or Brown Sauce, from the late curious Mr. *Harrison* of *Henley* upon *Thames*.

Cut your Hare in four or eight pieces, and slit the Head; fry it a little in Hog's Lard, and then put it to stew in an earthen glazed Vessel, with Gravey, half a pint of White-wine, Pepper, Nutmeg, Salt, a bunch of sweet Herbs, and a slice or two of Lemmon-Peel; keep this close covered, and stew it gently till 'tis tender, then strain off the Sauce, and brown it with fry'd Flower, or burnt Butter: pour the Sauce hot over the Hare, and serve it with a Garnish of Lemmon in Slices; but if you would have your Sauce of brighter Colour, instead of the burnt Butter, or fry'd Flower, thicken it with the Yolks of three or four Eggs. This is an excellent way of dressing a Hare, and more generally admired than any other.

This being the Season for taking Honey, I shall here set down the Method of making of Mead, after two ways, which are both extraordinary.

To make Mead, from Lady *G*.

Take eight Gallons of Water, and as much Honey as will make it bear an Egg; add to this the Rind of six Lemmons, and boil it well, scumming it carefully as it rises. When 'tis off the Fire, put to it the Juice of the six Lemmons, and pour it into a clean Tub, or open earthen Vessel, if you have one large enough, to work three Days; then scum it well, and pour off the clear into the Cask, and let it stand open till it has done making a hissing Noise; after which, stop it up close, and in three Months time it will be fine, and fit for bottling.

To make Hydromel, or Mead.

Take eight Gallons of Water, and as much Honey as will make the Water bear an Egg; put to this a quarter of a pound of Cloves tied in three or four pieces of Muslin or Linnen Cloth, and set it to boil till the Scum has done rising, scumming it as it rises; then take it off the Fire, and take out the Cloves, which may be wash'd and dry'd for other Uses, and pour your Mead into an open Tub to ferment for about three days, till the Violence of the Working is over; after which, scum it very well, and pour the clear into a Vessel, leaving the Bung open till it has done hissing, which you may know by holding your Ear close to it, for at a distance you can hardly discover it. When this hissing is over, stop it close, and let it stand three Months till it is fine, before you bottle it; remember in bottling this, as well as all other Liquors, that the Bottles must be clean, and perfectly dry, and that every Bottle be well cork'd. This will keep good several Years.

Besides this way of making Mead, there is another which I have approved to be very good, which, in all particulars, except the Water, is the same with this; and instead of the Water, put the like Quantity of small Ale-Wort, brew'd with pale Malt: but this will require less Honey than the former, and will require more time in the Vessel before it is fine and fit to bottle; but it will last many Years good, and will drink like *Cyprus* Wine when it is a Year old. In this Liquor, take particular care that your Cloves are fresh and sound, for else you must add a Quantity in proportion.

N.B. We may make these Meads in the Spring of the Year, as well as at this Season; only the advantage of making it now, is, that you have an opportunity of washing the Honey-Combs after the Honey is run off, and thereby will save Expence in Honey.

The Potatoe now begins to be gather'd, and is a very useful Root, being either boil'd or roasted in hot Embers; and after it is boiled, to be broiled, or after boiling it tender, and beaten in a Mortar, it is used to thicken Sauces, and for making of rich Puddings, as I am inform'd by a skilful Person in this way.

The Roots of red Beets now begin to come in season, and are very good boiled, and sliced, to be put in a Pickle of Vinegar only: thus you may keep them to garnish Sallads of small Herbs, and in some Intervals put Horse-Radish scraped. These Roots will hold all the Winter. The Root of the red Beet makes an excellent Dish, prepared after the following manner, which I got abroad.

To fry the Roots of Red Beets.

Wash your Beet-Roots, and lay them in an earthen glazed Pan, bake them in an Oven, and then peel the Skin off them: after this is done, slit them from the Top to the Tail, and cut them in the shape of the Fish call'd a Sole, about the thickness of the third part of an Inch; dip these in a thick Batter, made of White-Wine, fine Flower, sweet Cream, the Whites and Yolks of Eggs, rather more Yolks than Whites, some Pepper, Salt, and Cloves beaten fine, all well mix'd. As you dip every piece of Beet-Root in this Batter, strew them over thick with fine Flower mix'd with grated Bread, and Parsley shred small, and then fry them in Lard. When they are enough, let them dry, and serve them with a Garnish of Lemmon. These likewise may be put about stew'd Carps, Tench, or roasted Jacks, by way of Garnish, with scraped Horse-Radish, and pickled Barberries.

In the Heats of this Month, the following Jelly is used by a curious Gentleman abroad, who gave me the Receipt of it, under the Name of *The Jelly of Health:* It is of great use to weak People, and extremely pleasant.

To make the Jelly of Health.

Take some Calves Feet, according to the Jelly you design to make, and also get a Cock of the common Poultry kind; wash these well, and put them in a Kettle to boil, with a proportionable Quantity of Water, particularly taking off the Scum as it rises. When these Meats are boiled almost to pieces, it is a sign that your Jelly is boiled enough; but take care that it is not too stiff, which you may try by taking a little out with a Spoon, and then setting it to cool. Then pour the Liquor thro' a Sieve into a Stew-pan, and take off all the Fat; after which, put to the Liquor a proportionable Quantity of double-refined Loaf-Sugar, a small Stick or two of Cinnamon, three or four Cloves, and the Rinds of two or three Lemmons: boil all these together gently for about a quarter of an hour, till it is well-tasted, and then beat up the Whites of four or five Eggs, with the Juice of the six Lemmons, and pour them into the Jelly, stirring the whole a little time over the Fire; then let this Mixture stand still upon the Fire till it rises ready to boil over; at which time, you must take it off, and pour it into the Jelly-Bag, and as it runs thro' into a Pan set to receive it, pour it again into the Jelly-Bag for three or four times till it comes clear, and then let it drop into Jelly-Glasses. Sometimes, the above Gentleman told me, he has put a little White-Wine into the Liquor while the Meats were boiling in it, which he thinks helps it.

* * * * *

SEPTEMBER.

As this Month produces great numbers of Mushrooms in the Fields, it is now chiefly that we ought to provide ourselves with them for making of Ketchup, and Mushroom Gravey: And it is also a proper Season for pickling them. Indeed, where we have Mushroom-Beds, we may do these Works at any time of the Year. It is to be remark'd, that the best Mushrooms have their Gills of a Flesh Colour, even while the Mushrooms are in button; and as they tend to spread in their Head, or to open their Cap, the Gills turn redder, till at length, when their Heads are fully spread open, they will become quite black. These large-flap Mushrooms are still good for stewing or broiling, so long as they have no Worms in them, and the Gills are then in the best state for making Ketchup, or Mushroom-Gravey; altho' the red Gills will do, but the smaller Buttons are what most People covet for Pickling.

In the gathering of Mushrooms, we are sure to meet with some of all sizes; the very small for pickling, the large Buttons for stewing or making Mushroom-Loaves, and Mushroom-Gravey, and the large Flaps for broiling or making of Ragous, or stewing, and Ketchup: therefore to follow the common way, we should make two or three Parcels of them.

The cleaning of Mushrooms, or preparing them for any of the above Uses, will afford us nothing but what is useful; the Parings should be saved by themselves, to be wash'd, towards the making of what is called Mushroom Gravey; the Gills must be saved by themselves for making either Ketchup, or Mushroom-Gravey; and the Parts towards the Roots, and the Roots themselves, must be kept to dry in the Sun, or a warm Room, to raise Mushrooms from, especially if they are of a large good sort that has red Gills, for those which have white Gills, prove oftentimes unwholesome, and are apt to turn yellow when they are cut and put in Water: however, some People eat of this sort, and I have eaten of such a sort myself; but as there are some with white Gills that are deadly, it is dangerous for unskilful Persons to meddle with any of that fort: and therefore I thought it convenient when I was in *France*, to learn the Method of raising them in Beds, that we might be sure of our sort, and have them all the Year about: The Method of doing which, is in my *Appendix* to my *New Improvements of Planting and Gardening*, printed for Mr. *Mears*, at *Temple-Bar*.

The following Receipts for making of Mushroom-Ketchup, and Mushroom-Gravey,
I had from a Gentleman named *Garneau*, whom I met at *Brussels*, and by Experience find them to be very good.

To make Mushroom Ketchup.

Take the Gills of large Mushrooms, such as are spread quite open, put them into a Skellet of Bell-Metal, or a Vessel of Earthen-Ware glazed, and set them over a gentle Fire till they begin to change into Water; and then frequently stirring them till there is as much Liquor come out of them as can be expected, pressing them often with a Spoon against the side of the Vessel; then strain off the Liquor, and put to every Quart of it about eighty Cloves, if they are fresh and good, or half as many more, if they are dry, or have been kept a long time, and about a Drachm of Mace: add to this about a Pint of strong red *Port* Wine that has not been adulterated, and boil them all together till you judge that every Quart has lost about a fourth Part or half a Pint; then pass it thro' a Sieve, and let it stand to cool, and when it is quite cold, bottle it up in dry Bottles of Pints or Half-Pints, and cork them close, for it is the surest way to keep these kind of Liquors in such small quantities as may be used quickly, when they come to be exposed to the Air, for fear of growing mouldy: *but I have had a Bottle of this sort of Ketchup, that has been open'd and set by for above a, Year, that has not received the least Damage*; and some Acquaintance of mine have made of the same sort, and have kept it in Quart-Botles to use as occasion required, and have kept it good much longer than I have done. A little of it is very rich in any Sauce, and especially when Gravey is wanting: Therefore it may be of service to Travellers, who too frequently meet with good Fish, and other Meats, in Britain, as well as in several other parts of Europe, that are spoiled in the dressing; but it must be consider'd, that there is no Salt in this, so that whenever it is used, Salt, Anchovies, or other such like relishing things, may be used with it, if they are agreeable to the Palate, and so likewise with the Mushroom Gravey in the following Receipt.

Of Mushroom Gravey.

When you clean your Mushrooms, save the Parings, and wash them well from the Dirt, and then put to them the Gills that have been scraped from the large Buttons, and with a very little Water put them in a Saucepan, and stir them frequently till you have got all the juice from them; then strain the Liquor from them, and set it by to cool, or else till you have stew'd the Mushrooms that they were taken from, and then add the Liquor of the stew'd Mushrooms to the aforesaid Liquor, and boil them both together, with about 80 Cloves, about a Drachm of Mace, and two Drachms of whole Pepper to each Quart of

Liquor, which will be lit to take off the Fire when it has lost about a third part by boiling; then pass it thro' a dry Sieve, into a dry earthen Pan, and let it stand till it be quite cold before you bottle it, observing then that the Bottles be very dry, for if they happen to be wet, it will soon turn mouldy. When the Bottles are fill'd, cork them well with sound new Corks, and tye a piece of Bladder, that has been softened in warm Water, over every Cork as tight as possible, and set the Bottles in a dry Place; with this management it will keep a long time.

What I learn'd else from the above mention'd Gentleman, concerning the preparing of Mushrooms for eating, was, that they should be always used when they are fresh gather'd, and then only such as are without Worms, which may be easily perceived by cutting their Stems cross-wise; and also that as soon as the Peel is pared off, and the Gills, let the large Mushrooms be cut into pieces, of the bigness of Nutmegs, and thrown into Water, as well the Stems as the Caps, for they are both good; then wash them well, and stew them a Sauce-pan, without putting any Liquor to them, or Spice, or Salt, till they have discharged a great deal of their own Liquor, and, begin to grow tender; you will then find them shrink into a very narrow compass, and must have the greatest part of the Liquor poured from them, with which you may make the Mushroom-Gravey abovemention'd. The Mushrooms being thus prepared, put to them a Seasoning of Pepper, Salt, Mace, and such other Ingredients as will not rob the Mushrooms too much of their own natural Flavour, and stir them frequently till they are enough; then put a little White-wine and Butter to them, and they will make an excellent good Dish: or else they may be made brown with some burned Butter, or be made into a Ragout. As for the broiling of the Caps of the large Mushrooms, the same Person's Receipt directs to rub the Caps with Butter on both sides, and strew Pepper and Salt on them, and broil them till they are quite hot through, turning them two or three times on the Fire, they will make their own Sauce when they come to be cut. Another way which he directs, is to make a pretty thick Batter of Flower, Water, or Milk and Eggs beaten together with some Salt and Pepper, to dip them in, and then fry them like Tripe; and for their Sauce, he recommends Butter, a little White-wine, and some of the Mushroom-Gravey, to be well mix'd together.

Some of my Acquaintance, who have try'd these Directions, approve of them; and, for my own part, I think them as agreeable as any that I have eaten: but as the Taste is not alike in every one, I shall add an Observation or two more of Monsieur *Garneau's*, concerning the Mushroom, which I think not unworthy our notice. The Mushroom, says that Gentleman, is not only a good Groundwork for all high Sauces, but itself a good Meat to be dress'd after any manner, either to compose a white or brown Fricassee, or fry'd or broil'd, or baked in Pyes with common Seasoning, and stands in the room of Flesh better than any thing that has yet been found out.

This Month is likewise a good time, if it is not over-wet, to gather Mushroooms for drying; but they should chiefly be such as are newly open'd in their Caps, before the Gills turn black. For this end, take off the Gills very clean, and wipe the Caps with wet Flannel, and as soon as they are a little dry, run a String through them, and hang them at some distance from the Fire, turning them now and then till they are dry enough to be reduced to Powder. When they are thus dry'd, keep them in dry Bottles with wide Necks, close stopp'd, till you have occasion to use them in Sauces. Keep this in a dry place. Some dry them in Ovens after the Bread is drawn, but an Oven in its full heat will be too strong for them.

To pickle Mushrooms White.

Take a Quart of small Buttons of Mushrooms, cut off their Roots, and wash them well with a Flannel dipt in Water, and then fling them into clean Water, to remain there about two hours. In the next place, get ready some fresh Water in a well-tinn'd Vessel, or glaz'd Vessel, to which put your Mushrooms, and let them boil a little to soften; which being done, take out your Mushrooms, and presently put them into cold Water, and let them remain there till they are quite cold; after this, free them from the Water, and dry them well in a linnen Cloth, then put them either into a wide-neck'd Bottle, or glaz'd Earthen-Vessel, disposing here and there among them three or four Bay-leaves to a Quart, two Nutmegs cut in quarters, about a quarter of an Ounce of Mace, and boil as much White-Wine and Vinegar, in equal quantities, as will serve to cover the Mushrooms. This Pickle must be put to them cold, and the Bottle, or Earthen-Vessel, close stopt and ty'd down with a wet Bladder. The reason why the Spice should not be boiled with the Pickle, is, because the Mushrooms would change black by means of the boil'd Spices; and if this plain Pickle was to be pour'd upon the Mushrooms hot, it would immediately draw a Colour from the Spices, which would darken the Colour of the Mushrooms: therefore to fill up the glasses in the manner here related, is the best way to have your Mushrooms look clean and white.

This Month is the proper time to pickle Onions, which make an agreeable Pickle if they are prepared after the following manner.

To pickle Onions, from Mrs. *A. W.*

When your Onions are dry enough to be laid up in the House, take the smallest of them, such as are about the bigness of a small Walnut, and of that sort which we call the *Spanish* Onion, for these are not so strong flavour'd as the *Strasburgh* Onions; take off only the outward dry Coat, and boil them in one Water without shifting, till they begin to grow tender; then take them off the Fire, lay them in a Sieve or Cullendar to drain and cool; and as soon as they are quite cold, take off two other Coats or Skins from each, and rub them gently in a linnen Cloth to dry. When this is done, put them into wide-mouth'd Glasses, with about six or eight fresh Bay-leaves to a Quart, a quarter of an Ounce of Mace, two large Rases of Ginger sliced. All these Ingredients must be interspersed here and there in the Glasses among the Onions, and then boil your Vinegar with about two Ounces of Bay-Salt to each Quart, taking off the Scum as it rises, and letting it stand to be cold; pour it into the Glasses, and cover them close with wet Bladders, and tie them down; they will eat well, and look very white.

About the end of this Month, if the Season has been tolerable, the Grapes in our *English* Vineyards will be ripe, and then we must be careful to gather them in dry Weather, that the Wine may keep the better. I have already mention'd, in my other Works, the curious Vineyard near *Bath*, and that belonging to Mr. *John Warner* at *Rotherhith*, where good Wines are made every year; and also that at *Darking* in *Surrey*, belonging to Mr. *Howard*, which is a very good one: but as some years are less favourable than others to the Grape, as well with us as abroad, it will not be unnecessary to take notice of a few Particulars, which I have observ'd this year 1726, concerning the management of Vines, which I have only communicated to a few. I shall also set down a few Directions for the making of Wine, which have not been hitherto mention'd in any of my Works, or by Mr. *Evelyn*, or Mr. *Mortimer*.

As to the first, we are to observe, that the Situation of our Island occasions our Seasons to be more uncertain than on the Continent, or between the Tropics. The cold and wet Summer, 1725, prevented the ripening of our later kind of Grapes; and indeed I did not meet anywhere with a Grape that had its perfect Flavour, unless the Vines were forced; but yet there were abundance. However, this Year, 1726, on the contrary, there are very few Grapes, and those are likely to be very good, some being already ripe against common Walls, without Art; such as the white Muscadine the 24th of *July*, and black Cluster-Grape. And at Sir *Nicholas Garrard*'s Garden in *Essex*, I eat some of the black *Frontiniack* full in perfection, at the same time; and then the grisly and white *Frontiniack* Grapes, which are the latest kinds, were transparent, and within a little of being fit to gather: which is a Novelty so great, that has not been observ'd in *England* in my time; for the *Frontiniack* Grapes seldom ripen till the end of *September*, and then in a bad Year we cannot expect them without Art. However, the Vines in this worthy Gentleman's Garden are of long standing, and have been, by his own Directions, order'd and manag'd in a very artful manner for several Years. And tho' this Year generally we find so small a quantity in other Gardens, yet at this place there are as many as I judge are in the whole County besides. In most other places that I have observ'd this Year, the common way of management has been rather regarded than the rational part; and even the best Gardeners have fail'd in their Pruning the last Year, for the production of this Year's Fruit. I much wonder, that after the Demonstrations I have given from Facts, ever since the Year 1717, that Vines would grow and prosper well to be planted in old dry Walls; and the Instances I publish'd in the same Year, in my new Improvements, of Vines bearing best in dry Rubbish, or the most dry Soil: I say, it is surprizing, that some of those to whom I gave that satisfaction, should not guard against excess of Wet, especially when every one, who has judgment in the Affair of Vegetation, must know, that over-abundant Moisture will destroy the bearing Quality of any Plant, and more especially of such a kind of Plant as delights in dry mountainous Countries, as the Vine is known to do; but a common method of Management has so possess'd some People, that they will not give themselves leave to think that an Alteration of a Season from a dry to a wet, will occasion an alteration in a Plant. There is one Instance particularly, which I cannot help mentioning, relating to Vines, and the neccessity of keeping their Roots from Wet, which I observ'd this Year at *Twittenham*, at *John Robarts*'s Esq. This Gentleman has several Vines laid up against the side of his House, as full of Grapes as I have ever seen any; but at the bottom where they grow, the Ground is paved with Bricks for about ten or twelve foot from the Wall they are nail'd to. This Pavement, in the last wet Summer, kept the Roots from imbibing, or receiving too much Moisture, and therefore the Juices of the Vines were digested, and capable of producing Fruit this Year; whereas such Vines as were not growing in dry places naturally, or had their Roots defended from the violent Wet by accident, have few or no Grapes at all. My Observations this Year, in some places where there are Pavements, still confirms me in my Opinion; and where there was any tolerable Skill in Pruning, I am persuaded every one will find that there have been Grapes this Year, or now are on those Vines that have stood in paved places, where the Pavement defended the Roots from the wet of the last Year. And as I have already mention'd in this, and other Works, the neccessity of planting Vines in dry places, for regular Seasons; and these Instances showing us the advantage of doing the same in wet Seasons; I think one may reasonably judge, that Pavements made over such places where Vines are planted, as well as Rubbish and dry Ground to plant them in, is the best way we can take for them. This way, particularly in a wet Year, will keep our Vines from running into long Joints, and the Juices consequently in digesting, as we find by experience; for no long-jointed Shoots of Vines are fruitful as they ought to be, and rarely bear any Fruit at all. 'Tis the short-jointed Shoots that will bear Fruit plentifully; and where there is much Wet at the Root, you must expect very few short Joints, and also very little Fruit: therefore, in this case, the

Roots ought always to be defended from Wet.

This Year, 1726, was, at the beginning, a gentle and moist Spring, but *April* and *May* were hot; which brought every thing so forward, that our Harvest was about five or six Weeks forwarder than it has been for several Years past. The Case I have mention'd of the Grapes ripening naturally, was in proportion to the forwardness of the Harvest; every thing that I have observed in the same way was alike. The last Year was as extraordinary in the lateness of Crops, for then everything was as backward through the perpetual Rain we had in the Summer. Sometime or other this Memorandum may be of use, if my Papers last so long; however, for the present, consider how these two different Years have affected the Vine; the last wet Year made the Vines shoot strong and vigorous, and there was no Fruit this Year: nor was this only with us in *Britain*; but every where in *Europe*. The last Year produced such Floods, from the continued Rains at unexpected Seasons, as was never known in the memory of Man, the Vines shot vigorously; and this Year there were very few Grapes of the first Crop: but this Summer was so good and favourable, by its warm Months at the beginning of the Summer, that the Vines abroad shot out fresh Crops, or second Crops or Grapes, which made up for the other deficiency. I expect the next Year from hence, that the Vines will produce a full Crop of Grapes abroad, because this Year has settled the Juices, and digested them; but what Season there may be for ripening, is still uncertain, especially when we have the two last Years in view. But in our Gardens, I fear, we shall have worse success; for what this Year has done, will give the Gardeners generally a hard piece of work; for, as I imagine, there was little care taken in the beginning of the Year to lay up the Vines, especially because there was but a small, or no appearance of Grapes then; and the neglect of that Season in managing of Vines, will be the occasion of losing the Crop the next Year. What I say here about the management of Vines in the early part of the Year, I have already treated of in my other Works.

I shall now proceed to give some Particulars relating to the making of Wines of Grapes, which I believe may help those who make Wines in our *English* Vineyards, and make them stronger and richer than they have usually been.

Considering the uncertainty of Seasons, and that every sort of Grape will not always ripen without Art, it will be necessary to contrive how that Defect may be amended. The Richness of Wine depends upon the Ripeness of the Grapes; and therefore when Grapes have not had the advantage of a favourable Season to ripen, the Liquor press'd from the Grapes, may be amended by boiling; for this extraordinary Heat will correct the Juice, by evaporating the two great quantity of watery parts. This Method, however ripe the Grapes were among the ancient *Greeks* and *Romans,* was frequently, if not always practised; and is practised in those more Southern Climes, why is it not as reasonable in ours? But that this is not now practised any where in *Europe,* is no reason why

Wines may not be the better for it. I suppose the only reason why it is not now practised, is, because it would be an Expence and Trouble, more than the Masters of Vineyards have usually been at; and so long as they can sell their Wines at a constant Price, they do not care to go out of the way; but in a bad Season there is no doubt but even the Wines in *France* might be meliorated by boiling: As in the Instance of the *Frontiniack* Grapes, that are sour and unripe, and without Flavour, yet, by boiling or baking, they will gain the high Flavour that is found in them when they are well-ripen'd, by the Sun; but in baking or boiling unripe Grapes in the Skins, one must expect that the sourness of the Skins will communicate a sourness to the juices enclosed; but the Juices being press'd and boil'd, will ripen and become pleasant. In my *New Improvements of Planting and Gardening,* I have given large Directions for making of Wine of Grapes, and in this, have also given variety of Receipts for making of Wines of Fruits of our own growth; from whence we may learn the Use of boiling Juices of Fruits, and what will require fermenting by Yeast, and what do not. You will find that such Wines as are boiled with Sugar, are to be fermented with Yeast; and such as have Raisins for their foundation, will ferment in some measure of themselves. And especially observe, that while any Liquor is fermenting, the Vessel it is enclosed in must be kept open till it has quite done working; for if we should stop it up before that Action is over, it will certainly burst the Vessel; or if it has room enough, will turn sour, and be always thick and troubled. Again, all Wines, and other Liquors, must be stopt close as soon as they have done working, or else the Liquors will grow flat and dead. Some Wines will ferment six Weeks or two Months after they are in the Vessel, as one may know by the hissing noise which they make; but when that is done, then the ferment is over, and they should be closed up. But some Wines will ferment much longer than two Months, and then it is a sign that they stand too hot; then they must be put in a cooler place, or the outside of the Vessel frequently cool'd or refresh'd with Water, which will stop the ferment. Again, some will not ferment as they ought to do, and then they must be set in warmer places, which will raise the ferment.

In very bad Years we may help our Wines with a small quantity of Sugar, perhaps a Pound to a Gallon of Juice, to boil together; but whether we add Sugar or no, we must be sure to take the Scum off the Wines as it rises when they are boiling.

In the colder Climates, we ought not to press the Grapes so close as they do in the hot Countries, because in the colder parts of the World, and in places the most remote from the Sun, the Skins of the Grapes are much thicker, and carry a Sourness in them which should not be too much press'd to mix with the richer part of the Grape; but in the hotter Climes, the Skins of the Grapes are thin, and the Sourness rectify'd by the Sun, and will bear pressing without injuring the finer Juices.

There is one thing which I shall mention with regard to the Endeavours that have been used to make Wine in the Island of *St. Helena*; a Place so situate, that it lies as a resting-place between these Northern Parts, and the *East-Indies*, and so remote from other places, that could there be good Wine made there, it would be of great help and assistance to the Ships that sail that way: But I am informed by a curious Gentleman, who has had many good Accounts of that Place, that the Vines which have been planted there, are of such sorts, as bring the Grapes ripe and rotten on one side of the Bunch, and green on the other at the same time, which surely can never make good Wine. But upon enquiry, they are only such sorts of Grapes as grow in close Clusters, and therefore the side next the Sun must be ripe much sooner than the other; for the Climate there is so violent hot, that there are no Walls used behind them to reflect the Heat to ripen the Backs of the Bunches.

Therefore, I suppose that the best way to have good Wine made in those Parts, is to furnish that Place with Vines which may bring their Grapes in open or loose Bunches, such as the Raisin-grape, and some others, which do not cluster; for then the Sun would have an equal effect upon all the Grapes, and good Wine might be made of them: But the worthy Gentleman who told me of this, has, I hear, sent to *St. Helena* a Collection of such Grapes as will answer the desired end.

This is likewise the Month when Saffron appears above ground; sometimes sooner, sometimes later, according as the Season is earlier or later. This Year, 1726, I was in the Saffron Country, and in the beginning of *August* the Saffron-heads or Roots had shut up so long in the flowering part, that the Planters were forced to put them into the Ground: I mean, such as were design'd for new Plantations, which is sooner by near a Month than they used to sprout, though they lay dry in Heaps, the Weather had so great an effect upon them.

About *Littlebury, Chesterford, Linton,* and some other Places thereabouts, is certainly now the greatest Quantity of Saffron of any part of the Kingdom; the famous Place noted formerly for it, call'd *Saffron Walden,* being at this time without it. However, the People of the Places which I have named, do not forbear bringing it to *Walden* Market, or driving Bargains there for large Quantities of it, tho' the Market at *Linton* is look'd upon to be much the best. What I have said in my *Country Gentleman and Farmer's Monthly Director*, gives ample Inductions for the Management of Saffron, but I may here add a word or two more concerning it; which is, that considering how many Accidents the Saffron is subject to, that is dry'd upon the common Kilns, by the scorching of it by too hot a Fire, and the Unskilfulness of the Dryers; I do not wonder that there is so much Saffron spoiled. Where there are unskilful Hands employ'd in the drying part, one ought to provide such Kilns for them as are large enough to distribute the Heat moderately, and as constant as possible; which may partly be help'd by providing such a Fire as may be constant, and not give more Heat at one time than another; for there is a great deal of Judgment in that. I find, that by the common way, some Saffron is scorch'd, and some unequally dry'd, for which reason I have contriv'd such a Kiln as must necessarily answer the end which is proposed in the drying of Saffron; that is, to put it into a state of keeping with its Virtue in it, and to put it out of the danger of being scorch'd in the drying. This I shall publish in my *Natural History of* Cambridgeshire *and* Essex, which will soon appear in the World.

As for the way which is now commonly practised in the drying of Saffron, it is, when you have provided a Kiln, such as I have described in my *Farmer's Monthly Director*, with a Cloth made of Horse-hair on the top, strain the Hair-cloth tight, and lay on two Sheets of Saffron-paper, that is, a sort of Paper made on purpose for that Use, which is very large; and prepare a little Vessel with some Small beer, and as many Chives of Saffron as will make it of a deep Colour to stand by you; sprinkle over the Paper with a Brush or Feather dipt in this Liquor, and spread your Saffron upon it, either in a square or a round Figure, about three Inches thick, and cover the Saffron with two Sheets more of the same kind of Paper, and lay a woollen Cloth upon them, and over that a Board, which will cover the top of the Kiln: view this now and then, till you see that the Steam of the Saffron comes through the upper Papers. Then take off the Board and Woollen-cloth, and taking the Papers on each side with your Hands, turn the Saffron in the Papers, so that the under-side be uppermost; taking off presently after the Papers which were first the undermost, and then smooth down the side of the Saffron that was first next the Fire with a Knife, so that it lie all equal. Then cover it as it was at first, and after a little time turn the Saffron as you did before, and spread then the upper-side even with a Knife, as you did at first; then sprinkle your Saffron with the Brush dipt in the prepared Liquor upon the dry part's of the Cake, and cover it as before; let it lie then a little, and turn it as occasion requires, which may be sooner or later, as the Fire in the Kiln is quick or slow, minding every time, as you turn it, to sprinkle the dry parts with the Liquor; the more it shrinks, the oftner you must turn your Cake of Saffron, minding still to sprinkle the dry parts; and when it has shrunk about three fourths of the first thickness, lay a Stone or Weight upon the Board at the top of the Kiln, of about seven or eight Pound weight, the Board already being about ten or a dozen Pounds; when it is dry enough, take it off the Kiln, and the Paper it was dried in will be of good use; remember to keep your Fire gentle and clear. We may note, that a Gatherer of Saffron has this Year about ten Pence *per* Drain, and that about six Pounds, or six Pounds and a half of raw Saffron will dry to a Pound; but generally they allow only six Pounds of wet Saffron to a Pound of dry Saffron: but that depends upon the Dryers, who sometimes out of a Willingness to get Money, do not dry it so much as they ought to do. It is a Rule among the Saffron-Planters in *Cambridgeshire,* that sixteen Quarters of Saffron-Roots, or Heads, will plant an Acre; and that a full Acre this Year produces about seventeen or eighteen Pounds of dry Saffron, tho' the common rate is about sixteen Pounds.

About this time you have many green Melons upon the Vines which will not ripen; and besides, if they would, that Fruit would now be too cold for the Stomach; therefore it is advisable to pickle them, to make them imitate Mango's, which some prefer before Mango Cucumbers. The following is the Receipt to pickle them.

To pickle green Melons, in imitation of Mango.

The Mango is a Fruit brought to us from the *East Indies,* about the Shape and Bigness of a small Melon; it has a large Stone in it, and comes to us in a Pickle, which is strong tasted of Garlick, but approved by most People. When we gather Melons for this use, we must wash them and cut them, as directed for the Mango Cucumbers, then lay them in Salt and Water, shifting the Salt and Water every four and twenty Hours, for nine Days successively; after which, take them out and wipe them dry, and put into the inside of each, which has been already scraped, the same Ingredients directed for your Mango Cucumbers, and tie them up: then boil your Pickle of Vinegar, Bay-Salt, and Spices, with these Mangoes in it; scumming it as it rises, and with it a piece of Allum as directed in the Receipt for Mango Cucumbers, and afterwards follow that Receipt till your Melons are fit to use.

Now we have Wild-Ducks fit for the Table, and it is to be noted, that these should not be larded as Land-Fowls, in the roasting of them. It must be observed, that they be sent to Table with the Gravey in them; but before they are laid down to the Fire, it is practis'd in many places, to chop Onions, the Leaves of red Sage, and mix these with Pepper and Salt, to be put in the Belly of the Ducks; and when they are brought to Table, pour a Glass of Claret warm'd through the Body of the Ducks, which with some Gravey, that must be sent in the Dish, under the Ducks, will make a proper Sauce for them.

Another agreeable way of eating Ducks, is roasting them, and eating them with boil'd Onions; they are sometimes used in Soups, and baked, and they likewise eat very well when they are half roasted, and then cut to pieces and stew'd with their own Gravey and Claret.

Now Stubble Geese will be in season, after they have been taken up and fed for a Fortnight or thereabouts, in a close place, with Barley and Water; but during their Confinement, they must never want Victuals. Note, the Barley must have no more Water with it than will just cover it, and they must never have their Corn dry. If during the time of their feeding, you happen to let them out to ramble for a few hours, they will lose more good Flesh in that time, than they can regain in three Days; therefore when you have once put them up, keep them up till they are fit to kill: but if you would have them very fat, put them in a Coop for a Week or ten Days before you kill them, and feed them with Barley-Meal and Water, made almost as thick as Paste; and always let there be several of them together, for a single one will pine, and lose Flesh, instead of increasing it by Eating. As to the dressing of this Fowl while it is young, in the Spring, under the Character of a Green-Goose, it is fatted in a Coop with Barley-Meal and Water, and being kill'd and scalded when 'tis fat, 'tis roasted and eaten with green Sauce, or scalded Goosberries: but being full grown as at this time of the Year, is roasted, being first salted and pepper'd within side, and salted without side. Some put an Onion, and some Sage-Leaves into the Body of the Goose, when it is laid down to the Fire, and when it is brought to Table, it is serv'd with Apples stew'd and mash'd in a Plate by the Side; but for the Sauce in the Dish, there need be none but some Claret heated, and pour'd thro' the Body of the Goose, to mix with its own Gravey. Some also salt Geese, and boil them with Greens, as with other salt Meat; a Goose may also be bak'd in a Pye to be eaten cold. A Goose is to be kill'd, by pulling first the Feathers at the back of the Head, and cutting pretty deep with a sharp Penknife, between the back of the Head and the Neck, taking care that it does not struggle, so as to make the Feathers bloody, for that will spoil them: and 'tis to be noted, the Feathers of a full grown Goose are worth four Pence to be sold in the Country; this I had from a Gentlewoman in *Surrey.* In *Holland* they slit Geese down the Back, and salt them with Salt-Petre, and other Salt, and then dry them like Bacon; they eat very well, if they are boiled tender.

* * * * *

OCTOBER.

This Month is a noted Month for brewing of Malt Liquors especially. Brown, or high-dried Malt is to be used, as I have mentioned at large in the Month of *March*, under the Article of Brewing; to which I refer my Reader, to be fully satisfied of such Particulars relating to it, as seem to be the least consider'd, altho' they are the most contributing to the Perfection of Malt Liquors.

At this Season, Cyders, Mussels, Cockles, and such kind of Shell-Fish are good and in Season; as for the Oyster, it is not only to be eaten raw, but makes an agreeable Dish stew'd, or in Scallop-Shells; and besides, being useful in many Sauces, are extremely good when they are well pickled. Altho' the Oyster may seem foreign to a Farm, or some part of the Country, yet considering that we live in a part of the World surounded with a Sea that produces the best Oysters, and that they are a sort of Shell-Fish which we can keep a long time, and feed them, I think it necessary to take notice of them. About *Colchester* the Oyster-Pits are only small Holes about twelve foot square, by the side of the River, where the salt Water comes up, and has a passage into them at the height of the Tides; in these places the Oysters are laid, and there grow fat, and become green, by a sort of Weed which is called Crow-Silk: and this may be done any where, if there is a River with salt Water, as well as by *Colchester*, and be kept two or three Months; so that I wonder 'tis not practised in other places. But if we have not this conveniency, yet if we lay them in Salt and Water after the Shells are well wash'd, just when they come from the Sea, they will keep a Fortnight in pretty good order, if the Weather be cool, and they can have the open Air; but then the Salt and Water should be changed every four and twenty hours. The following Receipts are very good for preparing them for the Table.

To stew Oysters. From *Exeter.*

Take large Oysters, open them, and save their Liquor; then when the Liquor is settled, pour off the Clear, and put it in a Stew-Pan, with some Blades of Mace, a little grated Nutmeg, and some whole Pepper, to boil gently, till it is strong enough of the Spices: then take out the Spices, and put in the Oysters to stew gently, that they be not hard; and when they are near enough, add a piece of Butter, and as much grated Bread as will thicken the Liquor of the Oysters; and just before you take them from the Fire, stir in a Glass of White-wine.

Roasted Oysters in Scallop Shells. From *Exeter.*

Provide some large scallop Shells, such as are the deepest and hollowest you can get, which Shells are sold at the Fishmongers at *London*; then open such a Number of Oysters as will near fill the Shells you design, and save the Liquor to settle; then pour a moderate quantity of the Liquor into each Shell, and put a Blade of Mace, and some whole Pepper with it; after which, put into your Shells a small piece of Butter, and cover the whole with grated Bread: then let these on a Grid-Iron over the Fire, and when they are enough, give the grated Bread at the tops of the Shells a browning with a red-hot Iron, and serve them.

The same Person who sent the foregoing Receipts, concerning Oysters, advises another way of roasting Oysters, which I think is a very good one, and not much known. It is, to take large Oysters, open them, and hang them by the finny part on a small Spit, after having first dipt them in the Yolk of an Egg, and roll'd them in Crumbs of Bread; turn them three or four times before the Fire, and baste them gently with Butter, till the Crumbs of Bread are crisp upon them, and serve them hot. As for their use in Sauces, they are proper with Fish, and are sometimes used with Fowls; their own Liquor is always put in such Sauces where they are used. For pickling of Oysters, the following is an excellent Receipt.

To pickle Oysters.

Open a quantity of large Oysters, saving their Liquor, and letting it settle; then pour the Liquor clear off into a Stew-pan, and wash the Oysters in Water and Salt: after which, boil them gently in their own Liquor, so that they are not too hard. When they are enough, take them out, and add to the Liquor some Mace, a few Cloves, some whole Pepper, a little Ginger, and a Bay-Leaf or two, and let the Liquor boil, putting to it about a fourth part of White-wine Vinegar, letting it continue to boil a little more; then take it off, and let it stand to be quite cold. When the Oysters are cold, put them into Jars or Gally-pots, and pour the Liquor with the Spice cold upon them; then tie them down with Leather.

The Mussel and Cockle may be pickled after the same manner, only allowing this difference; *i.e.* that Cockles and Mussels are taken out of their Shells by setting them over the Fire, and opening them by the Heat; but before-hand the Shells must be wash'd very clean, and then must be put in the Sauce-pan without Water, they of themselves will soon produce Liquor enough: then as the Shells open, take out the Fish, and wash every one well in Salt and Water; but as for the Mussels, they must every one be carefully look'd into, and discharg'd from that part which is call'd the Beard, and also particular care must be taken to examine whether there are any Crabs in them, for they are very poisonous, and as they lie in the Mouth of the Mussel, may easily be discover'd; they are commonly as large as a Pea, and of the shape of a Sea-Crab, but are properly Sea-Spiders: the Mussels however where you find them, are not unwholesome, and it is only the eating of this little Animal, which has been the occasion of People's swelling after they had eaten Mussels, but the goodness of the Fish is well enough worth the Care of looking after that. When your Mussels or Cockles are all clean pick'd and wash'd, lay them to cool; and when their Liquor is well fettled, pour off the Clear, and boil it up with the same sort of Spices mentioned above for the pickled Oysters, with the same proportion of Vinegar; and letting it stand till it is quite cold, put your Fish into proper Pots, or little Barrels, and pour the Liquor upon them till they are cover'd with it, and stop them up close: they will keep good two or three Months, if the Liquor is now and then boiled up, but it must be always cold before it be put upon the Fish.

In the Management of Cockles for pickling, or for eating any other way, let the Shells be very well wash'd, and then lay the Cockles in a Pan of Salt and Water for two or three days, to scour themselves from the Sand that is in them at their first taking; but observe to shift the Salt and Water every day. The largest Cockles that I have observ'd on the *English* Coasts are those found about *Torbay,* which are sometimes brought to *Exeter* Market; the Fish is as large as a good Oyster, and the Shells of some are above two Inches and a half Diameter. Mussels and Cockles may likewise be stew'd and grill'd in Scallop Shells, as directed for Oysters. The Mussels after they are well pick'd are flower'd and fryed in some places, and eaten with Butter and Mustard, and the *French* make rich Soups of them.

As this is a Season when we have plenty of Quinces, I shall insert the following Receipt for making Wine of them, which is very pleasant.

To make Quince Wine. From Mrs. *E. B.*

Gather your Quinces when they are dry, and wipe them very clean with a coarse Cloth, then grate them with a coarse Grater or a Rasp, as near the Core as you can; but grate in none of the Core, nor the hard part about it: then strain your grated Quinces into an earthen Pot, and to each Gallon of Liquor put two Pounds of fine Loaf-Sugar, and stir it till your Sugar is dissolved; then cover it close, and let it stand twenty four hours, by which time it will be fit enough to bottle, taking care in the bottling of it that none of the Settlement go into the Bottles. This will keep good about a Year; observe that your Quinces must be very ripe when you gather them for this use.

Rabbits still continue in Season this Month, and besides the common way of dressing them, they may be larded, and drest in the following manner; which I had from a Gentleman in *Suffolk.* Make a Farce for them, like that mentioned for the Belly of a Hare in the preceding Month, and order its Management and Sauce as for a Hare. A young Rabbit, or Hare, is known by the tenderness of the Jaw-Bones, which will easily break by pressing with the Finger and Thumb.

Woodcocks are now in Season, and it is to be advertised of them, that they are to be only pull'd of their Feathers, and not drawn like other Fowls, but the Guts left in them; when they are roasted, they must be serv'd upon Toasts of Bread, upon which the Guts are spread and eaten, when they are brought to Table. The inward of this Bird eats like Marrow; this is generally eaten with Juice of Orange, a little Salt and Pepper, without other Sauce. The Legs of this Bird are esteem'd the most, and are therefore presented to the greatest Strangers at Table; but the Wings and Breast of a Partridge are the principal parts of that Fowl, for the Legs are full of Strings, like the Legs of Turkeys and Pheasants.

The Snipe is of the same nature with the Woodcock, and is ordered in every respect like it. These may be larded with Bacon upon the Breast, or else strew'd with Salt and Crumbs of Bread, while they are roasting. Besides the Sauce used for Woodcocks and Snipes, the aforesaid *Suffolk* Gentleman has the following which is Gravey with a little minced Anchovy, a Rocambole, some Lemon-Juice, and a little White-wine boiled together; and when it is strain'd, pour it in a Saucer, and serve it with the Fowls.

These Birds are in plenty among the woody parts of *England*, from *September* till the end of *March*, and then they all leave us at one time, except only such as have been lamed by the Sportsmen, and disabled for Flight; and then they will breed in *England*, as there are Instances enough. About *Tunbridge*, it is frequent to find them in Summer; and I have known the same in *Leicestershire*. I think if one could take Woodcocks here in Hay-Nets, as they do in *France*, and pinion them or disable a Wing, and then turn them loose again, we might raise a Breed of them that would stay with us; but I have experienced that they will not feed if they are confined in Cages or Aviaries, for they must have liberty to run in search of their Food, which they find for the most part in moist places, near Springs; for I have often taken both the Woodcock and the Snipe with such Snares as are made for Larks, by laying them in the Night on the Bank of Rivulets, or watery Trenches near Woods.

* * * * *

NOVEMBER.

Pheasants are still in season, and are now chiefly roasted, for they are not so frequently boiled, till about *April,* and then only the Hens when they are full of Eggs; but that, I think, is too destroying a way. The boiled Pheasants are generally dressed with Oyster-Sauce, or Egg-Sauce, but the roasted are either larded on the Breast with fine Bacon Fat, or else roasted and strew'd with Crumbs of Bread: these, says the *Suffolk* Gentleman, who sent me the foregoing Method of ordering the Woodcock and Snipe, should be served with the same Sauces that are used for Partridges. The Sauces in his Directions are within a trifle the same as those I have already set down in *September* for Partridges or Quails, so that I shall not repeat them here.

The Truffle, which I have treated of at large as to its manner of Growth and Season of Maturity, in my *Gentleman and Farmer's Monthly Director,* affords such Variety of agreeable Dishes, that I have taken care to send to a curious Gentleman abroad for the Receipt how to dress it: They are very plenty in our

Woods in *England,* as I understand by several who have found them this Summer by my Directions, and I believe will be much more so, since several curious Gentlemen have followed my Advice in propagating them. It is now, as well as in the two preceding Months, that we may find them of a fine Flavour; but they being something more in perfection in this Month than in the others, I think it the properest to give the Methods of ordering them for the Table in this place: The first manner is to broil them.

To broil Truffles.

The Truffle being brought in fresh, wash it well, and cut off the rough Coat on the outside: some of these will be as large as one's Fist, and they are the best for this purpose; but let them be of any size, as soon as the Coat is off, cut them through a little more than half-way, and put Pepper and Salt into the opening, and close it again; then wrap up each Truffle in wet Paper close, and broil them over a gentle Fire of Wood-Embers till you judge they are enough, which will be as soon as they are very hot quite through; let them be turn'd as occasion requires, that they may be all equally done, and then serve them to the Table in a folded Napkin. This is a very good way of eating them, but the other I have more frequently eaten.

To Stew Truffles in Wine.

The Truffles must be peel'd from the rough Coat on the outside, and well-wash'd; then cut your Truffles into Slices, and stew them in White wine, or Claret, which you please, with Salt, Pepper, and a Bay-leaf; or in the lieu of that, some *Jamaica* Pepper, and serve them. White-wine for this use is generally preferred.

To Stew Truffles after another manner.

Gather Truffles, peel them and wash them, and then cut them in Slices, after which fry them a little in a Stew-pan, with either Butter or Hog's-Lard, and a little Wheat-Flower; then take them out and drain them, and put them again in a Stew-pan with Gravey, a bunch of Sweet-Herbs, some Salt, Pepper, and Nutmeg grated; and when they have stewed a little in this, strain the Liquor, and dish them for the Table, garnished with Slices of Lemmon. Besides this way, they may be used in the same manner as Fowls are stewed or fricasseed, with brown or white Sauces, after they have been soften'd a little by boiling.

While I am speaking of the Truffle, I may well enough mention the Receipts for the management of the Morille. Altho' the Morille grows in *April*, which is the only time when it may be gather'd fresh, yet one may dress the dry'd ones now, by first softening them in warm Water and Salt for three or four Minutes; but, as observ'd before, they are best fresh gather'd. And again, I chuse to put the Receipts for their Management in this place, because they are so near a-kin to the Truffle. In the first place, I shall speak of drying them, which I have done in *England,* after the following manner: Gather, and wash them, and when they are well drain'd, then lay them in a Dish, and dry them by degrees in a gentle Oven; and when they are throughly dry, keep them in a dry place, and in a cover'd earthen glazed Pot; but when they are fresh, order them according to the following Receipts. And I am the more ready to give these to the Publick, because all such who know the nicest way of eating, may nor be disappointed in their Travels thro' *England,* and denied at the Inns such things as perhaps are as agreeable in that way, as any in the Country. Particularly I remember at *Newberry,* or *Spinhamland,* in the publick Road to *Bath,* I was at the most publick and noted Inn in that Road, and had got some very good Mushrooms, and the People there were of opinion that they were poisonous, or else did not know how to dress them, and by no means they would send them to the Table. I say, if such mistakes can be made in a place where so many People of fashion travel continually, it is not likely that Morilles or Truffles will be received with more favour than my Mushrooms; and I believe that some of the greatest Niceties of our Country may ever remain unknown, without a Work of this nature, which I have pick'd up inch by inch, *viz.* in my Travels. And besides, considering the strange disagreeable Compositions which one meets with in some of our Travels, as Sugar with a pickled Trout, and many more as ridiculous; I think this little Piece of Work not unworthy my Time. Again, there are many Families in *England* which have plenty about them, and do not know what to do with it; and therefore I think this the more necessary. But to come to my point, the Morille may be dress'd when it is either fresh or blanch'd in warm Water, according to the following Receipts, which I had from *France.*

To make a Ragout of Morilles.

The Morilles being fresh gather'd, take off the Roots, and wash them in many Waters, for the Wrinkles in their Tops harbour a great deal of Dirt and Sand; then slit them lengthways, and fry them a little in a Stew-pan, with Butter or Hogs-Lard, letting either be very hot when you put in the Morilles; then let them drain, and put them in a fresh Stew-pan with Gravey, in which shred some Parsley and Cherville very small, with a young Onion, some Salt, and a little Nutmeg: let these stew gently, and send them to the Table garnish'd with slices of Lemmon, or they may be sent to the Table in Cream, as we have already mentioned concerning other things in the same manner.

To fry the Morilles.

Prepare your Morilles as directed in the former Receipt, and boil them in a little Gravey gently; when they begin to be tender, take them out of the Liquor, and flower them very well, then fry them in Hog's-Lard: when they are thus prepared, make a Sauce for them of the Liquor or Gravey the Morilles were stew'd in, season'd with Salt, Nutmeg and a little Juice of Lemmon.

The following Directions I had from a Gentleman in *Suffolk.* The Turkey is now in good Season, and may be either boiled or roasted; when it is boiled, it is most commonly served with Oyster-Sauce, and when it is designed for roasting, it may be larded with fine Fat of Bacon on the Breast, or else well strew'd with Crumbs of Bread, having first made a Farce to fill the Hollow of the Neck, where the Crop lay; this Farce may be made of grated Bread, Spice, Salt, butter'd Eggs, and some sweet Herbs powder'd, the whole well mix'd and bound with the Yolk of a raw Egg; or the Liver of a Fowl may be boiled and chop'd small and put into it. The Receipt as I receiv'd it directs Beef-Suet chop'd small instead of butter'd Eggs; but Mr. *John Hughs,* a noted Cook in *London,* tells me that Suet should be avoided in these Farces, because it is apt to cool too soon, and offend the Roof of the Mouth, and therefore directs butter'd Eggs in their stead. As for the Sauce for the roasted Turkey, it must be made with Gravey, a Bunch of sweet Herbs, some Lemmon-peel, a Shallot or two, and some whole Pepper and All-spice boiled together and strained.

Concerning the Lark, which is now in Season, the abovemention'd Gentleman gives the following Directions: Let the Larks be pick'd only and not gutted, truss the Legs, with a Leaf of red Sage to every Lark between the Joints of the Legs; then with a Feather, dip'd in the Yolk of an Egg beaten, wash the Body of every Lark, and cover it well with Crumbs of Bread; after which, cut some thin Slices of fat Bacon, about three Inches long, and an Inch broad, and lay the Larks in a row, side to side, with a piece of this Bacon between every two Larks; then have small Spits about ten Inches long, and pass the Spits thro' the Sides of the Larks and the Bacon, so that you have half a dozen Larks upon each Spit, observing to have a piece of Bacon on both the outsides of the half dozen Larks; baste these well while they are roasting, and for the Sauce for them, fry some grated Bread crisp in Butter, and set them to drain before the Fire, that they may harden; serve these under the Larks when you send them to Table, and garnish with Slices of Lemmon. Some have their Lark-Spits made of Silver, and serve their Larks upon the Spits to the Table, by which means they keep hot the longer: you may eat them with Juice of Lemmon with the fry'd Crumbs, but some like such Gravey-Sauce with them as is directed for the roasted Turkey. Tho' the Guts are left in the Larks, yet they are not to be eaten.

In my Travels I observed a kind of Soup, which was very frequently used abroad, and quickly ready, that was very taking to most Travellers who delighted in savoury Dishes, which the People abroad call Soup *a l'Yvrogne,*

It is made as follows.

Take half a score Onions, peel them, and cut them in small Pieces into a Stewpan, and fry them brown with Butter, and a little Pepper and Salt; and when they are enough, pour such a quantity of Water upon them as you think proper to make a Soup of them; then let these boil together, and thicken it with as many Eggs as are neccessary, keeping it stirring to prevent the Eggs from Curdling. Some add to this a large Glass of White-wine, which I think makes it better tasted than 'tis without it: this is served with a *French* Role in the middle. At the same time I met with the following Receipt for Beef *A-la-mode,* which is as good as any I have eaten.

To make Beef *A-la-mode.*

Take a fleshy piece of Beef, without Fat, and beat it well with a Rolling pin, then lard it with pretty large pieces of Bacon-Fat, and if you please put over the Fire a little to fry till the outside is brown, and then put it to stew in a deep Stew-pan, or glaz'd Earthen-Vessel, with Salt, Pepper, Bay-Leaves or *Jamaica* Pepper, some Lemmon-Peel, half a dozen large Mushrooms, two Gloves of Garlick, or four or five Cloves of Shallot, half a Pint of Wine, and a Pint of Water; cover it close, and let it stew gently till it is tender: when it is enough, fry some Flower in Hogs-Lard, and add to it, with some Lemmon-Juice, or a little Verjuice. This is very good hot, but is for the most part eaten cold, cut in Slices of about half an Inch thick.

* * * * *

DECEMBER.

Now is the principal Season for killing of Hogs, as well for Pork as for Bacon, and likewise for Brawn. I have already in my other Works given Directions for making of pickled Pork and Bacon; so that I shall say little of it in this place, but give the Receipts for ordering some particular parts of Hogs. The following Receipt I received from *France,* concerning the preparing of the Jole of a wild Boar, and have had it try'd in *England* with the Head of a common Hog; and I find little difference, especially if the Hog has been fed with Acorns.

To dress a Hog's Head, in imitation of the Jole of a wild Boar.

Take a Hog's Head and burn it well all over upon a clear Fire, till all the Hair is burnt to the Skin; then take a piece of Brick, and rub the Head all over as hard as possible, to grind off the Stumps of the Bristles, and finish the whole with your Knife, and then clean the Head very well; when this is done, you must take out all the Bones, opening the Head in the under Part, and beginning with the under Jaw-Bones and the Muzzle; then cleave the Head, leaving only the Skin over the Skull to hold it together: take out the Tongue and the Brains. When thus you have taken away all the Bones, stab the Flesh with the Point of your Knife in many places on the inside, without wounding the Skin, and put Salt into every Incision, then join the Head together, and tie it well together with Packthread, and then wrapping it up in a Napkin, put it in a Kettle, with a large Quantity of Water, a large Bunch of all kinds of sweet Herbs, a little Coriander and Anise-Seeds, two or three Bay Leaves, some Cloves, and two or three Nutmegs cut in pieces, and some Salt, if you think there is any wanting; add likewise two or three large Onions and a Sprig or two of Rosemary. When this has boiled half enough, pour in a Bottle of Wine, and let it boil three or four Hours longer till 'tis tender; for it will not be so under seven or eight Hours boiling, if the Hog be large; and if it is a Boar's Head, that has been put up for Brawn, it will take more time to boil. Being boiled enough, let it cool in the Liquor, and then take it out and untie it, and lay it in a Dish to be carry'd cold to the Table, either whole or in Slices. If you will, you may salt it three or four days before you boil it.

To make Sausages, from Lady *M.*

Take the Flesh of a Leg of Pork, and mince it small, and to every Pound of the Flesh minced, mince about a quarter of a Pound of the hard Fat of the Hog; then beat some *Jamaica* Pepper very fine, and mix with it some Pepper and Salt, with a little Sweet-Marjoram powder'd, and some Leaves of red Sage minced very small; mix all these very well, and if you fill them into Guts, either of Hogs or Sheep, beat two or three Yolks of Eggs and mix with them, taking care not to fill the Guts too full, lest they burst when you broil or fry them: but if you design them to be eaten without putting them in Guts, then put no Eggs to them, but beat the Flesh and the Fat in a Stone Mortar, and work the Spice and Herbs well into it with your hands, so that it be well mix'd, and keep it in a Mass to use at your pleasure, breaking off Pieces, and rolling them in your hands, and then flowering them well before you fry them. If you use them in Guts, take special care that the Guts are well clean'd, and lie some time in a little warm White-wine and Spice before you use them; if any Herb happens to be disagreeable in this Mixture, it may be left out, or others added at pleasure.

The following Receipt to make Sausages of Fish for Fast-Days, I had at *Bruxelles*, which I have experienced to be very good.

To make Sausages of Fish.

Take the Flesh of Eels, or of Tench, and to either of these put some of the Flesh of fresh Cod, or of Pike or Jack, chop these well together with Parsley, and a few small Onions; season these with a little Salt, Pepper, Cloves in

Powder, a little grated Nutmeg, and, if you will, a little powder'd Ginger, with some Thyme, Sweet-Marjoram, a little Bay-Leaf, all dry'd and powder'd; and mix all these well together with a little Butter.

Then beat the Bones of the Fish in a Mortar, pouring in among them while they are beating, a Glass or two of Claret, which must afterwards be poured upon the above Mixture; then take the Guts of a Calf well wash'd and clear'd of the Fat, for in that condition I find there is no scruple to use them abroad: being well discharged of the Fat, fill these Skins with your Mixture of Fish, &c. tying them at both ends, and lay them for twenty four Hours in a Pickle of Wine and Salt, and taking them out from thence, hang them in a Chimney where they may be well smoak'd with a Wood-Fire, or burning Saw-dust for twenty-four hours, or longer if you please, provided you have allow'd Salt and Spices enough. When you would use them, boil them gently in White-wine, with a Bunch of Sweet Herbs; or in Water, with one third part White-wine, and Sweet-Herbs. These are served cold at the Table, and eat very well.

The Boars that were put up for Brawn, are now fit to kill. It is to be observ'd, that what is used for Brawn, is the Flitches only, without the Legs, and they must have the Bones taken out, and then sprinkled with Salt, and lay'd in a Tray, or some other thing, to drain off the Blood; when this is done, salt it a little, and roll it up as hard as possible, so that the length of the Collar of Brawn be as much as one side of the Boar will bear, and to be, when it is rolled up, about nine or ten Inches diameter. When you have rolled up your Collar as close as you can, tye it with Linnen Tape, as tight as possible, and then prepare a Cauldron with a large Quantity of Water to boil it: In this boil your Brawn till it is tender enough for a Straw to pass into it, and then let it cool; and when it is quite cold, put it in the following Pickle. Put to every Gallon of Water a handful or two of Salt, and as much Wheat-Bran; boil them well together, and then strain the Liquor as clear as you can from the Brawn, and let it stand till it is quite cold, at which time put your Brawn in it; but this Pickle must be renewed every three Weeks. Some put half small Beer and half Water; but then the small Beer should be brewed with pale Malt: but I think the first Pickle is the best. *Note,* The same Boar's Head being well cleaned, may be boiled and pickled like the Brawn, and is as much esteem'd.

This is a good Season to make what they call Hung-Beef: The way of doing it, is, to take the thin Pieces of the Beef, and salting them with Salt-Petre about two Ounces to a Pound of common Salt, and rubbing it well into the Meat, dry it in a Chimney with Wood Smoke. When this is throughly cured, it will be red quite through, which one may try by cutting; for if there is any of the Flesh green, it is not smoked enough. It is, in my opinion, better than any Bacon to be boiled and eaten hot.

This is what I shall say, concerning the use of such things as are generally found about a Gentleman's Country-Seat, or about a Farm, which I think will be very useful, tho' a little out of the common Road; and so I shall make no Apology for publishing such Receipts as I am sure are good. If I do not use proper Terms in some of my Receipts in Cookery, I have at least put my Receipts into such a Method, as I suppose will make them intelligible, and what any one may understand: But I must take notice before I conclude, that the meaning of publishing this, is to instruct those who may not have had opportunity of observing or collecting so much as I have done, and not any way pretending to inform those who are full enough of Knowledge already. However, I hope my Readers will be contented with what I have here given them, and meet with something that is New and Useful.

FINIS.

* * * *

* THE
COUNTRY HOUSEWIFE
AND
LADY's DIRECTOR,
IN THE
MANAGEMENT OF A HOUSE, AND THE
DELIGHTS AND PROFITS OF A FARM.

PART II.

INCLUDING

A great Variety of the most curious Receipts for Dressing all the Sorts of Flesh, Fish, Fowl, Fruit and Herbs, which are the Productions of a Farm, or from any Foreign Parts.

Contained in Letters, and taken from the Performances of the most polite Proficients in most Parts of *Europe*.

Now publish'd for the Good of the Publick, By R. BRADLEY, *Professor of Botany in the University of* Cambridge, *and F. R. S.*

To which is Added, From a Poulterer in *St. James's*-Market, the Manner of Trussing all Sorts of Poultry. Adorn'd with Cuts: Shewing, how every Fowl, Wild or Tame, ought to be prepared for the Spit; and likewise any kind of Game.

* TO
Sir *Hans Sloane,* Bart.

PRESIDENT OF THE ROYAL-SOCIETY.

This Piece of Oeconomy, or Management of the Houshold, is most humbly presented, by His *Most humble and most obedient Servant,* R. BRADLEY

* * * * *

THE INTRODUCTION.

There is nothing induces me so much, to publish this Second Part of Directions to prepare the Things about a Farm or Family, as the Encouragement my first Volume, in this Way, has met with in the World; which being now in the sixth Edition, has brought me many Receipts, from the Curious, which would be detrimental to the Publick if I did not offer them to the World. I must acknowledge my Gratitude, in this Piece, to several Persons of Distinction, and good Oeconomy, who have favoured me with their Assistance; and, as far as their Leave would suffer me, I have given their

Names or Signatures. Most of the Receipts I have been Witness to, at some Meal or other with them, or else in Publick Places have purchas'd; for I always thought that there was more satisfaction in eating clean and well, if one had good Provisions in a Place, than to have such Provisions good, and spoiled in their Management.

With the many Noblemen I am conversant with, and in the large Tract of Ground I have passed over, it may not be surprizing, that I have collected so great a variety of Things in this way; and there is no greater Happiness I enjoy, than to communicate to the World, what I love myself: but as the Proverb says, *there is no disputing about Tastes*, so that every one has still the Liberty of choosing or rectifying any thing as their Palate directs, when they have a good Foundation to go upon.

I think, if these Receipts had lain still in my Cabinet, they might after my death have been distributed to the World in a wrong Sense; but as I have particularly been present amongst many of them, I have taken the meaning of them in Writing; or if I had left them behind me, they might have been lost, which, I think, are much too good to be bury'd in Oblivion.

* * * * *

THE Country Lady's DIRECTOR.

PART II.

Since I have publish'd the Receipts I gathered together, with regard to the several Preparations of the Products of a Farm, for the Table; entitled, *The Lady's Monthly Director, &c.* (now in its sixth Edition:) I have received a great number of Letters relating to many Improvements that may be made to it, and am desired to publish them, in order to render my first Volume more compleat. And, as I find they will be of public Use, I shall begin with one concerning the Preservation of Flesh, Fowls and Fish from Putrefaction, or Stinking; which is too often the Case, in Summer-time, when it is rare to find any sweet Morsels, although they have undergone the Discipline of Salting. As for the common Notion, that Women cannot lay Meat in Salt, equally with success, at all Times, it is false; it is the Manner of doing it, and not the state of the Women who handle it, that makes it right; there must be a right way of Management to preserve it, and render it fit for the Palate, as the following Letter informs us.

To Mr. *Bradley*.

Sir,

I have not only read your Book call'd, *The Lady's Monthly Director*, but have tasted many elegant Dishes of Meat, ordered by the Receipts in it; but I think, as you are a philosophical Gentleman, you should have taken a little more Notice of the preservation of Flesh from Putrefaction: For in many places I have set down to a Dinner which has sent me out of the Room by the very smell of it; even, though I am so much of the *French* Taste, that I can bear the *Fumette*. The Husband, in this Case, has blamed his Wife; and the Wife has taken the opportunity of whispering to her Husband, that the Maid was not in right Sorts when she salted the Meat: but I am sure, I shall set you to rights in that Point.

I have taken pains in my Family, which consists of thirty Persons, to have my Wife order the Experiment to be made, and I am satisfied from her Arguments, that there is nothing in the Notion above. But now to the purpose. Let your Flesh-Meat be fresh, and take all the bleeding Arteries from it; then sprinkle it with common Salt, and let it lie in the Air for twelve Hours; but salt the Places, where the Arteries were, more particularly: then wipe your Meat dry, and make some Salt very hot, over the Fire, then rub in the Salt very well, and lay the Pieces of salted Meat one upon another, and it will keep for several Months.

Or with common Salt, rub the several Pieces of Meat briskly with it, after the Blood is out, and especially in the hollow Places lay Salt enough. So will you be sure to have your Meat sweet, either Beef or Pork.

To send *Venison* Sweet in hot Weather.

Give it a little Salt, and have the Haunches parted, taking out the Marrow and all the Veins, as they are called, that bleed; and then wipe all of it quite dry after you have wash'd it with Vinegar, and then powder it with Pepper, and in an open Basket send it up to *London*.

Sometimes Venison (meaning a Buck) comes up to *London*, not fit for the Table; to prevent which, order the Keeper, when he has killed it, to strew three or four Pounds of Pepper, beaten fine, upon it; and especially upon the Neck Parts of the Sides, after he has wash'd them with Vinegar and dried them well.

But if it stinks, when you receive it, wash it with Vinegar, and dry it, then pepper it and wrap it in a dry Cloth, bury it in the Ground, three foot deep at least, and in sixteen Hours it will be sweet, fit for eating; then wash off the Pepper with Vinegar, and dry it with a Cloth, and hang it where the cool Air may pass, and the blue Flies cannot come at it. *Query.* Is it not strange, that we see daily the Limbs of Horses hung up in Trees, and they do not stink, but remain good a long while fit for Dogs Meat? If any one will say, that Dogs all delight to eat Carrion, I must deny that; but that every sort of Dog will roll himself in Carrion, when he can find it, is certain.

To send *Partridges* a long way in hot Weather.

When you have killed your Partridges, take out the Crop, and the Artery which bleeds in the Neck, then fill the Place with Pepper; and the Mouths of the Fowls should be fill'd with the same, for these Parts take a taint sooner than the rest; the Vent too, ought to be taken care of, and open'd, and filled with Pepper, beaten grossly. *N.B.* This Pepper may be always wash'd away without leaving any Season or Flavour behind it, and is a certain Antidote against Corruption. So the same may be done with Pheasants, and you should likewise leave on their Feathers.

To keep an *Hare* a long Time.

As soon as 'tis kill'd and discharged of its Entrails, take care that all the Blood be dried away with Cloths about the Liver, for there it is apt to settle, then dust the Liver well with Pepper; and fill the Body with Nettles, or dry Moss, for these will not raise a ferment as Hay and Straw will do, when they come to be wet; then fill the Mouth with Pepper, and it will keep a long time.

To keep *Wild-Ducks* fresh.

Draw them, and fill the Body with red Sage, after the inside is well pepper'd; and likewise pepper the inside of the Mouth, leave on the Feathers. A Goose may be serv'd the same way.

But if they be too long kept, or through want of Care, they should receive a taint; then, when they are pull'd, wash the Inside very well, with Vinegar and Water, and dry it well with a Cloth; and scrape away, if need be, what are call'd the Kidneys; then strew the Inside afresh with Pepper, and hang them up for an Hour or two, where the Air may pass through them.

Some in such a case will put an Onion into the Body, which does very well towards restoring it to a freshness; then wash out all, and prepare it for the Spit.

Helps towards the Preservation of *Fish.*

If you would keep Fish long, kill them as soon as they are out of the Water, and take out their Gills; then fill their Heads as much as may be, with Pepper, and wipe them very dry, and pack them in dry Wheat-Straw.

T. R.

To make *Wine* of *White Elder-berries,* like *Cyprus* Wine from Mrs. *Warburton* of *Cheshire.*

To nine Gallons of Water, put nine Quarts of the Juice of White Elder berries, which has been pressed gently from the Berries, with the Hand, and passed thro' a Sieve, without bruising the Kernels of the Berries; add to every Gallon of Liquor three Pounds of *Lisbon* Sugar, and to the whole Quantity put an Ounce and a half of Ginger, sliced, and three quarters of an Ounce of Cloves; then boil this near an Hour, taking off the Scum, as it rises, and pour the whole to cool, in an open Tub, and work it with Ale-Yeast, spread upon a Toast of white Bread, for three Days, and then tun it into a Vessel that will just hold it; adding about a Pound and a half of Raisins of the Sun split, to lie in the Liquor till we draw it off, which should not be till the Wine is fine, which you will find about *January*. This Wine is so like the fine rich Wine brought from *Cyprus*, in its Colour and Flavour, that it has deceiv'd the best Judges, These Berries are ripe in *August*, and may be had at the Ivy-House at *Hoxton*.

To make *Wine* of *Black Elder-berries,* which is equal to the best *Hermitage* Claret; from *Henry Marsh*, Esq. *of Hammersmith.*

Take nine Gallons of Spring Water, and half a Bushel of Elder-berries, pick'd clean from the Stalks; boil these till the Berries begin to dimple, then gently strain off the Liquor, and to every Gallon of it put two Pounds of good *Lisbon* Sugar, and boil it an Hour; then let it stand to cool, in an open Tub, for if it was to cool in the Copper, or Brass Kettle, it was boil'd in, the Liquor would be ill-tasted. When it is almost cool, spread some Ale-Yeast upon a Toast of White Bread, and put it into the Liquor, to work three Days in the open Tub, stirring the Liquor once or twice a Day, and then tun it in a Vessel of a right size, to hold it: At the same time add to every Gallon one pound of Raisins of the Sun whole, and let them lie in the Cask till the Wine is drawn off.

Such a small quantity of Wine, as is here directed, will be fit to bottle the *January* next after it is made, but larger Casks should not be drawn off till *March* or *April*.

A Receipt from *Barbadoes,* to make *Rum;* which proves very good.

In *Barbadoes* the Rum is made of the Scum and Offal of the Sugar, of which they put one ninth part, or eighth part, to common Water, about eighteen Gallons, all together, in a wooden open Vessel or Tub; cover this with dry Leaves of Palm, or for want of them, with the Leaves of *Platanus* or the Leaves of Fern in *England*, or the Parts or Leaves which Flagg-Brooms are made of. Let this remain for nine Days, till it changes of a clean yellow Colour, and it will be then fit to distil; then put it into an Alembic, and you will have what we call the Low-Wines. A Day or two after distil it again, and in the Cap of the Still, hang a small muslin Bag of sweet Fennel-Seeds, and the Spirit will be of a fine Flavour. Some will use Anniseed in the Bag, and some use a little Musk with the sweet Fennel Seeds, or else distil the Spirit twice, *viz.*, once with the sweet Fennel-Seeds, and the next with a little Musk.

N.B. The wooden Vessels, or open Tubs, must not be made of any Wood that is unwholesome, or sweet-scented; such as Deal, Firr, or Manchineel.

In *England*, Treacle may be used with equal Success, and is cheap enough to get a good livelihood; as appears by the several Ways mention'd above, that have been privately experienced.

To make *Citron-Water,* from *Barbadoes.*

Take Citron, or Lemon Flowers, for the word Citron in *French* signifies Lemon; though we generally in *England* esteem the large Lemons to be Citrons, and the middle-siz'd we call Lemons, and the smallest of that race is call'd the Lime. In these, however, there are as many varieties as we have in Apples, one is finer flavour'd than the other. The Oranges too are of as many different Sorts, the Rind of one pleasanter than the other, and the Juice likewise, and so are the Flowers various in their Smells, some more odorous than others; yet all these are used indifferently, according to the Kinds that happen to grow upon the several Estates, where the Citron-Water is made, and this is the Reason why one Sort is better than another; and therefore, those who have the most pleasant Sorts, make the best Waters of this Kind.

We must take, either of Citron, Lemon, or Orange-Flowers, four Ounces to a Gallon of clean Spirit, or *French*-Brandy; put these in the Spirits, with two Pounds of white Sugar-Candy, beaten fine: then take of the best Citron-Peels, or Lemon-Peels, six Ounces, and let them steep in the Spirits till the Liquor is strong enough of every Ingredient; and when that is done, pour it off, through a Sieve. And in some places they put about half a Drachm of Musk to six Gallons of Liquor; and this has been sold for sixteen Shillings the Quart in *London.*

To make fine *Vinegar.*

There is no doubt but the making of Vinegar will be a considerable Article, seeing that few of our fine Preparations for the Table can be made without it. A Gentleman of great note has given me the following Receipt for it, *viz.*

To nine Gallons of Water, put eighteen Pounds of *Malaga* Raisins, chopt a little, Stalks and all; put this into a Cask, bound with Iron Hoops, and place it in the warmest Exposure you can find in the open Air: then take a *Florence* Flask, divested of its Straw, and put the Neck of it into the Bung-hole, fixing it as close as may be, with some Linnen-Cloth, and a little Pitch and Rosin melted together. By this Means, if the Weather prove fair and warm, your Vinegar will be fit for Use in three Weeks time. The use of the Glass, is, that in the heat of the Day it will fill itself with the Liquor, and when the cool of the Evening comes on, that Liquor will again be return'd into the Cask; by which means the Liquor will become sour much sooner than it will otherwise do. As soon as it is clear, draw it off.

To make *Irish Usquebaugh;* from Lord *Capell's* Receipt, when he was Lord Lieutenant of *Ireland.*

To every Gallon of *French*-Brandy, put one Ounce of Liquorice sliced, one Ounce of sweet Fennel-Seeds, one Ounce of Anniseeds, one Pound of Raisins of the Sun split and stoned, a quarter of a Pound of Figs split, two Drachms of Coriander-Seeds, let these infuse about eight or nine Days, and pour the Liquor clear off, then add half an Ounce of Saffron, in a Bag, for a Day or two, and when that is out, put in a Drachm of Musk. If when this Composition is made, it seems to be too high a Cordial for the Stomach, put to it more Brandy, till you reduce it to the Temper you like. This is the same Receipt King *William* had when he was in *Ireland.*

To make Green *Usquebaugh.*

To every Gallon of *French*-Brandy put one Ounce of Anniseeds, and another of sweet Fennel-Seeds, two Drachms of Coriander-Seeds. Let these infuse nine Days, then take of the Spirit of Saffron one Drachm, distil'd from Spirit of Wine, mix with the rest; infuse during this time some Liquorice sliced in Spirits, one Pound of Raisins of the Sun, and filter it; put then a Quart of pure White-Wine to a Gallon of the Liquor, and when all is mix'd together, take the Juice of Spinach boil'd, enough to colour it; but do not put the Spinach Juice into the Liquor till it is cold. To this put one Pound of white Sugar candied, finely powder'd, to a Gallon of Liquor.

To make a *Cabbage-Pudding;* from a Gentlewoman in *Suffolk,* as it was written by herself.

Sir,

You will excuse me, if I send you a Receipt for a Pudding, which is accounted so agreeable by my Acquaintance, that they think it worth a place in your Book, call'd, *The Lady's Monthly Director,* in the Management of the several Products of a Farm. It may as well be made by People of the lower as of the higher Rank.

Take a Piece of boil'd Beef, which is not always done enough; the Parts of it which are the least done, and chop them small: take as much boil'd Cabbage as you have Meat, and chop that as small as the Beef, season this with Pepper and Salt, and two or three Eggs beaten, to mix it up in the manner of farced Meat. Whatever else of seasoning you like, put it to it; and when it is made into a thin Paste, put the Mixture into a Linnen-Cloth, and boil it till it is enough, then serve it to the Table. But this Pudding is much better made with raw salt Beef and boil'd Cabbage, for is makes an extraordinary Paste, and is much softer and fuller of Gravey than the first.

N.B. If it is of the first Sort, the quantity of half a Quartern Loaf of fine Bread, may boil an Hour, and the latter Sort may boil an Hour and a half.

I am Yours, C. B.

Serve it with Butter and Gravey, with Lemon-Juice.

Of the *Gourmandine-Pea,* and its several Ways of Dressing.

P.S. You have mention'd in one of your Books a sort of Pea, which is call'd the Gourmandine, or Gourmand; which I suppose one may call, in *English,* the Glutton's Pea, because we eat all of it. For the Pods of it are very sweet and have no Film, or Skin in them, so that the Cods may be as well eaten as the Peas themselves; for which reason, when we have drawn the Strings from them, as we do from Kidney Beans, you may broil them upon a Gridiron, and serving them with gravey Sauce, they are very good; or to cut them into Pieces, and fry them with Mutton Steaks; or else you may fry them with Beef, and they are still better. But the best way, is to cut them cross, as you do *French*-Beans, and stew them in Gravey with a little Pepper and Salt, there is not any thing in my Opinion can eat better, and to be put in a gravey Soop, are incomparable; especially, if they have been parboil'd, and rubb'd dry, and then fry'd in burnt Butter.

The smallest dwarf crooked Sugar-Pea, that you recommend, is of the same quality, but rather better, for all these Uses, being somewhat sweeter than the former, and the Pod fuller of Pulp.

C. B.

To make *Verjuice* of Grapes, unripe, or of Crab-Apples; from *J. S.* Esq.

Take Grapes full grown, just before they begin to ripen, and bruise them, without the trouble of picking them from the Bunches; then put them in a Bag, made of Horse-Hair, and press them till the Juice is discharged; put this Liquor into a Stone Jar, leaving it uncover'd for some Days, then close it and keep it for use. This Verjuice is much richer than that of the Crab-Apple, and has a much greater influence in the way of Callico-Printing; but is harder to come at, few People being willing to gather their Grapes unripe; but where there is a large Quantity, it is well worth while. *N.B.* It will do well, if the Liquor is put into common Casks, but is nicer to the Palate if it is kept in glazed Jars of about eight or nine Gallons, and the Berries might then be pick'd from the Stalks. Keep this in a good Vault, and it will remain good for three or four Years as Verjuice; but a little more time will make it lose its Sourness, and it will become like Wine.

The Verjuice of Crab-Apples should be made of the wild Crab, which produces Thorns on its Branches, and brings a small round Apple, such as are common to be planted for Fences. I am the more particular in this, because some Apples, which are call'd Wildings, are supposed to have a sharp juice, but such will soften by keeping a Year or two. Take the Crabs, I speak of, in *October*, and grind them in a Mill, such as they use for making Cyder; then press the Liquor, and put it into Vessels like the former. Besides the agreeable Taste this has, as an *Agresta* at the Table, it is good for the Callico Printers.

A dry Travelling Powder, for Sauce, or Pocket-Sauce. From *Mynheer Vanderport* of *Antwerp*.

Take pickled Mango, and let it dry three or four Days in the Room; then reduce it to Powder by means of a Grater. Take of this Powder six Ounces, to which add three Ounces of Mushrooms, dry'd in a gentle Oven, and reduced to Powder, by beating in a Mortar; add to this, a Dram of Mace powder'd, half as much Cloves powder'd; or in their room, a large Nutmeg grated, and a Dram of black Pepper, beat fine: mix these Ingredients well together, and sift them through an open HairSieve: and half a Tea spoonful, or less, of the Powder will relish any Sauce you have a mind to make, though it be a quart or more, putting it into the Sauce, when it is warm. To this, one may add about nine Grains of sweet Basil, dry'd and powder'd; or of Summer sweet Marjoram powder'd. If we use this Sauce for Fish, it is extremely good, adding only a little Anchovy Liquor and white Wine.

To preserve *Grapes* all the Winter.

Take an Earthen Jar, well glaz'd, that will hold about six Gallons, or more; then dry some Oats, a little, in the Sun, upon Leads if you can, so that they have lost some part of their Moisture; lay them then two Inches thick, at the bottom of the Jar, and upon them, your Bunches of Grapes, gathered full ripe and dry; and if in any Bunch there is a rotted Grape, cut it off, and see that your Bunches are quite clean in their Berries; and besides, that all the Parts you have cut the Grapes from, are quite dry. Lay these on the Oats, and upon them put two Inches thick of Oats, dry'd as before; and on them again, a Layer of Grapes, and so the Oats upon them, continuing this Practice till the Vessel is full. Then take a Cork, well soak'd in Oil, and stop it close in the Jar, and seal it up with Pitch, Bees-Wax, and a little Rosin, melted together, and keep it in a cool Place; but to bury it three Foot under ground, is better.

A Collar of *Mutton* roasted. From *St. Edmund's-Bury* in *Suffolk*.

Take a Coast of Mutton, which is the Neck and Breast together, skin it in the whole Piece; then parboil it, and prepare a Mixture of Crumbs of Bread; Lemon-Peel grated, a little Pepper, Salt, Nutmeg, or sweet Marjoram powder'd, which answers the End of most Spices, or else a little dry'd sweet Basil, which we call *Bush-Basil*, in the Gardens. To this, add the Yolks of six hard Eggs, beat in a Mortar, with six Ounces of Butter; mix this with the other Ingredients; then take the inside of the Mutton, and cover it with this Mixture, and roll it up as close as can be, and secure it in the Roll; so that it may be close for the Spit. It must be spitted through the Middle length-ways, and basted with Butter, salting it every now and then, and the Gratings of Crusts of Bred should be sprinkled upon it, with the seasoning above. Just before it is enough, when it is taken off the Spit, serve it with strong Gravey and Lemon or Orange Juice, and garnish with Lemon or Orange sliced; or when Oysters are in season, add fry'd Oysters: *viz.*

To fry *Oysters* for a Plate, or the Garnish of the foregoing Dish.

Make a Batter of Eggs and Flower, Crumbs of Bread, and a little Mace, beaten fine. Stew some large Oysters in their own Liquor gently, and wipe them dry, and flower them: dip them, after this, in the Batter, and fry them in very hot Butter, or Lard, or Seam of an Hog; and they will be incrustated, or cover'd, with a sort of Paste, which will be very agreeable, either for a Plate, or to garnish a Dish. If we have them alone, serve them with some of the Liquor, a little Butter, some White Wine, boiling first some Spices in the Liquor.

Of a *Sturgeon,* how it ought to be cured, for cold Meat, or dressed hot for the Table.

The Sturgeon is a Fish commonly found in the Northern Seas; but now and then, we find them in our great Rivers; the *Thames,* the *Severn* and the *Tyne.* This Fish is of a very large size; even sometimes to measure eighteen Foot in length. They are in great esteem when they are fresh taken, to be cut in Pieces, of eight or ten Pounds, and roasted or baked; besides, to be pickled and preserv'd for cold Treats: And moreover, the Caviar, which is esteem'd a Dainty, is the Spawn of this Fish.

To Cure, or Pickle, *Sturgeon;* from *Hamborough.*

Take a Sturgeon, gut it and clean it very well, within side, with Salt and Water; and in the same manner clean the Outside, wiping both very dry with coarse Cloths, without taking any of the great Scales from it: then take off the Head, the Fins and Tail; and if there is any Spawn in it, save it to be cured for Caviar. When this is done, cut your Fish into small Pieces, of about four Pounds each, and take out the Bones, as clean as possible, and lay them in Salt and Water for twenty-four Hours; then dry them well with coarse Cloths; and such Pieces as want to be rolled up, tie them close with Bass-strings, that is, the strings of Bark which compose the Bass Mats, such as the Gardeners use: for that being flat, like Tape, will keep the Fish close in the boiling, which would otherwise break, if it was tied with Pack-Thread. Strew some Salt over the Pieces, and let them lie three Days; then provide a piece of Wicker, made flat, aid wide as the Copper or Cauldron you will boil your Fish in, with two or three Strings, fasten'd to the Edges, the Ends of which should hang over the Edges of the Copper. The Pans we generally boil our Fish in, are shallow and very broad; then make the following Pickle, *viz.* one Gallon of Vinegar to four Gallons of Water, and to that quantity put four Pounds of Salt. When this boils, put in your Fish; and when it is boil'd enough, take it out, and lay it in single Pieces, upon Hurdles, to drain, or upon such Boards as will not give any extraordinary Taste to the Fish. Some will boil in this Pickle a quarter of a Pound of whole black Pepper.

When your Fish is quite cold, lay it in clean Tubs, which are call'd Kits, and cover it with the Liquor it was boil'd in, and close it up, to be kept for Use.

If at any time you perceive the Liquor to grow mouldy, or begin to mother, pass it through a Sieve; add some fresh Vinegar to it, and boil it: and when it is quite cold, wash your Fish in some of it, and lay your Pieces a-fresh in the Tub, covering them with Liquor as before, and it will keep good several Months. This is generally eaten with Oil and Vinegar.

To prepare the *Caviar,* or *Spawn,* of the *Sturgeon.*

Wash it well in Vinegar and Water, and then lay it in Salt and Water two or three Days; then boil it in fresh Water and Salt; and when it is cold, put it up for Use. This is eaten upon Toasts of white Bread with a little Oil.

To Roast a piece of fresh *Sturgeon;* from Mr. *Ralph Titchbourn,* Cook.

Take a piece of fresh Sturgeon, of about eight or ten Pounds; let it lie in Water and Salt, six or eight Hours, with its great Scales on: then fasten it on the Spit, and baste it well with Butter for a quarter of an Hour; and after that, drudge it with grated Bread, Flour, some Nutmeg, a little Mace powder'd, Pepper and Salt, and some sweet Herbs dry'd and powder'd, continuing basting and drudging of it till it is enough. Then serve it up with the following Sauce, *viz.* one Pint of thin Gravey and Oyster Liquor, with some Horse-Radish, Lemon-Peel, a bunch of sweet Herbs, some whole Pepper, and a few Blades of Mace, with a whole Onion, an Anchovy, a spoonfull or two of liquid Katchep, or some Liquor of pickled Walnuts, with half a Pint of White Wine: strain it off, and put in as much Butter as will thicken it. To this put Oysters parboil'd, Shrimps or Prawns pickt, or the inside of a Crab, which will make the same Sauce very rich; then garnish with fry'd Oysters, Lemon sliced, butter'd Crabs and fry'd Bread, cut in handsome Figures, and pickled Mushrooms. *N.B.* If you have no Katchep, you may use Mushroom Gravey, mention'd in the first Part of your Treatise, or some of the travelling Sauce in the same Book, or else a small Tea spoonful of the dry Pocket-Sauce.

To Roast a Collar, or Fillet, of *Sturgeon;* from the same.

Take a piece of fresh Sturgeon; take out the Bones, and cut the fleshy Part into Lengths, about seven or eight Inches; then provide some Shrimps, chopt small with Oysters; some Crumbs of Bread, and such seasoning of Spice as you like, with a little Lemon-Peel grated. When this is done, butter one side of your Fish, and strew some of your Mixture upon it; then begin to roll it up, as close as possible, and when the first Piece is rolled up, then roll upon that another, prepared as before, and bind it round with a narrow Fillet, leaving as much of the Fish apparent as may be. But you must remark, that the Roll should not be above four Inches and a half thick; for, else one Part would be done enough before the Inside was hardly warm'd: therefore, I have sometimes parboil'd the inside Roll before I began to roll it.

When it is at the Fire, baste it well with Butter, and drudge it with sifted Raspings of Bread. Serve it with the same Sauce as directed for the former.

A Piece of fresh *Sturgeon* boiled; from the same.

When your Sturgeon is clean, prepare as much Liquor to boil it in, as will cover it; that is, take a Pint of Vinegar to about two Quarts of Water, a stick of Horse-Radish, two or three bits of Lemon-Peel, some whole Pepper, a Bay-leaf or two, and a small handful of Salt; boil your Fish in this, till it is enough, and serve it with the following Sauce.

Melt a pound of Butter; then add some Anchovy Liquor; Oyster Liquor; some White Wine; some Katchep boil'd together with whole Pepper and Mace strain'd; put to this the Body of a Crab, and serve it with a little Lemon-Juice. You may likewise put in some Shrimps, the Tails of Lobsters, cut to Pieces, stew'd Oysters, or Cray-fish cut into small Bits: garnish with pickled Mushrooms and roasted or fry'd Oysters, Lemon sliced, and Horse-Radish scraped.

To make a _Sturgeon-_Pye; from the same.

Put to a quartern of Flour, two Pounds of Butter, and rub a third Part in; then make it into a Paste with Water, and roll the rest in at three times, then roll out your Bottom, and when it is in the Dish, lay some Butter, in pieces, upon it; and strew on that, a little Pepper and Salt. Then cut your Sturgeon in Slices cross-ways, about three quarters of an Inch thick, seasoning them with Pepper, Salt, Nutmeg and Lemon-Peel grated, till your Pye is full, and on the Top lay on Pieces of Butter; then close it, and put in, just before it goes to the Oven, some White Wine and Water; and when it is bak'd, serve it: garnish it with sliced Lemon, or Orange.

To butter *Crabs,* from the same, for Garnish for the foregoing Dishes, or to be served by themselves.

Take middle-siz'd Sea-Crabs; break the Claws, and pick them; then take out the Body, free from all the Films and boney Parts; mix these together with some Pepper and Salt, to your mind; and when you have heated some White Wine over the Fire, put your Mixture into it, and stir it well together, and keep it warm in a gentle Oven, till you want it for Use: and just before you use it, pour into your Mixture a little melted Butter, and stir it well in; then clean your Shells, as well as possible, in hot Water, and put in your Mixture, and serve it to the Table hot. Or this Mixture may be serv'd on a Plate, upon Sippets, with Slices of Lemon or Orange. You should fry the Sippets.

The Manner of Pickling and Drying of *Sheeps* Tongues, or *Hogs* Tongues, which they call *Stags* Tongues; from a celebrated Practitioner of forty Years standing in *London*.

The Sheeps Tongues, which are commonly bought in the *London* Markets, are the best, if they are the Tongues of Wethers, fed in low Lands; being the largest, as they are taken from the largest sort of Sheep: but the Tongues of all Sorts of Sheep are good enough to be worth Pickling. But there is this Difference in the Value, that one large Tongue, well cured, will sell for three Pence, while the smallest Sort, cured in the same manner, will only sell for Three Half-pence, or a Penny. These Tongues are bought in Quantities of the Carcass Butchers, about *Whitechappel*, and other Butchers about Town, who kill from One hundred to Six hundred Sheep in a Day, each Butcher; and they know very well how to cut out the Tongues, with all their Parts to advantage: but they are afterwards trimm'd, when we receive them, into a more regular Shape; by those who cure them. When we are about this Work, there is one thing necessary to be observ'd, especially in hot Weather, but always it is best to be done; which is, cut the fleshy Part of the Bottom of the Tongue lengthways, and you will find, towards the Root, an Artery, which as soon as 'tis cut will bleed, and joining to that is a kind of Sweet-bread; take these out, as clean as you can, without disfiguring the Tongue; otherwise the Tongues will have an ungrateful Smell, and putrify: so, that if you deal by Wholesale, they will be return'd upon your hands, or be a trouble to the Family where they are made. Wash these well, after trimming, in Salt and Water, and then salt them with common Salt, well dry'd, in an Iron Kettle; one pound to half an Ounce of Salt-Petre, or Nitre, powder'd and well mix'd. Rub them well with the Mixture, and lay them close together in a Tub, or glaz'd earthen Vessel; and, after a few Days, when they are salt enough, take them from the Pickle, and when they are a little dry, tie them by the Tips, half a dozen together; and hang them up in a Chimney, where Deal Saw-Dust is burnt, till they are smoked enough, to be cured for boiling; then boil them in their Bunches, and let them dry for Sale. But to come a quicker Way to cure these Tongues, in the Pickle, as we do generally, is to make a Brine or Pickle in the following manner; that is, take a quantity of Water, and make a Pickle of it with common Salt, boil'd till it will bear an Egg; and then put in to every Pound of Salt, half an Ounce of Nitre, or Salt-Petre; and when the Pickle is cold, throw in your Tongues: which is the quickest Way. But for drying of them, the Smoking-Closets will do perfectly well, only we have not always those Conveniencies.

The *Smoking-Closets,*

It is to be observ'd, from your own Writings, That the Smoking-Closets are of great use in curing of Hams; and they are no less useful in drying of Tongues.

I have, in a place, in the Country, one of them in a Garret, where we enclose a Room of ten foot Square, where is a Chimney, into which, by a Register, we let in the Smoke from the Fire, which is made on a Hearth, on the ground Floor; so that the Smoke then does not come too hot on the Tongues, and so preserves them from turning rusty. This is much the best way of curing them, and one may cure, in such a Room, fourscore dozen at a time. This Place, likewise, we cure our Hung-Beef in. We have try'd some Sheeps Tongues, salted only in a Brine of common Salt, and dry'd in such a Room; and they are very red, and well tasted, though there is no Salt-Petre used in the Pickle.

A *Carp* Pye. From Mrs. *Mary Gordon.*

Put to a quartern of Flour a pound and a half of Butter, rubbing a third part in; and make it into a Paste with Water: then roll in the rest of the Butter, at two or three times, and lay your Paste in the Dish, putting some bits of Butter, on the bottom Paste, with some Salt and Pepper, at discretion.

Then scale and gut your Carp, and wash it with Vinegar, and dry it well; and make the following Pudding for the Belly of the Carp: *viz.* Take the Flesh of an Eel, and mince it very small; add some grated Bread, some dry'd sweet Marjoram powder'd, two butter'd Eggs, a small Anchovy minced, a little Nutmeg grated, and some Salt and Pepper; mix this well, and fill the Belly of the Carp with it, and for the remaining Part, make it into Balls. Then cut off the Tail and Fins of the Carp, and lay it in the Crust, with the Balls about it; some Mushroom Buttons, Oysters with their Fins taken off, and some Shrimps, a few Slices of Lemon, and some thin Slices of fat Bacon, a little Mace and some bits of Butter: then close it, and before you put it into the Oven, pour in half a Pint of Claret. Serve this Pye hot.

To make Biscuits of *Potatoes.* From the same.

Boil the Roots of Potatoes, till they are tender; then peel them, and take their weight of fine Sugar, finely sifted; grate some Lemon-Peel on the Sugar; and then beat the Potatoes and Sugar together, in a Stone Mortar, with some Butter, a little Mace, or Cloves, finely sifted, and a little Gum Dragon, steeped in Orange-Flower-Water, or Rose-Water, till it becomes a Paste; then make it into Cakes with Sugar, finely powder'd, and dry them in a gentle Oven.

To make *Biscuits* of Red *Beet-Roots;* from the same; call'd the *Crimson Biscuit.*

Take the Roots of Red-Beets, and boil them tender; clean them, and beat them in a Mortar with as much Sugar, finely sifted; some Butter; the Yolks of hard Eggs, a little Flower; some Spice, finely beaten, and some Orange-Flower-Water, and a little Lemon-Juice. When they are well mix'd, and reduced to a Paste, make them into Cakes, and dry them in a slow Oven.

To boil *Onions,* that they shall lose their strong Scent, and become as sweet as Sugar in their Taste. From the same.

Take the largest Onions, and when you have cut off the Strings of the Roots, and the green Tops, without taking off any of the Skins, fling them into Salt and Water, and let them lie an Hour; then wash them in it, and put them into a Kettle, where they may have plenty of Water, and boil them, till they are tender. Then take them off, and take off as many Skins, as you think fit, till you come to the white Part, and then bruise them, if you will, and toss them up with Cream or Butter, if you use them with boil'd Rabbits, or under a roasted Turkey; but in the last Case, this Sauce should be serv'd in Basons, or on Plates. You may also bruise them, and strain them through a Cullendar, and then put Cream to them; which is esteem'd the nicest way for a Turkey; or if you keep them whole, you may warm them in strong Gravey, well drawn, with Spice and sweet Herbs; and when that is done, thicken the Gravey with burnt Butter, adding a little Claret, or White Wine; or, for want of that, a little Ale. This is a Sauce for a Turkey roasted, or roast Mutton, or Lamb.

Hungary-Water. From Mrs. *Du Pont,* of *Lyons;* which is the same, which has been famous, about *Montpelier.*

Take to every Gallon of Brandy, or clean Spirits, one handful of Rosemary, one handful of Lavender. I suppose the handfuls to be about a Foot long a-piece; and these Herbs must be cut in Pieces, about an Inch long. Put these to infuse in the Spirits, and with them, about an handful of Myrtle, cut as before. When this has stood three Days, distil it, and you will have the finest Hungary-Water that can be. It has been said, that Rosemary Flowers are better than the Stalks; but they give a faintness to the Water, and should not be used, because they have a quite different Smell from the Rosemary; nor should the Flowers of Myrtle be used in lieu of the Myrtle, for they have a scent ungrateful, and not at all like the Myrtle.

The Manner of making the famous *Barcelona Snuff,* as it was perform'd at the *Lyon* at *Barcelona;* from the same. This is also call'd *Myrtle Snuff.*

Take *Seville* Snuff, and prepare a dry Barrel, that has not had any Wine in it, or of any Scent; then cut the fresh Tops of Myrtle, and lay a layer of them at the bottom of the Cask, an Inch or two thick; then lay Snuff on that as thick, and lay on more Myrtle, two Inches; then again, put on Snuff, and so fill the Barrel in the same Manner, *Stratum super Stratum.* Then press it down with a Board, that will fit, and set three Weights upon it of a quarter of an Hundred a-piece, and let it stand four and twenty Hours; then turn it out, and sift it, flinging the Myrtle away; then put it into the Cask, as before, with fresh Myrtle, and serve it so three times, and sift it off. When this is done, add to every ten Pounds of Snuff, one pound of Orangery Snuff, and mix the whole very well, and after three days, put it into glaz'd Pots, well pressed into them, and stopt close; or else into Leaden Pots: which last is rather the best.

To make *Orangery Snuff*. From the same.

Take *Seville* Snuff and Orange-Flowers, fresh gather'd early in the Morning. And in a glaz'd Earthen Vessel, lay a Layer of the Flowers, then a Layer of Snuff, then a Layer of Flowers; and so on, till the Pot is full. Press it down very gently, and let the Mouth of the Pot be open for twenty-four Hours; then turn all out, and sift your Snuff, and lay in fresh Flowers, with Snuff, in the same manner as before; and at the end of four and twenty Hours sift it off again, and repeat the same the third time: being sure that the Flowers do not remain longer than twenty-four Hours, else they will sour the Snuff. In making this Snuff, you ought to allow at least a pound for Waste, for the Flowers will gather a great deal of it.

To make *Orange-Butter*. From the same.

Take Hogs-Lard (or as in some Places, call'd Hogs-Seame) wash this well in Spring-Water, beating it all the while with a piece of Wood; then take Orange-Flowers, fresh gather'd, and melt the Lard gently, and put about a quarter of a pound of the Flowers into a pound of Lard; let them remain ten Minutes, gently keeping them warm over the Fire; then strain it off, and when the Lard is again cold, beat it, and wash it with Orange-Flower-Water. Then melt it gently a second time, and put in fresh Flowers, in the same manner as before, and it will become of a yellow Colour; and, when it is cool, beat it again with a wooden Paddle and Orange-Flower-Water, and then put it into Pots for use. I should remark, that the Lard should be melted by putting it in a glazed Vessel, and melting it by putting the Vessel into boiling Water.

To make Flour of *Mustard*.

Those who live in the Country, or go to Sea, have frequent occasion to use Mustard, when there is no opportunity of getting it without extraordinary Trouble. It is a Sauce seldom thought on till the Minute we want it; and then, according to the old Way of making it, if we are lucky enough to have Mustard-Seed in the House, we must spend an Hour in the Ceremony of grinding it in a wooden Bowl, and an Iron Cannon-Bullet, according to the old Custom; or, if we have Mustard by us, ready made, if it has stood a Week, it is then of no value, if it is in small quantity. But to obviate this Difficulty, the Invention of grinding Mustard-Seed in a Mill, and thereby reducing of it to Flour, to be made fit for the Table in an instant, has been very well received: for by that Contrivance we have it always fresh, and full of brisk Spirits, and may only make just what we want without any spoil, as long as we keep a Stock of this Flour by us.

There are two Sorts of Mustard: *viz.* The white Sort, which is a large Grain, and not so strong; and the black Sort, which is a small Grain. That which I account the best, is from the wild Mustard, commonly found growing in *Essex*, which sells the best in the Markets. But from whatever Place we have it, regard should be chiefly had to its being free from Mustiness, which happens from the gathering the Seed wet, or in the Dew, and laying it close together before it is thresh'd. When this Seed is dry and sweet, grind it in a Mill, such as a Coffee-Mill; but the Mill must be fresh, and free from any Flavour or Taint: it should not indeed be used with any other thing. When you have ground a sufficient Quantity, pass it through a pretty open Sieve, and the next day put it into Vials with open Mouths, pressing it down close; stop them well, and keep it for use. When you want good Mustard for the Table, take a spoonful or two of this Flour, and as much boiling Liquor from the Pot, where Beef or Pork is boiled, as will make it of the Consistence you desire, stirring it well till it is mixt for your Purpose; or for want of such Liquor, boil a little Salt and Water together, and mix your Mustard-Flour with that; but in either of these Ways you must observe, that while your Mustard is warm, it will last better.

Some who do not love their Mustard overstrong, put equal Quantities of the white and black Mustard-Seed into the Mill, and then the Flour will not be so poignant to the Palate, and will have a brighter Look. If your Mill be set very sharp, the Flour will be so fine, that it need hardly be sifted.

To keep *Anchovys* good for a long time. From Mrs. *M. N.*

As the People in the Country have not always the conveniency of a Market near them, and the Anchovy is often required for Fish-Sauce; so should every Family keep a quantity by them. They should be large, and fresh brought over when we buy them, and feel firm to the Finger; neither should they have their Heads on, for they are then more apt to turn rancid and stink; and if we buy them in large Quantities, the frequent opening the Pot we keep them in will subject them to Change. But to prevent this, as the Liquor falls or shrinks, add Vinegar to them, which will continue them firm and free from Rotting for two Years.

To Roast a Shoulder of *Mutton* like *Venison.* From the same.

Take a Shoulder of Mutton, and skin it; then lay it in the fresh Blood of a Sheep, well stirr'd with a little Salt, as it is bleeding, for six or eight Hours. When you have done this, wash it in Water and Salt, and at last with Vinegar; or else you may steep it in an Infusion of warm Water, a Gallon, and half a quarter of an Ounce of *Brazil*-Wood rasp'd. You may steep it in this Liquor for four Hours, or else you may let it pass half an Hour in a gentle Oven with Water and Salt, and a small Piece of *Brazil*-Wood in it; either of which will give it a Colour: but I think the two last are better than the Blood. Roast it then for its time, basting it well with Water and Salt, till it is near enough, and then give it a little sprinkling of Salt and raspings of Bread, with some Flour well mixt. The Sauce for this is Claret boil'd with Cinnamon, sweetned with a little Sugar and Crumbs of Bread grated: but some will use the Claret, Sugar and Cinnamon without the Crumbs, in Saucers; as it is now the most common way in Noblemens Families to do Venison. But in the Dish with the artificial Shoulder of Venison, put a strong Gravey of Beef; or made of some of the Beef-Glue which you have recommended in your Book.

To make a *Hare-Pye,* for a cold Treat. From the same.

Take the Flesh of an Hare, and beat it in a Marble Mortar; then add as many butter'd Eggs as will almost equal the Quantity of the Hare's-Flesh. Mix these together with a little fat Bacon cut small, some Pepper and Salt, and a little powder of Cloves and Mace, or sweet Marjoram, to your Pleasure, and mix them very well; then lay in your Paste, and butter it well at the bottom with some seasoning, strew'd upon it, and lay in your Preparation, and cover it with Butter; then close it, and serve it when it is cold.

To preserve *Ginger,* and reduce the common *Ginger* for that purpose. From the same.

Take the large Roots of Ginger, and pour scalding Water upon them; and when that is cool, pour on some more scalding Water: and so repeat the same till the seventh or eighth time, or till you find the Ginger soft, and very much swell'd. Then warm some White Wine, and put it in that, for a few Hours, stirring it frequently while it is in any of the Liquors. Boil the last Liquor with fine Sugar to a Syrup; then put in your Ginger, and boil it for some time; then set it by till the next day, and repeat the boiling of the Ginger, adding every now and then a little White Wine, till the Ginger begins to look a little clear; and when it is cold, put it into Glasses, or glazed Jars, stopping it close.

Marmalade of *Oranges* and *Lemons.* From the same.

It is necessary to boil the Rinds of each in several Waters, till the Bitterness is lost, and that they are reduced to a tenderness, such as you like; then beat them in a Marble Mortar with as much of the Pulp of Golden-Pippins, or Golden-Rennets, as you think proper. Then take their weight of Sugar well powder'd, and a Pint of Water to every Pound of Sugar; boil your Sugar and Water, and when you have made a Syrup, put in your Pulp, and boil them all together till they are clear. Then put in the Juice of Oranges and Lemons, so much as will give you the Taste you desire; then boil it over again till it jellies, and put it into Glasses, Keep this in a dry Place.

To make *Syrup* of *Mulberries.* From the same.

Press out the Juice of Mulberries with your Hands, and pass it through a Sieve; and when it has stood to settle, pour off the clear, and put to it, its Weight of fine Sugar; put this into a Gallypot, and set that Pot into a Kettle of hot Water, which should be kept simmering near two Hours: stir the Syrup every now and then with a Silver Spoon, and take off what Scum may rise at Times, upon it; when it is enough, let it stand till it is quite cold, and then put it into clear dry Bottles with large Mouths, and stop them close. Keep this in a dry Place.

It is to be remark'd, that besides this Syrup is very cooling; its use is to colour stew'd Apples, or Puddings, or any sweet Preparation made with Flour or Fruit: for in itself it carries no Flavour that will be predominant over that of another Fruit.

Of *Syrup* of *Raspberries, Currans,* or other Fruits. From the same.

These Syrups are made like the former, by pressing out the Juice with the Hands; because if the Seeds are broken, they would have an ill Taste. Treat these in the making just in the same way as the former, and use them in the same manner, to colour any sweet Preparation; but remember, where you put any of the Raspberry Syrup, the Flavour of the Raspberry will prevail.

To make a _Raspberry-_Pudding. From the same.

Take a Pint of Cream, and grate into it four Penny *Naples* Biscuits; then take the Yolks of eight hard Eggs chopt and broken small; then beat four Eggs and put in two spoonfuls of Flour, and as much Powder of double-refined Sugar; then put in as much Syrup of Raspberries as you think proper to give it a Flavour and a Colour. If you find that your Composition is not thick enough, you may grate in more *Naples* Biscuit. Mix all this well together, and, if you will, make a fine Crust roll'd thin and laid in a Dish, and bake it in a gentle Oven.

Parsnip-Cakes. From the same.

Scrape some Parsnip-Roots, and slice them thin, dry them in an Oven and beat them to Powder; mix them then with an equal quantity of Flour, and make them up with Cream and Spices powder'd; then mould them into Cakes, and bake them in a gentle Oven. *N.B.* The sweetness of the Parsnip Powder answers the want of Sugar.

To make *Raspberry* bak'd Cakes. From the same.

Take Potatoes and boil them, and when they are peel'd, beat them in a Marble Mortar with half the Quantity of fine Sugar powder'd; then put in some of your Raspberry Syrup, till it is coloured with it, and make up your Cakes in fine Sugar powder'd. Then dry them, or bake them, in a gentle

Oven, *Note*, these Cakes should be made thin.

Of *Ortolans*. From Mr. *Renaud*.

The *Ortolan* is a Bird brought from *France*, and is fed in large Cages with Canary-Seeds till they become a lump of Fat; and when they are fully fatted, they must be killed, or else they will feed upon their own Flesh. When we kill them, you must take them by the Beak, and holding it close between your Finger and Thumb, the Bird will be stifled in about a Minute; then pick off the Feathers even those of the Head, and pass a fine Skewer through them, just under the Wings, and roast them quick; setting small Toasts under them to drip upon. Serve them with strong Gravey, and as much White Wine hot, and garnish with Slices of Lemon and Raspings of Bread sifted and toasted before the Fire.

To make *Sugar Comfits* of any Sort. From Mrs. *Anne Shepherd* of *Norwich*.

The Seeds which we generally make Comfitts of, are Carraways, Coriander and Anise-Seeds; these, when they are cover'd with Sugar, are call'd Comfits, (*Confects*).

The Instruments to be employ'd for this Use, are first a deep-bottom'd Bason of Bell-Metal, or Brass, well tinn'd, to be hung over some hot Coals.

Secondly, You must have a broad Pan to put hot Coals in.

Thirdly, Provide a Brass Ladle to pour the Sugar upon the Seeds.

Fourthly, You must have a Brass Slice to scrape off the Sugar that may chance to hang upon the side of the hanging Bason.

Then take care that your Seeds are dry, or dry them well in your hanging Pan.

To every quarter of a Pound of Seeds use two Pounds of fine Sugar beaten; unless to Anise-Seeds, use two Pounds of Sugar to half a Pound of Seeds.

To begin the Work, put three Pounds of fine Sugar into the Bason with one Pint of Water, to be stirr'd well together till the Sugar is wet; and boil it gently, till the Sugar will rope from the Ladle like Turpentine, and it is enough. Keep this however warm, upon warm Embers, that it may run freely in a ropy Way from the Ladle upon the Seeds.

When this is ready, move the Seeds briskly in the Bason, and fling on them half a ladle-full at a time of the hot Sugar, keeping the Seeds moving for some time; which will make them take the Sugar the better, and be sure to dry them well after every covering, by moving the Bason, and stirring the Comfits. In an Hour, you may make three Pounds of Comfits: you will know when they are coated enough with Sugar, by their becoming as large as you would have them. There is no certain Rule, but our own Fancies, for the Size of them. *Note*, Till they are as you would have them, cast on more melted Sugar, as at first, and keep them stirring and shaking in the Pan, drying them well after every Coat of Sugar.

If you would have ragged or rough Comfits, make your Sugar so liquid, that it will run from the Ladle; and let it fall upon the Seeds about a Foot and a half high. Let it be very hot, for the hotter it is, the rougher will be your Comfits; and for all that, the Comfits will not take so much Sugar as one may imagine from their Appearance. Put on at each time only one Ladle-full, and in ten times repeating it your Comfits will be perfectly well coated.

For plain Comfits; let not your melted Sugar be too hot at first, nor too thick; neither pour it on the Seeds too high: but the last two or three Coverings may be thicker and hotter.

As for Coriander-Seeds, which are large, three Pounds of Sugar will only cover a quarter of a Pound of them.

While your are at work, you should keep your melted Sugar in good Temper, that it may not gather into Lumps, or burn to the bottom of the Pan; and to prevent its growing too thick at any time, put to it a spoonful or two of Water, gently stirring it now and then with your Ladle, keeping your Fire very clear under your Pan. When your Comfits are made, put them upon Papers in Dishes, and set them before the Fire, or in a declining Oven, which will make them look of a Snow white; when they are cool, put them in Boxes, or in crystal Bottles.

To make *Comfits* of various Colours. From the same.

If you would have your Comfits of a red Colour, infuse some red Saunders in the Water till it is deep colour'd enough; or else take some Cochineel, and infuse it till the Liquor is red enough; or put some Syrup of Mulberries with Water to the Sugar.

If of a yellow Colour; use Saffron in Water, which you are to mix with the Sugar.

If Green; take the Juice of Spinach, and boil it with the Sugar: so will your Comfits be of the several Colours above-mention'd.

To preserve *Orange* and *Lemons-Peels* in Jelly. From the same.

Cut some of the fairest Oranges and Lemons in halves; then scoop out all the Pulp and Inside, and boil them in several Waters till they are so tender, that you may pass a Straw through them; then wash them in cold Water.

Boil then the following Preparation: *viz.* The Quantity of a Quart of Water to every Pound of Peel; and in it some thin Slices of Golden-Pippins, or Golden Rennets, till the Water becomes slippery. Then to this Water, add as much Sugar as will boil it to a strong Syrup; then put in your Peels and scald them, and set them by till the Day following, and boil them again till the Syrup will jelly. Then put your Peels into your Glasses, and put into your Syrup the Juice of three large Oranges, and one Lemon strain'd, and boil it till it will make a stiff Jelly, and pour it upon your Peels. When this is quite cold, then put Papers over the Glasses, and keep them in a dry Place.

You may also pare the Rinds, in Rings or Slices, and boil them as before; and in every respect treat them as you are directed to preserve the halves of Oranges.

To preserve *Orange-Flowers* in Jelly.

Gather your Orange-Flowers, in the Morning early, when they are just open, and take the Leaves of them. Boil these gently in two or three Waters, passing them every time through a Sieve: shift the Waters often, to take out the too great bitterness, but don't boil them too soft, nor to lose their Whiteness. When this is done, make a strong jelly'd Syrup with Water and fine Sugar, and add some Juice of Lemon or Orange to it; then pour it on the Leaves of the Orange-Flowers; and when it is cold, cover your Glasses with Paper. N.B. You may thicken your Syrup with the Pulp of Pippins.

_Lemon-_Cakes. From Mrs. *Anne Shepperd* of *Norwich*.

Take out the Pulp of Lemons, as little bruis'd as possible; then boil some Sugar to a candied height, and put to it the Pulp and Juice, and stir it quickly; then put it into a Stove or into hot Sand. When you observe that it begins to candy on one side, then turn them out of the Glasses with a wet Knife on the other side, and let that candy too, in the same manner; when all is done, put them in a Box between Papers, and keep them in a dry Place.

Tripe of *Eggs*. From Mr. *Fontaine*.

Take the Whites of Eggs, and beat them very well in a Porringer; prepare then some hot Water and Vinegar with a little Salt, and then put in the Eggs, till they are hard; then cut them in pieces about an Inch square, and then take some White Wine, and as much Water and some Salt. Put this in a Pan, and heat it over the Fire with a little Parsley, an Onion and some Spice; when it is hot, serve it up with Butter and Mustard, and it will eat like Tripe: or else you may serve it like a Ragoust, with the following Sauce; *viz*.

Sauce for the Artificial *Tripe* in *Ragoust*. From the same.

Take strong Gravey made of Beef, and the Ingredients which are mention'd in the drawing of Gravey. Warm it with a little White Wine, and thicken the

Sauce with burnt Butter: then, when the Eggs are warm'd, pour the Sauce over them.

Bacon Froize, or *Fraise.* From Mrs. *Bradbury.*

Cut fat Bacon in small Pieces, about an Inch long, and then prepare ten or a dozen Eggs well beat; put in a little Milk, some Spice, at pleasure, and some Flour; then put some Lard or Seam of an Hog into a Pan, and make it very hot; and when it is so, pour in the Mixture, and clap a dish over it, after you have thrown some of the Seam upon it. When the Froize is done enough on one side, turn it with the Dish, and fry it till it is quite enough. Then serve it with a garnish of sliced Lemons and a little Butter, first letting it drain.

Clary and *Eggs,* From the same.

Take eight or ten Eggs; beat them well in a Porringer; then take some Clary Leaves, and chop them small; add a little Pepper and Salt, and some Onion chopt small. This Mixture must be fry'd in hot Lard or Hog-Seam, and serve it with Slices of Lemon.

To stew a *Pig.* From the same.

Roast a Pig till it is hot; then take off the Skin and cut it in pieces; then take some White Wine and good Gravey, and stew it with an Onion, some Pepper, Salt, some Nutmeg, a little sweet Marjoram, and some Elder Vinegar, with some Butter; and when it is enough, lay it upon Sippits, and garnish with sliced Lemon.

To stew a *Pig* another way. From the same.

Roast a Pig till you can take off the Skin; cut it then in small pieces, and stew it in White Wine, with a bunch of sweet Herbs, an Onion, some Pepper and Salt, a few Cloves, or a little sweet Marjoram powder'd. When it is enough, strain off the Liquor it was boil'd in, and in some of that put some Mushrooms, and thicken it with Cream, and it will make an excellent Dish. You may garnish it with sliced Lemon and pickled Barberries.

To make a *Fricassee* of Sheeps Trotters.

Clean them very well from the Hair; then wash them in Vinegar and Water; then take out the Bones, and boil them in Salt and Water with a little Lemon-Peel. When they are hot, give them either of the following Sauces. For a white Sauce, take the following: *viz.*

Take some Water, with some Salt, a few sweet Herbs, some whole Pepper, some Lemon-Peel and a bit of Horse-Radish, a Shallot, and a little White Wine. When it is strong enough relish'd, then strain it off, and take a little of it, and mix it with Butter to thicken it, or Cream would do better, about half a

Pint: pour this over the Sheeps Trotters with a few Capers, and serve it up with Slices of Lemons.

A brown *Fricassee* of Sheeps Trotters.

Dress them as before, and when they are fit for Sauce, then take some Hogs Lard, and make it very hot in a Pan, then put in your Trotters, when they are well covered with Flour, and when they are done enough, pour over them a Sauce made of Gravey, some Claret and some Mushrooms thickned with burnt Butter. This will make a good brown Fricassee; and serve it up with a garnish of Lemon sliced, Barberries pickled, some raspings of Bread lifted, and toasted before the Fire.

To make a *Lumber-Pye.* From *Exeter.*

Take a Pound of lean Veal, free from Strings, shred it very small, season it with Cloves and Mace powder'd, some powder of dry'd sweet Herbs, some Lemon-Peel grated, some Pepper and Salt, three large spoonfulls of grated Bread, a little Juice of Lemon, and five or six butter'd Eggs. Mix these Ingredients well together into a Paste or as a farced Meat for Balls about the Bigness of small Wallnuts; then take two or three large Veal Sweat breads, and cut them in pieces; then provide a Pint of Mushroom Buttons well clean'd, and the Yolks of eight hard Eggs cut in halves, a dozen Coxcombs well scalded and clean'd: lay these with a seasoning of Pepper and Salt in a good Paste that covers the bottom of your Dish; first laying bits of Butter on the Paste at the Bottom. Some will put about half a Pound of Currans into this Pye; but every one to their Fancy. When your Ingredients are disposed in your Dish, lay on about four Ounces of Marrow, and the quantity of six Ounces of Butter, and then close it.

Just before you set it in the Oven, pour into your Pye half a Pint of Water; and as soon as you take it out, pour in half a Pint of White Wine warm'd, and serve it hot.

To make *Orange* or *Lemon* Tarts. From Mrs. *J. S.*

Take the Rinds of half a score Oranges or Lemons, and salt them four Hours; then boil them in four or five Waters till they are tender, and beat them in a Marble Mortar till they are reduced to a Pulp; then squeeze in the Juice of as many of the Oranges or Lemons as you think fit, and sweeten the whole very well with fine Sugar, and boil it till it is thick, stirring it while it boils, that it may not burn; then let it stand till it is cold, and put it into your Paste. When you serve it, strew fine Sugar over it. Serve it cold.

To make *Lemon* Cheesecakes. From Mrs. *M.N.*

Grate the Rind of a large Lemon, into the Yolks of eight raw Eggs, being first very well beat; then add a quarter of a Pound of fine Sugar well beaten and sifted, and four Ounces of fresh Butter; warm these gently over a Fire, keeping it stirring all the while till it begins to thicken; then take it off, and put it in the Coffins made of puff Crust, and bake your Cheesecakes in a gentle Oven.

To make *Orange* or *Lemon* Cheesecakes, another way. From the same.

Take the Rind of a large Lemon or Orange, and boil it in four or five Waters till it is quite tender, and free from its Bitterness; then either shred it or beat it very fine in a Marble Mortar with the Yolks of eight hard Eggs, six Ounces of Loaf-Sugar finely powder'd, and a spoonfull of Orange-Flower-Water: mix this then with as much Cream, and two Eggs beat, as will render it of the Consistence of Cheesecake-meat before it is baked; then put it into your Coffins, and bake them in a gentle Oven. You may put in Currans if you please, but they are generally omitted: however, if you like to have them, let them be first plump'd a little over the Fire in Sugar and Water.

The best way for these Cheesecakes is to make the Coffins in Patty-Pans, and fill them with the Meat near an Inch thick.

The Proportions mention'd above will serve to direct for a large quantity.

To make *Cheesecakes.* From Lady G.

Take a Quart of tender Curd, and drain it from the Whey; then break it small; then take a quarter of an Ounce of Mace finely powder'd, and eight Ounces of fine Sugar sifted, eight Yolks of Eggs well beaten, four Ounces of blanched Almonds beat fine in a Marble Mortar with Rose-Water, or Orange-Flower-Water, and grate four penny *Naples* Biscuits into a Pint of Cream, and boil them together over a gentle Fire, stirring it all the while till it is as thick as an hasty Pudding; then mix with it eight Ounces of Butter, and put it to the Curd, but not too hot: mix then all well together, and put it in your Paste.

A *Sorrel* Tart. From the same.

Wash some Spinach and Sorrel Leaves in two or three Waters, for they are apt to gather Dirt; then either shred them, and squeeze the Juice out through a Cloth, or else beat them in a Mortar of Marble, and strain off the Juice; about half a Pint of Juice will be enough: then shred into it about a Quart measure of the same Herbs, and add six Ounces of fine Sugar beaten, and some Spice, with the Yolks of six hard Eggs bruised, and well mix'd with it, and two Eggs raw well beaten; then put in half a Pint of Cream, stirring it well, and put it in a Paste, then bake it in a very gentle Oven. When it is done, sift on some fine Sugar, and garnish with Orange and Lemon sliced; you may put in some Orange-Flower-Water, if you think convenient.

To make *Umble Pye*. From *Mr. Thomas Fletcher* of *Norwich*.

Take the Umbles of a Deer and boil them tenderly, and when they are cold, chop them as small as Meat for minc'd Pyes, and shred to them as much Beef-Suet, six large Apples, half a Pound of Sugar, a Pound of Currans, a little Salt, and as much Cloves, Nutmeg and Pepper powder'd as you see convenient; then mix them well together, and when they are put into the Paste, pour in half a Pint of Sack, the Juice of two Lemons and an Orange: and when this is done, close the Pye, and when it is baked, serve it hot to the Table.

To Stew Peaches. From the same.

Take Peaches when they are so ripe that they begin to smell; then pare them and slit them, and the Sorts I recommend will leave the Stones. Put these in a Silver Plate, or on such a one as will not communicate any ill taste to them, and pour over them a Syrup made of Pippins, Water and Sugar boil'd till it is a Jelly, and add a little White Wine; then stew them gently over a clear Fire till they are tender; and serve them with fine Sugar sifted upon them. In some Cafes they pour Cream upon them.

Red *Peach Tarts*. From the same.

Take your Peaches, as before directed, and order them as you did before in paring them and slitting them; then lay them into the Coffins, and when you have sifted on them some fine powder'd Loaf-Sugar, pour over them some Syrup of Raspberries or Mulberries, and bake them gently: they will be tender and very highly flavoured, if you put Raspberries to them, and finely colour'd; but to have them more of their own Taste, put Syrup of Mulberries to them, and they will be finely colour'd. The Coffins or Crust ought to be made of melting Paste, with fine Sugar in it.

Bitters to be drank with Wine.

Take a Quart of clean Spirit, or good Brandy, and put into it an Ounce of Gentian Root sliced, one Ounce and a half of dry'd Orange-Peel, and one Drachm of *Virginia* Snake-Root; add to this half a Drachm of Cochineel, and half a Drachm of Loaf-Sugar; which last will heighten the Bitter to admiration. A little of this Bitter in a Glass of White Wine creates an Appetite.

To Stew *Wild-Ducks*. From *Amsterdam*.

When your Ducks are ready prepar'd for the Fire, rub their Inside with Pepper, Salt, and a little powder of Cloves, a Shallot or two, with a lump of Butter in the Belly of each of them; then lay them in an earthen glazed Pan, that will just hold them, and put three Quarters of a Pound of Butter under and over your Ducks: then pour in a Pint of Vinegar, and as much Water with some Salt, Pepper, some Lemon-Peel, some Cloves whole, a bunch of sweet Herbs, and covering the Pan close, let them stew three or four Hours. Then pass the Liquor through a Sieve, and pour it over your Ducks; and serve them hot with garnish of Lemon sliced and Raspings of Bread sifted. This Method serves likewise for Easterlings, Widgeons, Teal and such like.

To Stew a salted Brisket of *Beef.* From Mr. *La Fontaine.*

To a Pound of common Salt, put one Ounce of Salt-Petre, and rub your Beef well with it, and let it lie a Week; then lard the Skin of it with Bacon-Fat, and lay it in a Stew-pan that will shut close. Cut a Lemon in half with its Rind, and lay a-part on each side the Beef; then put in a bunch of sweet Herbs, some whole Cloves, half a Nutmeg sliced, some Pepper, an Onion, or three or four Shallots, half a Pound of Butter, a Pint of Claret, and a Quart of Water; shut your Pan close, and let it stew gently five or six Hours till it is very tender.

Then having some boil'd Turnip cut in dice, flour them and fry them brown; then pour off the Liquor the Beef was stew'd in, and having passed it through a Sieve, thicken it with burnt Butter, and mix your fry'd Turnips with it, and pour all together over your Beef; garnish with Lemon sliced, and Raspings of Bread sifted, and serve it hot, it is an excellent Dish.

Neck of *Mutton* ragou'd. From the same.

Take a Neck of Mutton clean from Bones, and strip it from the Skin; salt it a little, and let it lie till the next day. In the mean while, bake the Bones with a slice or two of fat Bacon, a Faggot of sweet Herbs, some Spice, a little Salt and some Lemon-Peel, with half a Pint of Water, and half a Pint of Claret, to cover them; then lay your Mutton in a Pan, and when your baked Gravey is passed through a Sieve, pour it into the Pan to the Mutton; but first lard the fat Part of the Mutton with Lemon-Peel, and the leaner Part with Fat of Bacon; then strew some grated Bread and Spice over the Mutton, which will not be cover'd with the baked Gravey; and when you have closed your Pan, stew it gently four Hours. Then lay it in the Dish, and when you have thickned the Sauce with burnt Butter, put a Pint of Mushroom Buttons, either fresh and parboil'd, or pickled, into it, and toss them up till they are hot; then pour them all over your Meat, and serve it hot, garnish'd with Lemon sliced, red Beet-Roots pickled and sliced, Capers, and Horse-Radish scrap'd.

Stew'd *Beef* in *Soup.* From the same.

Take four Pounds of Beef, indifferently lean, and cut it in eight or ten Pieces. Put these into a Pan that may be close cover'd, and then about three Quarts of Water, and a Pint of White Wine, some Pepper and Salt, some Powder of dry'd sweet Marjoram, a few Cloves powder'd, half a dozen small Turnips cut in Dice, a Carrot or two cut in the same manner, the white Part of a large Leek shred small, some Leaves of white Beet, two Heads of Sallery shred, and a Piece of Bread-Crust burnt; cover close, and stew this for six Hours, and serve it hot. You may garnish with Lemon sliced.

To dress the *Liver* and *Crow* of an *Hog*. From Mrs. *Johnson* in *Devereux-Court*.

However this Dish may seem dispiseable, yet if it is well dresed, few of the savoury Dishes exceed it. The Liver and Crow of an Hog, with the Sweet-Breads, should be used presently after the Hog is kill'd, and the Liver cut in Lumps, twice as big as a Walnut, and not in thin Pieces as most do; for then they will become hard in the Dressing. The Crow must likewise be cut in Slips about the breadth of two Fingers, and so must the Sweet-Breads; then parboil the Pieces of Liver, and make a thick Batter of Flour, Water and Eggs, mixing a little Salt with it, and prepare some red Sage shred very fine; some grated Bread, and some Pepper beaten: mix these together, and when you have some Butter, or Lard, very hot in your Frying-Pan, dip the Crow and Sweet-Bread in the Batter, and immediately dip your Pieces in the Mixture of Bread, Sage, &c. and throw them into the Pan. When these are enough, lay them to drain before the Fire, and then dip the Bits of Liver into the Batter; and after that, into the crumb'd Bread, and give them a turn or two in the Pan, over a quick Fire: then drain them like the others, and serve them hot with Butter and Mustard.

Sea-Larks or *Oysters,* roasted on Spits or Skewers. From the same.

Take large Oysters, and wash them from Dirt; then dip them in Batter made with Milk, Flour, Powder of Mace, some Eggs and a little Pepper; then dip them again in Crumbs of Bread grated, and some Mace powder'd, and put them on a fine Skewer, broad-side to broad-side, or upon Silver Lark Spits; and when they are at the Fire, flour them well, and baste them with Butter till they are enough. Prepare for them, while they are Roasting, the following Sauce: Take Crumbs of Bread, a little Pepper and Salt, and a Blade or two of Mace with a little Nutmeg, and boil them in some of the Oyster-Liquor till the Bread is tender and like a Pulp, and tastes well of the Spice; then put in a Glass of White Wine, and mix it well, and serve it hot, in a Plate, with the roasted Oysters over the Sauce.

A Shoulder of *Mutton* or *Lamb,* roasted with a Farce of *Oysters*. From Mr. *Norman,* late Cook in *Norfolk*.

Take a Shoulder of Mutton or Lamb, of the smallest size, and slip up the Skin almost to the Leg-Joint; then cut the Flesh from the Bone, on the upper side, and mince it very small, take part of that, and as many Oysters parboil'd without their Fins, and chopt a little; then have some Mace powder'd, and a little Salt and Pepper, with some grated Lemon-Peel, and some grated Bread, with the Yolk of an Egg, or two; and make this into a Paste, and lay it into the Places where the Flesh was taken out; and you may add to this Paste a little Fat of Bacon cut small, or a little Butter. Then skewer the Skin on all sides, over the Farced Meat, and lard the Skin and the fleshy Parts below with Lemon-Peel, and some will lard in Lemon Thyme likewise. Then fix it on a Spit with Skewers, and roast it, well basted with Butter and well floured. The Sauce for this should be stew'd Oysters, some Mace, stew'd Mushrooms, a little Gravey, and some White-Wine, with Crumbs of Bread; then serve it hot, garnish'd with sliced Lemon, and Red Beet-Root pickled and sliced.

Stew'd Veal, with white Sauce; from the same.

Take some Lean of a Leg of Veal, and cut it in thick Slices, then stew them in Water and a little Salt, with some Mace, and a little Nutmeg, and a Bunch of sweet Herbs. When they are almost stew'd enough with the Gravey in them, put to the Liquor they were stew'd in, a Glass or two of White Wine, and a little Lemon Juice, or Orange Juice, with a little Mushroom Gravey, or Liquor of stew'd Mushrooms. When this is done, have some Mushroom Buttons, that have been stew'd white in their own Liquor, and Spice, with a Bay-Leaf; then strain the Liquor, and put some in the Sauce: and when it is hot, put some thick Cream to it, with the Mushrooms; and then serve it hot with a Garnish of sliced Lemon.

Hard *Pease-Soup.* From the same.

There are many ways of making Pease-Soup. In great Families it is sometimes made of Beef, but a Leg of Pork is much preferable; and in smaller Families the Bones of Pork, as they are called. And the Shin and Hock of a Leg of Pork, after they have made Sausages, may be had at the Sausage-Houses: these boil'd for a long time, will afford a strong Jelly Broth, but they are hard to be met with. However, when they are to be had, you have the Directions for a Broth. Then pass the Broth, hot, through a Sieve, and put into it half a Pint of slit Pease to a Quart of Liquor; or a Quart of whole Pease to three Quarts of Liquor. The Difference between one and the other, is, the slit Pease will open in the Liquor, when we boil it, and the other ought to be broken through a Cullender, when they are boil'd: but the slit Pease are the best; and when you put them into the Liquor to boil, add to every Quart of Liquor as much Sallery as you think proper, cut small; some powder of dry'd Mint, some powder of dry'd sweet Marjoram, some Pepper, and some Salt, to your mind, and let these boil till the Sallery is tender. This is to be done, if we boil a Leg of Pork, after the Pork is out of the Pot; but if we make the Soup from the Bones, boil these Ingredients afterwards in the Liquor. When you serve it, put a *French*

Role in the middle of the Dish, and garnish the Border of the Dish with rasp'd Bread sifted. Some put in All-spice powder'd, which is very agreeable: and one might add the Leaves of white Beets, And in serving, put in toasted Bread, cut in Dice; but the last is out of fashion.

To make green _Pease-_Pottage, with *Milk*. From the same.

Take a Quart of green Pease shell'd, and boil three Quarts or two Quarts of Milk, as you please to have them thick with Pease; and add some Pepper largely beaten, a little Salt, some dry'd Mint, and sweet Marjoram in powder, and a little whole Spice beaten. Boil these together till the Cream rises, and then stir it, and serve it hot. *N.B.* The Pease should be boil'd first, if there is any opportunity; and for that Reason, if when we have a Dish of Pease, we leave any, they may be put into the Milk, and boil'd the Morning following, and indeed it is the best to have the Pease boil'd first.

To make an artificial *Crab* or *Lobster*. From Mr. *F.* of *Buckingham*.

I Suppose you have by you the large Shells of Sea-Crabs clean'd; then take part of a Calf's Liver, boil it and mince it very small, and a little Anchovy Liquor, and but very little, to give it the Fish-taste. Mix it well with a little Lemon Juice, some Pepper, and some Salt, with a little Oil, if you like it, and fill the Shells with it; and then the outside Parts of the Liver, being a little hard, will feel to the Mouth like the Claws of the Crab broken and pick'd, and the inner Parts will be soft and tender, like the Body of a Crab. One may serve this cold, and it will deceive a good Judge, if you do not put too much of the Anchovy Liquor into it. It is very good cold; but if you would have it hot, take the following Receipt.

To make artificial hot butter'd *Sea-Crabs*.

Have the great Shells of Crabs clean, and prepare some Liver, as before; or if you cannot get Calf's Liver, get a Lamb's Liver, or a young Sheep's Liver will do tolerably well. Boil these, and shred them as directed before, and put a little Anchovy Liquor to them; then add a little White Wine, some Pepper and Salt at pleasure, and some other Spice at discretion, with Butter necessary to make it mellow, over a gentle Fire, or a little Sallet Oil, if you like Oil. Then add a little Lemon Juice in the Shells, stirring the Mixture together. Then serve them up hot with Lemon sliced.

To make artificial *Crabs*. From M. *De la Port* of *Lyons* in *France*.

Take some of the White of a roasted or boil'd Chicken's Breast, and shred it very small; then add some Roots of Potatoes boil'd and beat into Pulp. Mix these together, and grate a little Lemon-Peel upon it, and add a little Anchovy Liquor to it, with some Oil; and put a little Lemon-juice to it, or Vinegar, with some Pepper and Salt, serve it upon Sippits, garnish'd with sliced Lemon. These may be butter'd in Shells as the Former, but the first is rather the best.

To make artificial *Lobsters.* From the same.

Practise the same Method with either of the former; and to imitate the Tail of the Lobster, put in the Tails of Shrimps, Buntings, Prawns or Cray-fish; the last cut in pieces, and serve them either upon Sippets in a Plate, or in the large Shell of the Lobster.

N.B. This is a sort of Salmy, or Salmy-Gundy, as they call it in *England;* but is very much like the Thing we want: and I think, if the Shrimps, or others, were put into the first, it would make it better than putting in the Anchovy Liquor; but if they are to imitate a Crab, they must, (*i.e.* the Shrimps or Prawns) be chopt very small.

To imitate *Cherry-Brandy,* without *Cherries,* very Good.

Take a clean Spirit, or some good *French* Brandy, one Gallon, and infuse in it the Tops of Laurel, one good handfull till it tastes like the Kernels of Cherries; then put in a quantity of Mulberry Syrup, enough to colour it, and make it pleasant to the Taste. A good Judge will not find the difference between the Right and the Wrong. *N.B.* When the Brandy is strong enough of the Laurel-Buds, pour it off.

To make *Cherry Brandy.* From Mr. *Cent-Livre.*

Take black Cherries, when they are at the cheapest, and pulling them from the Stalks, put them into a Cask of Brandy, a Pound to each Quart of Brandy, and one Pound of fine Sugar to each Gallon. Let it stand for some time, and draw it off. It will be very rich.

To make *Ratafia.* From the same.

Take the Kernels of Apricots, to do it in the highest way, about one hundred and fifty, and bruise them a little; then put them into three or four Quarts of Brandy, and let them steep four or five Days: then strain them off, and add as much fine Sugar powder'd, as will make it sweet to your Taste. If you find that the Brandy is too strong of the Kernels, put some more Brandy to it before you sweeten it.

Memorandum, If you cannot get Apricot or Peach-Stones, enough for your use, you may use the Kernels of Plum-Stones, Cherry-Stones, or Prunes, and they will make little difference, in great quantities. Break the Shells, and put in Shells and all.

To make Artificial Ratafia.

To a Gallon of Spirits or Brandy, put in two handfuls of the Buds of young

Laurel-Branches; infuse this till the Liquor is of a taste as you would have it: then pour off the Liquor, and sweeten it to your Fancy with fine Sugar powder'd. This is a way that a Distiller, who is dead, practised a long while, as well as the making of Gin, or Geneva Brandy, with infusing the Tops of the Juniper Plant in common Spirits. These I told him of, and it is now at my own disposal, and therefore give it to the World. The Ratafia tastes exactly as if the Kernels of Apricot or Plum-Stones had been used.

To make *Salmy,* or with us *Salmy-Gundy.* From Lady *M.*

Take the Breast of a Turkey, a Chicken, or the Lean of some Veal that has been roasted rather than boil'd; but if that happens, it will still do. But however it is, take none of the Skin, nor any Fat. Mince this very small about half a Pound, and then take off the Skin of a pickled Herring, and mince the Flesh of it very small, or for want of that, cut the Flesh of some Anchovys very small; then cut a large Onion small, an Apple or two as small as the rest. Mix these Meats together and laying them in little Heaps, three on a Plate, let some whole Anchovys curl'd or upright, in the Middle, and garnish with sliced Lemon, Capers and other Pickles, with red Beet-Roots pickled and sliced. This to be served cold; and when you eat it, use Oil, Vinegar, and a little Mustard.

To serve up pickled *Herrings.* From the same.

Take large pickled Herrings, take off the Skin; then take the Flesh from the Bones, on each side, all in one piece, crossing them every half-inch. Then lay the Parts next the Head, in the middle of the Plate, spreading their Bodies to the outside, like a Star, garnishing them with the Roots of red Beets sliced, Lemon sliced, and Berberries pickled. This is commonly eaten with Vinegar, and Bread and Butter, but Onion and Pepper is sometimes used.

Marmalade of *Peaches.* From the same.

Take Peaches, well grown and almost ripe; pare them, and take their Flesh clean from the Stones. Lay them with a little Water into a Stew-Pan, and add three Quarters of their weight of fine Sugar powder'd. Let this stew till the Peaches are tender, and then mash them with a Spoon, letting them boil gently all the while, till the Whole becomes thick, almost like a Paste; then take it out, and cool it in a *China* Dish, or earthen glazed Pan; and when it is cold, put it into Glasses, and cover them over with white Paper.

White _Peach-_ Tarts. From the same.

Make some Coffins of sweet Paste, and when they are gently baked, and cold, fill them with the above-mention'd Marmalade of Peaches, and serve them.

Apricots preserv'd for Tarts. From the same.

Take Apricots of the largest kind, When they begin to turn to Ripeness, pare them and discharge them from the Stones. Cut them in Halves, and stew them with a little Water, and their weight of fine Sugar powder'd. Boil these gently over a clear Charcoal Fire, till the Liquor becomes of the Consistence of a Jelly, and the Apricots are clear. Then when they are cool, put them up in glazed Gallypots, or in Glasses. If you use them for Tarts, put them in Coffins of sweet Paste, and cover them, and put them in the Oven, till they are hot through. Then serve them with double-refined Sugar grated over them. These may be either serv'd hot or cold. The Jelly of this kind, in the Glasses, may be serv'd as a Sweetmeat in a Desert.

Memorandum, If, when these Fruits are ripe, you can have any Apples near ripe, pare them, and slice them free from the Core, and stew them in as much Water as will cover them, and their weight in fine Sugar, till by boiling and stirring, the whole becomes of a Jelly; then in this, when it is clear, stew your Apricots, or Peaches, till they are what you desire. *N.B.* You may always colour these with Syrup of Mulberries, which gives no additional Taste.

Plums to make _Marmalade _of. From the same.

There are several sorts of Plums, which are fit for this use. And though they differ in colour, that is, some red and some white, yet the Marmalade made of any of them will be white, for the Colour is only in the Skin; and that if it was to be used, could give no Tincture; but in our Case, we do not want it. The Sorts are either the *Bonum Magnum,* as it is call'd, which is a large, long, red Plum, with a Pulp very tender, but sour, when it is raw from the Tree. Another is a large Plum, rather yellowish than white, when it is ripe, and of the former Shape, like an Egg, which is called by some the Egg-Plum; but more particularly the white *Holland* Plum, and is so called by the Gardeners. These two have a Flesh and Juice much like one another, and make a fine Shew in a Dish by way of Desert; but are in my Opinion only fit for stewing. However, the Skins will part easily from 'em, when they are ripe, and they both quit the Stone freely. Take these and peel them, and divide them; then put them in a little Water and their weight of fine Sugar, made into a Syrup, over a gentle Fire: put them in when the Liquor is only warm, and when they are cover'd with the Syrup, stew them gently, if you would preserve them in their Shape; and put them, with the Syrup, into Glasses as soon as they are clear, or else mash them into the Syrup, and let them boil till they become like a Paste; keeping all stirring while they are over the Fire, or else they will burn to the Pan. This Marmalade is good to be serv'd in Glasses as a Sweet-meat in a Desert, or to be put into Coffins for Tarts, or to be brought upon the Table in Saucers among the other Sweet-meats in a Desert.

To stew *Cucumbers.* From the _Devil-_Tavern, *Fleet-street.*

Take a dozen large green Cucumbers, that are not too full of Seed; pare them, and slice them; then take two large Onions, and shred them indifferently small. Put these in a Sauce-Pan, and set them over the Fire to stew, with as much Salt as you think convenient; stir them now and then, till they are tender, and then pour them into a Cullender to drain from the Water, and are as dry as possible you can make them; then flour them, and put some Pepper to them. After this, burn some Butter in a Frying-Pan; and when it is very hot, put in your Cucumbers, and stir them continually till they are brown; then put to them about a Gill of Claret; and when that is well mix'd with them, serve them hot, under roast Mutton or Lamb; or else, serve them on a Plate, upon Sippits fry'd and dip'd in Mutton or Beef Gravey.

To Farce *Cucumbers*. From the same.

Take large Cucumbers and pare them, then scoop out all the Seeds, first cutting off one End, then prepare the following Farce for them. Take the Hearts of some Cabbage-Lettuce stew'd tender in Salt and Water, drain them well, and chop them small, and cut some Onion very fine, shred a little Parsley that has been boil'd tender, and a Mushroom pickled; and add a little All-Spice finely powder'd, and some Pepper, a little Salt, and some Fat of Bacon chopt small. Mix these well together, with the Yolk of an Egg or two, according to your Quantity, and stuff the Cucumbers full of it. Then tie the Ends, that were cut off close, with Packthread, and stew them in Water and Salt till they are tender; then drain them and flour them, and fry them brown in Hogs-Lard very hot, and let them drain; then take off the Threads that hold them together, and lay them in your Dish, and pour the following Sauce over them: *viz*. Take Gravey well season'd, and as much Claret; boil these together, with some Lemon-Peel, and All-Spice; and thicken this Sauce with burnt Butter. These are good to be serv'd with Mutton Cutlets, as well as alone.

To make a *Shropshire* Pye.

Take a couple of Rabbits, and cut them in pieces; season them well with Pepper and Salt; then cut some pieces of fat Pork, and season them in like manner. Lay these into your Crust, with some pieces of Butter, upon the bottom Crust, and close your Pye. Then pour in half a Pint of Water, and red Wine mixt, and bake it. Some will grate the best part of a Nutmeg upon the Meat, before they close the Pye, which is a very good way. This must be serv'd hot.

To make a *Shropshire* Pye, another way. From Lady *H.*

Take Rabbits and Pork, cut and season'd as above; then make a Farce of the Rabbits Livers parboil'd, and shred small; some fat Bacon shred small, some sweet Marjoram powder'd, some Pepper and Salt, and made into a Paste, with the Yolks of Eggs beaten; and then make this into Balls, and lay them in your Pye, amongst the Meat, at proper Distances. Then take the Bottoms of three or four Artichokes boil'd tender, and cut in Dice; and lay these likewise amongst the Meat. Put in also some Coxcombs blanch'd; then close your Pye, and pour in as much Wine and Water as you think convenient. Bake it, and serve it hot.

To make artificial *Coxcombs.* From Mr. *Renaud.*

Take Tripe, without any Fat, and with a sharp Knife pare away the fleshy part, leaving only the brawny or horny part about the thickness of a Cock's Comb. Then, with a Jagging-Iron, cut Pieces out of it, in the shape of Cocks Combs, and the remaining Parts between, may be cut to pieces, and used in Pyes, and serve every whit as well as Cocks Combs: but those cut in form, please the Eye best; and, as Mr. *Renaud* observes, the Eye must be pleased, before we can taste any thing with Pleasure. And therefore, in Fricassees we should put those which are cut according to Art.

Calf's Liver stuffed and roasted. From the same.

Take a Calf's Liver, the Morning it is kill'd, and make a hole in it, with a large Knife, to run length-ways, but not quite through it; then make a farced Meat, or stuffing for it, of some of the Liver parboil'd, and some Fat of Bacon cut very fine, some fresh Lemon-Peel grated, some sweet Herbs powder'd, and some butter'd Eggs, as much as may be necessary, to mix with the other Ingredients; then add some grated Bread, and some Spices finely beat, with some Pepper and Salt: then fill that part that you cut in the Liver with this farced Meat; and cut other Places if you will, and fill them likewise. You may then lard the Liver, if you will, with Bacon Fat, and roast it, flouring it very well, and basting it with Butter, till it is enough. But it is reckon'd rather better by some, when the Liver is stuffed, to brush it over with the Yolk of an Egg, and strew upon it raspings of Bread sifted, some Flour, some dry'd sweet Herbs powder'd, and some Spice; and then enclose the Whole with the Caul of Veal; so roast it, and it will make an excellent Dish. To be served hot, either with Venison Sauce, made of Claret boil'd with Cinnamon, and sweeten'd with Sugar, or with Gravey Sauce, with a little Wine in it.

To roast a *Calf's* Liver, another way. From Mrs. *M. N.*

Take a Calf's Liver, as before, and stuff it as above, only with this Alteration in the Stuffing. Shred some Veal-Suet very small, and add to that some grated

Bread, Spice, and dry'd sweet Herbs finely powder'd, with some Currans plump'd, and a little Salt; then make this into a Paste, with some Eggs beaten; and when you have stuffed what Parts you please, with the Mixture, roast it, basting it well with Butter, and strewing on, now and then, some of the above Mixture, as far as it can be in powder, or admit of strewing. Then serve it hot, with melted Butter and Lemon-Juice, or Verjuice, and garnish with Lemon sliced, and pickled Berberries.

Cream Custard. From Lady *H.*

Boil a Quart of Cream, with some grated Nutmeg, and a little Mace finely powder'd; then beat the Yolks of twelve Eggs, with half as many Whites, with a little Salt: then add a spoonfull of Sack, and one of Orange-Flower Water, or Rose-Water: then put about six Ounces of fine Loaf-Sugar beaten fine, and well sifted; and mix all together, when the Cream is not too hot; then pass it through a fine Sieve, and bake it in *China* Cups.

To imitate the fat Livers of *Capons* roasted. From the same.

Take a Calf's Liver fresh, and cut it in pieces, in the shape of large Capons Livers. Dip every one in Flour, and spit them on Lark-Spits, the flat Sides against each other, but minding to put between them a slice of fat Bacon. Roast them, and baste them well with Butter, and drudging them often with rasped Bread sifted, and flour with a little Salt. When they are enough, serve them with the following Sauce. Take two or three Necks of Fowls, if you have them, or else, a little clean Beef Gravey, a little Water, a little Ale, or small Beer; an Onion and some Pepper and Salt: then strain off the Sauce, and pour it into the Dish before you lay in your Livers, and garnish with Slices of Lemon, sliced Beet-Roots pickled, and sifted raspings of Bread. These do well likewise to be laid about a roasted Chicken.

To make *Pound Cakes.* From the same.

Take a Pound of double refined Loaf-Sugar beaten and sifted; then beat eight Eggs and stir the Sugar in them; then melt a Pound of Butter, and stir that in with the rest, and then stir in a Pound of Flour, some Mace finely beat, with some Nutmeg grated, and some Sack, and Orange Flower Water; beat these all together for an hour and a half till all is well mix'd; then stir in some Currans plump'd a little. To make good the name of the Cake, there should be a Pound of a sort. Some put about a quarter of a Pound of Caraway Comfits; but every way is good. Bake these in little Pans, in, a gentle Oven, and when they are quite cold, turn them out, and keep them in oaken Boxes, with Papers between them, in a dry Place.

To make a Six Hour Pudding. From the same.

Take a Pound of Beef Suet, pick'd clean from the Skins and bloody Parts, and chop it pretty small; then take a Pound of Raisins of the Sun, and stone them; then shred them, and mix them together: add to them a large spoonfull of Flour, and six Eggs beaten, a little *Lisbon* Sugar, some Salt, and some Cloves, and Mace, beaten. Then mix these well together, and make two Puddings of them, tied up in Cloths well flour'd; boil them six Hours, and serve them with Sugar and Butter in Cups. This will cut very firm, and not taste at all greasy. And if you save one cold, cut it in Slices, and lay it upon a Grid-Iron, under Beef while it is roasting, and it eats very well with Beef Gravey hot.

To make a *Venison* Pasty. From the same.

Take six Pounds of Cambridge potted Butter, and rub it into a peck of Flour, but do not rub in your Butter too small; and then make it into a Paste, with Water: then butter your Pan well, and when your Paste is roll'd out thick, lay it in the Pan, preserving only enough for the Lid. The *Cambridge* Butter is mention'd, because it is a little Salt; or else, if you use fresh Butter, there should be some Salt put into the Crust. When that is prepar'd, take a side of Venison, and take off the Skin, as close as can be, and take the Bones out quite free from the Flesh; then cut this through length-ways, and cut it cross again, to make four Pieces of it; then strew these Pieces with Pepper and Salt, well mix'd, at discretion: and after having laid a little of the Pepper and Salt at the bottom of the Pasty, with some pieces of Butter; then lay in your pieces of Venison, so that at each Corner the Fat may be placed; then lay some Butter over it, in pieces, and close your Pasty. When it is ready for the Oven, pour in about a Quart of Water, and let it bake from five a Clock in the Morning till one in the Afternoon, in a hot Oven. And at the same time put the Skin and the Bones broken, with Water enough to cover them, and some Pepper and Salt into a glaz'd earthen Pan, into the same Oven; and when you draw the Pasty, pour off as much as you think proper, of the clear Liquor, into your Pasty. Serve it hot, but it is properly a side-board Dish, and the Carver ought always to take the Services, of the Pasty, from the Corners where the Fat is, to do honour to the Master and his Park.

To roast a *Hog's* Harslet. From the same.

Take a Hog's Harslet, as soon as the Hog is kill'd, lay aside the Lights, and cut the Liver in thick Slices, and the Heart in thinner Pieces; then take some of the Crow of an Hog, and cut that in Pieces equal with the rest. Then take the Sweetbreads, with some of the Sticking-Pieces, as they are called, and some Slices of fat Bacon. Dip these into Eggs beaten, and then dip them again into grated Bread, some red Sage chopt small, and some Pepper and Salt, with a little sweet Marjoram, or sweet Basil powder'd; then put the Pieces, broad-side one to another, upon a small Spit, always observing to put the Bacon next the Heart, and the Crow next the Liver; then wrap them up in a Cawl of Veal, and roast it. Put these Pieces as close as you can together, and when it is done, serve it with some melted Butter and Mustard, with a little Lemon-Juice.

To make Cream of *Raspberries*. From Mrs. *Heron*.

Take thick Cream, a Quart, and put to that, either some Raspberry Syrup, or some Jamm of Raspberries; but the Syrup will mix much easier with it: however, the Jamm of Raspberries is accounted the best by some, because that has the Seeds in it. But I think, that Syrup of Raspberries is better, because all is smooth, and the Cream tastes sufficiently of the Raspberries. One must serve this with the Desert. But if you use the Jamm of Raspberries, you must beat it with some of the Cream a good while before it will mix; and then put it to the other Cream, and stir it a little, and it will mix.

Artificial Cream, to be mix'd with any Preserves of Fruit. From Mrs. *M. S.* of *Salisbury*.

Take a Quart of Milk, and when it is boil'd, put in the Yolks of eight Eggs well beaten with the Whites of six. Put not in the Eggs while the Milk is too hot, lest they curdle. Then, when they are well mix'd, set them over a gentle Fire, and stir them all the while; and when you perceive them to be thick enough, put into them what quantity you please of Syrup, or Jamms of Apricots, Peaches, or Plums, or Cherries, or Oranges, Lemons, or other Fruits, stirring them well till they partake enough of the preserv'd Fruit's taste, and then serve them up, in *China* Basons, cold, in a Desert, without any Ornament of Flowers.

To make Sweet-meat *Cream*. From the same.

Take either clean Cream from the Dairy, or else make the foregoing artificial Cream, and slice preserv'd Apricots, or preserv'd Peaches or Plums, into it, having first sweeten'd the Cream well, with fine Loaf Sugar, or with the same Syrup they were preserv'd in. Mix these well, and serve them separately, cold, in *China* Basons.

To embalm *Pidgeons*. From a Lady in *Suffolk*.

This Receipt was communicated in this manner: *viz.* Sir, I have seen the Method you propose to embalm Partridges, in your *Farmer's Monthly Director,* and have tried it so far, that I have kept them, done that way, a Month. I had then a mind to try what I could do with Pidgeons; and as soon as they were kill'd, I was diligent to take out all the Blood, and wash them, and dry them, as is directed, with warm Cloths, both inside and outside. I then laid them in Pans of earthen Ware, and cover'd them with melted Butter, which kept them very well, for a long time. I wash'd the Necks of the Pidgeons, when the Crops were taken out, with Vinegar, and dry'd them. Then I used them as you direct for Partridges, and they kept sweet a Month, fit for Roasting; and they eat the same as if they were fresh kill'd. This I send you word of, because you may know how far your embalming of Partridges has taken Effect, and to tell you, the Lady who told you of it, understood very well what she did. As for my part, I used fresh Butter; but you did not say whether it should be salt or fresh, and I try'd Pidgeons, because they are Fowls which decay sooner than any. If you think this worth your Notice,

I am,
Your humble Servant.
S. F.

To preserve *Pidgeons* another way. From the same.

Take Pidgeons fresh kill'd; wash them from the Blood, and take off the Flesh, as clean as you can from the Bones, and discharge all the Inside: then season them well with Pepper and Salt, with a little Mace and Nutmeg grated, and boil them in equal quantities of Vinegar and Water, till they are very tender with Cloves, or other Spice, as you like, and if you add a Bay-leaf or two it will be better. When your Pidgeons are boil'd tender enough, take them from the Fire, and when the Liquor is cold, lay your Pidgeons in a large Gally-pot, and pour the Liquor upon them, and cover them up close with Leather, and they will keep a long time.

An Attempt to preserve *Cucumbers,* for Stewing, in the Winter. From the same.

Sir,

You have often told me, that you was a Lover of Cucumbers, and more especially stew'd, than any other way; which I find many others of my Friends come into. I propose, that you should pare and slice Cucumbers as usual for stewing; and then with a little Salt and Pepper, with their own Liquor stew them in a Sauce-Pan till they are a little tender; then pour them into a Cullendar, and when they are drain'd well from the Liquor, boil some White Wine, with Water, half one, and half the other, with whole Pepper; and when the Liquor is cold, put the Cucumbers into a Gally-pot, and pour the Liquor over them: and, if you put a little Oil upon the Liquor, I am persuaded they will keep several Months. I wish it may be try'd, for I have thought of it; and according to my Judgment it may be fit to use, any time in the Winter, for stewing.

When you use these, pour away all the Liquor, and let them pass through a Saucepan with a little Salt and Water, till they are tender, as you would have them; then drain them again in a Cullendar, and fry them brown, with burnt

Butter, first flouring them, and a little Pepper; and when they are enough, put in a Glass of Claret, or a Glass of White Wine.

I am,
Your humble Servant.
　S. F.

Pippin Tart. From the same.

Cut some golden Pippins in halves, pare them, and take out the Cores; then stew them with half their weight of Sugar, and some Lemon-Peel, cut in thin long Slices, and Water enough to cover them. When they are clear, they are enough; then set them by to cool, and strain off the Liquor, or Syrup, and put that in a Pan to stew gently, with some candy'd Lemon and Orange-Peel, in slices; then have a sweet Paste prepared in a Dish, and lay in your Pippins, and pour the Syrup, and Sweetmeats, over them, and bake them in a gentle Oven; and when it is hot, pour some Cream either pure or artificial over them, and serve them to the Table.

To Pickle *Marygold-Flowers.* From Mr. *T.* of *Buckingham.*

Though the Marygold Flower is of old date in Pottage; yet it continues still its stand among the useful things of the Kitchen, and cannot more easily be worn out, according to the custom of the Country, when the Country Folks make Broth. Mint with Pease, Fennel with Mackarel, and such like, cannot be forgot. And as the Marygold-Flowers are used in Porridge, I send the Receipt how to pickle them. Strip the Flower-leaves off, when you have gather'd the Flowers, at Noon, or in the Heat of the Day, and boil some Salt and Water; and when that is cold, put your Marygold-Flower Leaves in a Gallypot, and pour the Salt and Water upon them; then shut them up close till you use them, and they will be of a fine Colour, and much fitter for Porridge than those that are dry'd.

Seed-Cake. From the same.

Make some Paste of fine Flour, such as you would make for light Bread, with Yeast. Take five Pounds of this Dough, Without Salt in it, and cover it before a Fire for half an Hour, to make it rise; then take two Pounds and a half of fresh Butter melted, and five Eggs beaten well with half a Pound of fine *Lisbon* Sugar. Mix these well with your Paste, and work it till it is as light as possible; and when your Oven is very hot and clean, strew into your Cake a Pound of smooth Caraway Comfits; then put some Butter on the Sides and Bottom of your Pan, and put in your Cake, and one Hour and a quarter will bake it. When it comes out of the Oven, cover it with Cloths of Linnen till it is cold; then put it, the next Day, a little while into an Oven. *N.B.* You must be sure to put in the Sugar after the Butter. One may put on an Iceing if one will.

To make Orange-Chips. From the same.

Take some fresh Oranges about *February,* and pare them very thin; they are then very cheap. Boil them in several Waters till they are tender, and have lost their Bitterness; then put them into cold Water for twelve Hours or more. Then make a Syrup for them in the following manner. Take about their weight of fine Sugar powder'd, and mix it with as much Water as it will take in, or a little more. Boil this, and scum it well; then drain the Orange-Peels from the Water they were steep'd in, and put them in a glaz'd earthen Vessel, and then pour the boiling hot Syrup upon them, letting them remain so till the Day following; then pour the Syrup from them, and boil it afresh, and pour it on a second time, and repeat the same work till your Peels are very clear, and the Syrup very thick; and then dry them in a Stove, and they will be fit for use, in the Condition we buy them. One may candy Lemon-Chips after the same manner.

To make *Hartshorn-Jelly.* From the same.

Take six Ounces of Harts-horn Shavings; put them into two Quarts of Water, and two or three bits of Lemon-Peel, and set this in a Sand-heat, for six or eight Hours, or let them infuse about ten Hours upon hot Embers. Then boil it briskly, and when you find it will jelly, as you may do, by taking out a little of the Liquor in a Spoon, and cooling it; then strain it off, and add to it about half a Pound of double-refined Sugar powder'd very fine; about a Gill of Sack, or two or three spoonfuls of Mountain Wine, the Juice of two Lemons; then set this on a slow Fire, and as it heats, beat the Whites of two Eggs to a froth, and put it into the Pan, where the Jelly is, at times as it rises; and then, when it just boils up, take it from the Fire, and it will be clarified. Then pour it by small quantities into the Jelly-bag, and let it drop or run into some Receiver; but it will be apt to run thick at first: then take that which is first run, if it be thick, and pour again into the Jelly-bag, and you will find it come clear. Then place your Glasses to receive it, and change the full one for another, which you must carefully watch, that your Glasses be not soil'd in the least, for the Beauty of this, in one particular, is its transparency; and again, it should not be too stiff. Some only take the Harts-horn Shavings, six Ounces to two Quarts of Water, and boil it gently till the Liquor will jelly, without the expence of a Sand-heat, or setting it on hot Embers. The boiling it is the best way, but requires more Patience.

To make a Tart of the *Ananas,* or *Pine-Apple.* From Barbadoes.

Take a Pine-Apple, and twist off its Crown: then pare it free from the Knots, and cut it in Slices about half an Inch thick; then stew it with a little Canary Wine, or Madera Wine, and some Sugar, till it is thoroughly hot, and it will distribute its Flavour to the Wine much better than any thing we can add to it.

When it is as one would have it, take it from the Fire; and when it is cool, put it into a sweet Paste, with its Liquor, and bake it gently, a little while, and when it comes from the Oven, pour Cream over it, (if you have it) and serve it either hot or cold.

Marmalade of *Pine-Apples,* or *Ananas.*

When you have small Pine-Apples in Fruit, which are not noble enough to be brought to the Table, twist off their Crowns, and pare them; then slice them, and put them into a Syrup of Water, Sugar, and Pippins; and boil them with half their quantity of Sugar added to them, with a little White Wine, breaking them with a Spoon, as they boil, till they come to a Mash, or are a little tender. Then take them from the Fire, and put the Marmalade into Glasses to keep, and cover every Glass with white Paper, preserving them in a dry Place.

To dress the Giblets of a *Tortoise,* or *Sea-Turtle.* From a *Barbadoes* Lady.

Take the Head, the Feet, and the Tail, of either of these, and taking off their Scales, stew them three or four Hours, in Salt and Water, till they are almost tender; then broil them a little with Pepper and Salt on them, and then put them into a Stew-pan with a Shallot, and some Spice and sweet Herbs, according to your Taste; some strong Gravey, and some Wine, and thicken the Sauce, taking out the bunch of sweet Herbs. You may put then some Juice of Limes to them, or Chadocks or Lemons, to make them fine. *N.B.* This is a dainty Dish, if they are broil'd, after the first stewing, because as they are sinewey, the Sinews ought to be a little scorched by broiling, or else they will not be so tender as one would have them.

There are two Sorts of Tortoises, the Land, and the Sea-Tortoise; but the Sea-Tortoise or Turtle, is what I mean, which is that which we have about the *West-Indies.* This is a fine Animal, partaking of the Land and Water. Its Flesh between that of Veal, and that of a Lobster, and is extremely pleasant, either roasted or baked. There are some of these Creatures that weigh near two hundred Weight. They are frequently brought to *England* in Tubs of Sea Water, and will keep alive a long time.

To roast a Piece of *Turtle,* or *Tortoise.* From the same.

Take a piece of the Flesh of about five or six Pounds, and lay it in Salt and Water two Hours; then stick a few Cloves in it, and fasten it to the Spit, baste it at first with Wine and Lemon-Juice; and when it is near enough, drudge some Flour over it, with the raspings of Bread sifted; and then baste it well, either with Oil, or Butter, strewing on, from time to time, more Flour and Raspings till it is enough; then take the Liquor in the Pan, and pouring off the Fat, boil it with some Lemon-Peel, and a little Sugar and Salt, and pour it over the Turtle. So serve it hot.

To make a *Turtle,* or _Tortoise-_Pye. From the same.

Cut the Flesh of Turtle, or Tortoise, into Slices, about an Inch thick; then take Cloves beaten fine, with some Pepper and Salt, and a little sweet Herbs, and season your Pieces with them; then lay them in your Crust, with some Lemons sliced, and a quarter of a Pint of Oil-Olive pour'd over them, Or else some Butter laid in bits upon them. In the cutting your Pieces, distribute your Fat and Lean, equally as may be; and though the Fat is of a greenish colour, it is yet very delicious: then close your Pye, and just before you put it in the Oven, pour in some White Wine, and bake it in a gentle Oven till it is tender. Then serve it hot.

To preserve *Ginger-Roots.* From the same.

Take Roots of Ginger, as we have them dry in *England*; wash them well, and lay one Pound of them to steep, ten or twelve Days, in White Wine and Water, stirring them every Day. Then take two Quarts of White Wine, and about half a Pint of Lemon-Juice, and boil them together a quarter of an Hour; then add two Pounds and a half of fine Sugar, and boil it to a Syrup, taking off the Scum as it rises; then put in your Ginger, and boil it a quarter of an Hour; then let it cool in a glazed Pan till the next Day, and then boil it again in the Syrup for half an Hour, and let it cool, as before, till the Day following, and repeat the boiling and cooling till your Ginger is clear, and put it into your Glasses, and cover them with Papers. It makes a fine Sweet-meat for the Winter.

To preserve *Ginger-Roots,* fresh taken out of the Ground. From the same.

As Ginger is very common in the *West-Indies*, so the Roots are either preserved or pickled, when they are fresh taken out of the Ground, and we have now Ginger, growing in Pots, almost in every Garden where there is a Stove; and in a Year's time a single Root will almost fill a Pot; so that one might easily have enough of our own, to preserve every Year. We must take them up, when they have no Leaves upon them; and then scald them in Water, and rub them with a coarse Cloth till they are dry; then put them into White Wine and Water, and boil them half an. Hour; then let them cool, and boil them again half an Hour. Then make a Syrup with White Wine two Quarts, half a Pint of Lime or Lemon-Juice, and two Pounds and a half of fine Sugar, with two Ounces of the Leaves of Orange-Flowers. When these boil together, put in your Ginger, and boil it gently half an Hour; then let it cool in an earthen glaz'd Vessel, and continue to boil it every Day, and cooling it till the Roots of your Ginger are clear. Then put it up in Gallypots, or in Glasses, and cover them with Papers, to keep for use.

To make Paste of *Pippins,* or other fine Apples. From the same.

Take large Golden-Pippins, or Golden-Rennets, and scald them, with their Skins on; then pare them, and take out the Cores, and beat them in a Marble Mortar very well, with a little Lemon-Peel grated. Take then their weight of fine Sugar, and a little Water, and boil that in a Skillet to a candy height; then put in your Apples, and boil them thick in the Syrup till they will leave the Skillet, and when it is almost cold, work it up with fine Loaf-Sugar powder'd, and mould it into Cakes, then dry them.

To preserve *Cornelian-Cherries.* From the same.

Take Cornelian-Cherries, when they are full ripe, and take their weight in fine Sugar powder'd; then put these into your preserving Pan, and lay a Layer of Sugar, and another of Fruit; and so on till you have laid all in, covering them with Sugar; then pour upon them half a Pint of White Wine, and set it on the Fire, and as soon as the Sugar is all melted, boil them up quick, and take off the Scum as it rises, stirring them every now and then: and when the Fruit is clear, they are enough. Then put them into Glasses, and cover them with Papers.

To make *Marmalade* of *Cornelian-Cherries.* From the same.

When your Cornelian-Cherries are full ripe, take out the Stones, and to every Pound of Fruit, take its weight of fine Sugar powder'd. Wet it with White Wine, and boil it to a candy'd height; then put in your Fruit, with the Juice that comes from them; then boil them very quick, and stir it often, scumming it clean; and when you see it very clear, and of a good Consistence, put it into a glaz'd earthen Pan; and when it is almost cold, put it into Glasses, and cover them with white Paper, and keep it in a dry Room. *Note,* If you let any of these sharp Fruits stand to cool in your Sweet-meat-Pans, they will take an ill taste from them.

To make *Jamm* of *Damsons.* From the same.

Take Damsons, full ripe, a Gallon; pick them from the Stalks, that may happen to be about them, and the Leaves that are sometimes gather'd with them: then take near their weight of Sugar, and about a Quart of Water, and boil them well together, and put in your Damsons, and boil them till they are tender, breaking them with a Spoon, all the while, till the whole is thicken'd. Then put it in Gallypots, and set it to cool; then close the Pots down with Leather.

To preserve *Currans* in *Jelly.* From the same.

Take some of the large *Dutch* red or white Currans, when they are ripe, and pick them from the Stalks; then, with a Pin, pick out the Stones; or, you may, if you will, leave them on the Stalks, if they are large Bunches, but still pick out the Kernels. Then take their weight in Sugar, and wet it with a little Water, and add a little Syrup of Raspberries to it; then boil it to a Syrup, scumming it as it rises: then put in your Currans, and boil them up quick, shaking them often, still taking off the Scum as it rises. They will be enough done to put up, when the Syrup will jelly, as you may try by putting some in a Spoon, and letting it cool. When you find this, pour out all into Glasses, when it has cool'd a little. If your Currans are pick'd from the Stalks, or if they are in Bunches, then let the Syrup be half cold, and pour it into the Glasses; and then put in your Bunches, placing them as you would have them situated, and as it cools, they will fix in their several Stations; cover the Glasses then with white Paper.

Note, The red Currans ought to be done by themselves, and the white by themselves, for both together will make a disagreeable Mixture.

To dry *Apricots*. From Mrs. *Walsingham* of *Suffolk*.

Chuse for this use, the large Turkey or Roman-Apricot, almost ripe; Stone them, and pare them; then throw them into cold Water, with the Parings; weigh the pared Apricots, and prepare an equal weight of fine Sugar powder'd; then put some of the Water the Apricots were steep'd in, to the Sugar, and boil them to a candy'd height: you may then put in your Apricots, and boil them till they are clear, and when they have lain a few Days, in the Syrup, lay them upon a fine Wyre-Sieve, and dry them in a warm Place. Then, when they are done, put them in oaken Boxes, with Papers between them.

To stew a Rump of *Beef*. From Mrs. L——

Take a small Rump of Beef, lay it in a long Pan, deep enough to allow your Beef to be cover'd; then put to it a Pint of Ale, a Quart of Claret, half a Pint of Verjuice, or the Juice of two large Lemons; and as much Water added, as will make Liquor enough to cover it, a Crust of Bread burnt, an Anchovy, some bits of Lemon-Peel, a bunch of sweet Herbs, two large *Hertfordshire* Turnips cut in dice, two large Onions cut in halves, some Pepper and Salt, a Nutmeg sliced, a few Cloves, and a little Mace. Stop this close, and let it stew, at least, five Hours; then lay your Beef in the Dish, and pass the Liquor through a Sieve, and fill the Dish with it; garnishing with Turnips, cut in Dice, boil'd tender, and then fry'd in Hog's-Lard, and sliced Lemon, or you may bake your Rump of Beef, if you will, for it is much the same. And this way you may likewise bake or stew a Leg of Beef, or an Ox-Cheek, only break the Bones of the Leg of Beef, and take out all the Bones of the Ox-Cheek, and take especially Care to clean it, for it requires some nicety to do it well.

Pepper-Mint Water, From the same.

Take Pepper-Mint six handfuls, cut it a little, and infuse it two Days in six

Quarts of clean Spirit; then draw it off in a cold Still, marking every Bottle, as it fills, with a Number, for the first Bottle will be far the strongest, the second less strong, and the third weaker than the second; and so as we draw off more, they will be still weaker, till at last it becomes almost insipid, and somewhat sourish, but take none of that; then cover the Mouth of your Bottles with Papers prick'd full of Holes, and let them stand a Day or two; then pour your first Bottle into a large earthen glaz'd Pan; and to that the second, and then the third, and the fourth, and so on, till by mixing they all become of a sufficient strength; then put them in Bottles, with a Knob or two of double-refin'd Loaf-Sugar, and cork them close. This is an incomparable pleasant Dram, tasting like Ice, or Snow, in the Mouth, but creates a fine warmth in the Stomach, and yields a most refreshing Flavour.

This Sort of Mint is hard to be met with; but is lately cultivated in some Physick Gardens at *Mitcham*. It must be kept well weeded, and the top of the Bed, where it grows, must, when we cut it, be pricked up, a little, with a small Fork, or the Earth made fine with a Trowel; because the Runners, of this sort of Mint, shoot along upon the Surface of the Ground, and so at the Joints strike Root, which is contrary to other Sorts of Mint, which shoot their Runners under ground.

Damson-Wine to imitate *Claret*. From the same.

Take nine Gallons of Water, make it scalding hot, and pour it upon six and thirty Pounds of *Malaga* Raisins well pick'd from the Stalks. The Raisins should be sound, or they will spoil your Wine. While the Water is yet hot, put into the Liquor half a Peck of Damsons full ripe, and pick'd clean of the Stalks and Leaves, to each Gallon of Liquor; then stir them all together in the open Tub we make this Infusion in, and continue stirring them twice a Day for six Days. Keep this Tub cover'd with a Cloth all that time: then let it stand five or six Days longer, without stiring, and then draw it off: and if it is not deep-colour'd enough, put a little Syrup of Mulberries to it, and work it with a piece of White-Bread toasted, and spread with Yeast or Barm, in an open Vessel; and then tun it, keeping the Bung of the Vessel open till the Wine has done singing in the Cask. Then slop it close, and let it stand till it is clear, which will be in two or three Months; then draw it off. Some will just give their Damsons a scald in the Water before they pour it on the Raisins, which is a good way.

To Cure a *Lap-Dog,* when he continues drowsy some Days, and cannot eat. From the same.

If you find a Lap-Dog to be sleepy, and will not take his Victuals for two or three Days; or if he eats, and as often discharges it soon after; take a large Tea-spoon-full of Rum or Brandy, and as much Water, and holding his Head up, and his Mouth open with one Hand, pour it down his Throat. This is quantity enough for one of the smallest Dogs, and will cure him in less than half an Hour; but as the Dogs are larger, you may give to the biggest a large spoonful of Rum or Brandy equally mix'd with Water, and so in proportion to the size of the Dog. It is a sure Remedy.

Dog-Grass, or *Couch-Grass,* or *Twitch-Grass,* necessary to be had, growing in Pots in *London,* to cure *Lap-Dogs,* that are sick, in the Summer. From the same.

Couch-Grass is one of the Gardener's Plagues, and is in every Garden too much. Take a Clump of this, and set it in a large Garden-Pot, and letting it stand as airy as possible, water it gently every other Morning. There is one sort of it, which is finely variegated, the Leaves appearing like striped Ribbons. This fine sort is at the Ivy-House at *Hoxton,* where it may be put in Pots at any time. This, or the other, should be put to a Dog, at any time, when he is sick, and he will eat it greedily, and cure himself; but for want of this Help, which favourite Lap-Dogs in *London* want, they lose their briskness. I believe it would be worth some poor Woman's while to sell this Grass, in *London,* where so many fine Lap-Dogs are kept, and indulged so much, that they cannot be taken abroad to search their Physick; while those of the larger kind take their way abroad, in the Mornings, at their pleasure. This, Sir, I send you with some other Receipts, because Dogs are not a little useful about a Farm, and the little ones are no less agreeable to their Keepers. And I am sure, if you publish these, they will prove very acceptable to many Ladies, and Gentlemen, who are Admirers of these faithful Creatures.

I am, &c. J. L.

Lisbon or *Portugal-Cakes.* From the same_,_

Take a Pound of double-refin'd Loaf-Sugar beaten fine, and past through a fine Sieve. Mix this with a Pound of fine Flour; then rub into these a Pound of fresh or new Butter, till your Sugar and Flour looks like Bread-Crumbs; then add, two or three spoonfulls of Orange-Flower-Water, and about ten spoonfuls of Canary-Wine: then beat ten Eggs, till their Whites are whipt to Snow, and mix the Eggs, with the rest, with a quarter of a Pound of blanched Almonds beaten in a Marble Mortar, with some Orange-Flower Water; and when you have butter'd your Pans well, fill them half full with this Mixture, and bake them, if you make them without Currans, or else fill the Pans fuller, first plumping the Currans, which should be in proportion, as you please.

Imperial Florentine. From *Mr. Byecorf* at *Augsburgh.*

Cut the leanest part of a Leg of Veal, in thin Slices, and beat them with the Back of a Knife, as you would do *Scots* Collups; then season the Cutlets with

Cloves, Pepper beaten fine to powder, some Pepper and Salt, with some Nutmeg grated, a little dry'd sweet Marjoram powder'd, or some sweet Basil. Lay this Mixture pretty thick upon them, and roll them up with a little Piece of fat Bacon, in the middle; then lay in your Paste to the Dish, and over the Bottom strew a little Pepper, Salt, and Nutmeg, with some Balls of farced Meat, with bits of Butter, placed here and there. Put in then your rolls of Veal, with some Cocks-Combs blanched, a quarter of a Pint of Mushroom Buttons pickled, some Slices of Lemon, with half a Pint of White Wine, and about a Pint of Water; then close your Pye, and when it is baked, serve it hot. *N.B.* Before you close it, put some bits of Butter on the top of your Rolls of Meat.

To make Farced Meat, for the foregoing *Florentine*. From the same.

Take the Lean of a Leg of Veal, chop it small, and beat it well in a Marble Mortar, with as much Fat of the Kidney of Veal; and then put some Pepper, Salt, Cloves, Nutmeg, Powder of dry'd sweet Marjoram, and some Mushrooms, chopt as you please; then add as many Eggs, beaten as you think proper, with some grated Bread, to make it into a Paste, and roll this Mixture into Balls. Some instead of the Kidney-Fat of Veal, will chop the same quantity of fat Bacon.

To make a Tart of white *Beet-Cards*. From the same.

Take some white Beet-Cards, (or Leaves) as much Spinach-Leaves, and the same quantity of *French* Sorrel, which has a round Leaf. Chop these small, or if you beat them all together in a Marble Mortar, it is better; then strain out the Juice, and put it amongst the same proportion, or quantity, of the same Herbs, fresh cut, that is, put the Liquor to as many Herbs as you cut before, and shred them; then add to them about five Ounces of good Sugar, and you may put as much Currans. Mix these well, and bake them; then pour over it, while it is hot, some Cream that has been boil'd thick, and serve it hot: but if you use raw Cream, from the Dairy, you must mix it with the Ingredients, and then strew fine powder'd Sugar over it, but serve it hot, let it be which way you will.

To make a Preserve of *Quinces*, white in *Jelly*. From the same.

Make a Syrup of Golden-Pippins, or Golden-Rennets; and to make that, pare your Apples, and core them, but never use two sorts together, for one will be soft before the other is half done. Always take this for a Rule in Apples, Onions, and Turnips; they should be all of one kind, and all from the same Place, or else you will be disappointed. Boil your Apples with their weight in Sugar, and as much Water as will mix with it: boil this to a Jelly, and in the mean time, pare your Quinces, and cut them in Quarters, taking them clear off the Core; then boil them, first in fair Water, till they are a little tender, and then put them into the boiling Syrup, and keep them gently boiling half an Hour, or what one might more properly call stewing. If the Quinces are not then clear, boil them again, the next Day, in the same Liquor; and when the Quinces are as clear as they can be, which is never very much like other Fruits, but we should rather say tender, put them into Gallypots, or Glasses, and pour the Syrup, or Jelly, over them, to keep; and as soon as they are cold, then put Papers over them.

To Candy whole *Orange,* or *Lemon-Peels.*

Take some of the fairest Oranges, or Lemons, and cut a small hole in the top of them; then scoop out all the Pulp, as clean as possible; lay these in Water to steep eight or ten Days, shifting them to fresh Waters twice a Day; then boil them in several Waters, till they are tender enough to run a Straw through them. Then take one Pound of double-refin'd Loaf-Sugar to each Pound of Peel, and a Quart of Water: then make your Syrup, and boil your Peels in it eight or ten Minutes, and let them stand in your Syrup five or six Days, in an earthen glaz'd Vessel, for it would spoil in a Brass or Copper Pan: then to every Pound put one Pound more of Sugar into your Syrup, and boil your Peels in it, till they are clear; then put them into Gallypots, and boil your Syrup till it is almost of a Candy height, and pour it upon your Peels; and when it is cold, cover it. The same manner they preserve the Peels of green Oranges, Lemons, and Limes, in *Barbadoes.*

To stew *Soles.* From *Yarmouth.*

Take the largest Soles you can get, gut them, and skin them; lay them then into a Stew-pan, and pour in about a Pint of good Beef Gravey, and as much Claret; some bits of Lemon-Peel, an Anchovy or two, a stick of Horse-Radish, a bunch of sweet Herbs, a large Onion, half a large Nutmeg, some Cloves and Mace, whole Pepper, and Salt, with a little bit of Butter. Then stew these till the Fish is enough, and pour off the Liquor, through a Sieve, and thicken it with burnt Butter, having first put to it the Juice of a Lemon. Then pour the Sauce over the Fish, and garnish with Lemon sliced, and the Roots of red Beets pickled and sliced, with Horse-Radish scraped, and fry'd Bread.

A Hash of raw *Beef.* From Mr. *Moring* at the Blue-Posts *Temple-Bar.*

Cut some thin Slices of tender Beef, and put them in a Stew-Pan, with a little Water, a bunch of sweet Herbs, some Lemon-Peel, an Onion, with some Pepper, Salt, and some Nutmeg. Cover these close, and let them stew till they are tender; then pour in a Glass or two of Claret; and when it is warm, clear your Sauce of the Onion, Herbs, *&c.* and thicken it with burnt Butter. It is an excellent Dish. Serve it hot, and garnish with Lemon diced, and red Beet-Roots, Capers, and such like.

Thin *Beef-Collups* stew'd. From *Oxford.*

Cut raw Beef in thin Slices, as you would do Veal, for *Scots* Collups; lay them in a Dish, with a little Water, a Glass of Wine, a Shallot, some Pepper and Salt, and a little sweet Marjoram powdered; then clap another Dish over that, having first put a thin slice or two of fat Bacon among your Collups: then set your Mess, so as to rest upon the backs of two Chairs, and take six Sheets of whited-brown Paper, and tear it in long Pieces; and then lighting one of them, hold it under the Dish, till it burns out, then light another, and so another till all your Paper is burnt; and then your Stew will be enough, and full of Gravey, Some will put in a little Mushroom Gravey, with the Water, and the other Ingredients, which is yet a very good way.

Stew'd *Beef-Steaks.* From the *Spring-Gardens* at *Vaux-Hall, Surrey.*

Take good Rump-Beef Steaks, and season them with Pepper and Salt; then lay them into the Pan, and pour in a little Water; then add a bunch of sweet Herbs a few Cloves, an Anchovy, a little Verjuice, an Onion, and a little Lemon-Peel, with a little bit of Butter, or fat Bacon, and a Glass of White Wine. Cover these close, and stew them gently, and when they are tender, pour away the Sauce, and strain it; then take out the Steaks, and flour them, and fry them; and when you put them in the Dish, thicken the Sauce, and pour it over them. This way was much approved.

To make *Cologn's-Geneva.* From *Cologn.*

Take good Brandy, one Gallon; then take two Pounds of Juniper-berries fresh gather'd, and full ripe. Press these till you perceive a greenish Liquor come from them; then put them into the Brandy, and let them remain about ten Days: then pour them through a Cloth of coarse Linnen, and squeeze it, and when you have the Liquor, if you find it too strong, you may add to it some more Brandy, and half a Pound of fine Sugar to a Gallon. Then put it in Flasks, or Bottles.

Then take the Pressings, and infuse them again in Brandy, for six or seven Days, and distil them. This they call double *Cologn's* Gin, and the best is sold in *Holland,* at three Shillings and Six-pence *per* Quart.

To make *Scots-Snuff,* or pure *Tobacco-Snuff.* From Mr. *Hyslop.*

Take the Leaves of good Tobacco, and spread them open; then dry them gently in the Sun, or before the Fire, and strip them from the Stalks; when the leafy part will crumble, between the Fingers; then put it into a Mill, and with a Pestle rolling about it, the Tobacco will presently be ground, as fine as Snuff; or else, if you have never a Mill, when your Tobacco will break between the Fingers, lay it on an oaken Table, and pass the flat side of a Knife over it, backwards and forwards, as if you was whetting it, pressing it hard, and you will make fine Snuff. This I mention here, because, sometimes, the Snuff-takers are without Snuff, and remote from any Place where it may be had, and would give any Money for it; which was my Case, when I learn'd this Receipt, and by the last Means was presently supplied: we may make it likewise of cut Tobacco dry'd before the Fire.

Or if we raise Tobacco in our Gardens, pick the Leaves from the Stalks, towards the Root, when they are full grown, tie six in a bunch together, and hang them up to dry in the Shade; then dip them in Water, or some Beer or Ale, and hang them up again to dry, and then press the Leaves one upon another, in their Bunches, in a Box or Tub, as hard as possible; and in a few Months time, they will make very good Snuff, being order'd as above directed.

Butter turned to *Oil* recovered. From Mrs. *M. N.*

There are some Lands, as well as some Treatments of Butter in the Dairy, that makes the Butter so very fat and greasy, that it is hard to melt, without running to Oil; while, on the other hand, there is a sort of Butter, which cuts as firm as Wax; and even this will sometimes turn to Oil in the melting, but very seldom. However, when it so happens, pour your oil'd Butter into a Porringer, and letting it stand a little, melt a little fresh, and as soon as it is liquid, pour into it, by gentle degrees, at times, some of the Butter that was oil'd before, keeping your Sauce-pan shaking all the while; and if you find it any way difficult to be recovered, pour in a little Milk, and shake them together, and it will recover. *Memorandum*, A Sauce-pan that is very thin at the Bottom is apt to oil Butter, let it be ever so good.

Orange or *Lemon-Cakes*. From the same.

Take some preserv'd Orange or Lemon-Peels, wash'd from their Syrup; then beat them, in a Marble Mortar, to a Pulp, adding a little Orange-Flower Water to them, and a very little Gum-Arabic to it powder'd, this will become a Paste; then mould it into Cakes, with double-refined Sugar beaten fine, and dry them; they must then be laid in Boxes, between sheets of white Paper, and kept in a dry Place.

To dry *Plums,* of any sort, without *Sugar*. From the same.

Take a Wyre Sieve, and gather your Plums, not too ripe, nor in the heat of the Day; run a Needle through the Skin of each of them, and lay them on the Sieve, so as not to touch one another. Put your Sieve then into a declining Oven, and let it stand twelve Hours; then set it by, and repeat the same the second and third time, and if the Plums are large, then it may be they will require the fourth or fifth time; but turn them every time, when you are going to put them in the Oven. They will dry by this Means so well, that you may keep them all the Winter, for use, in Boxes, in a dry Place. *Memorandum*, Some of them will candy on the Outsides. The Mussel-Plum is a very good one for this use.

The *Shropshire* and *Worcestershire-Dish*. From the same.

Sir,

If you would please all People, by the several Receipts you publish, you ought to have the particular Dish that is the Favourite of every County. In *Worcestershire* and *Shropshire*, the following is in esteem, and I believe you will oblige several Gentlemen and Ladies of these Parts, if you would insert it in some of your Works.

Take some good middling Bacon, and fry it; then put in some Calf's Liver, and cut it in thick Pieces, pepper it, and salt it; and when it is enough, for it must not be fry'd hard, have ready prepared some Cabbage-Lettuce, some white Beet-Cards, or Beet-Leaves, and some Spinach-Leaves, and chop them together, with some Parsley, but not too small; then chop some Onion, and mix with the rest; then throw them into your Frying pan, with a piece of Butter, when the Bacon and Liver is out, and fry them till they are tender, and as brown as may be; putting in a spoonful of Verjuice, or the Juice of a Lemon, a little before they are enough. And having kept the Liver and Bacon hot all the while, pour these Herbs over them, which ought to be in good quantity.

Fine *Cakes* to keep. From the same.

Take a Pound of fine Sugar powder'd, and somewhat less than a Quart of Flour. Rub these with a Pound of fresh Butter, and mix it with three or four Yolks of Eggs, with some Orange-Flower Water, and a little Ale-Yeast: set this Paste before the Fire to rise, and roll out your Cakes thin, while the Paste is hot; then cut them into what Shapes you please, and prick them on the top, and bake them in a gentle Oven. They will keep a long time and are very good.

To make *Penzance-Cakes*. From the same.

Take the Yolks of Eggs well beaten, put to them some Mace finely powder'd, with a few spoonfuls of Wine, a little Salt, and as much Sugar as you please; then add as much Flour as is necessary, and a small quantity of Ale-Yeast, and work your Dough pretty stiff; then add some fresh Butter, broken in little bits, and work it in till all the Paste has partaken of it, and the Dough becomes as stiff as at first. Make your Cakes then, and bake them. They will keep some time.

To make Crystal candy'd *Sweet-meats*. From the same.

When we propose to make these candy'd Sweet-meats, we must first know what Fruits, Flowers, *&c.* are proper for them, and how those ought to be gathered and prepared.

First of all, to begin with the Flowers. Take Orange-Flowers, or Lemon, or Citron-Flowers; gather them, when the Dew is upon them, in the Morning, because the Leaves of them will be then full, and then they are best to use, when the Leaves are pick'd off, and then the Dew will be gone; but if they lie a Day, they will shrink, turn bitter, and of a yellowish brown Colour. Take these Leaves fresh pick'd, and pour the following Composition upon them.

You may take also some Orange, or Lemon, or Citron, preserved, and dry'd, and cut them in small pieces. Or Apricots dry'd and cut into small pieces, or such sorts as are a little hard in themselves will do. If one was to cut some Pine-Apple, or Ananas, simply or preserv'd, and cut that in pieces, it would be entomb'd in a Rock of Sugar; or Currans preserv'd upon their Stalks may do, if you think it worth while; but Orange-Flower-Leaves do very well. It is a fine Candy to carry in the Pocket.

Then to begin your Business. Take one Pound of double-refined Loaf-Sugar beat small, and finely sifted; mix this with four or five spoonfuls of Orange-Flower-Water, and about half a Drachm of Gum-Arabic finely beaten; then put three spoonfuls of White Wine, and mix all together, and boil them in a glazed earthen Vessel till the Liquor will hardly run, or at least run in Ropes; then have small Jars of earthen Ware glazed, and put into each of them the several sorts of Fruits, and Flowers, you would inclose in candy'd Sugar, making those Jars very hot, and immediately pour the Liquor upon them, and stop them close; then put the Jars into a Stove, for a fortnight or more, and you may then break the Jars, and your several Fruits and Flowers will be inclosed in a crystal like Candy, such as white Sugar Candy. And then with a slight blow of an Hammer, break these Candies into Pieces of about a Finger's length, and keep them in Glasses stopt close, in a dry Place, and they will remain good several Years. The little Pots must be broken of course.

To make a *Hackin*. From a Gentleman in *Cumberland*.

Sir,

There are some Counties in *England*, whose Customs are never to be set aside; and our Friends in *Cumberland*, as well as some of our Neighbours in *Lancashire*, and else-where, keep them up. It is a Custom with us every *Christmas*-Day in the Morning, to have, what we call an Hackin, for the Breakfast of the young Men who work about our House; and if this Dish is not dressed by that time it is Day-light, the Maid is led through the Town, between two Men, as fast as they can run with her, up Hill and down Hill, which she accounts a great shame. But as for the Receipt to make this Hackin, which is admired so much by us, it is as follows.

Take the Bag or Paunch of a Calf, and wash it, and clean it well with Water and Salt; then take some Beef-Suet, and shred it small, and shred some Apples, after they are pared and cored, very small. Then put in some Sugar, and some Spice beaten small, a little Lemon-Peel cut very fine, and a little Salt, and a good quantity of Grots, or whole Oat-meal, steep'd a Night in Milk; then mix these all together, and add as many Currans pick'd clean from the Stalks, and rubb'd in a coarse Cloth; but let them not be wash'd. And when you have all ready, mix them together, and put them into the Calf's-Bag, and tye them up, and boil them till they are enough. You may, if you will, mix up with the whole, some Eggs beaten, which will help to bind it. This is our Custom to have ready, at the opening of the Doors, on *Christmas*-Day in the Morning. It is esteem'd here; but all that I can say to you of it, is, that it eats somewhat like a *Christmas*-Pye, or is somewhat like that boil'd. I had forgot to say, that with the rest of the Ingredients, there should be some Lean of tender Beef minced small.

The *Northampton-Cake.*

Take a Peck of Flour, and a Pound of fine Sugar beaten well into Powder, and sifted; then add a quarter of an Ounce of Cloves, half an Ounce of Cinnamon, and a large Nutmeg, and beat them to powder; put to this some Orange-Flower-Water, or Rose-Water; then take five or six Pounds of Currans well pick'd, and rub'd dry with a coarse Cloth, but not wash'd. Put these with your Fruit, and a little Salt into the Flour; then take as much Cream as you think proper: then melt two Pounds of Butter, to mix with it, and add a Pint of Canary-Wine, and kneed it with some fresh Ale-Yeast, till it rises under your hand. Have your Oven hot before you put it in the Hoop for Baking.

Of the Baking of Fruit. From Mr. *L. M.*

It is to be observed, that all Fruits that are ripe require little baking, and those which are of the hardest, or most unripe Sorts, ought to have a long and gentle baking. In Pears, for example, when we have some of those, which ripen in the Autumn, they will bake with a Tart; for as they are ripe of themselves, they require very little baking, for Ripeness is one degree tending to Rottenness; and as that is done by heat gently, so the Oven brings that to a certain height, suddenly, with its safeguard of Sugar; that the Fruit comes to its full flavour, with the additional beauty, from the Sugar. It would have done a great deal by Nature itself, if the Tree had stood in a place agreeable; but much more would it be for those baking Pears, as we call them, if they had the advantage of a good Climate; one may guess then how much difference there is between one and the other. In the tough and hard Pears, one ought to bake them twice, that is, once with a little Water and Sugar, in as hot an Oven as they bake Bread in; and then put them in Pyes, and bake them over again, so will they become tender, well tasted, and of a fine colour. But be it as it will, as soon as either of these come out of the Oven, pour some Cream over them, and mix it with them, if they are to be served hot, mashing the Fruit all the while; but if they are to be served cold, then only pour some Cream over them, when they just come from the Oven, and let it remain till you serve it cold.

There is one way which is practised by some, and that is, to break the hard Pears, just when they are taken out of the Oven, in the Pye; for else the outsides, though the Rind is off, will be hard, and tough: then pour on the Cream. It is to be noted, that all ripe Apples require less baking, and less Sugar, than the hard Apples, which do not become ripe till some Months afterwards. When an Apple, or Pear, for example, is as ripe as it can be in our Climate, it will have some softness, and some sweetness in it, and therefore will require less baking, as baking is only a sort of ripening; and so on the other hand: but we are providentially provided with both Apples and Pears, which are, some ripe sooner, and some ripe later; even that by the end of *July*, we have some ripe, and some remain hard and sour till *June*. We ought be apprised of the Sorts, to take them in their several Seasons, and not to take the Winter Fruits, for baking, when we have ripe Fruits by us. Many thousand Bushels of Fruit are lost for want of this Caution.

So at any time, when you use Apples, or Pears, for Tarts, Puddings, or Sauces, let them be all of one Sort, and ripe; for, if they are ripe, or towards it, they will soon soften; and if you put two Sorts together, one will be in Pulp very soon, and the other will be hard for an Hour or two, and at length will not be soft. *Memorandum,* This is not to be disregarded.

To make Paste. From Mrs. *Peasly.*

There are many sorts of Paste made, and among them, are some which are made with Eggs, according to the old fashion; but these are always hard, when they are baked, though they will fly and crackle in the Mouth, but they taste like Sticks: while, on the other side, leave out your Eggs, and use Butter and Water only, as in the following Receipts, and your Paste will melt in the Mouth, and be agreeable to the Taste.

If you would have a sweet Paste; then take half a Pound of Butter, and rub it into about a Pound of Flour, with two or three Ounces of double-refined Sugar powder'd, and make it a Paste, with cold Milk, some Sack and Brandy. This is a very good one.

You may also make an hot Paste, for minced Pyes, or such like, by taking a quantity of Flour as you like, and break a Pound or two of Butter into a large Sauce-pan of Water; and when the Butter is melted, make an hollow in the midst of the Flour, and scumming off the Butter, throw it, at times, into the Flour, with some of the boiling hot Water along with it; then, when you have enough for your use, work it into a stiff Paste, and lay it before the Fire, cover'd with a Cloth, and cut off such bits as you want, just when you are going to use them. This Paste does very well for raised Pyes. Some will make this Paste by breaking in a Pound of Butter into a quarter of a Peck of Flour, and then pouring on it some scalding hot Water, enough to work it to a stiff Paste. As for Tarts, one may make the following Puff-Paste. Rub in some Butter into your Flour, and make it into a Paste with Water, and when it is moulded, roll it out till it is about half an Inch thick; then put bits of Butter upon it, about half an Inch asunder, and fold your Paste together, and then fold it again: then roll it again till it becomes of the thickness it was before; and then lay bits of Butter on it, as before directed, and fold it as mention'd above, and roll it again to the thickness of half an Inch; then put on the rest of your Butter, and fold it up, and roll it for the last time, doubling it, and rolling it twice, before you use it. This is very good for Puffs, Puddings, or Petty-Patees.

As for Meat-Pyes, or Pasties, they require another sort of Paste, which is made thus. Rub seven Pounds of Butter into a Peck of Flour, but not too small; then make it into a Paste with Water. It is good for Venison-Pasties, and such like great Pyes.

To dress a Dish of Fish in the best manner. From the same.

To make one of these grand Dishes, you ought always to have some capital sort of Fish, for the middle of the Dish; such as a Turbut, a Jowl of fresh Salmon, a Cod's Head, or a Pike boiled; and this must be adorn'd either with Flounders, Whitings, Soles, Perch, Smelts, or Gudgeons, or Bourn Trouts, which are the small River Trouts, or young Salmon-Fry, according as you can meet with them. This kind of Dish is call'd a Bisque of Fish.

To boil Fresh *Salmon.*

If you have fresh Salmon, you wash it with Salt and Water, and according to the Fashion, leave all the Scales on, though some take them off, to prevent that trouble at the Table; for the Skin of the Salmon, is the fattest part of the Fish, and is liked by most People. Lay your Fish thus prepared, into the Pan, where you boil it, and pour in Water, with a sixth part of Vinegar, a little Salt, and a stick of Horse-Radish; this should be boiled pretty quick: thus far for boiling fresh Salmon. The grand Sauce for it you will see at the end of these Receipts, for preparing the several sorts of Fish for the Bisque but if it is served alone, then let the Sauce be as follows. Take a Pint of Shrimps, a Pint of Oysters and their Liquor, and half a Pint of pickled Mushrooms; or else take Shrimps, and the Bodies of two middling Sea-Crabs, or of a couple of Lobsters, the Tail of the Lobsters to be cut in Dice, but use which you have by you. If you have Oysters, stew them a little, in their own Liquor, with some Mace, and whole Pepper, then lay by the Oysters, and put Mushroom Pickle to the Liquor, and dissolve two Anchovies in it; then melt what quantity of Butter you think fit, and mix your prepared Liquor with it, adding a little White Wine, or that may be left out. I should take notice, that just before you melt your Butter, put your Oysters, Shrimps, and Mushrooms, &c. into your prepared Liquor to boil up, and then mix all together. *Note,* The Bodies of the Crabs being well stirred in the Liquor, will thicken it, and render the whole very agreeable.

To boil *Turbut, Flounders,* or *Plaise, Pike,* or a *Cod's-Head,* or *Whitings.*

When your Fish are gutted and well wash'd: put them upon your Fish-Plate; the Jacks or Pikes, whether small or great, must have their Tails skewer'd into their Mouths, so that they make a round figure, which is the Fashion. Then put your Fish into the Kettle, into as much Water as will cover them. Put into this Water, an Onion, with some Cloves stuck in it, some Mace, some whole Pepper, a little bunch of sweet Herbs, a stick of Horse-Radish, and half a Lemon. When your Liquor boils, add a little Vinegar, or Verjuice; and when your Fish are boiled enough, let them drain before the Fire. The Sauce for these, if they are served singly, is that directed for the Salmon, or else some melted Butter, Anchovies dissolved in Water, over the Fire, and some Shrimps; or for want of them, if you can get any of the small Crabs, such as they sell in *London,* about eight or ten a Penny, and no bigger in their Bodies than to contain the quantity of a Golden-Pippin. Take the Inside of the Bodies of these, and thicken your Sauce with them. Or if you have Cray-fish, take the Bodies of them, and mix them well with your Sauce, and cut the Tails in small bits, as big as Pease. The foregoing way of boiling Fish gives them a relish.

To fry *Soles, Flounders, Plaise, Whitings, Smelts,* and *Gudgeons,* or such like.

Take a large quantity of Hog's-Seam, or Lard, and melt it in a Pan, till it is very hot; then put in your Fish, prepared as follows; but first you may fry some Bread, in Lengths, as big as one's Finger, to drain for a Garnish.

As for Soles, skin them, and gut them, then flour them well, and toss them into the Pan, turning them once, when you see the upper side of a yellow Colour. When they are enough, put them into a Cullendar to drain before the Fire.

Flounders are only to be gutted, and the Skins wash'd with Water and Salt, and being well dry'd with a Cloth, flour them, and fling them into the Pan, and use them as you did the Soles.

The Plaise are to be done in the same manner as the Flounders.

Whitings must be treated in the same manner as the former.

Smelts must be only rub'd with a coarse Cloth, and then flour'd, and thrown into the Pan.

Gudgeons must be scaled and gutted, well dry'd and flour'd, and thrown into the hot Lard: but take care in all these that you have a quick Fire under them, and not too many in the Pan at one time.

You have now all your Furniture for your Bisque of Fish; but to fry them still crisper, and better, use Sallad-Oil instead of Hogs-Lard; or if you have neither of these, you may use good dripping of Beef, or Mutton, but there must be enough of it, and it should be as hot as possible, in the Pan, when you throw your Fish in. Serve these with melted Butter, and Anchovy Liquor, with Shrimps, or Oysters, if they are single.

To broil *Whitings*.

Clean your Whitings, with Water and Salt, after they are gutted, and drying them thoroughly, flour them well, then lay them on the Grid-Iron, first rubbing it with a little Chalk. As you find them enough on one side, turn them, and serve them, if they go to the Table alone, with Butter melted, some Anchovy Liquor, and Oyster Sauce; these may make one of your grand Dishes of Fish, but fry'd and boiled is enough, because there is never a Dish of this kind, but there are many more at the same Treat, which will give the Cook a great deal of difficulty, and besides you must still in this Dish have some Spitchcot-Eels.

N.B. I forbear to mention here the manner of dresing Spitchcot-Eels, as they are already set down in the first part of this Book.

When you fry Whitings, skewer their Tails in their Mouths; and some take off their Skins.

The Grand Dish of Fish, and its Sauce.

When we have prepared these things, with regard to the grand Dish we design, then make the following Sauce: *viz.*

Sauce for a Bisque of Fish.

Take a Pint of Gravey, two or three spoonfuls of Mushroom Katchep, and a spoonful or two of Mushroom Pickle; then add about a Gill of White Wine, half an Onion, a slice of Lemon with the Peel, two Anchovies shred, some

Cloves, and Mace. When these have boiled half a quarter of an Hour, take out the Onion, and Lemon, and thicken your Liquor, with about three Pounds of Butter, rub'd in a little Flour; then put in the Body of a Crab, or Lobster, Shrimps, Oysters, and Mushrooms, and it is ready to pour over your Fish: but some rather chuse to serve this Sauce in Basons, lest it be too high for every Palate. However, when you have disposed your Fish well in the Dish, garnish with fry'd Bread, Horse-Radish scraped, fry'd Parsley, Lemon sliced and pickled, red Beet-Root sliced, and serve it up hot. If your Sauce is serv'd in Basons; then take care to have one Bason of plain Butter: but if all your Company happens to like the rich Sauce, your Dish of fish will make a much better appearance to have some of the Sauce pour'd over it, before you lay on your Garnish. Remember to lay your Spitchcot Eels near the edge of the Dish.

To broil *Herrings,* so as to prevent their rising in the Stomach. From the same.

Take fresh Herrings, scale them, gut them, and wash them; and when they are well dry'd with a Cloth, strew them with flour of Ginger, as you would any Fish with Flour, then broil them; and when they are enough, the taste of the Ginger is quite lost: then serve them with Claret, Butter, Salt, and Mustard, made into a Sauce, and they will not at all disturb the Stomach.

A white *Fricassee* of *Rabbits.* From the same.

Take three or four young Rabbits and cut them to pieces, then put them in a Stew-pan, with four Ounces of Butter; then season them with some Lemon-Peel grated, a little Thyme, a little sweet Marjoram, Pepper, Salt, and a little *Jamaica*, Pepper beaten fine. Let these be close cover'd, and stew them gently, till they are tender; then take about half a Pint of Veal-Broth, an Onion, some Lemon, a Sprig of sweet Marjoram, and some Spice, to your mind, and put to it half a Gill of White Wine. Boil these together six or seven Minutes, then pour away the Butter, in the Stew-pan, and strain your Veal Gravey through a Sieve; then beat the Yolks of four Eggs, with half a Pint of Cream. Then put some of the Broth, by degrees, to the Eggs and Cream, keeping them stirring, lest they curdle, and you may put to it some Parsley boil'd tender, and shred small; then put it to the Rabbits, and toss them up thick with Butter, adding some pickled Mushrooms, and serve them hot with a Garnish of sliced Lemon, and red Beet-Root pickled.

A *Neat's-Tongue* roasted. From the same.

Take a large Neat's-Tongue, that has lain three Weeks in Salts mixed in the following manner. Take a quarter of a Pound of Salt-Petre, half a Pound of Bay-Salt, and three Pints of common Salt. This is enough to salt four Tongues: let them be rubb'd well with this Mixture, and kept in a cool place. Take, I say, one of these Tongues, and boil it till the Skin will come off; and when it is stript of its Skin, stick it with Cloves, about an Inch asunder, then put it on a Spit, and wrap a Veal-Cawl over it, till it is enough; then take off the Cawl, and just froth it up, and serve it in a Dish with Gravey. *Note*, The Cawl will keep the outside tender, which otherwise would be hard. One must serve with it, in Saucers, of the following: Grate a Penny-Loaf into about a Pint of Water, and half as much Claret; then boil it thick, with two or three chips of Cinnamon, then sweeten it to your mind, as you please: strew some sifted raspings of Bread about the Dish, and garnish with Lemon sliced.

To dress a *Cow-Heel*. From the same.

Take out the Bones, and clean it, cut it to pieces, and wash it; then flour it, and strew over it a little Pepper and Salt, then fry it brown in Hog's-Lard, made very hot in the Pan. Prepare at the same time some small Onions boiled whole, till they are tender, and pull off as many of the Coats or Skins, till you see them pure white; then make a Sauce of Gravey, some White-Wine, Nutmeg, and a little whole Spice, with a little Salt and Pepper, and thicken it with burnt Butter. Let your Onions, when they are skin'd, be made hot in Milk, and lay them whole in the Dish, with the Cow-Heel, and pour the Sauce over the whole. Some who have strong Stomachs will slice Onions, and flouring them well, fry them with with the Cow-Heel, but this must be fry'd in Butter.

To make *Marmalade* of *Quinces*. From the same.

Take the large *Portugal* Quinces, pare them, and take out the Cores; then cut each Quince in eight Parts, and throw them in Water; then boil the Parings, and such of the Quinces as are of the worse sort, in two Quarts of Water, till the Liquor is reduced to half the quantity: when this is strain'd, put the Liquor into your Preserving-Pan, with a Pound of fine Sugar powder'd, with two Pounds of Quinces: boil these gently, till they are tender. Then if you design your Marmalade for mixing with Apples in Pyes or Tarts, put to them a Pound more of Sugar to each two Pounds; break them with a Spoon, and boil them briskly, keeping them stirring all the while: then put them hot into the Gallypot, when they are thick, and of a reddish Colour. To heighten their redness, and keep them from burning to the bottom, put into the Pan four or five pieces of pure Tin, as big as Half-Crowns. But if you would have your Marmalade fine for Glasses, then, when they are boil'd tender, take them out of the Liquor, and beat them well in a Marble Mortar, and rub them through a Sieve; then put to them a Pound of fine Sugar, and stir them well in the Liquor; boil them quick, stirring them all the while, till they grow thick.

Memorandum, While they are boiling the second time, put in some pieces of Tin, as before, and when they are enough, pour them hot into your Glasses or Cups, first taking out the Pieces of Tin; and when your Marmalade is cool, cover your Glasses and Cups with white Paper.

Boil'd *Tench*. From the same.

Take Tench, fresh from the Pond, gut them, and clear them from their Scales; then put them into a Stew-pan, with as much Water as will cover them, some Salt, some whole Pepper, some Lemon-Peel, a stick of Horse Radish, a bunch of sweet Herbs, and a few Cloves; then boil them till they are tender, and when they are enough, take some of the Liquor, and put to it a Glass of White

Wine, and a little Lemon-juice, or Verjuice, and an Anchovy shred. Then boil it a few Minutes, and thicken it with Butter rubb'd in Flour, tossing up a Pint of Shrimps with the Sauce, and pour it over the Fish. Serve it with garnish of fry'd Bread, cut the length of one's Finger, some Slices of Lemon and Horse-Radish scraped, with some pickled Mushrooms, if you will, or you may toss up some of them in the Sauce.

To bake *Tench*. From Lady G.

Take your Tench, fresh from the Pond, gut them, and clean them from the Scales; then kill them, by giving them an hard stroke on the back of the Head, or else they will live for many Hours, and even jump out of the Pan in the Oven, when they are half enough. Then lay them in a Pan, with some Mushroom Katchep, some strong Gravey, half a Pint of pickled Mushrooms, as much White-Wine as Gravey, three or four large Shallots, an Anchovy or two, two or three slices of fat Bacon, some Pepper, Cloves, and Nutmeg, at pleasure, a little Salt, some Lemon-Peel, and a bunch of sweet Herbs; then break some bits of Butter, and lay them on your Fish, then cover all as close as you can, and give them an Hour's baking.

When they are enough, lay them in a hot Dish, and pour off the Liquor, and strain it, only preserving the Mushrooms; then add to it a spoonful of Lemon-Juice, and thicken your Sauce with the Yolks of four Eggs, beaten with Cream, and mix'd, by degrees, with the Sauce. Pour this over your Fish, and serve it hot with a Garnish of BeetRoots sliced, some slices of Lemon-Peel, and some Horse-Radish scraped.

To roast a *Westphalia-Ham*. From the same.

Boil a Westphalia-Ham, as tender as it will be, with the Gravey in it; then strip off the Skin, put it on a Spit, and having done it over with the Yolk of an Egg, strew it all over with raspings or chippings of Bread finely sifted, and mixt with a little Lemon-Peel grated. Baste it well when it is before the Fire, and drudge it frequently with the above Mixture till it is enough. Some, instead of Roasting it, will prepare it, with a good covering of the aforesaid Mixture, and set it an Hour in the Oven, which answers full as well. Then serve it, with boiled Pidgeons, *Russia* Cabbages, if you can get them, or Sprouts of Cabbages, curll'd, as big as Tennis-Balls, or Collyflowers, or Brocoli. This is an excellent Dish, especially, if the Cabbages, or Collyflowers, are toss'd up with Butter and Cream, but the Brocoli must only have the Butter pour'd over them.

A Neck of *Mutton* and *Broth*. From *L. P.* Esq.

The Method of this Broth was first from a mistake, where instead of boiling a Neck of Mutton, as directed, the Cook roasted it. The Gentleman was in a hurry for it, and call'd in half an Hour for his Neck of Mutton and Broth; but the Cook had only that Neck in the House; which she was roasting, and was then above half done: however, she takes it from the Spit, and cut it in pieces, which she presently set over the Fire, with the Gravey that came from it, with a small quantity of Water, and serv'd it up with some Turnips, as soon as possible. The Relish which the Meat had gain'd by roasting, gave the Broth so good a flavour, that it is recommended since that time, by the Gentlemen who eat of it, where-ever they go; but with this addition, that they take four or five *Hertfordshire* Turnips, pare them, and cut them in dice; then boil them in the Liquor with the half roasted Mutton; and when they are enough, take them out of the Liquor, and draining them a little, flour them, and adding a little Salt, fry them either in Butter very hot, or in Hog's-Lard, and then serve them with Pottage.

Boil'd *Venison,* with its Furniture. From Mr. *L. L.*

Take an Haunch of Venison, salt it well, and let it remain a Week, then boil it, and serve it with a furniture of Collyflowers, *Russia* Cabbages, some of the *Hertfordshire* Turnips cut in dice, and boiled in a Net, and toss'd up with Butter and Cream, or else have some of the yellow *French* Turnips, cut in dice, and boil'd like the former; or we might add some red Beet-Roots boiled in dice, and butter'd in the same manner. Place these regularly, and they will afford a pleasant Variety both to the Eye and the Taste.

Frogs, a white *Fricassee* of them. From Mr. *Ganeau.*

Take large Frogs, and cut off the hinder Legs, strip them of the Skin, and cut off the Feet, and boil them tender in a little Veal-Broth, with whole Pepper, and a little Salt, with a bunch of sweet Herbs, and some Lemon Peel. Stew these with a Shallot, till the Flesh is a little tender; then strain off the Liquor, and thicken it with Cream and Butter; then serve them hot with the Cream, and some Mushrooms pickled, toss'd up with the Sauce, they make a very good Dish, and their Bones being of a very fine Texture, are better to be eaten than those of Larks. But we have in many Places an Aversion to them, as, in some others, some People have to Mushrooms.

Frogs, in a brown *Fricassee.* From the same.

Prepare the Frogs as before, and flour them well; then put them into a Pan of hot Lard, and fry them brown. Then take them and drain them from the Liquor they were fry'd in, and make a Sauce for them of good Gravey, some Lemon-Peel, a Shallot or two, some Spice beaten, a bunch of sweet Herbs, an Anchovy, some pickled Mushrooms and their Liquor, and some Pepper and Salt.

Toss up these, thick with Butter, and pour the Sauce over them, putting first a little Claret to it, and some Lemon-Juice. Garnish with broiled Mushroom-Flaps, and Lemon sliced.

Snails, to be dressed with white Sauce. From the same.

Take the large *German* Snail, early in the Morning; put them, shells and all, into Salt and Water, for a few Hours, till they purge themselves: then put them into fresh Salt and Water, for a few Hours more, and repeat that a third time, then give them a gentle boil in Water and. Salt, in their Shells, and you may then pick them out, with a Pin, as you do Perwinkles, Then stew them in Veal-Broth, with some Cloves, a little Sack, some Mace, and a little Salt. Stew these a little while, and then pour over them this Sauce thicken'd with Cream and Butter, and grate some Nutmeg upon the Sauce, and serve them hot.

Snails, to be drest with brown Sauce. From the same.

Take the same sort of Snail, as above mention'd, and clean it as before; then give them one turn, when they are flour'd, in some hot Butter, or Lard, and drain them. Then pour into the Pan, when, the Liquor is out, some strong Gravey, a Glass of Claret, some Nutmeg, some Spices, and a little Salt, with a little Lemon-Peel grated; and when the Sauce is strong enough, then strain the Sauce, and thicken it with burnt Butter, Then serve them up hot, with a Garnish of sliced Lemon, and some Sippits fry'd in Lard.

A *Gammon* of a *Badger* roasted. From Mr. *R. T.* of *Leicestershire.*

The Badger is one of the cleanest Creatures, in its Food, of any in the World, and one may suppose that the Flesh of this Creature is not unwholesome. It eats like the finest Pork, and is much sweeter than Pork. Then, just when a Badger is killed, cut off the Gammons, and strip them; then lay them in a Brine of Salt and Water, that will bear an Egg, for a Week or ten Days; then boil it for four or five Hours, and then roast it, strewing it with Flour and rasped Bread sifted. Then put it upon a Spit, as you did before with the *Westphalia* Ham. Serve it hot with a Garnish of Bacon fry'd in Cutlets, and some Lemon in slices.

To make minc'd Pyes, or _Christmas-_Pyes. From Mrs. *M. C.*

Take an Ox-Heart, and parboil it, or a Neat's-Tongue, boil'd without drying or salting, or the Inside of a Surloin of Beef; chop this small, and put to each Pound two Pounds of clean Beef-Suet, cleaned of the Skins and Blood, and chop that as small as the former; then pare, and take the Cores out of eight large Apples, and chop them small, grate then a Two-penny Loaf; and then add two or three Nutmegs grated, half an Ounce of fresh Cloves, as much Mace, a little Pepper and Salt, and a Pound and a half of Sugar; then grate in some Lemon and Orange-Peel, and squeeze the Juice of six Oranges, and two

Lemons, with half a Pint of Sack, and pour this into the Mixture. Take care to put in two Pounds of Currans to every Pound of Meat, and mix it well; then try a little of it over the Fire, in a Sauce-pan, and as it tastes, so add what you think proper to it: put this in an earthen glaz'd Pan, and press it down, and you may keep it till *Candlemas,* if you make it at *Christmas.*

Memorandum, When you put this into your Pyes, press it down, and it will be like a Paste.

When you take these Pyes out of the Oven, put in a Glass of Brandy, or a Glass of Sack or White Wine, into them, and stir it in them.

Plum-Pottage, or *Christmas-Pottage.* From the same.

Take a Leg of Beef, and boil it till it is tender in a sufficient quantity of Water, add two Quarts of red Wine, and two Quarts of old strong Beer; put to these some Cloves, Mace, and Nutmegs, enough to season it, and boil some Apples, pared and freed from the Cores into it, and boil them tender, and break them; and to every Quart of Liquor, put half a Pound of Currans pick'd clean, and rubb'd with a coarse Cloth, without washing. Then add a Pound of Raisins of the Sun, to a Gallon of Liquor, and half a Pound of Prunes. Take out the Beef, and the Broth or Pottage will be fit for use.

Amber-Rum, from *Barbadoes;* an extra-ordinary way of making it, from that Country.

Take the Preparation of the Scum and Dregs of the Sugar-Canes. Let them ferment, and distil them with the Leaves of the *Platanus,* or Plain-Tree; then put them into a Still again, and hang some Amber powder'd, in a Muslin Bag, in the Cap of the Still, and let all the Steam pass through that, and it will be incomparable good Rum.

A boiled *Goose* with its Garniture. From the same.

Take a young fat Goose, and salt it, and pepper it, for four Days or a Week; then boil it as you would do other Victuals, till it is tender; then take it from the Pot, and put about it some *Hertfordshire* Turnips boiled, being first cut in dice, some Carrots boiled, and cut in dice, some small Cabbage-Sprouts, some red Beet-Roots cut in dice, some *French* yellow Turnips cut in dice, or such other Roots, or Herbs, as you like best. Collyflowers, if they are in season, will do well; but they must all be toss'd up with Cream and Butter, except the *Hertfordshire* Turnips, which should, after they are boiled, be dry'd in a Cloth, and well flour'd; then fry them in hot Lard, or hot Butter, drain them well, and serve them with the same Sauce.

Memorandum, If you have any of the yellow *French* Turnips, cut them in dice to boil, and when they are enough, treat them in the same manner as you are directed, for the *Hertfordshire* Turnips. Take care in the buying of the *Hertfordshire* Turnips, for they are all white; but they require a longer boiling than the red-ringed Turnips: the red-rings are soft presently, when they are good, and the others are near an Hour in boiling, and, even then, feel hard to the Spoon.

Viper-Soup. From Mr. *Ganeau.*

Take Vipers, alive, and skin them, and cut off their Heads; then cut them in pieces, about two Inches in length, and boil them, with their Hearts, in about a Gallon of Water to eight Vipers, if they are pretty large. Put into the Liquor a little Pepper and Salt, and a Quart of White Wine to a Gallon of Liquor; then put in some Spice, to your mind, and chop the following Herbs, and put into it: Take some Chervill, some white Beet-Cards or Leaves, some Hearts of Cabbage-Lettuce, a Shallot, some Spinach-Leaves, and some Succory. Boil these, and let them be tender; then serve it up hot, with a *French* Roll in the middle, and garnish with the raspings of Bread sifted, and slices of Lemon.

Ketchup, in Paste. From *Bencoulin* in the *East-Indies.*

There is a Kidney-Bean, we have here, which has a fine relish in it, as the *Indians* say, but in fact there is none but what they give it by Art. This Bean, when it is full ripe, is taken out of the Shells, and boiled to a Pulp, and that Pulp strain'd till it becomes like Butter; then they put some of all the Spices into it, in Powder, as, Nutmeg, Cloves, Mace, and Pepper, Garlick, and Orange-Juice, or some Mango Pickle. This being well mix'd together, makes an agreeable Sauce, when it is put in any warm Liquor.

To dry Plums with Sugar. From Mr. *Girarde.*

Take large white or red Plums, such as the white *Holland's*-Plum, the *Bonum magnum*, the Royal Dolphin or Imperial Plum. Cut these, and take out the Stones, and to every Pound of Plums, put three quarters of a Pound of Sugar: boil your Sugar with a little Water, to a candy height; then put in your Plums, and boil them gently on a slow Fire; then set them by to cool, and then boil them afresh, taking care that they do not break; then let them lie in their Syrup, three or four Days, and then lay them upon Sieves, to dry, in a warm Oven, turning them upon clean Sieves, twice a day, till they are dry. Then wash them off the clamminess of the Sugar with warm Water, and dry them again in the Oven; and when they are cold, put them up in Boxes, with Papers between them, and keep them in a dry Place.

To make small *Almond-Cakes.* From the same.

Take some Orange-Flower-Water, or Rose-Water, with about two Grains of Amber-Gris, and beat these with a Pound of blanched Almonds, in a Marble

Mortar; then take a Pound of fine Sugar powder'd, and finely sifted, and put most of it to the Almonds, when they are well beaten, and mix it well. Then make your Cakes, and lay them on Wafers, and set them in a gentle Oven, on tin Plates; and when they are half baked, boil what Sugar you have left, with some Rose-Water, to a candy height, and, with a Feather, wash the Cakes over with this Liquor, and close your Oven, and let them stand a few Minutes longer.

To preserve *Bullace*. From the same.

Take your Bullace before the Frost has taken them; let them be fresh gather'd, and clear Fruit, scald them in Water: then take their weight in fine Sugar, with a little Water, and boil it to a Syrup; then put in your Bullace, and boil them till the Syrup is very thick, and your Fruit very clear.

To preserve green *Peaches*. From the same.

In some Gardens, where the Trees are pruned and ordered, by a skilful hand, it is often that a Tree will be so full of Fruit, that it is necessary to take away some, when they are green, that the others may swell the better. As this sometimes happens with Peaches, so I shall here direct how to preserve them. Scald your green Peaches in Water, then, with a Cloth, rub the Down from them; then put them, in more Water, over a slow Fire, and let them stew till they are green, keeping them cover'd. Then take their weight in fine Sugar, and with some Water, boil it to a Syrup, taking off the Scum as it rises; then put in your Peaches, and boil them till they are clear, and put them up, with the Syrup, in Glasses, or Gally-pots; and when they are cold, cover them with Paper. Note, You must gather your Peaches before the Stone is hard in them, which you may know by putting a Pin through them.

To preserve *Goosberries*. From the same.

The best Goosberries, for this Work, are the white *Dutch* Goosberry, and the Walnut-Goosberry. Take these, just when they are beginning to turn ripe, pick off the Flower-tuft at the Ends, and stone them; then take to every Pound of Fruit, one Pound and a quarter of fine Sugar beaten and sifted. Boil the Sugar with a little Water to a Syrup, taking off the Scum as it rises; then put in your Fruit, and boil them quick till they are clear, and put them in Glasses, boiling the Syrup a little more; then pour it upon them, and when it is cold, cover your Glasses close with Paper.

To candy *Eringo-Roots*. From Mr. *Lufkin* of *Colchester*.

Take the fairest Roots of Eringo, fresh taken out of the Ground, wash them clean, and boil them in several Waters till they are very tender: wash them again, and rub them with a Cloth, to dry as much as they will bear, without breaking, or bruising; slit them, and take out the Pith, and twist two together, like a Screw. Then take to every Pound of Root two Pounds of fine Sugar powder'd, of which Sugar take one Pound at first, and boil it with some Rose-Water, to a Syrup; and then put in your Roots, and boil them till they are clear; then wet the rest of your Sugar with Rose-Water, and boil it to a candy Height; then put in the Roots, and let them boil, shaking them often over the Fire, and when you think they are enough, take them from the Fire, and shake them till they are cold, and almost dry; then lay them upon Dishes to dry thoroughly, and when they are done, put them up in Boxes with white Paper, under and over them, then keep them in a dry place.

To preserve *Grapes* in *Syrup*. From the same.

The best Grapes for this use, are those of the Fronteniac Kind, of which there are the white and the blue, and the red, which seldom come to ripen in *England*, with their pure flavour. But as Heat is the occasion of ripening; so, though they want it with us, from the Sun, we may make good that deficiency by Fire, which will answer the end fully, and bring them to the highest perfection of Taste, therefore the Sweet-meat made of these is excellent; besides these Grapes for preserving, the *St. Peter* and the Warner Grapes are very good, and I may mention the grizled Fronteniac, which is a noble Grape, when it is ripe, as well as the others. And for the other Sorts of Grapes, they are not fit for preserving, unless I take in the Raisin Grapes, red and white, and the *Lombardy* Grape; all which are full of Pulp, and seldom ripen. These are your sorts, and now to proceed.

Take your Grapes, gather'd in a dry Day, though they are not ripe. You may guess when we come to the end of *September*, and they are not so, they never will be ripe: pick them then from the Stalks, and stone them carefully, without breaking much of the Skin, save the Juice; then take the weight of them in fine Sugar powder'd, and boil your Sugar with some Water, wherein Pippins have been boiled before, first straining your Water, and boil them to Syrup, taking off the Scum as it rises. And when the Scum rises no more, put in your Grapes, and boil them quick till they are as clear as Crystal, I mean the white Grapes; but the red Sorts, let them boil till they are clear, and that the Syrup will jelly; then put them into Glasses, and when they are cold, cover them close with white Paper; but mark your Papers, which are of the Fronteniac Kinds, for they will have a very different Flavour from the other Sorts, an high richness that is much admired. However, though the other Kinds of Grapes, mention'd in this Receipt, may want a flavour by themselves, you may add some Orange-Flower Water to the Syrup, you make for them, which will give them a fine taste.

N.B. Take care that when you make this Preserve, you use only one sort at one time.

To dress a *Calf's-Head* in a grand Dish. From Mrs. *E. Sympson.*

Take a large Calf's-Head, and divide it, cut off the Muzzle, and wash it well; then take the Brains, and wash them, and dry them, and flour them, and put them in a Cloth, and tye them up. Boil these till they are half done; then take them from the Kettle, and cut the Flesh off one side of the Head, in slices, like harsh'd Meat, and the other side of the Head must remain whole, and mark'd only with a sharp Knife, cross-ways. The Brains must lie till the rest are prepared.

Take then the harsh'd part, and with some of the Liquor it was boil'd in, put a Glass of White Wine, a little Mushroom Ketchup, a little Nutmeg grated, and a little Mace beat fine, some Pepper and Salt, some grated Lemon-Peel, and stew them together with a bunch of sweet Herbs, and some Butter. When it is enough, put in a little Juice of Lemon, and thicken it with Cream and Butter, in some of the same Liquor, with the Liquor of Oysters parboil'd, a Pint of Oysters, and as many pickled Mushrooms, which must be toss'd up with your Sauce, when you thicken it, remembring to cut the Eye in pieces, amongst the Harsh.

Then for the other side of the Head, when you have cut the Flesh cross ways, in Diamonds, about an Inch over, beat the Yolks of two or three Eggs, and with a Feather past over it, cover it with the Yolks of Eggs, and then drudge upon it the following Mixture.

Take some Raspings of Bread sifted, put to them some Flour, a little Pepper and Salt, with some Mace and Nutmeg, in powder, and a little sweet Marjoram powder'd, or shred small. Mix these well together; then set it in an Oven, with some bits of Butter upon it, till it is enough, or before a brisk Fire, till the drudging is brown: this must be laid in the middle of the Dish, and the Harsh round it. The Brains must be cut in pieces, and strew'd with a little red Sage cut very small, and a little Spice and Salt; and then every piece, dip'd in a thick Batter, made of Eggs, Flour, and Milk. Fry these well in hot Hog's-Lard, or for want of that, in hot melted Beef-Suet; then take Oysters, a little stew'd in their own Liquor, with Mace, and a little whole Pepper; take off their Fins, and dip them in the same Batter, and fry them as directed above for the Brains. There must be likewise some Pieces of Bread cut the length of one's Finger, and fry'd crisp; all these are by way of Garnish. One may likewise boil some Skirret-Roots, and peel them, and then dip them in the Batter, and fry them crisp. As for the other part of the Garnish, it must be red Beets pickled and sliced, and Lemon sliced.

_Calf's-Head-_Pye. From the same.

Take a large Calf's-Head, divide it, and when it is well cleaned, boil it half enough; then cut it in large slices, and slit the Eyes, season it with Nutmeg, Pepper, Salt, and some powder of dry'd sweet Herbs; then lay it in your Paste, with some Pepper and Salt, at the Bottom, with some bits of Butter; then put in the Yolks of twelve hard Eggs, and a farced Meat made in the following manner. Take some Lean of Veal, shred it very small, then take some Eggs butter'd, and a little Pepper and Salt, with other Spice beaten, and some sweet Herbs in powder. Mix this with the Yolk or two of raw Eggs beaten, and make it into a Paste. Then roll it into Balls, and lay a good number of them into the Pye, amongst the Meat; and, if you will, put in half a Pound of Currans well pick'd, and only rubb'd in a Cloth, without washing. Then close your Pye, and just before it goes to the Oven, pour in a Gill of White Wine, and half a Pint of Water; bake it and serve it hot, and you may add, if you will, the following Liquor, *viz.*

Take half a Pint of White Wine, and as much Water, with the Juice of a Lemon. Boil these together a Minute or two, then take the Yolks of four Eggs, and beat them well, a quarter of a Pound of Butter, and as much Sugar as you like to make it palatable. Then mix them well together, taking care that it does not curdle, and pour it into your Pye just before you serve it.

Note, One may put into this Pye, Cock's-Combs blanched, and some Citron or Lemon-Peel candy'd, if you design it for a sweet Pye; but it is very good, whether we make it a sweet Pye or not.

To bake a *Calf's-Head.* From the same.

Take a Calfs-Head, wash it clean, and divide it; then beat the Yolks of four or five Eggs, and beat them well, and with a Feather, trace that Liquor over the out-side of the Head, and strew over it some raspings of Bread sifted, some Flour, some Pepper and Salt, some Mace and Nutmeg powder'd, with some sweet Herbs powder'd, with a little Sage shred small, and the Brains cut in pieces, and dip'd in thick Batter; then cover the Head with some bits of Butter, and pour in the Pan some White-Wine and Water, with as much Gravey, and cover it close. Then bake it in a quick Oven, and when you serve it, pour on some strong Gravey, and garnish with Lemon sliced, red Beet-Root pickled and sliced, and some fry'd Oysters, and fry'd Bread.

To make Spirit of *Lilley* of the *Valley.* From *Norway.* N.B. This serves in the room of *Orange-Flower-Water,* in 'Puddings, and to perfume *Cakes;* though it is drank as a Dram in *Norway.*

Gather your Lilley-of-the Valley Flowers, when they are dry, and pick them from the Stalks; then put a Quarter of a Pint of them into a Quart of Brandy, and so in proportion, to infuse six or eight Days; then distil it in a cold Still, marking the Bottles, as they are drawn off, which is first, second and third, &c. When you have distill'd them, take the first, and so on to the third or fourth, and mix them together, till you have as strong as you desire; and then bottle them, and cork them well, putting a lump of Loaf-Sugar into each Bottle.

Things to be provided, when any great Family is going into the Country, for a Summer. From Mr. *R. S.*

Nutmegs.
Mace.
Cinnamon.
Cloves.
Pepper.
Ginger.
Jamaica-Pepper.
Raisins.
Currans.
Sugar *Lisbon.*
Sugar-Loaf Lump.
Sugar double-refin'd.
Prunes.
Oranges.
Lemons.
Anchovies.
Olives.
Capers.
Oil for Salads.
Vinegar.
Verjuice.
Tea.
Coffee.
Chocolate.
Almonds.
Chesnuts.
French Pears.

Sir, I send you this as a *Memorandum*, because when some People go into the Country, many of these Things may be forgot, and it is sometimes the Case, that one must send a Mile or two for what is wanted of them.

I am Yours, R. S.

To salt a *Ham* in imitation of *Westphalia,* &c.

Take an Ham of young Pork, and sprinkle it with Salt for one Day, that the Blood may come out; then wipe it dry, and rub it with the following Mixture.

Take a Pound of brown Sugar, a quarter of a Pound of Salt-Petre, half a Pint of Bay-Salt, and three Pints of common Salt. Mix all these together, and stir them in an Iron Pan, over the Fire, till they are pretty hot, and then rub your Ham with it. Turn your Ham often, and let it lie three Weeks; then dry it in a Chimney with Deal Saw-Dust.

To make artificial *Anchovies*. From Mr. *James Randolph* of *Richmond*.

About *February* you will find, in the River of *Thames*, a large quantity of Bleak, or in *August* a much larger parcel in Shoals. These Fish are soft, tender, and oily, and much better than Sprats to make any imitation of Anchovies from. Take these, and clean them, and cut off their Heads, and lay them in an earthen glazed Pan, with a Layer of Bay-Salt under them, and another over, a single Row of them; then lay a fresh row of Fish, and Bay Salt over that; and so continue the same *Stratum super Stratum*, till the Vessel is full, and in a Month you may use them, and afterwards put Vinegar to them. But they will be like Anchovies without Vinegar, only the Vinegar will keep them. Turn them often the first Fortnight.

Apple-Dumplings in an extraordinary way. From Mrs. *Johnson*.

Take Golden-Rennets ripe, pare them, and take out their Cores; then cut the Apples into small pieces, and with a large Grater, grate in a Quince, when it has been pared and cored: for if you was to slice in a Quince, to your Apples, in large pieces, the Quince would not be boil'd equally with the Apples; for the Quince is of a tough Nature, and will not boil under twice the time that the Apples will: therefore to grate them, will be enough to give their flavour to the Apple, and make all enough at one time. Put what Sugar you think proper into each Dumpling, when you take it up, and the necessary quantity of Butter. It will then eat like a Marmalade of Quince.

Note, The Crust, or Paste, for these Dumplings, must be of a Puff-Paste made with Butter, rubb'd into Flour, and for some other Parts of the Butter, break them into the Paste, and roll them three times, and put in the Apples to the Crust, tying them into a Cloth well flour'd, and boiling them. It may be understood before, that when they are taken up hot, the Ceremony of sugaring and buttering is necessary.

Apple-Dumplings made with Sweet-meats. From the same.

Take fair Apples ripe, pare them, and take out the Cores; then slice them thin, and with a large Grater, grate in some candy'd Orange or Lemon-Peels, and you may put in also some powder'd Clove or Cinnamon, and a little grated Quince, or Quince Marmalade. Put these together, the Apples being first cut in small pieces, into a Puff-Paste, and tye it up in a Cloth. These must be sweeten'd with *Lisbon*-Sugar, when they are taken up, and melted Butter pour'd in: for if you use Loaf-Sugar, though it is powder'd, some of it will be harsh in the Mouth; and the *Lisbon*-Sugar, which is the fattest sort of Sugar, will not, but will give a good flavour to your Fruit.

An *Hog* barbecued, or broil'd whole. From *Vaux-Hall, Surrey.*

Take an Hog of five or six Months old, kill it, and take out the Inwards, so that the Hog is clear of the Harslet; then turn the Hog upon its Back, and from three Inches below the place where it was stuck, to kill it, cut the Belly in a strait Line down to the Bottom, near the joining of the Gammons; but not so far, but that the whole Body of the Hog may hold any Liquor we would put into it.

Then stretch out the Ribs, and open the Belly, as wide as may be; then strew into it what Pepper and Salt you please.

After this, take a large Grid-Iron, with two or three Ribs in it, and set it upon a stand of Iron, about three Foot and a half high, and upon that, lay your Hog, open'd as above, with the Belly-side downwards, and with a good clear Fire of Charcoal under it. Broil that side till it is enough, flouring the Back at the same time often. *Memorandum*, This should be done in a Yard, or Garden, with a Covering like a a Tent over it.

When the Belly-part of the Hog is enough, and turn'd upwards, and well fix'd, to be steady upon the Grid-Iron, or Barbacue, pour into the Belly of the Hog, three or four Quarts of Water, and half as much White-Wine, and as much Salt as you will, with some Sage cut small; adding the Peels of six or eight Lemons, and an Ounce of fresh Cloves whole.

Then let it broil till it is enough, which will be, from the beginning to the end, about seven or eight Hours; and when you serve it, pour out the Sauce, and lay it in a Dish, with the Back upwards. *Memorandum*, The Skin must not be cut before you lay it on the Gridiron, to keep in the Gravey; neither should any of the Skin be cut, when you have any Pork roasted for the same Reason.

Beef, or *Pork,* to be salted for boiling immediately, from the *Shambles.* From Mr. *J. P.* Chymist.

Take any piece of Beef you desire to boil, or Pork for the same, dressing it fresh from the Shambles, or Market, and salt it very well, just before you put it into the Pot; then as soon as your Meat is salted, take a coarse Linnen Cloth, and flour it very well, and then put the Meat into it, and tye it up close. Put this into a Kettle of boiling Water, and boil it as long as you would any salt piece of Beef of the same bigness, and it will come out as salt as a piece of Meat, that had been salted four or five Days: but by this way of salting, one ought not to have pieces of above five or six Pounds weight. *N.B.* If to half a Pound of common Salt you put an Ounce of Nitre, or Salt-Petre, it will strike a redness into the Beef; but the Salt-Petre must be beat fine, and well mix'd with the common Salt.

_Potatoe-_Puddings, made with Sweet-meats. From Mr. *Moring, Temple-Bar.*

Take some clean Potatoes, boil them tender, and when they are so, and clean from their Skins, break them in a Marble Mortar, till they become a Pulp; then put to them, or you might beat with them some slices of candy'd Lemons and Oranges, and beat these together with some Spices, and Lemon-Peel candy'd. Put to these some Marrow, and as much Sugar, with Orange-Flower Water, as you think fit. Mix all together, and then take some whole candy'd Orange-Peels, and stuff them full of the Meat, and set them upon a Dish, in a gentle Oven; and when they have stood half an hour, serve them hot, with a Sauce of Sack and Butter, and fine Sugar grated over them.

_Potatoe-_Pudding baked. From *Mr. Shepherd* of *Windmill-Street.*

Boil some fair Potatoes till they are tender; then, when they are made clean, bruise them in a Marble Mortar, till they become a Paste, with some Mace powder'd, some Sugar, and the Pulp of Oranges, with a *Naples* Biscuit or two grated in, and a large Carrot grated. Add to these some Orange-Flower Water; and when all these are well mix'd, put to them some butter'd Eggs, with some slices of Butter laid upon your Pudding, when it is put into the Dish, or Pan. A little baking will serve for it; and when it is enough, serve it hot, with a garnish of sliced Lemon or Orange. Some will put this into a Paste, but not cover it.

To make *Whipt Syllabubs.* From Mrs. *Cater* of *Salisbury.*

To a Pint of Cream put a Gill of Canary-Wine, and two Ounces of Loaf-Sugar finely beat, and a slice or two of Lemon; then with a clean Whisk, whip it together, adding a little Milk, as it grows thick: then have your Glasses clean, and put into each of them three or four spoonfuls of any sorts of Wine, red in some, and white in others, sweeten'd with fine Sugar powder'd; then fill your Glasses with the Froth of your Cream, as it is whipt up.

Of the fashionable Tables, for Persons of Rank, or Figure, where five Dishes are serv'd at a Course. From *S.G.* Esq.

The Tables I shall speak of, are so order'd, as to save a great deal of trouble to the Mistress of the Family, as well as to the Guests; for with this Table every one helps himself, by turning any Dish he likes before him, without interrupting any body. You must have first, a large Table with an hole in the Middle, of an Inch Diameter, wherein should be fix'd a Socket of Brass well turn'd, to admit of a Spindle of Brass, that will turn easily in it. The Table I speak of, may be, I suppose, five or six Foot diameter; and then have another Table-board made just so large, that as it is to act on the Centre of the first Table, there may be near a foot vacancy for Plates, &c. on every side. Then fix the Spindle of Brass in the Centre of the smaller Table, which Spindle must be so long, as, that when one puts it in the Socket of the great Table-board, the smaller turning Table may be about four Inches above the lower Board; so, that in its turning about, no Salt, or Bread, or any thing on the Places, may be disturb'd. These Tables have Cloths made to each of them; the upper, or smaller Table, to have an whole Cloth to cover it tight, and fasten'd close, so that none of the Borders hang down; and the Cloth for the under Table, or great Table, must have an hole cut in the middle of it for the Spindle of the upper Table to pass thro' into the Brass Socket: and when this is rightly order'd, and every necessary Furniture of the great, or lower Table, set by every Plate; then the upper Table, which will turn, may be furnish'd with Meats. It remains only then, in some Places, for the Lady of the House, to offer the Soup; but after that, every one is at liberty to help themselves, by turning the upper Table about, to bring what they like, before them.

I am Yours, S. G.

The Manner of killing and salting *Oxen,* in the hottest Months, for the Sea, that the *Beef* may keep good. From a Contractor with the Commissioners of the *Royal-Navy.*

Sir,

I have often read your Books, and particularly your *Lady's Monthly Director,* relating to the Management of the several Products of a Farm, but you have not taken notice of the Preservation of Flesh, as I expected.

I send this therefore, to inform you, that upon the setting out of a Fleet in *June,* it was thought difficult to salt the Beef; but it was done, to full Satisfaction, by the following Method.

We killed an hundred Oxen, in *June,* towards the Close of the Evening, and let them hang up whole, till the next Evening: then, when the Cool comes on, cut out the Messes, and by every Stand have a Punchin of Brine, and throw them into it as soon as they are cut, and in about three Minutes after that, take them out, and salt them well. *Note,* These Pieces will by these means lose their bloody Parts, in great measure, and be capacitated to receive the Salt much better than otherways, and then put them up. *Memorandum,* We had not, out of all this quantity, above three Pieces fail'd, though the Weather was extreme hot.

_Cheshire-_Pye with *Pork*. From Mr. *R. J.*

Take some salt Loin of Pork, or Leg of Pork, and cut it into Pieces, like Dice, or as you would do for an Harsh. If it be boiled or roasted, it is no matter; then take an equal quantity of Potatoes, and pare them, and cut them into dice, or in slices. Make your Pye-Crust, and lay some Butter, in pieces, at the bottom, with some Pepper and Salt; then put in your Meat and Potatoes, with such seasoning as you like, but Pepper and Salt commonly, and on the Top some pieces of Butter. Then close your Pye, and bake it in a gentle Oven, putting in about a Pint of Water, just before it is going into the Oven, for if you put in your Water over Night, it will spoil your Pye.

To bake *Herrings* in an extraordinary manner. From Mrs. *M. N.* of *Shrewsbury.*

Take fresh Herrings, and when they are scaled and cleaned, put them in a glazed earthen Vessel, where they can lie straight; then put in as much of the following Liquor as will cover them, *viz.* an equal quantity of fine pale and old strong Beer, with Vinegar, which is the best, or else all Vinegar, or as some do, put two parts of Vinegar and one of Water; any of these will do well. Then put in some Bay-Salt, such a quantity as you think will season it to your mind, and to that a tenth part of Salt-Petre, which will not make it salt, but give it a fine relish: to these put two or three Bay-Leaves, a bunch of sweet Herbs, some Cloves, or *Jamaica* Pepper, and some whole Pepper; then cover your Pan, and bake it in a quick Oven, with Bread. These must be eaten cold; they are excellent for a Country Breakfast, especially, if they are warm of the Spice, and if they are well done, the very Bones will dissolve.

To draw *Gravey* for a private *Family*. From the same.

Take some fleshy part of Beef, without Fat, and cut it in pieces about the bigness of Pidgeons Eggs; then flour it well, and put it in a Sauce-Pan, with a little fresh Lard, or a little Butter, a little Onion sliced, some Powder of sweet Marjoram, and a little Pepper. Cover all close, and stir it now and then till the Gravey is come out enough, and then pour on it some Water, when the Gravey is brown, and stir all together, and let them boil some time; then strain it off, adding a little Lemon-Juice.

Another *Gravey*, for a private Family, where there is not an opportunity of getting *Beef* to make it of.

Take some Butter, and some Onion, cut small, put it in a Sauce-Pan, and set it over the Fire till the Butter melts; then drudge in some Flour, and stir it well, till the Froth sinks down, and then it will be brown; you must then have ready prepared the following Mixture to throw in, *viz.* some good old Beer, and as much Water, an Onion cut small, some Pepper and Salt, a small Anchovy shred, a little Lemon-Peel grated, a Clove or two, and, if you have it, a little Mushroom Liquor, or Liquor of pickled Walnuts; then let them all simmer together a little while, and it will produce a thick good Gravey.

The Manner of Trussing a *Rabbit* for Boiling.

[Illustration: Fig. 1]

Cut the two Haunches of the Rabbit close by the Back-Bone, two Inches, and turn up the Haunches, by the Sides of the Rabbit; skewer the Haunches through the lower Part of the Back, as at A; then put a Skewer through the utmost Joint of the Leg at B, and so through the Body, and through the other Leg, so that the end of the Leg reaches the Shoulder-Blade. Then truss up the Shoulders high, and let the Pinnions be carried back, to take the Legs at B, and lie between them and the Body; and under the height of the Pinnions, put a Skewer, and bend the Neck backwards, and pass the Skewer through all, at C, so that it supports the Blade-Bone, and holds the Head up.

The Manner of Trussing a Single *Rabbit* for Roasting. From Mr. *W. N.* Poulterer.

[Illustration: Fig, 2]

You case the Rabbit all, excepting the lower Joints of the four Legs, and those you chop off: then pass a Skewer through the middle of the Haunches, after you have laid them flat, as at A; and the Fore-Legs, which are called the Wings, must be turn'd, as at B; so that the smaller Joint may be push'd into the Body, through the Ribs. This, as a single Rabbit, has the Spit pass'd through the Body and Head, but the Skewer takes hold of the Spit to preserve the Haunches. But to truss a couple of Rabbits, there are seven Skewers, and then the Spit passes only between the Skewers, without touching the Rabbits.

To make a *Pheasant* of a *Rabbit,* truss'd in such a manner, that it will appear like a *Pheasant,* and eat like one, with its Sauce. This is called, by the topping *Poulterers,* a *Poland-Chicken,* or a *Portugal-Chicken.* But it is most like a *Pheasant,* if it is larded. From Mrs. *Johnson,* at the famous Eating-House in *Devereux-Court* near the *Temple.*

[Illustration: Fig. 3]

Take a young Rabbit full grown; case it all, excepting the Fore-Feet, chop off them, and the Head, as close as may be, but strip the Skin from the hind Legs, even to leave the Claws on them. These Claws are not unlike the Claws of a Pheasant, and some good Judges may be deceiv'd by their first Look, for they are little different from the Legs of the Fowls we design to imitate. Then turn the Neck-part of the Rabbit, the Breast inwards, to the Scut or the Rump, leaving the Rump somewhat short, but to appear; then will the Rabbit appear in the Shape above, *viz.* B is the Scut, or Rump, of the Rabbit, and C is where the Neck comes; then will the Part mark'd F, appear like the Breast of a Fowl: but you must put up the stript Legs of the Rabbit, over each side of the Neck of it, and tie all together, with a String, as mark'd H H. So will the Hind-Legs of the Rabbit appear like the Legs of a Fowl, and where you see the Letter G mark'd, the Back of the Rabbit is broken. D, is what represents the Back-Side of the Fowl, and E is the Appearance of the Wings, which are supposed to be stuck into the Back, where two large Orifices are made, but the Bones of the Wings, of the Rabbit, must be taken out. A, shews the Legs as they ought to be tied, and O O Directs to the Points of the Skewers which are to run through it.

[Illustration: Fig. 4]

Fig. 4. will shew you the Back of the same, when it is truss'd, with the Appearance of the Skewers, o, o, o, o, with the Orifices, wherein are the supposed Bones of the Wings. If this is larded on the Breast, I think it best, and it should be served with the following Sauce, if it is roasted.

When this is thus prepared, you may stick a Pheasant's Tail-Feather at the Scut, and roast it as you would do a Pheasant, basting it well with Butter, after it is drudg'd well with Flour; then make the following Sauce for it. Take some strong Gravey, and put a little Lemon-Peel into it, with some Spice, and a little Wine; then take a few Buttons of Mushrooms pickled, and thicken it with burnt Butter, so that the Sauce becomes like one fit for a Ragout, or *Ragoo,* as the *English* pronounce it. Pour this over the Fowl or Rabbit, which you please to call it, and serve it hot, with a Garnish of Lemon sliced, and pickled Red Beet-Roots sliced.

Of Trussing a *Pidgeon.* From the same.

[Illustration: Fig. 5]

Draw It, but leave in the Liver, for that has no Gall; then push up the Breast from the Vent, and holding up the Legs, put a Skewer just between the bent of the Thigh and the brown of the Leg, first having turn'd the Pinnions under the Back: and see the lower Joint of the biggest Pinnions, are so pass'd with the Skewer, that the Legs are between them and the Body, as at A.

A *Goose* to Truss. From the same.

[Illustration: Fig. 6]

A Goose has no more than the thick Joints of the Legs and Wings left to the

Body; the Feet, and the Pinnions being cut off, to accompany the other Giblets, which consist of the Head and Neck, with the Liver and Gizzard. Then at the bottom of the Apron of the Goose A, cut an hole, and draw the Rump through it; then pass a Skewer through the small part of the Leg, through the Body, near the Back, as at B; and another Skewer through the thinnest part of the Wings, and through the Body, near the Back, as at C, and it will be right.

The Trussing of an *Easterling*. From Mr. *W. N.* Poulterer of St. _James's-_Market_, London._

[Illustration: Fig.7]

A Duck, an Easterling, a Teal, and a Widgeon, are all trussed in the same manner. Draw it, and lay aside the Liver and Gizzard, and take out the Neck, leaving the Skin of the Neck full enough to spread over the Place where the Neck was cut off. Then cut off the Pinnions at A, and raise up the whole Legs, till they are upright in the middle of the Fowl B, and press them between the stump of the Wings, and the Body of the Fowl: then twist the Feet towards the Body, and bring them forwards, with the bottom of the Feet towards the Body of the Fowl, as at C. Then take a Skewer, and pass it through the Fowl, between the lower Joint, next the Foot, and the Thigh, taking hold, at the same time, of the ends of the stumps of the Wings A. Then will the Legs, as we have placed them, stand upright. D is the point of the Skewer.

The Manner of Trussing a *Chicken* like a *Turkey-Poult,* or of Trussing a *Turkey-Poult*. From. Mr. *W. N.* Poulterer of St. _James's-_Market._

[Illustration: Fig. 8]

Take a Chicken and cut a long slit down the Neck, on the Fore-part; then take out the Crop and the Merry-Thought, as it is call'd; then twist the Neck, and bring it down under the Back, till the Head is placed on the side of the Left-Leg; bind the Legs in, with their Claws on, and turn them upon the Back. Then between the bending of the Leg and the Thigh, on the Right side pass a Skewer through the Body of the Fowl; and when it is through, run the Point through the Head, by the same Place of the Leg, as you did before, as at A: you must likewise pull the Rump B through the Apron of the Fowl. *Note,* The Neck is twisted like a Cord, and the boney part of it must be quite taken out, and the Under-Jaw of the Fowl taken away; neither should the Liver and Gizzard be served with it, though, the Pinnions are left on. Then turn the Pinnions behind the Back, and pass a Skewer through the extreme Joint, between the Pinnion and the lower Joint of the Wing, through the Body, near the Back, as at C, and it will be fit to roast in the fashionable manner. *N.B.* Always mind to beat down the Breast-Bone, and pick the Head and Neck clean from the Feathers before you begin to truss your Fowl.

A Turkey-Poult has no Merry-Thought, as it is called; and therefore, to imitate a Turkey the better, we take it out of a Chicken through the Neck.

[Illustration: Fig 9]

Fig. 9. Shews the Manner how the Legs and Pinnions will appear when they are turn'd to the Back; as also, the Position of the Head and Neck of the Chicken, or Turkey-Poult.

The manner of Trussing an *Hare* in the most fashionable Way. From Mr. *W. N.*

[Illustration: Fig. 10]

Case an Hare, and in casing it, just when you come to the Ears, pass a Skewer just between the Skin and the Head, and by degrees raise it up till the Skin leaves both the Ears stript, and then take take off the rest as usual. Then give the Head a Twist over the Back, that it may stand, as at A, putting two Skewers in the Ears, partly to make them stand upright, and to secure the Head in a right Disposition; then push the Joint of the Shoulder-Blade, up as high as may be, towards the Back, and pass a Skewer between the Joints, as at B, through the bottom Jaw of the Hare, which will keep it steady; then pass another Skewer through the lower Branch of the Leg at C, through the Ribs, passing close by the Blade-Bone, to keep that up tight, and another through the Point of the same Branch, as at D, which finishes the Upper-Part. Then bend in both Legs between the Haunches, so that their Points meet under the Scut, and skewer them fast, with two Skewers, as at O O.

A Fowl trussed for Boiling. From Mr. *W. N.* Poulterer, &c.

[Illustration: Fig. 11]

When it is drawn, twist the Wings till you bring the Pinnion under the Back; and you may, if you will, enclose the Liver and Gizzard, one in each Wing, as at A, but they are commonly left out. Then beat down the Breast Bone, that it does not rise above the fleshy Part; then cut off the Claws of the Feet, and twist the Legs, and bring them on the out-side of the Thigh, towards the Wing, as at B, and cut an Hole on each side the Apron, just above the Sidesman, and put the Joints of the Legs into the Body of the Fowl, as at C: so this is trussed without a Skewer.

To Truss a *Pheasant* or *Partridge*. From the same.

[Illustration: Fig. 12]

Both the Pheasant and Partridge are trussed the same way, only the Neck of the Partridge is cut off, and the Neck and Head of the Pheasant is left on: the

Plate above shews the Pheasant trussed. When it is drawn, cut off the Pinnions, leaving only the stump-bone next the Breast, and pass a Skewer through its Point, and through the Body near the Back, and then give the Neck a turn; and passing it by the Back, bring the Head on the outside of the other Wing-Bone, as at A, and run the Skewer through both, with the Head landing towards the Neck, or the Rump, which you please: B is where the Neck runs. Then take the Legs, with their Claws on, and press them by the Joints together, so as to press the lower Part of the Breast, then press them down between the Sides-men, and pass a Skewer through all, as at C. Remember a Partridge must have its Neck cut off, or else in every thing is trussed like a Pheasant.

To boil an artificial *Pheasant,* with *Sellary.* From Mrs. *Johnson, Devereux-Court* near *Temple-Bar.*

Prepare a Rabbit in the same manner as above directed, only it must not be larded; then boil it, and give it the following Sauce. Take six or seven Roots of Sellary, and boil them, when they are well clean'd from Dirt, till they are tender, then cut them into pieces of about two Inches long, and toss them up with strong Gravey thicken'd with burnt Butter. Pour this over the artificial Pheasant, and serve it hot, well impregnated with Spice. Then garnish it with Lemon sliced, or sliced Orange, and some fry'd Bread, and some Slices of pickled red Beet-Roots; or round the Edges of the Dish, strew some sifted raspings of Bread.

THE END.

* * * * *

INDEX TO PART II.

A.

Anchovies, how to keep a longtime.
Artificial Lobster.
Artificial Ratefia.
Abricots, preserved in Jelly.
  Ditto, for Tarts.
Artificial Creams.
Abricots, dry'd.
Almond-Cakes, small.

Apple-Dumplings, in an extraordinary way.
  Ditto, another way.
Anchovies, artificial, made.

B.

Broil'd Whitings.
Beef, to salt, immediately.
Beef, hash'd raw.
Biscuit, of Potatoes.
Butter'd Crabs.
Barcelona-Snuff, to make.
Bacon-Froize.
Brown Fricassee of Sheep's-Trotters.
Bitters for Wine.
Brisket of Beef, to stew.
Beef, to stew, in Soup.
Beef, a Rump, to stew.
Beet-Card Tart.
Beef-Collups, from *Oxford*.
Beet-Steaks, stew'd.
Butter, recover'd from Oil.
Bisque of Fish.
Badger, its Gammon roasted.
Bullace, preserv'd.

C.

Cyprus-Wine, imitated.
Citron-Water, from *Barbadoes*.
Cabbage-Pudding.
Collar of Mutton, roasted.
Cakes, sweet, made of Parsnips.
Ditto, made of red Beet-Roots.
Comfits, to make.
  Ditto, to make in Colours.
Caviar, to pickle or preserve.
Collar of Sturgeon roasted.
Carp-Pye.
Currans in Syrup.

Cakes, baked, of Raspberries.
Cakes, of Lemon.
Clary and Eggs.
Cheese-Cakes, of Lemon.
  Ditto, Orange.
  Ditto, Good.
Crab, artificially made.
  Ditto, another way.
Crabs, butter'd.
  Ditto, artificial, butter'd.
Cherry-Brandy, artificial.
Ditto, right.
Cucumbers, to stew.
  Ditto, to farce.
Cocks-Combs, artificial.
Calf's-Liver, stuffed and roasted.
  Ditto, another way.
Cream-Custards.
Capons Livers imitated.
Creams of Raspberries.
Cornelian Cherries, Preserves
  Ditto, in Marmalade.
Currans in Jelly.
Cakes, from *Lisbon.*
Cakes, of Orange.
Cakes, fine,
  Ditto, from *Penzance.*
Ditto, from *Northampton.*
Cow-Heel dress'd.
Calf's-Head, dress'd in a grand manner.
Calf's-Head-Pye,
  Ditto, baked.
Creams, artificial.
Cream, with Sweet-meats.
Cucumbers, to preserve in the Winter.
Cologn's Gin, to make.
Candy'd Orange-Peel.
  Ditto, Lemon-Peel.
Claret, Hermitage, to imitate.
Cheshire-Pye.
Chicken, to truss.

D.

Damsons in Jamm.
Damson-Wine.
Dog-Grass.

E.

Eringo-Roots, to candy.
Easterling, to truss.
Extraordinary Tables.

F.

Fish, to keep, a long time.
Fruit, baked.
Flounders, dressed.
Frogs, white Fricassee.
Ditto, brown Fricassee.
Florentine, Imperial.
Farced-Meat.

G.

Gravey, drawn quick for a private Family.
Gravey, rich, made without Flesh.
Ginger-Roots, preserv'd, Green.
Goose, to truss.
Grapes, preserved in Syrup.
Geneva, from *Cologn,* to make.
Gourmandine-Pease, dress'd several ways.
  Ditto, broil'd.
Grape, to keep the Winter.
Ginger, to preserve.
Green-Pease Pottage.
Gudgeons, to dress.
Grand Sauce for Fish.
Goose, boiled.
Green-Peaches preserved.

Goosberries, preserved.

H.

Hermitage-Wine, to imitate.
Hare-Pye.
Hungary-Water, to make.
Hare, to keep.
Hard Pease-Soup.
Herrings, pickled, to serve.
Hog's-Harslet roasted.
Hartshorn Jelly.
Hash of raw Beef.
Hackin, from *Cumberland.*
Ham, Westphalia, roasted.
Hams, Westphalia, artificially made.
Hog barbacued.
Herrings, broiled, not to make sick.
Hare to truss.
Herrings, baked in an extraordinary way.

K.

Katchep, in Paste, to make.

L.

Lemons in Marmalade.
Lemon-Peels, preserv'd in Jelly.
Lemon-Cakes.
Lumber-Pye.
Lap-Dog, to keep in Health.
Liver and Crow.

M.

Mustard, of several Sorts.
Mustard-Seed-Flour.

Marmalade of Peaches.
  Ditto, of Plums.
Marygold-Flowers, preserved.
Marmalade of Pine-Apples.
Marmalade of Quince.
Mutton, the Neck in Broth, an extraordinary way
Mutton, the Neck ragou'd.

N.

Neats-Tongues, roasted

O.

Oysters, fry'd.
Oranges in Marmalade.
Orangery Snuff.
Orange-Butter.
Onions, boil'd.
Ortolans, to dress.
Orange-Peels, preserved in Jelly.
Orange-Flowers, preserved in Jelly.
Orange-Tarts.
Orange-chips.
Oxen, to kill and salt in hot Weather.

P.

Peach-Tarts, white.
Pepper Mint-Water.
Pidgeon, to truss.
Potatoe-Puddings.
Provisions, to take into the Country.
Plums, dry'd with Sugar.
Plum-Porridge.
Pyes, minced, or *Christmas*-Pyes.
Paste, to make, of all Sorts.
Plums, dry'd.
Pippin Paste.

Pine-Apples, in Marmalade.
Pine-Apple-Tarts.
Peach-Tarts, red.
Pheasant, to keep sweet.
Powder'd, Sauce.
Pig, to stew.
  Ditto, to stew another way.
Preservation of Flesh from tainting,
Plum, Marmalade.
Pound-Cakes.
Pudding, six Hours.
Pidgeons, embalm'd.
Pidgeons, preserved.
Pippin-Tart.
Pickled Marygold-Flowers.
Partridges, to keep, a long time in hot Weather
Pheasant, to truss.

Q.

Quinces, preserved.
Quince, Marmalade, red.
Ditto, White.

R.

Rum, to make.
Rum, with Amber.
Rabbit trussed for Roasting.
  Ditto, for Boiling.
  Ditto, truss'd like a Pheasant.
  Ditto, to roast with Mushrooms.
  Ditto, to boil.
Raspberry-Pudding.
Ragout of Tripe.
Ratafia, to make.
  Ditto, artificial, to make.
Rabbits, white Fricassee.

S.

Sturgeon, cured.
Sturgeon, pickled.
Ditto, fresh, to roast.
Ditto, fresh, to boil.
Ditto, fresh, in a Pye.
Sheeps-Tongues, pickled.
Smoaking-Closets, for Hams.
Sorts of Mustard.
Shoulder of Mutton roasted like Venison.
Syrup of Mulberries.
Syrup of Raspberries.
Sheeps-Trotters, fricasseed.
Sorrel-Tarts.
Stew'd Peaches.
Stinking, of Flesh, prevented.
Stew'd Wild-Ducks.
Sea-Larks, or Oysters, roasted on Spits.
Shoulder, of Mutton, farced.
Salmi, or Salmi-Gundy.
Shropshire-Pye.
Ditto, another way.
Seed-Cake.
Sick Lap-Dog, to cure.
Soles, to stew.
Scots Snuff, to make.
Shropshire-Dish.
Salmon-boiled.
Soles, fry'd.
Snails, fry'd.
Snails, with white Sauce.
Ditto, with brown Sauce.
Sweet-meats, candy'd.
Syllabubs, whipt.
Spirit of Lilly-of-the-Valley.
Stew'd Veal.
Sauce for a Bisque of Fish.

T.

Turkey-Poult, to truss.
Teal, to truss.
Tripe, made of Eggs.
Tortoise, or Turtle, the Gibblets dress'd.
Tortoise, or Turtle-Flesh, to roast.
 Ditto, in a Pye.
Turbut, to dress.
Tongue, to roast.
Tench, boiled.
Turnips, from *Hertfordshire,* to dress.
Turnips, yellow, from *France,* to dress.
Tables, extraordinary, for Treats.

U.

Vinegar, to make.
Usquebaugh, the yellow sort.
Usquebaugh, the green Sort.
Verjuice.
Umble-Pye.
Venison, to keep.
Venison-Pasty.
Venison, boiled.
Viper-Soup.

W.

Wild-Ducks, to keep.
Wild-Ducks, to recover from stinking.
Wild-Duck, to truss.
Widgeon, to truss.